the other side

kim holden

Published by Do Epic, LLC

ISBN: 978-1-945443-05-3

Cover designer: Brandon Hando

Editor: Lori Sabin

Proofreaders: Christine Estevez and Monique Tarver

ALSO BY KIM HOLDEN:

THE BRIGHT SIDE SERIES

Bright Side

Gus

Franco

STANDALONE NOVELS

All of It

So Much More

DEDICATION

*This book is dedicated to
anyone and everyone touched by
the darkness of depression.*

*To quote "My Blood"
by Twenty One Pilots,
"I'll grab my light and go with you."
You are not alone.*

PROLOGUE OF NIGHTMARES

Past, June 1985
Toby

Once in seventh-grade health class, I performed CPR on a dummy. I wasn't particularly dedicated to the experience or my technique, but I vividly remember the unnatural drag of chapped lips against an alcohol-swabbed, rubbery mouth and the lazy pressure of palms against a pliable, equally as lazy rib cage. My counting was sloppy. My armpits were sweaty with the judging eyes of my teacher in my peripheral, and my cheeks were hot with the ridiculing snickers of my classmates in my ears. I also remember the thought creeping into my mind—and my addled, overprotective subconscious trying to force it out as I tried to ignore the whole embarrassing scene—that this go-through-the-motions-worst-case-scenario bullshit lesson couldn't possibly be anything like the real thing.

I was right.

It wasn't.

WHEN I WAS SIXTEEN, IN A HELLHOLE HOUSE IN WASH Park, I performed CPR on the only person I'd ever loved unconditionally. My lips were covered in tears; her mouth was coated in blood. Each breath I forced into her limp, lifeless shell sucked out what remained of my tattered soul, but I would've gladly surrendered it if it meant trading my life for hers.

The first five minutes my counting was precise, my hands clasped one atop the other, thrusting the heel of my palm down into her sternum with determined execution. I remember the first thrust being met with the unexpected resistance of rib cage that made me stutter with the hesitation of not wanting to inflict more harm on her frail, decimated body. That was quickly replaced by the incessant, bloodcurdling commands freely flowing from the overbearing, but almost nonexistent optimistic corner of my mind, *Do it or you're going to lose her!* The thrusts deepened, the sensation of the protective cage of bone bowing to a point near breaking brought bile to the back of my throat, but my pace remained steady.

The second five minutes I abandoned counting. And pace. Breaths were sobs exhaled between desperate ultimatums and threats into her lungs from mine.

"You can't leave me, Nina! You can't! I can't do this without you! If you go, I go!"

Thrusts were fueled by desperation but felt powerless. She was gone and I knew it.

Inescapable despair, hopelessness, and reality slipped in through the door on the backs of the paramedics answering my 911 call, like thieves in the night sent to negate their own well-intentioned efforts.

I conceded and they took over the futile attempt to save our lives. Or take them.

Nina was already dead.

And though my heart was still beating, so was I.

PART ONE

One Side of the Story

CHAPTER ONE

Two years later...

Present, February 1987
Toby

I'm an asshole. Ask anyone. It's a fact; predictable, like the sun rising in the east every morning and setting in the west every night.

"You're an asshole, Toby."

Told you.

I don't respond, because my roommate, Cliff, will continue. The only thing Cliff likes more than the sound of his own voice is stealing. His fingers are stickier than a toddler with an ice cream cone on a hundred-degree day. I just walked in the door from school and he's standing on the inside, not the side I prefer him on, of my bedroom door with the padlock that should be securing it from invasion in one hand and a cassette tape in the other. I suspected he could pick locks; I really don't like being proven right in this case. Glancing at the rosary beads resting against his chest, framed between two upraised hands, I wonder, once again, if he's aware he's a hypocrite or if he's just comfortable with the fact. I'm guessing it's the latter, but with him, it's hard to tell.

He rattles the cassette in his left hand hard enough to get my attention but not hard enough to damage his precious Sex Pistols. "I've been looking for this for two weeks. *Two weeks, you asshole.*"

"Forgot I had it." I didn't forget. I've been listening to it every night while I draw. It's a copy of a copy...of a copy...the quality so horrible that I have to turn the volume on my boom box up to twenty, and even then, Johnny Rotten's angry rants sound like gentle whispers. Normally, Cliff steals brand new cassettes from the Record Bar store at the mall because, according to the symbol drawn in permanent black marker on the back of his denim vest, he's an anarchist who likes "sticking it to the man." Which again seems at odds with the rosary around his neck—hypocrite, I'm telling you. It's more likely because Record Bar has no security cameras, unlike the indie music store, Wax Trax, in our neighborhood. That, and there's a code among thieves: no one steals from Wax Trax. It just isn't done. This Sex Pistols tape is a sacred exception to his *I steal everything* rule; he paid good money for it. Money he stole, but still money. He brags endlessly that it's a recorded copy of the original vinyl that belonged to Malcolm McLaren's cousin's sister, or something like that. I guarantee you it isn't, but it's a waste of time to try to argue logic with him. He's not the brightest crayon in the box.

"You didn't forget. You were just hoping I wouldn't notice you stole it."

True. "Borrowed." I was hoping he wouldn't notice I stole it.

"You're a liar," he growls as he carelessly drops the padlock to the floor where it leaves a divot in the worn, peeling linoleum, and stomps through the kitchen like a pouting preteen girl. He's a short, pudgy, acne-riddled, fourteen-year-old with a lopsided mohawk he shaved himself, and he's carefully chosen clothes to match his disingenuous attitude. In his mind he's menacing, but in reality, he's harmless. Except for the stealing. And the lock picking, apparently.

He's right. I lie. It's cheap entertainment. But I never lie about anything important. Because the important stuff I don't talk about at all. The list of important stuff is short. Mainly, it revolves around a calendar, *The Count-Out,* I call it, folded up in my wallet. It's sandwiched between a condom on one side and imaginary money on the other. I'll tell you about it later, when the time is right. When I feel like I can trust you with my secret.

I drop my backpack on the sleeping bag on the floor in my room, lock the door behind me with the tainted padlock, which now seems futile, and make my way to the answering machine on a rickety chair that sits below the telephone mounted on the kitchen wall. The message button on the answering machine is flashing. It's always flashing. A desperate distress call the tenants of this fine establishment, an ancient Victorian house that's been converted into five apartments, know will be answered but rarely with the news they want, or for that matter, need. You see, I'm the superintendent for this dilapidated pile of shit I call *home sweet home.* Did I mention I'm a sarcastic asshole? You'll see soon enough. Darkness within gestates; sarcasm is the result. It's how I breathe. My black soul is the wolf, *the asshole* is the sheep's clothing.

I'm seventeen and have never had a home. Have I always had a roof over my head? Most nights, yes. Was it a clean, habitable environment suited for humans? Sometimes. Was it a place that felt like home? Never. My current situation, until the fifth of June when I graduate from East High School, houses me in the roomy kitchen pantry of apartment 3A. The attic apartment is a kitchen surrounded by two cramped bedrooms, a bathroom, and the kitchen pantry—it's minimal. I used to have the second bedroom, but when Cliff moved in, I volunteered to give it up because he has more stuff and he's Johnny's family. And before that, I used to live in apartment 1A with my mom. She was evicted almost two years ago and disappeared and I had nowhere to go. Our landlord, Johnny, offered me a job as the building super (because he's usually too drunk to deal with calls), paying me with room and board and a little cash in my pocket every Friday. I live like a king—yes, that was sarcasm again.

I press play and listen as my afternoon is dictated to me.

Message one: "The water is rising, Toby! It's pouring in through the window! I've seen *The Poseidon Adventure*, I know what's going to happen! The ship's going down! We're all going to dro—" It's Mrs. Bennett downstairs in apartment 2B, on the second floor of a building in a landlocked state, I might add, which makes oceanic waves pouring in through the window an impossibility. At least once a week she calls in a panic and asks me to save her from herself. I tap the *next* button and make a mental note to knock later and make sure she's not alone.

Message two: "Toby, get down here. The fridge ain't workin' again—" It's Mr. Street in apartment 1B. I tap the next button because the gist of his tragedy has been relayed—he's pissed his Pabst is lukewarm.

Message three: "Toby, Johnny here." He always tells me who it is, as if I won't recognize the familiar, slurring voice barking orders at me. "New tenants in unit 2A. Meet them at four o'clock. Keys are on the kitchen counter. I need these renters, so don't screw this up." Stunted sentences punctuated with condescension against the background soundtrack provided by the drunk patrons of Dan's Tavern—this is the daily one-sided dance between us.

The blinking, red message light dies out. Only three SOS calls today. It's a banner day. And it's Friday. I glance at the clock hanging on the wall above the stove. It's shaped like a rooster. Cliff calls it the *cock clock* because he's clever like that. It's covered in layers of grease and dust. I wonder how long it's been hanging there because I've never seen anyone cook on that stove to generate grease splatters. It reads fifteen past four. I'm late to let the new tenants in. I have a thing about being late and Johnny knows it, which is why he told me to meet them at four o'clock. He knows I don't walk in the door from school until a few minutes after four. He knows when I realize I'm already late, I'll start sweating (yes, my pits are damp) and the nail-biting will begin (yes, they're disgustingly short and hurt from my neurotic attacks). Most people don't pay close enough attention to notice my reactions. Johnny has an odd talent for picking up on my ticks. Grabbing the keys from the counter and the toolbox from on top of the refrigerator, I head out the door.

I bound down the stairs and notice there's no saltwater seeping from under Mrs. Bennett's door when I walk past so I save her for last. Apartment 2A is on the second floor and is furthest from the stairs. A figure is sitting on the floor in front of the door with their legs outstretched. I squint, because my eyesight is far from 20/20 and glasses aren't a luxury I can afford, and decide the figure is female and alone. The closer I get I can see her hands resting in her lap, her head bowed exaggeratedly so that her incredibly long blonde hair pools on the hardwood floor on either side of her.

When I step over her legs that are punctuated with scuffed, black Dr. Martens boots, I notice her startled reaction to my momentary invasion of her personal space, but I don't acknowledge it. I walk directly to the door, slide one of the two identical keys on the ring in the dead bolt lock, and open it. Leaving the keys dangling in the lock, I step aside with my back still to her so she can enter.

She stands but makes no attempt to walk past me to enter the apartment. At the same time I turn to face her, she thrusts out her hand. It hangs in the air between us, suspended resolutely but shaking like a delicate kite riding a violent wind. I grip it with my own and shake firmly, more to quiet her tremors than to return the act of civility.

"Too much caffeine this afternoon, I guess," she says playfully to acknowledge the jitters. I'm painfully aware of my damp palm and release immediately, when she adds, "Thanks. I'm Alice."

I hear an odd combination of hope, confidence, and nerves in the lilt of her soft voice. It's almost enough to draw my eyes to hers. But making eye contact at close range would require bravery, which I lack. I have bravado for days—bravado that usually translates into perceived arrogance—but no actual bravery to back it up. My mom always said I was a coward; I hate to admit she's right. But she's right. So I keep my gaze trained on the floor and bite my thumbnail instead, all while I speed walk back down the hall to escape before she turns around and tries to initiate conversation. It's not that I dislike conversation, I dislike that it's a two-way street. I prefer to watch and listen like a spectator. From afar. Okay, maybe I do dislike conversation.

"Thanks," she calls again. It's louder and clearer this time. The hope and confidence muffling the nerves.

For a second, I feel a twinge—pity knotting up like unstrung fishing line—behind my ribs for her, as I think, *Say goodbye to hope, this is the place it comes to die.* I contemplate calling back with my name as I hit the stairs to descend to Mr.

Street's, but I figure what's the point? She'll find out I'm an asshole soon enough if she doesn't already know, no need for pretense and the showy pageantry of manners now. She may as well get the real Toby right off the bat.

Mr. Street opens the door in a dress shirt and pants cloaked, as always, in a clean, but shabby, brown terry cloth robe that looks out of place. A beer in one hand, his pipe in the other. The tobacco smoke swirling around him smells faintly of cinnamon today.

"What took ya so long?" he asks.

I glance at the television and realize he's watching *Taxi Driver* and that this is his best Robert De Niro impersonation. Which is a little disturbing because Mr. Street is, indeed, a taxi driver. He grandiosely calls himself an actor but says driving a taxi puts some money in his pocket between the "theater work." In the three months he's lived here I've been presented with poor representations of many movie characters. Some I know, some I've never heard of. He sucks at all of them. No wonder he's a taxi driver. I'm also one-hundred-percent sure I've never met the real Mr. Street.

I don't answer him and walk through his spotless apartment making a beeline for the fridge. It's a bulbous, turquoise relic from the fifties. Grasping the long lever-action pull, I jerk the door open to take a look inside. There's a six-pack of Pabst Blue Ribbon neatly lined up on the top shelf, the cans' placement methodical and precise. I picture him unpacking them into the fridge with the intimate touch most men reserve for a lover's body. The thought is too perverse, Mr. Street caressing beer cans with his bony fingers, so I stop and focus on the task at hand. The only other things in the fridge are a few stray individually wrapped American cheese slices and an open package of hot dogs sitting in a pool of their own unnatural, watery juice. I bet he doesn't even cook them. I bet he eats them straight from the package. Maybe he wraps them in a cheese slice if he's feeling gourmet. When I have a diversion, this is the kind of crap my racing mind drifts to and gets tangled up in— the filthy dietary habits of the thespian boozehound on the first floor. My life is pathetic.

He's hovering behind me. I can feel the itch of his stiff robe on my elbow.

"Well, what's wrong with it?" he demands. His breath is a conflicting mixture of tobacco and toothpaste, not a hint of hops despite the beer in his hand. Maybe it's a prop.

All I can assess so far is that the chamber inside is room temperature instead of cold.

I set my toolbox down on the floor and mutter, "Gimme a minute."

I want to tell him I forgot my crystal ball upstairs, but I'm feeling charitable and keep my mouth shut and close the door. Stepping to the side, and away from him, I wrench the behemoth of an appliance away from the wall and inspect the coil and motor on the back. I've attempted to repair this ancient thing twice this month, to limp it along to its inevitable death.

I've always been pretty good at fixing things because it was a necessity growing up. We never had much and what we did have was secondhand and usually way past its prime. I started tinkering when I was young because I was curious to find out how things worked but also because I liked things like a toaster that actually toasted. All of that came in handy when I was forced to be handy with this job.

Pushing it back against the wall, I steal a glance at Mr. Street and he's looking on expectantly, though the De Niro malice he's channeling in his eyes makes it appear sinister instead of innocent.

"Nothing I can do. I'll start looking for a new one."

He throws his hands in the air incredulously, foam sloshing

out of the can, and soaking into his pristine attire. "How long will that take?" He has the attitude down today. Kudos for that. Though when he registers his shirtsleeve sponging up the beer spill, he grumbles softly and surprisingly out of character, "Shit."

I shrug, pick up my toolbox from the floor, and head for the door. Truth be told, I hate confrontation. It's another thing that makes me sweaty. But bravado masks it, in the combination of standing tall and silent. I feel like an imposter when I do this, a fraud, but it always works. The other person perceives my posturing as me asserting power, instead of me hiding behind armor. That works for me.

The De Niro voice is ranting at me again as I exit. I tune it out because I know it's for effect and make my way up the stairs to 2B and Mrs. Bennett. The screaming from my quads is persistent and gains momentum with each step; my legs are tired.

I knock loudly on Mrs. Bennett's door. Her hearing is dismal.

She opens the door in a flourish. Physically, she's spry and able, I think that's what makes me so sad that her mind is a sieve; the pairing seems cruelly unfair.

"Toby!" she shouts with glee.

There's the rare spark of recollection in her eyes. The glimmer of awareness flickers brightly like a flame behind her irises, illuminating them with a fierce vitality. When she's in full control of her mind, it shines like a beacon in her eyes.

"Mrs. Bennett," I greet. I've known her and her grand-daughter, Chantal, who lives with her, for the seven years I've lived in this building. I like her. I'm not sure it shows, but I do. "Everything okay today?" I ask.

She nods enthusiastically. "Oh yes, it's a fine day. Chantal's feeding the baby in her room, but she'll be out in a minute so you can see them." I inwardly, reflexively wince—it hurts and always will—while she continues, "We're going to sit down to dinner while we watch the end of *Oprah*. Would you like to join us?" She offers me dinner at least once a week.

I decline every time. "No, thanks. I need to get back upstairs and do my homework."

I'm lying, I don't have any homework. Family, its essence, is strong in this apartment and I can only take it in short bursts. The comfort that lives inside is as overwhelming as the aroma of the fried chicken wafting out of the kitchen like a dizzying fog sent to lull me in to a false sense of security and make me believe in fairy tales. *Short bursts*, I remind myself as my stomach rumbles with hunger, and I pry away from her kindness and merciful lack of judgment.

She daintily flutters her bony hand at me, her wrist flexing up and down rapidly like dragonfly wings. "Good night, Toby."

I raise my hand in response, but my wrist and hand remain fixed stiffly in place like the mask on my face. "Night."

I know I should say something about Chantal and the baby, but I don't. Guilt takes another stab. Mrs. Bennett should think I'm a monster, but she doesn't. Another stab. And another. I'm riddled with it—a series of open, infected, invisible wounds.

She sighs quietly before the door closes completely and I hear her faint, pensive words. "That poor boy needs to sleep, he always looks tuckered out."

And here I always thought the constant purple circles under my eyes made me look tough instead of strung out and holding onto sanity by a frazzled thread. I guess I was wrong.

I return the toolbox to its rightful place of prestige on top of the fridge. For a lone, turbulent moment I regard my bedroom door with longing and consider skipping my weekly Friday night routine in favor of trying to sleep. The allure of routine and avoiding a head-on collision with insomnia wins out quickly and absolutely. I need to quiet my thoughts, not exacerbate them with stillness and silence.

Zipping up my sweatshirt and pulling the hood up because it's like blinders, I walk out the door on a mission for Dan's Tavern down the street. Let the numbing commence.

Johnny is easy to spot when I walk in the door; the place is relatively empty. The nine-to-fivers are just getting off work and won't stream in for another hour or so, even those with shaky hands and desperate need. I stride toward him like a man on a mission and take a seat on the empty stool next to him at the bar. As soon as I'm seated, the sensation of being stationary does little to ease my persistent ball of nerves, it only aggravates. My mind tends to accelerate when I'm sedentary, instead of the other way around. Doubt, guilt, hopelessness, and helplessness rushes in and crushes with brutal force. It's the reason I try to keep busy all the time: distraction dulls and enables me to function.

He tilts and tips his chin in my direction. "Asshole." When I moved in with him, he asked me what I like to be called.

I told him, "Asshole," because that's how I felt. It stuck, though he never says it with much conviction.

"Mr. Street's fridge finally gave up the ghost," I greet in return.

He nods solemnly. He knew this day was coming.

"My money," I add, sounding every bit the asshole he's labeled me. It's usually a request, asking my employer for my weekly paycheck. Today my fuse is burned out and spent, so it's a demand instead.

He fingers some bills in the chest pocket of his dirty flannel. There's sanctity in his touch; it's a ritual. He does it every time he parts with money, a silent prayer on his tongue already mourning the separation. His lips move minutely as he slips two tens and a five from his pocket, and with a final longing glance, tosses them in my direction.

I snatch them up and nod at the bartender, Dan, to get his attention. The balls of my feet are resting on the railing under the bar and my heels bounce involuntarily in anticipation.

I want to yell, "I can't do this anymore! I can't make it until June! I want out now!" But Johnny isn't a mind reader, thank God, and doesn't know my plan, so a hissy fit would only serve to feed the *This Kid Is Mental* title I try to avoid. I mean, *I* know I'm a head case, but I don't want to give others a peek in to the crazy going on inside my skull. So, I sit in silence, like I always do, and accept the watery beer that Dan sets in front of me. The pint glass is hazy, the telltale signs of a half-ass dish-washing job. Tugging the cuff of my sweatshirt down to cover my palm, I make a few swipes at the rim in an attempt to clean it before bringing it to my lips. It's lukewarm and tastes like misery. Next to me, Johnny points the open end of the pack of cigarettes in his hand in my direction and shakes one loose, as he ironically coughs a raspy, lung-rattling cautionary tale. I take it without a second thought and reach for the lighter on the bar in front of him. Lighting it, I inhale deeply, earnestly, wishing that the smoke filling my lungs could cloud my mind instead. But I guess that's what the beer is for. I only smoke when I drink. And I only drink on Friday nights. And only at Dan's because happy hour is from five to eight, which means a pint costs a quarter. The added bonus being that Dan never cards me. I'm tall and even though I have a baby face, my surly atti-tude ages me, and the purple bruises under my eyes, let's not forget those. It's only when I smile that I look my age, at least that's what I've been told. It's been years since I hinted at a smile so I wouldn't know.

Johnny leaves the pack of cigarettes on the bar between us. It's unspoken I can help myself. Not sure why he's so generous with them because he sure as hell isn't generous with anything else, maybe he's trying to kill me.

By beer number three and cigarette number four, the bar is starting to fill up as tortured souls file in like lambs being led to slaughter. Some bars are Friday night destinations for fun and celebration, Dan's is a destination for sedation and eradication. It's a place to hide out and forget for a while.

Johnny sits on the same barstool day in and day out. I know why he chose it—the barstool—it backs to a wall, and he has a full view of the bar and the door leading outside. No one can sneak up behind him here. Even drunk he's on guard. It took me a long time to figure him out because he doesn't talk about it, but I've seen the camouflage jacket with his last name on it that hangs on the bedpost in his room. I know he served in Vietnam and I'm assuming by the way he acts that he never made it out. The shell sitting next to me that smells like beer, cigarettes, and ruination boarded a plane home, but the real Johnny Stockton vanished a lifetime ago.

Just as the bliss of a warm buzz begins to descend on me, the hinges on the front door creak and a brunette walks in with everything I'm looking for. Even from across the bar and through the haze of cigarette smoke, her sagging shoulders, shuffling pace, and tight frown tell me she's carrying something heavy, the weight of it bearing down like her pockets are filled with bowling balls. Her eyes flit around the room; it's obvious she's never been in here, she's looking for a place to land before she draws any attention to herself. Too late.

I watch her for no more than two minutes before I know she's the one. Every Friday night I survey the crowd, like I am right now. Most guys look for shallow attraction on the outside; I look for deep devastation on the inside, so brutal it seeps out. I look for the woman whose vulnerability is flying high above her, whipping in the wind like a white flag on a battlefield. I seek out the broken.

I introduce myself, and because I'm mildly drunk my approach is softened, less awkward, more mature. The words flow freely when I drink, which is a bonus. She's meek and shy until she gets a few beers in her and then she loosens up. Like pulling at stray yarn on a worn sweater, she begins to unravel. As it happens it's a seesaw, she goes up and I come down. Because the moment I take that seat next to her no more alcohol passes my lips.

Her name is Jessica. She's twenty-four, recently moved here from Philly, and lives with her older sister. She's also newly single. The way she talks about her ex is amiable, but the terror in her eyes isn't. It's a tattletale. I listen to her words. I listen to her eyes. And I decipher the truth between them. The more she drinks, unbidden honesty coaxes the two to blend into middle ground and my suspicions are confirmed. She ran away. Because he beat her.

I don't say much, I'm the listener, remember? But as we approach the fine line of the precipice I try to avoid, I tell her the same thing I've told all the others: "You deserve better."

I'm talking about her past company and her present.

When she's done talking, and there's a discernable level of balance between her state of drunkenness and the lightening of her worry, I ask Dan to call us a cab.

You're waiting for me to dish on what happened next, aren't you? You want all the juicy details? Too bad. I'm an asshole *and* a gentleman.

It's after one in the morning when I walk in the front door of the Victorian on Clarkson and head up the stairs. My feet are tired after the long trek from Jessica's. So is the rest of me. But I'm tucked away into that quiet corner of my mind that rarely allows me to feel—different, better; I try not to put a label on it because it's temporary—but I *feel*.

When I jab the key in the lock to Johnny's apartment, I'm praying he isn't here and that Cliff is asleep.

Johnny's bedroom door is open and he's not in it. A reprieve. The same cannot be said for Cliff.

The stench of burnt microwave popcorn is an unwelcome guest in the kitchen. Cliff's bedroom door is open. His TV is blaring and he's watching me. I can feel his beady eyes like tractor beams.

"Did you get any?" he calls out crudely.

He's talking about sex. He asks a variation on the question at least once a week. Not as if he's living vicariously through me, but as if it's a link of camaraderie he and I share.

I don't dignify the question with an answer. I never do. I grit my teeth instead.

"Applause finally got *Sid and Nancy*." Applause is the video rental store down on Colfax. Cliff's been stalking it for weeks trying to get his grubby mitts on the story of his hero.

I can't help my shock. "*They rented to you?*"

He was banned from further VHS rentals until he pays late fees he racked up when he kept a movie ten days past its return date.

Pride twists his lips into a smirk and I know before he says the words that they didn't. "Stole it." He sings the reply, he's so proud of himself. "They're not getting this one back. She's mine."

I raise my eyebrows, more to acknowledge my body's pleas to get it into a swift state of slumber than to congratulate his thievery.

"Watch. If you want." His words are flippant. His tone isn't.

He wants me to watch it with him. He *really* wants me to watch it with him. He's a Sex Pistols zealot and he wants to baptize me with their debauchery by watching the true story unfold on film.

"I know how it ends." Both of them drug addicts. Both of them dead. I read articles on microfiche at the library last week. I'd been listening to the band and was curious. When I'm curious, I read everything I can. I get obsessive. Ask me anything about the Sex Pistols, I can probably answer it.

"Sid Vicious is a legend," he says it knowingly, the camaraderie in his voice again.

I shake my head and mutter, "Legend is the last word I would use to describe him," and shuffle past his door to mine and unlock my padlock. Cliff needs a new role model.

Door shut behind me in my room, I toe off my shoes and shed my sweatshirt and jeans. There's no window, no light, so I crawl into my sleeping bag by feel. Then I replay the events of the evening after Jessica and I left Dan's until I drift off to sleep.

And I dream nondescript dreams about nothing important.

No nightmares.

No voices.

It's beautiful.

CHAPTER TWO

PRESENT, February 1987
    Toby

I'M A CREATURE OF HABIT, A FAN OF ROUTINE.

Today is Sunday and Sunday means one thing: a trip to Mile High Comics.

It's early; Cliff and Johnny must still be sleeping because I haven't heard their bedroom doors open. I'm in the bathroom. I tend to linger when I'm in here because it's my favorite room in the apartment. I know how weird that sounds, especially when it's a bathroom shared by three guys, two of which are pigs. I'll let you guess where I fall in that equation. And I'll be offended if you choose incorrectly. But the bathroom is spacious, has a window, and a lock on the door. Privacy paired with hot water, fresh air, and sunlight. I'm not claustrophobic in my bedroom, but I can't deny that my time in the bathroom feels like an escape. It's also the place I try to chase away the images that race through my nightmares. The steaming water loosens my tight muscles but does little to loosen the tightly wound tormenter (aka my memory) inside my skull. I can't escape it, blood stains for a lifetime.

After a long shower, I shave, brush my teeth, and comb the tangles out of my wet hair—it's getting long and hangs in my eyes, I need a haircut.

I return back to my room in a towel wrapped around my waist, pull the string that hangs in the middle of the space to turn on the single bulb in the ceiling overhead, and shut the door behind me. The illumination is weak. The bulb burned out last week and I replaced it with the only one I could find in the basement supply room. It's twenty watts, basically a night-light. A candle would probably give off more light. Hanging the towel on a hook next to the door to dry, I turn to see what I have in the way of clean clothes.

Shelves line one wall and I like to keep them orderly. My life is divided into compartments: clothes, school stuff, an old boom box I filched when Johnny evicted the tenants in 2A last year, three cassette tapes, drawing stuff, comics, more comics, my skateboard, my backpack, and a small box of Nina's stuff. The opposite wall is covered in my drawings. I rotate them out continually. It's not that I'm a self-absorbed admirer of my work —I don't have a window, so the change of scenery is welcome. The narrow space between those two walls is about five feet, just wide enough for my sleeping bag and the two-inch pad of foam it's lying atop, a pillow, a desk lamp, and a pillowcase in the corner that I use as a laundry bag. I do laundry once a week, the bag is full.

Dressed, I grab my backpack and skateboard before exiting and securing my bedroom door with the not-Cliff-proof padlock. I'm two steps away from the door when the phone rings. I sigh, because I was seconds away from freedom, and answer it. "Hello."

"May I please speak to Toby?" The voice is female, scratchy like she's just woken up or has a cold, and unexpectedly pleasant.

Which trips me up because I'm not usually on the receiving end of unexpectedly pleasant. "This is Toby," I answer clumsily.

"This is Alice."

Alice? I wait, hoping she'll keep talking because I can't place the name.

"Alice in 2A," she adds.

Oh, *Say goodbye to hope* Alice, the new tenant. "Right," I confirm, mostly to myself.

"Um...Johnny said if we...you know...if we had any issues to call...you." Her voice is soft again like it was when I met her, but the hesitation sounds like she's the type of person who hates asking for help.

"Yeah." I pause, but when she doesn't continue, I ask, "What's the problem?"

"The toilet won't flush. I'm sorry to bother you, but...it's... urgent...if you know what I mean..." she trails off.

"I'll be down in a few." I hang up the phone before she can say anything else, unlock the useless padlock again, stow my backpack and skateboard, lock up, and grab the toolbox from on top of the fridge instead.

The door is open at 2A when I approach, but I knock anyway before I step inside.

"Toby?" Alice calls, which is odd because she's standing six feet inside the door looking right at me. Doesn't she recognize me? Not that I'm the sort of person who's memorable, but we met less than forty-eight hours ago.

"Yeah," I snip. I'm already irritated that my trip to the comic store has been delayed and now I can't figure out what's going on here. Is she messing with me? Does she have short-term amnesia? Is she high?

Again, she's staring directly at me when she says, "Come in."

I step inside, into the cramped living room that's void of furniture except one small love seat with more exposed foam than upholstery and four milk crates filled with records. I leave the door open, feeling it's better for both of us if I do.

She turns and starts walking toward one of the two bedrooms. I stop and watch her instead of following. Her steps are short in length and she barely lifts her feet off the hardwood, she's cautious. And her arms are stretched out in front of her slightly at waist height, fingers fluttering up and down slightly like she's playing a piano.

I assume she's going into her bedroom to leave me alone to do my thing, and normally that's exactly what I would do, but for some reason I say, "I'll take a look at the toilet."

At the doorway she stops, points, and says with mild confidence, "Yeah, it's right in here."

I don't know what to say, so I go with the obvious. "That's a bedroom."

She turns toward my voice behind her and a pair of red splotches blossom on her cheeks. "Sorry, I'm still getting used to the layout and I'm still half asleep. Next door to the left, isn't it?" she asks sheepishly.

I nod, noticing her pajamas are a pair of boxer shorts and a ragged, thin Siouxsie and the Banshees T-shirt.

She pauses like she's waiting for me to speak.

I pause, realizing the distinct shape of every curve and color housed inside her white, threadbare shirt is veiled slightly, but unequivocally unconcealed, and drop my eyes to the boxers. Nope, not any better, they're thin too. Red bikini panties are a siren beneath the pale blue and white stripes. I drop my eyes lower to her knees and am met with stark ivory skin wrapped around mile-long legs. Jesus, the temptations are never-ending.

When I, thankfully, see her hands begin to feel their way along the wall, I clear my throat because embarrassment—not for her but for me, the callous asshole and apparent pervert—is clogging it. She's blind.

I vocally answer in the affirmative, "Yes, next door to the left," and silently tuck the undeniable attraction away because it's been overshadowed by the blunt reality of my shame.

"Thanks," she says on a sleepy smile as her hand floats over the opening of the bathroom door.

Giving her time to enter the tiny bathroom, I wait until she decides where she's going to stand before I enter and shimmy past her.

"Sorry," she says when I brush her arm with mine.

She's trying to shrink into herself to make more room for me even though her back is already up against the wall, but she's not timid. She's self-assured; there isn't an ounce of unease in her.

Which is probably because all of the unease in the universe has been absorbed into my bloodstream. I'm sustaining myself on it at the moment, and it sucks.

"It's okay. The room's small." Not sure why I added that part. She may be blind, but she can get a sense of space by touch. This room is small enough that if you stand in the middle with arms outstretched, parallel walls are easily touched on both sides. I'm an idiot.

"It is," she agrees. "I like it that way."

Lifting the lid on the back of the toilet, I don't comment and take a look inside. The chain connected to the flapper that lifts it up and down is broken; one of the links is cracked and split in two. I dig around in the toolbox and find a small coil of stainless steel wire and snip off two inches of it. The chain will need to be replaced but making a temporary link out of this wire should work for a while. The water in the tank is cold when I submerge my hands, so I make quick work of it.

"Can it be fixed?" she asks.

I replace the lid and flush the toilet to answer her question. When I look in the mirror over the sink, I see a wide smile break out on her face like the sound of that toilet flushing is the best answer she could've hoped for. I'd guessed her early twenties, but wearing this smile it's obvious she's younger, probably my age. This is the first time I've really looked at her. She's pretty. Really pretty.

"That was quick. You're a lifesaver, thank you." Her voice sounds different, happier.

I understand the relief. When the only toilet in the apartment isn't working, it's kind of a bummer. But the thing about Alice is that every word she utters emits emotion. Her words seem to carry more weight and reveal more than most people's do; they're not frivolous. She doesn't hide. I've never known a blind person before, maybe everything shifts around when one of your senses is stifled and you get a superpower in some other area. It's interesting. *She's* interesting.

Accepting thanks has always made me uncomfortable. I've never spoken the phrase, *you're welcome*, because the thought of it brings heat to my cheeks. Gratitude, whether sincere or the reaction of unconscious, trained manners, shines a momentary spotlight on me—I hate that. So I never acknowledge a thank you, I just move on. After quickly washing my hands in the sink, I would usually walk out and leave without saying anything more. But somehow, I can't bring myself to do it with her.

"It's a temporary fix. I'll ask Johnny to get the part to fix it the right way this week though." I almost add, *I'm leaving*, but then I decide to pick up my toolbox from the floor and squeeze by her instead.

But when she says, "Sorry," again when I graze her arm, I blurt, "Bye."

To which she immediately responds, "Bye, Toby. Thanks again." Her voice sounds more awake now, the husk faded and replaced by softness.

The second *thank you* sends me speed walking for the door. I turn the dial on the inside knob to lock before I pull it closed behind me.

MY SKATEBOARD RIDE TO THE BUS STOP IS CONSUMED WITH thoughts of Alice: beautiful, confident, friendly, but also *alone*. I've been to that apartment twice and she's been alone both times. Where are her parents? I was a latchkey kid myself, hell, I've lived with my drunk, most-of-the-time absent landlord for almost two years because my mom split, but the difference is I've never been helpless. Not that she's helpless, she just seems...I don't know...vulnerable. Like she could use some assistance. And suddenly I'm angry for her. I believe that ideal families only exist on television, because I've never seen one in real life. Why can't parents just *parent*?

I'm still dwelling on it on the bus, but as soon as I step through the door of Mile High Comics, every stray thought vanishes. This is the place I get lost for an hour every week. I've always equated the smell of newsprint paper and ink with more than the entertainment factor that comics provide. The earnest search for the next great storyline is a quest. The enormous number of painstaking hours that went into creating each and every volume housed in this store feels like a sacrifice; the visual overload that the presentation of cover after cover provides is a gift. Every illustrator's artwork is as unique and individual as a fingerprint, their style precise and identifiable—that's my favorite part because it's further proof that human beings aren't carbon copies and there are never duplicates. I categorically memorize illustrators and their work, analyzing and appreciating. Todd McFarlane is god-like.

I do a slow walk-through of the store, meandering down each aisle like it's my first visit. I know the owner probably thinks I'm a lunatic, but he leaves me alone and doesn't follow me anymore now that he knows I'm not going to tuck something into my backpack that I didn't pay for. After my walk-through, I go back to whatever section captured my attention the most (that is, unless there's a new issue in the Dark Knight series, because it's a given that I'll go home with that) and I slip every book off the shelf one by one to look, careful to only touch the corners and not leave smudgy fingerprints on the slick cover. Time is irrelevant here, at least for a while. But around the hour mark, my conscience starts harping on me. *Your time is up. You've been here long enough. You like being here, and you know you don't deserve that.*

I don't.

So, that's when I make my decision, pick the comic that's going home with me, pay the grouchy curmudgeon behind the counter, and leave knowing this is likely the last time I will come here.

The entire journey back to the Victorian on Clarkson I feel guilty.

Guilty I enjoyed myself.

Guilty I was gone and not available for work if something happened.

Guilty I spent the dollar that I could've spent on food or something else.

Guilty I chose Amazing Spider-Man over Usagi Yojimbo.

Guilty that maybe I don't feel guilty enough.

You name it, I feel guilty about it.

Guilt and me, we're conjoined. One. When it isn't stabbing me, I drag it around like a ball and chain.

WHEN I ARRIVE BACK AT THE VICTORIAN ON CLARKSON, I walk up the first flight of stairs as stealthily as I can, tiptoe down the hall to 2A, and listen at the door. Okay, I don't literally tiptoe, but I'm cautious of how lightly I tread my beat-up Chuck Taylors. When I hear the melody of a cordial conversation, male and female, coming from behind the door, I turn and immediately go up to 3A, satisfied she's no longer alone.

CHAPTER THREE

Present, February 1987
  Toby

Mondays are always hard; a hectic start to the week is inevitable. It snowed last night, so I was up extra early to shovel and salt the stairs and sidewalk. Snow also means I can't ride my skateboard to school, which doubles my travel time. Trudging a mile through half a foot of snow in sneakers isn't my favorite thing in the world.

By the time I arrive at East High School, my fingers and toes burn with numbness and my face stings from the cold. Usually I'd stall at my locker until a minute before the bell, but due to my frozen predicament, I walk directly to Miss Montgomery's English classroom. There's one table in the second row that butts up to the radiator, and even though I normally sit in the back row, today that warm and toasty seat will be mine. When your walk to school is a mile long, you stake out things like this for days Mother Nature decides to assert her authority and be a pain in the ass.

The quiet solitude the extra time before the bell provides vanishes when I hear voices approaching the door a fraction of a second before it opens. I don't look up; my eyes are focused on the desktop and my thawing legs and feet stretched out under it. That is until Miss Montgomery says, "You're welcome to sit at the table nearest the door. It's directly in front of you, Miss Eliot." There's a pause, and Miss Montgomery coaches, "That's it, the chair's just around on the other side; you're facing the rear wall of the classroom now."

It's then that my eyes drift up and see Alice feeling her way around the desk. She props her white cane up against the side of the desk and removes her backpack and places it under the desk, before sitting down.

"Thank you," she says, the same way she said it to me in her bathroom, like she means it.

"You're welcome, dear. Don't be afraid to speak up if you need anything at all." Miss Montgomery has always been nice, accommodating—most kids walk all over her like a doormat because of it. She's one of those people who's oblivious to how the rest of the world views her. Blissfully unaware that she's the butt of jokes and constantly mocked. I admire her ability to tune it all out.

"Thank you," Alice repeats. Again, she means it.

When Miss Montgomery walks toward her desk on my side of the classroom, she greets, "Good morning, Mr. Page."

My eyes don't lift to greet her in return, but my chin does. I don't talk much; she knows it and doesn't expect more out of me.

Pulling papers from her beat-up, leather satchel, she walks my way. Standing in front of me she rifles through the stack, humming something upbeat. When the humming stops, a folder is slid into my view on the tabletop. It's my *Walden* essay. We read the book last month and then took a rare field trip to the mountains near Boulder so she could immerse inner city kids in the sights and sounds of pine trees and tranquility. She didn't think we could appreciate Henry David Thoreau wholly unless we "frolicked in the bosom of nature." Which made me want to immediately ban *frolic* and *bosom* from the English language because they should never be used in *any* sentence, let alone the *same* sentence.

"The only *A* in the class. The writing was splendid. Well done. I would like to hear more of your thoughts during class. Participate, Mr. Page, you have a lot to say. Dazzle us."

Of course when I'm being told to talk, the last thing I'm going to do is respond with actual words. I do my work, I study, I read, and I do it all well, but I will not participate in class. I don't react and tuck the unopened folder in my backpack; all the while, I can hear my mom's drunk, grating voice in my head: *You think you're so smart, don't you? Well, I've got news for you, you ain't. You'll never amount to anything, you stupid little shit.* I could replay insults for hours and never get a repeat because I have fifteen years' worth of them in my memory bank courtesy of Marilyn Page.

The humming recommences and Miss Montgomery returns to her desk knowing she's lost the battle but feeling good about her effort.

The solitude gone, I'm anxious for the room to fill. Anxious for bodies to flow in and blot out my line of sight to Alice, because I can't stop stealing glances. Every time I pull my gaze back to my desktop, it's as if there's a tug-of-war and she pulls it back toward her. Except she doesn't know I'm here, she can't see me. Which means she's not pulling—*I'm pushing.* I'm also, apparently, a voyeur. But my curiosity seems to get the better of me where she's concerned. It's not that I want to know her, but that I want to know *about* her. Is it as hard as I imagine it would be to be blind? What's her homelife like? Where did she move here from? Is she wearing red panties again? This makes me uncomfortable because I'm rarely so focused on one person unless it's Friday night at Dan's. Usually the only people I attempt to puzzle out are people I have some sort of a stake in, people I'm constantly surrounded by like Cliff and Johnny. And I only pay attention to them to try and stay a few steps ahead of their shenanigans. I never fixate...until now. Everyone else in my life is filler. For the most part, I ignore filler.

Speaking of grade-A filler, Jessie Tolken drops into the seat next to me with the distinct sluggishness of a stoner who whole-heartedly earns his title. He looks in my direction and his eyes look glazed, almost dreamy, as does the dopey smile on his face. He's feeling no pain and flying high. Ether: the unmistakable scent is strong and it's clinging to him like he's still holding the rag soaked in it to his nose, huffing. It's also invading my space, which is unfortunate because I know what this shit does. Last semester, Gina Ramirez and Alicia Fogle traipsed into American history, sat down behind me and bathed me in the remnant fumes for an hour. When I walked out of class, I couldn't feel my limbs and my mind floated somewhere outside my body, hallucinations at the ready. I can still remember stumbling on the stairs, and when I dropped my books, the noise I registered in my fogged-up brain sounded more like I'd dropped two hundred instead of two. The sound echoed in the corridor for what seemed like forever. My senses toyed with me in the hour that followed—some heightened, some muted—and then I felt nauseous for the rest of the day. I hated it. I can't figure out why drugs are so appealing to some people. I mean, sure I drink, but drugs are different. They just are. I already feel like I'm not in control of my thoughts most of the time, with my depression holding me hostage inside my own skin, but willingly handing over the last of my control to chemicals and rolling the dice with the unpredictability of drugs, is terrifying. I consider moving away from Jessie, but the heat seeping through my clothing and into my bones where the left side of my body is pressed up against the radiator is enough to tether me in place.

I spend the entire class period with my elbow on the desk, chin resting in the hammock of my cupped palm, breathing shallowly, nose and mouth, through the cuff of my sweatshirt that's pulled up over my hand.

The makeshift poly-cotton blend filter works well because when I stand up post-bell, I'm a tad light-headed, but other than that, I'm fine. I'm fine until I walk past Alice sitting in her seat by the door and I don't say anything. I feel guilty about that the entire walk to my next class. Guilty because I took advantage of her—she couldn't see me. I walk past people all day, every day, and don't acknowledge them, even the few who used to acknowledge me. But they *can see me* snubbing them, that's the difference. They know I'm being an asshole. Alice *doesn't.* To her, I'm the guy who fixes things, who makes things better.

That's definitely not me.

I only make things worse.

When lunch rolls around, I scan the halls for her. I even walk to the lunchroom and peek in through the window in the door but don't see her. Not sure why I'm stalking, I just need something to do. Something to keep my thoughts diverted away from the darkness. I don't eat during lunch. I more than qualify for the free lunch program in the cafeteria, but free lunches are a peanut butter and jelly sandwich, an apple, and a carton of milk. That's different than the hot lunch you receive if you actually have the money to pay for it, and believe me, people notice. They notice you're poor and can't afford to pay for lunch. That's not the part I'm worried about—my clothes, pretty much everything about me—already advertises I'm poor like a neon sign, and I don't give a rat's ass, because *I am*. I always have been. The part I worry about is being judged for taking a handout. I don't take handouts. They make me feel like a *complete* failure. I'm already a card-carrying member of the *Fuck-Ups Association*; I don't need any additional help with that.

I decide to go to the library because there's an alcove in the back corner where no one ever goes. Comfy couch and all, it's a respite about once a week. I like to keep my lunch landing spots on rotation and usually I end up walking, wandering. I, myself, love routine I think because my mom never provided it when I was younger. But in a setting like school where everything is routine and predictable, I like to mix things up. That means finding new spots to escape to; it's a game to discover places the masses avoid. I know every square inch of this school, public and private. As I walk through the library, I notice a few people milling in the aisles. Two girls are rifling through the shelves, searching for their next read. I can appreciate their dedication; I'm the same way around comics. And then there's a guy and girl in the biography section making out. He's backed into a corner and her hands are lost inside his coat, up his shirt. I can appreciate their dedication as well; nothing obliterates the outside world like surrendering all senses to the depths of a kiss. A kiss should feel like you've been plunged into an abyss that you may never surface from, or it isn't worth doing.

Sitting at a table alone at the opening of the alcove I'm headed for, is a girl. Slouched down, her back is to me and her long hair spills over the back of the chair like a waterfall. Headphones wrap her ears and must be delivering something serene because she looks asleep; she's utterly relaxed and unmoving.

The closer I get, the static hum tingles in my eardrums. And when I'm directly behind her, I pause because the volume is turned up so loud I can make out every word. It's Echo and the Bunnymen, "The Killing Moon," which drags my pause out because good music has the power to control me entirely, it's soul-steering. I'm pushing the limits of a typical pause toward what feels like lingering—I don't linger—so I move on and tuck into the corner of the couch in the alcove.

The back of the sleeping girl's head is visible in the two-inch gap between the top of the books on the third shelf and the bottom of the fourth. I'm staring at her, not luridly ogling her physically, but mildly envying the sounds being fed to her ears by those headphones. A great song is like catnip, a few notes can wind my insides up like a top, and always leaves me wanting more. Never mind that there are no good radio stations in Denver, no way to dial in new wave or punk on demand. I rely on my paltry cassette collection, trips to Wax Trax to hang out and listen to whatever they're playing over the in-store speakers, or on the off chance that I'm near a TV late on Sunday nights and can catch *Teletunes* on public television. *Teletunes* is basically poor man's MTV but with way better music, all crammed into an hour a week. There's no Martha Quinn, but seeing Depeche Mode videos is a fair trade. Music is fleeting; it's chance. So when I hear a good song, it feels like fate because it can't be planned or predicted. Like the universe has turned it on to flirt with me, to blindfold my dark thoughts and lord over them, lulling them into a submissive union for three or four minutes.

Sleeping girl shifts in her seat before sitting up straight to remove her coat. The shifts she makes to wrestle it off give me a glimpse of her face. It's Alice. I wonder if she's hiding, escaping, or enjoying the silence. A quick look at the clock on the cinderblock wall tells me there are twenty minutes remaining in the lunch period. Twenty minutes to sit twenty feet from Alice and pretend I'm not here.

The librarian assistant materializes from nowhere, tapping Alice on the shoulder, to which she startles because the librarian assistant moves around these stacks with the stealth of a cheetah. "Alice, you have about twenty minutes left before the bell rings to end lunch period. I need to run down to the main office, but I'll be back in time to escort you to your next class."

"Okay, thanks," Alice replies.

I know I was the one looking for her, but I only make it ten minutes before I start to feel claustrophobic. Like Alice's presence has shrunken the space and sucked out half of the oxygen supply. Guilt pokes the steely point of a sharp blade to my brain.

I need to leave...her...me...*this*, whatever it is...needs to go away.

I prefer walking around with a familiar grip on the shield of hopelessness and my depression in control, to taking in the world around me with bland interest only when survival deems it necessary.

Alice making me uncomfortable is *un*necessary.

Except the few bars I stole of the song she was listening to, *that* was necessary.

CHAPTER FOUR

Present, February 1987
Toby

It's Friday. I'm audibly sighing. Can you hear it?

Cliff's bedroom door is open when I arrive home from school, and he's sitting on his bed, right in the middle. His legs are crossed and his back is rigid. Cliff's posture is always ramrod straight; it makes him look nervous and guilty, like he's bracing to get busted for something. It doesn't pair well with his I-don't-give-a-shit, punk rock attitude. He's a fraud. The sheets are in disarray and he's only wearing a pair of sweatpants. I wonder if he went to school today or if he ditched again. He's staring at me, or rather through me, the blank look in his beady little eyes tells me he's not taking me in.

I have a decision to make, address the zombie-like stare or ignore it.

Easy choice—I ignore it and set my backpack down on the linoleum floor next to the answering machine chair and press the button that will relay Friday's tales of woe. One crisis at a time.

"Toby, Johnny here, chain for 2A's toilet is on the counter. Fix it before you do anything else." The familiar slur is absent, but he's grouchier than normal. I didn't think that was possible. "Stopwatch is running—" He hesitates and then adds after a huff, "Just get it done," and hangs up abruptly.

Second message: "Toby, this is Chantal." For a moment my stomach drops because Chantal never calls, her grandma calls. If she needs to talk to me, she always comes to 3A to talk to me in person. Which means something is really wrong. "I have a huge favor to ask. I'm sorry, but can you please stop by when you get home from school?" Well, that wasn't exactly comforting.

When the distress light on the answering machine dies out after her words, I don't waste any time in beating my feet down the stairs to Chantal. The broken toilet will have to wait.

I knock and then grasp my hands behind my back to still the nerves vibrating in them. My pits are growing damp beneath my jacket too. *Great.*

The baby's cries grow impossibly loud as I picture Chantal moving toward the door holding him. When she opens the door, the shrieks are pained. I know nothing about babies, but he rarely cries, and it's never like this, not even close. And Chantal? I've seen prizefighters on the losing end of twelve rounds look better. She obviously hasn't slept. Her hair is a mess, and her shirt is covered in spit-up. Exhaustion, fear, and sadness are whittling away at her. She gently strokes the head of the listless, angry boy with splotchy, tear-soaked cheeks in her arms with a patience that doesn't seem possible given the situation. She tries to smile at me, but her tired mouth can't be bothered to lift.

"Toby, thank God. Joey's running a fever, he has been for

two days now, and I'm out of formula for tonight. Grandma's not having a good day and I can't leave him with her to run to the store to get some." Her chin is quivering in unison with her voice. The request comes out accompanied by stress-induced tears. "If I give you some money, can you run down to the QuikMart and get some?"

I nod once and I can't take my eyes off the five-month-old in her arms. I'm wondering if he's so pissed off because he's hungry or so pissed off because he's sick. It hurts to think of either option. He isn't wearing anything except a kitchen towel pinned in place instead of a diaper. Which means she ran out again.

She walks to her purse on the coffee table, pulls out her coin purse, and proceeds to empty its contents into my open palm. A few neatly folded dollar bills and three pennies drop out. Her lips pinch together tightly and the chin quivering starts up again when she looks at what I'm sure is everything she has to her name lying in my hand. "It should be enough for the small container."

I drop my chin so my eyes slip away from the sad scene to the floor, and nod once, before turning and walking out the door and down the stairs. I run all the way to Dan's Tavern and slow only when I enter its smoky interior. Johnny is perched on his stool in the corner backed up to the wall, a half-empty glass of beer in his hands, and a striking scowl on his face.

Usually I wait for him to talk first, but today I don't.

"My money," I demand.

He glances at the clock on the wall behind the bar and back at me suspiciously. "It's only four twenty, you fix that toilet?"

I lie, "Yes."

"Bullshit." He always knows when I'm not being honest. And it's really inconvenient right now.

"My money," I try again.

He shakes his head, sets the beer on the bar top and reaches for his pack of cigarettes and his Zippo. "Not until that toilet is fixed." Lighting his cigarette, he hands the lighter over to me when I slip one from the pack.

After I take that first drag, I fix him with my best I-don't-have-time-for-this stare.

He matches it and time drags on. Too long—I'm sweating again.

Finally, his patience wears out. I'm making him uncomfortable standing in his personal space, and he huffs. "Fine, but listen to me, you're not ordering a beer. You're going back home and you're fixing that goddamn toilet."

Nodding once while I take a long pull on the Pall Mall, I swipe up the bills he tosses on the bar and stuff them in my pocket next to Chantal's.

"Joey needs formula," I add, my eyes darting to meet his.

The scowl begins to retreat, but I turn away before it dissolves and something softer replaces it. The sunlight is jarring when I step back outside, and I take one last drag on the cigarette and flick it into the street while I jog around the corner to the QuikMart.

The baby section is small. There are two different brands of formula and I'm not sure which one to get. It's been a few weeks since I bought some and either the brands are different or the packaging is. I take five seconds to deliberate, it's essentially a speed round of, "Eeny, meeny, miny, moe..." and pick one. I grab one more necessary item on my way and when the dude behind the counter (I don't know his name but I've always called him Dick in my mind...because he is) casts his judging eyes on me and chuckles under his breath, I look away and toss one of the tens Johnny gave me on the counter. He drops the change, a few odd coins, in my open palm and hands me the plastic bag. Pocketing the money, I take my purchase from him.

Before I can put some safe distance between myself and Dick and his patronizing attitude, he calls out, "You know how to use those, kid?" He's laughing again.

And I'm sweating. Again. While I raise my middle finger up high over my head on the way out the door.

He laughs harder.

When I'm out the door and past the store windows, I run.

Hanging the plastic QuikMart bag on 2B's doorknob, I knock loudly and walk up the stairs before Chantal opens the door. She'll thank me, I don't want that. And my heart can't take seeing Joey sick again.

Cliff hasn't moved from his position on his bed. Again, I know the thing to do would be to ask him what's wrong. We don't do that in 3A. Johnny, Cliff, and I tiptoe around each other and pretend feelings and emotions don't exist. Johnny and I have mastered putting up walls and keeping quiet. Cliff's approach is a little more ostentatious...okay, it's a lot more because he can't keep his mouth shut. Which makes his present silence that much more disturbing.

But I forge on. *One crisis at a time*, I remind myself. The toilet is next. Besides, I try not to get involved in people's lives, because A: I'm cursed, my mother always said so. I make things worse. And B: I'll be gone soon anyway, long-term anything is out of the question.

After two rounds of knocking, I let myself into 2A with the master key. No one is home. I leave the front door open, because I make a habit of doing that when the tenant isn't home, or if the only tenant in the apartment is a female. The transparency feels safe, necessary even. I don't need any trouble.

The toilet fix is quick and I'm almost done when I hear footsteps walking down the hall. My test flush muffles the voice coming from the other room. I can't make out the words, but the voice is too low to belong to Alice. The quicker I wash my hands and get out of here, the better. But before I twist the hot water knob on the faucet, there's a guy wearing a head to toe glare, ripped jeans, a wool coat, and black eyeliner to match his black hair, standing in the doorway. His eyes are slinging violent threats and promises, and he's pointing a grisly looking, dull steak knife at me. I don't like seeing them paired together.

"Who the fuck are you and what are you doing in my apartment?" he spits, while looking cool as a cucumber wielding a weapon in one hand and a guitar case in the other.

I instinctively raise my hands up in surrender so he doesn't take a swipe at me. "I'm Toby, the building super. I'm working on your toilet," I splutter.

His eyes narrow and then drop to my toolbox on the floor. "Oh."

I note that it takes five or six seconds before he lowers the threatening, but likely ineffective, blade.

I, in turn, lower my nonthreatening, and likely ineffective, hands. Grabbing my toolbox and skipping the handwashing, because I'll do it somewhere free of cutlery shanks, I wait for him to step aside and clear my path to freedom.

He nods his head at the toilet. "Alice said it broke a few days ago. Is it finally fixed?" His voice sounds oddly friendly now. He's set down the guitar case, but he's still holding the knife.

The obvious disparity, and the fact that he nearly made me wet myself, is what prompts my jackass, knee-jerk response by answering his question with a question, "Did you hear it flush?"

A smile breaks out in response to my obvious sarcasm and he nods on a laugh that's more chest vibration than actual sound. "Touché, Toby."

I raise my eyebrows, widen my stance, stand tall, and wait because I don't know where this is going. He may have several years on me, but I have at least four inches on him and I'm going to use them. I'm not going to make threats, but you better believe I'm going to posture until he lets me out of here. I'm a coward at heart, remember? All bravado.

He laughs again soundlessly. "Alice said you were cool." He raises his eyebrows and shrugs and the gesture tells me Alice has this maniac wrapped around her little finger. "I think she was right," he says before offering his knife-free hand in peace. "I'm Taber."

I nod once and engage in a quick, firm shake, still unhappy he hasn't put the knife down. But monumentally unhappier with the news that Alice doesn't live here with her parents, she lives here with her *boyfriend*. Who's familiar with weapons. And plays guitar. And who gets to see her in that see-through Siouxsie and the Banshees T-shirt every damn night. *Screw Taber.*

Stepping aside, he's the picture of relaxed, full-on grinning at me now.

I don't buy it and leave the apartment without another word, my cheeks and body burning with the unbidden memory of his girlfriend's silhouette under her PJs. His grin was probably a taunt because he's a mind reader and could see my indecent thoughts.

The QuikMart bag is gone from Chantal's door when I walk past and hit the stairs two at a time. Cliff is still mopey when I reenter 3A, but so am I, so I chalk his gloom up to too much weed and don't spare him a second glance after I put the toolbox back up on top of the fridge, wash my hands, lock up my backpack and skateboard I left sitting on the kitchen floor, and head for the door.

For Dan's Tavern.

For several pints of warm, weak beer.

For obliteration.

And for the woman I'll go home with tonight.

When I claim the stool two down from Johnny's at Dan's, he still looks grumpy. And his beer is still half empty. Both don't bode well for conversation, but I want one of his cigarettes, so I remain to endure.

"Is it fixed?" he asks.

I nod as I click the lighter, breathe through my Friday night indulgence, and gesture to Dan to bring me a beer.

"Was anyone there?"

I turn my head to look him in the eye so he can see the weight of my answer without speaking a word. We do this a lot, Johnny and me.

"You met Taber?" he asks on an almost gleeful sigh.

I'm still staring at him when I answer, "He pulled a fucking knife on me."

Because he's an ex-military-man's-man, the bastard actually half smiles.

Flicking ash in the ashtray in front of me, I shift my gaze back to the bar, shake my head, and mutter, "Shut up."

Dan delivers my first means-to-dull-all-things-for-a-few-hours. I swipe at the edge of the glass with the cuff of my shirt to clean it up and take a gulp, happily leaving the Taber story to die out.

Until Johnny says, "Don't let his appearance fool you, he's harmless."

I don't look at him when I say, "He's a psycho."

He clears his throat. "He's just trying to take care of Alice. Do you blame him? She's a sweet girl, you've met her."

I eye him wearily, but then mutter, "It was only a dull, steak knife," because I'm glad someone is looking out for Alice.

Johnny eases back into the wall behind him and settles into his natural state of guarded, stubborn speechlessness, and I focus my attention on the mirror behind the liquor bottles on the back of the bar. I have a full view of the place from this seat and can inconspicuously watch every patron who strides in and stumbles out. Upon entry and exit, all of them carry their burdens and problems around like Samsonite luggage packed to bursting. I imagine them stuffing in yesterday's firing or last week's eviction, on top of being bullied as a child or an alcoholic parent, and then sitting on it to force the latches to close.

It's a slow night, and I'm on my sixth or seventh cigarette and third and final beer—funds are a little light this week due to my extra, but necessary, purchase at the QuikMart—when she walks in. Shoulders thrown back to pitch confidence and her breasts like an ad campaign, but her eyes tremulously bouncing all over the room and their unwillingness to land on anyone for more than a nanosecond, negate it. I stand and make my move.

When I'm this buzzed, words come easy. I've been doing this every Friday night for a little over a year; and it's not like it's scripted, but it is highly predictable. There's a natural progression, an ebb and flow, a give and take. I sober up, while she descends gently into drunkenness. I lead the conversation until I sense her need to open up the imaginary suitcase filled with real burdens and to start playing show and tell with them. That's when I shut up and I listen.

And I listen.

And I listen some more.

When inebriation saturates enough to soothe her and I feel like her suitcase of burdens has been *un*burdened, and I've heard the man's name who helped her pack it in the first place, (his name was Gerald, by the way, and he should be in jail) I tell her she deserves better. I tell her that her past doesn't have to be her future. I also assure her that her present—*me*—is all wrong for her, and temporary but safe. She nods with a meek smile that I believe is genuine because it's paired with glassy, trusting, but earnest eyes. The trust is the part that kills me every time because she truly believes I'm a good guy.

And I know I'm not.

The night plays out...and on...as always.

Dan calls us a cab at my request.

I offer her my hand.

She takes it.

And holds it tight, in a grip that feels like naked truth, the entire ride to her place.

The cab ride always ends with this distinct look from her—no matter the woman's age, race, or facial features, the look is identical and unmistakable—it's trust, before I pay the fare and lead her out.

That's where story time ends. I'm an asshole and a gentleman, if you recall. What happens next is mine. Mine to hold onto and carry me into the only restful night's sleep I'll get all week.

CHAPTER FIVE

Present, March 1987
   Toby

There's a Canadian bacon Party Pizza in the oven and my eyes are glued to the cock clock over the stove impatiently waiting out the twelve-minute bake time. I consider pulling it out early, but I like a crispy, verging on charred, crust, so I wait.

When the time is right—or wrong, based on the crappy outcome—this happens:

I palm a ratty potholder, open the oven, and shove my greedy, hungry hand inside.

At the same time, the front door opens so forcefully that it crashes against the wall, only to rebound back in the glowering face of Cliff, whose meaty hands catch it and slam it back so he can stomp in.

My concentration and the potholder slip, my hand connects with the 450-degree oven rack when Johnny enters on

Cliff's heels. My, "*Shit!*" matches his, "*Cliff!*" in tone and annoyance. While I'm shaking my hand violently and shouting every curse word I know in my head, Johnny marches through the kitchen shouting every curse word he knows at Cliff, intermittently sprinkling in:

"What were you thinking?"

"You're going to end up just like your father!"

"You can't do this again or they'll take you to juvie!"

"You're almost fifteen years old, Cliff, it's time to grow up!"

They're in Cliff's bedroom now. Neither is listening, both are yelling over the top of each other like it's a competition to see who can fill the room with the most rage. From where I stand, they're both winners because it's boiling out and overflowing into the kitchen. A quick once-over of my hand and I see glistening, pillow-y blisters puffing up like the Pillsbury Doughboy along the inner creases of my fingers. Jerking the dish towel from the rod over the sink, I soak it in cold water and wrap it around my fingers. Dripping water all over the floor, I awkwardly fish my cheesy masterpiece out of the oven with the potholder and my left hand. Once on the waiting plate on the counter, I turn the oven off, close the door, and make my way out on the fire escape that functions more like a balcony with door access instead of just a window. It's cold out here, but I can't listen to them fight.

My mother was a yeller.

I'm not. Yelling twists my guts and fills my head with obnoxiously loud static. It makes me sweat.

And even though it's freezing out here, I'm sweating. I've only heard Johnny yell one other time, it takes a lot to get him there; Cliff got caught shoplifting then too.

Forcing the crispy crust to fold in half, I pick it up with my uninjured hand and take a big bite. The cheese burns the roof of my mouth, but that's child's play compared to the pain blazing through the blisters on my hand. It's dangling at my side, the towel and my nerve endings dripping.

"Hello? Is someone up there?" The voice is calm, at odds with everything going on, as if there's a barrier of peace that exists between here and there.

Looking down through the metal grating, I realize my dish towel is raining down on Alice standing below, and I rest my hand over the railing to divert it.

"Hey, Alice." I hate salutations because I'm a minimalist where words are concerned and most greetings are unnecessary when you're face-to-face with someone. But everything is different with Alice.

"Toby?" she questions.

I leave my plate behind and start down the ladder stairs connecting our fire escape to hers. I stop three rungs from the bottom and sit down, cooling pizza in one hand, and burning flesh in the other.

Her voice is quieter, she knows I'm close. "It smells like pizza."

"It is," I say, chewing through another bite and then for some unknown reason, I add, "Do you want some?" It's been years since I shared food with anyone.

She shakes her head. "No, thanks, I ate some spaghetti a little while ago."

I want to ask her if she cooked the spaghetti. And if Taber's home. Hell, I want to ask her lots of things, which is strange, but I settle on, "What are you doing outside? It's freezing."

She tips her head to the side slightly and then straightens it, like she's really thinking about my question. "I like being outside, it feels like possibility. Especially at night, because in the dark we're all the same..." she trails off, but she's not feeling sorry for herself. She's just talking. Sharing.

I'm not sure what to say. I don't have shallow conversations with people, let alone deep ones. But I can't leave her unfinished sentence dangling. "Have you always been blind?"

She shakes her head faintly and her long blonde waves rustle like fall leaves in the wind. "No, I started losing my sight two years ago. It's progressive. In another year, it will be gone entirely."

What strikes me the most about this information is the way it's delivered: all facts, no sadness, and a little of the hope I've come to associate with her. How can you be hopeful when your world is going dark?

It's obvious she doesn't expect me to respond when she continues and recites my question back to me with a teasing smile. "What are you doing outside? It's freezing."

"Talking to you," I answer to avoid the truth.

But if there's one thing Alice is, it's direct. "And avoiding the fight?"

Occasional loud bursts can still be heard from inside, one story up, so I give in to honesty. "Yeah, that too."

"Is it your dad, Johnny?" she asks gently.

It doesn't sound nosy. I get the feeling it's how she gathers information since she can't see.

"Johnny isn't my dad." I realize how vague my answer is after it's out. She knows nothing about me. Nothing about anyone in this big old house, except her knife-wielding, ninja boyfriend. "We aren't related, I just rent a room from him," I clarify.

"Who's he fighting with?"

"Cliff." One word won't be enough for her; I know there will be another question, so after taking a bite of pizza, I continue, "His nephew. He took him in a little over a year ago when Cliff's dad went to jail."

"Oh." The news saddens her, I can hear it. She feels sorry

for him even though she's never met him. "Where's Cliff's mom?"

"She died when he was nine or ten." I can't remember the last time I had a conversation this long. Or this private.

"Oh." Another compassionate, quiet response. She slides her gloved hands in the pockets of her puffy, cobalt blue coat.

She remains quiet for a few minutes while I finish my pizza, and my butt goes numb from the cold metal rung I'm sitting on. My right hand is numb now too, but I welcome the damper on the pain.

"Are the stars out, Toby? Is it a clear night?" Her head is tipped back, eyes closed, a slight smile smudges her rosy lips and cheeks, and moonlight bathes her.

I don't think I've ever seen anything so gorgeous in my life. She's the picture of serenity, aglow. Her hair is brushing the backs of her thighs as it sways in the light breeze.

I don't know if the stars are out. I don't know if it's clear. But the way she looks, I know she wants to imagine there's a sky filled with a million stars overhead, so I lie, and it feels like truth: "Not a cloud in the sky. They're all out."

Her cheeks round out slowly and her teeth are revealed, bright white in the moonlight. She's a contrast in shadows. "It's breathtaking, isn't it?" she asks.

I haven't looked up at the sky. I haven't taken my eyes off of her, but I don't lie this time. "Yes." *Breathtaking.*

We stay like this—her looking up, me looking down—both appreciating. I've never stared at someone like this, for this long, and when it starts to feel wrong, like I'm invading her privacy, I stop.

Like she knows there's a shift, she asks, "What makes you happy, Toby?"

Nothing. The severely depressed and happiness don't cross paths. "Um...I don't know." I could've lied; it's what I would've done with anyone else. I could've said comics or drawing or music, but those things don't make me happy, they prop me. They prolong me. They keep me alive. For now.

She tips her chin back down, and the moonlight glow on her skin disappears, but her smile remains. "What do you mean you don't know? Something has to make you happy."

You shouldn't make assumptions about me, I want to say, but instead I ask, "What makes you happy?"

"Evasion—" She takes a step toward me and I instinctively put my hand out like she's too close to the railing and needs protecting. Which is stupid because she navigates well on her own, and even if she collided with the railing there's no way she would fall over it. As if choreographed, I retract my hand at the same time she reaches for the railing, and I avoid an embarrassing collision by mere dumb luck. Taking one more step into what is now my personal space, she stops with her shins resting against the bottom rung, my heels resting on the second, my frozen butt on the third. This close we're almost eye-to-eye, she's taller than I remember. When she stills, she finishes her sentence, "—isn't an answer, Toby. I'll let it slide for now, but know there will come a time when I ask you that question again in the future and I expect an answer." Her smile is teasing but somehow, I know she means it, and then she tilts her head like she's thinking through her answer. "The endless possibility in a starry sky; 'Close To Me' by The Cure at deafening volume; swimming in an outdoor pool alone when the water inside is warmer than the air outside; the way white-hot sunshine on a blazing summer day can make you feel alive; the unapologetic chill of piano keys and the cooperative submission of guitar strings; lyrics and notes in my head willing and anxious to become anything I want them to be; meeting someone and not having to put effort into becoming friends because it's a given that we already are, like destiny already sorted us ahead of

---

time." She pauses and a breathy laugh escapes. "I'm going to shut up now, I could go on all night."

I'm staring at her again and I wish she would go on because in this moment I never want Alice to lose this. I don't want her to be *Say goodbye to hope* Alice. I want her to be *Never lose hope* Alice.

"They stopped fighting," Alice whispers.

I nod, it's habit, but then I whisper, "Yeah." The quiet is suddenly intimate, like Alice can see through me, see my hopelessness, see that we're polar opposites, so I stand abruptly. "I better go inside and warm up."

The serenity slips but doesn't vanish. "Okay, me too. Thanks, Toby. We should do this again."

Because I don't acknowledge thank yous, and because I'm the antidote to happiness, and because I don't let people in because I taint them, and because she has a boyfriend, I leave and go back inside without saying a word.

Alice remains on her fire escape below for another minute, her face pointed toward her endless possibilities in the sky, eyes closed, smile in place, looking angelic in the moonlight again, before she turns and disappears through her door.

Yes, I watched.

And I almost smiled too.

Almost.

CHAPTER SIX

Present, March 1987
Toby

It's late, after two in the morning. I've been drawing in my room for several hours now, working on a pencil drawing of the Dark Knight battling the Joker. It's dark, all of my art is. Blistered fingers make my grip unorthodox. It's like drawing with a mitten on, but I refuse to stop until it's done. Avoiding sleep means avoiding nightmares, obviously. It's a nightly duel. My hope being that if I'm exhausted enough when I drift off, my body will put all of its energy into restoring itself and my mind will forget to torture me.

New Order is playing quietly from my boom box and I'm sitting against the wall with my sketchbook resting on my thighs. Bent legs provide an easel. The desk lamp is on the floor next to my sleeping bag, pointed like a spotlight directly on the stark white paper that's being continually covered in shades of black, gray, fists, and fury. Eyelids heavy, concentration waning, and the details in decline, I give up. For tonight.

Stripping off my T-shirt, I give it the sniff test. No stink, it will go another day, so I fold it up and place it on top of a sweatshirt, a pair of jeans, and a T-shirt on my clothes shelf. Then I strip off my jeans and don't need a sniff to know they need to meet the laundry bag. I've been wearing them for four days, it's time. Jeans off, I take my wallet from my back pocket and set it on a shelf next to my backpack. Then I reach in the front pocket and pull out a piece of paper that's been folded over so many times it's as thick as it is wide. Unfolding it is a process, and I pry a pushpin from my art wall and stab it through the creased paper into the back of the door because that's where I put reminders. It's an order form for graduation announcements that was handed out in first period this morning. I only need one announcement, but the minimum quantity I can order is ten. I've already filled out the form, but I'll have to wait until Friday when I get paid to turn it in.

Before I tuck away in my sleeping bag, I reach for my wallet because I haven't crossed today off the calendar yet. Remember, I told you I'd tell you about *The Count-Out* calendar in my wallet when the time was right? I guess it's time. You may as well know. Opening it, I slip out the paper that's tucked between the lonely condom and a lonely dollar bill. This paper is sacred; it's literally my life, what's left of it anyway. *The Count-Out*. A calendar that ends on the fifth of June and a list of the things that need to happen between now and then because though I'm suicidal, I'm also somewhat selfish. The list isn't long:

A kiss I feel in my soul
Redemption
Graduate with my mom watching

Blacking out March sixth with a pencil on my handwritten calendar, I don't have to count to know how many days are left. Ninety-one. I've been doing this countdown for almost two years, it's ingrained. When you're counting down to the end of your life, it's always blindingly and purposefully at the forefront of your mind.

Ninety-one days left to endure and survive.

Ninety-one days left to rewind and endlessly replay the nightmare, awake or asleep.

Ninety-one days left to try to make some things right.

Ninety-one days left to prove a point.

Another ninety-one days that I got...

And Nina didn't.

CHAPTER SEVEN

The happy beginning of horror

Past, December 1984
Nina's Protector

I watch Nina every day. I try to talk to her. I try to guide her. She rarely listens. I sound like a nag, overbearing, possibly even a creeper, right? I like to think of myself as stubborn. I'm not a quitter, I fight until the end. You'll see.

Nina's turning thirty-one today—a milestone. They're all milestones because, in full disclosure, I didn't think she would make it this far, though I'd hoped with everything in me that she would. Her thirty-one years have been a ragged patchwork of bad decisions and regrets held together loosely by fragile, weary threads. The past clings to her and clouds her mind so completely that it governs her present and foretells her future. She can't escape it. Her mind and body are stone...her past a powerful river moving over them. You know the power of water over stone when you add in time as a factor—I don't have to tell you which one wins out. She also lives with a mind that vacillates in and out of balance depending on whether or not she's taking her medication. The medication is necessary. She sees it as optional. That makes every day a constant uphill battle. A battle that we fight together.

Her two best—an assessment I do not share—friends have been begging her all week to go out with them tonight.

"You only turn thirty-one once! Let's celebrate!" they said.

Celebrations are reserved for other people, people who deserve them. That's what Nina thinks.

I boldly tell her she's wrong, that she deserves to celebrate just as much as anyone else. I also add that I think she should find someone else to celebrate with, like Toby, but she ignores me.

In the end, she gives in to their pleas. She always gives in.

The bar is full when they arrive, bustling with the excitement of a Friday night and the possibility of...well, that depends on the person, I suppose. The prospects are varied and endlessly abundant though. Some safe, some not. Some smart, some not. I cringe, bite my tongue, and wait for Nina to decide. I'm endlessly patient. Until I'm not. I'm reaching my limit as my nerves burn down like a fuse on a stick of dynamite. Situations like this always put me on edge with Nina. There are too many choices. Too many things could potentially go wrong.

Two drinks turn into four drinks. The women dance until they're sweaty, and as hard as Nina fought coming out tonight, she's beginning to enjoy it.

By drink number six, she starts to believe that maybe she does deserve to celebrate. The music is loud in her ears. The lights flicker over the dance floor, the strobe of it adding to the dizzying effect of the alcohol thrumming through her veins. It's at this moment that I see something I haven't seen in her in a very, very long time. I see happiness. Not the fake smile she slaps on at work to get through her shift because customer service requires it—and because she, in turn, requires a paycheck. And not the half smile she conjures for her friends, that one's forced and only masks the dull ache she houses inside. No, the happiness she's allowing herself to feel right now is rare. It radiates out of her like sunshine. So stunning, I'm in awe.

So in awe, that I don't notice the body brushing against the back of hers at first. But when I do, I'm on guard again. I'm suspicious. It's a good thing I don't work in law, because my motto would be *guilty before proven innocent.*

But he's moving cautiously. When she turns to face him, she gasps quietly. It's the quiet gasp of surprise and appreciation. There's mutual attraction, no doubt. I can see it spark in both their eyes. It's fascinating to watch, the tennis match of flirtation. They dance an entire song playing cat and mouse with their glances, locking gazes for microseconds before smiling sheepishly and darting eyes away. By the second song he leans in, his lips brushing the hair covering her ear, and introduces himself—*Ken.* I watch her shiver with pleasure at the contact and the rumble of his voice and I sigh dazedly...and smile...and tell myself that he's different. Ken is different.

There's only a moment's hesitation when I ask myself, *He'll be good to her, right?*

And then I look at her face, so unnaturally happy. The kind of happy I've waited years to see and I stand down and answer my own question. *He'll be good to her. Ken is different.*

CHAPTER EIGHT

PRESENT, March 1987
Toby

JOHNNY HOLDING THE BASE OF THE LADDER DOES LITTLE to quiet the voice in my head reminding me second by second that this ladder is ancient and the ground is thirty feet down. My threshold on this ladder before my brain intervenes, says, *What in the hell do you think you're doing?* and starts locking down muscular cooperation, is around twenty feet. Ten feet above *Hell, no* height is not a good time, it's rebellion between body, mind, and pride. There is no way I'm ever going to tell Johnny I'm afraid of this sketchy ladder, or heights, or *whatever*, because I try not to give him ammunition to further judge me. Unfortunately, he already knows I feel responsible for Nina's death. I keep all the rest to myself. I bury it where the outside world can't see.

"Is the bracket broken? Or is the wood rotten?" Johnny yells from below. He's looking up with one hand on the ladder and the other now shielding his eyes from the bright midday sun directly overhead.

Two hands, chief! I want to scream, but instead I level my voice so I don't sound like a frightened five-year-old, and respond with a simple, "Yes."

"Yes? Which is it?" he asks, still with a single hand affixed nonchalantly to the stairway to my paranoia.

"Both," I answer, as I remove the screwdriver from my back pocket and begin to unscrew the half of the bracket that's still attached to the house. It's mangled. Last night the wind kicked up and rattled this stretch of downspout unmercifully, until the old bracket and the old house decided to part ways. The downspout clanged against the house for hours, I heard it, but it was the middle of the night, and I didn't want to be anywhere near this ladder in that wind. Bracket loose, I stick it in my back pocket with the screwdriver and screw then make my way down to solid ground.

Three rungs from the bottom, I beat him to the question I know he'll ask. "I'll make a new bracket and reattach it a foot lower where the wood isn't as rotten."

Johnny nods and the quiet draws my eyes to his, which I rarely do. They look tired, which isn't new. And a little irritated, which isn't new either. But they also look clear, no bloodshot weaving through the whites, and sober. It's rare he goes hours at a stretch without a drink. They also look haunted in an entirely new way, like whatever tortured him from within is no longer muted. It's at the surface and it's intense.

I want to ask him how long he's been without a drink. Ask him if the war broke him like I suspect it did. Ask him if he thinks he'll ever get over it. Ask him about his biggest regrets. But I don't because giving our demons a voice, acknowledging them, isn't something we do. I walk back around the house, in through the front door and into the basement, and try to ignore the tremor I saw in his hands and the fact that he's sweating buckets.

The new bracket takes thirty minutes to make and when I return to the backyard and my vertical nemesis, I don't expect that he'll be there. I expect him to be gone, like he always is. Disappeared to Dan's Tavern or wherever he goes these days to escape this old house. Cliff. Me. His life. Wherever he goes to still the tremors and sate his addiction's need.

But he's still standing in the same spot next to the ladder like he hasn't moved. The closer I get, I hear it. The raised voices coming from up above. We're both good at ignoring chaos; it's part of living in this house. Sometimes tenants are quiet like Mrs. Bennett and Chantal. And sometimes tenants verbally spar like it's their full-time job. We do our best to tune it out, unless it gets physical, then we call the cops and Johnny usually evicts them. He doesn't tolerate violence.

Johnny isn't looking up, but I can tell he's eavesdropping, or trying to. When I'm up the ladder seven or eight feet, he steps into place and holds it with two hands as I ascend. The aggression seeping out of the house gets louder and thicker the higher I climb. Three distinct voices: One female bellowing self-righteously about knowing what's right (Which makes me skeptical. If you're right, you don't yell about it until you're red in the face and someone believes you. Volume doesn't change minds, it closes them.), one male infuriatingly challenging that maybe she doesn't (His is a tired, but fiery fight. It sounds a decade old, like it's on a loop, defense more than offense.), and Alice (Louder than normal, a pleading roar to be heard. The passion is pure and distilled—her hope rivaling the bellowing cynicism.).

Cynicism doesn't hear hope.

Cynicism doesn't consider hope.

Cynicism just yells louder.

Because maybe if it yells loud enough, hope will fade away.

When I reach maximum height, I'm near a window in their apartment and the words are clear. It's a distraction from my own fear, but I'd gladly trade it back for Alice's sake. I hurriedly install the new bracket while I try to ignore the argument that I can't.

"I'm happy here with Taber—why can't you accept that?" Alice asks.

"Because I'm your mother, Alice. You need to come back home. I'm trying to be logical—why can't anyone else do the same?" The self-righteous woman challenges angrily.

I have a feeling that for most of her life, people have gone along with what she wants. It sounds like she isn't used to not getting her way and she's livid about it.

"I hate to break this to you, Rachel, but sometimes what you consider logical *isn't*. It's tunnel vision and fixation and it makes everyone else around you miserable." The male voice sounds like he's at the end of his rope and is ready to explode.

"Someone has to be logical, Taber!" she screeches. "You want to live in your make-believe world of music and debauchery? *Fine!* But you're not going to drag Alice into your disastrous life and brainwash her to follow you down the road to failure. You have no future and Alice's isn't in music."

Judging by his reaction to the outburst, he's heard this assessment one hundred times before, possibly verbatim. "Alice is so damn talented. *Why can't you see that? Why can't you support that?*" he pleads, defending Alice but not himself, even though Alice's mom's words were scathing. And as much as I don't like him, I admire him for it.

Alice butts in before her mom can counter, and she sounds steely. "Taber gets me to school every day. I'm doing well in all of my classes. We've written three new songs this week. We have a gig next weekend that will pay next month's rent and put groceries in the fridge for a few weeks. This is my dream. If you can't support it, fine, but let me live it in peace, *please.*"

"Dreams are folly, they're the things children chase and believe in. You want to be treated like an adult, *then start acting like one.* Being in a band isn't a viable future." It's not cruelly said, which is the saddest part. It's her mom's absolute. *Her* logic. It's obvious her mom's never had a dream.

Thank God I'm almost done because I don't know much about Alice, but I'm pretty sure her mom is seconds away from delivering an oblivious fatal blow. *Alice is about to have her spirit crushed! Don't let that happen, Taber!* I want to yell.

"What is that supposed to mean?" The steel is gone, but Alice isn't letting her mom see the hurt. Yet.

But I can feel it coming.

"Ignore her," Taber reassures, even though he knows she can't. Not with it all blasting at her.

"I guess I have to play bad cop, be the reasonable one. Be the *adult,*" she spits the word. That was for Taber. They all have roles to play, apparently. "You should be at home, Alice. You shouldn't be focused on music; we should be focused on finding another doctor—"

"You promised, Mom." Alice cuts her off on an angry, wobbly, threatening breath like she's been punched in the stomach.

"*You're not doing this to her again, Rachel,*" Taber warns. "She's not a pet project, *she's your daughter.* You promised after the last doctor that you accepted the prognosis. *Alice's eyesight can't be restored.* No one wishes it could be more than me. *But. It. Can't.* It's a medical impossibility." The desperation, utter sadness, and unimpeded anger in his voice reveal that he would do anything for Alice. Anything to protect her.

Respect—he has my respect.

"I refuse to accept that," her mom says defiantly as she dismisses his pleas.

"You refuse to accept *me*! I'm blind, Mom! Stop treating it like a death sentence!" Alice unleashes vulnerability and truth and acceptance and it's at once both glorious and agonizing to hear because her hope is being contaminated by the doubt being forced on her.

It's met with a rushed response that only sees its own logic and ignores her daughter's wishes, needs, and dreams. "You want the big picture, little girl? Your blindness means you're more likely to be discriminated against, it means you'll never live on your own, it means you're more likely to be the victim of a crime, it means you're more likely to be unemployed than employed, it means you will never work in a visual career. Without sight, your *dreams* are *impossible*. Am I getting through to you? Do you hear me?"

Silence.

The final turn of my screwdriver meets resistance. The bracket is secure. I need to climb down this ladder, but I can't. Not until I hear Alice speak. I want to hear *her hope* ignore her mom's denial.

Instead I hear a door open, and a faint but caustic, "Loud and clear. *I love you too, Mom*," from Alice, as the door slams shut and rattles on its hinges.

"Alice, you can't walk away from this discussion!" her mom yells.

"*Rachel*." Her name is a rumbling warning. Taber's fuming. "I know you're not happy she's here with me. Believe me, I know you want her as far away from me as she can get. But I love her. I take care of her, I always have. And I accept her exactly the way she is, because you seem to have forgotten that Alice is the most special person you've ever met or will ever have the pleasure of knowing. Now, *get out of our home,*" he growls.

"Are you going to follow her?" She still hasn't grasped what she said and how it broke her daughter's heart, instead she's testing Taber. Pushing him. Again.

"*No,*" he says forcefully. "She's pissed off and broken-hearted, she needs to take a walk and blow off some steam."

"She shouldn't be walking alon—"

Taber cuts off her warning with a knowing, "*She'll. Be. Fine.* She's eighteen years old, for Christ's sake, and she's better at navigating the downtown streets than you would be with your eyes wide open. *I. Trust. Her. With. Herself.* Now, get out." His voice sounds exhausted when it drops several decibels, and he begs, "Please, just get out."

I'm done. I can't listen anymore, I need to find Alice. In the fight, her mom needs to be right above all else. She needs to persuade everyone to see the world the way she does. She needs to ignore reality and believe in miracles that would fix a daughter who she can't see is already perfect in all the ways that matter.

When I reach the bottom, I hand Johnny the screwdriver and take off running for the front of the house. He doesn't question me, or try to stop me, or tell me to mind my own business—he takes the tool and nods. The nod is, *Go.* At the sidewalk, I spot her two houses down. Her pace is quick and her white cane is sweeping back and forth ahead of her at double speed, like she'd rather use it to beat someone senseless than to find obstacles in her path. My jog up the sidewalk toward her is purposeful, but when I'm beside her, I don't know what to say.

Alice does. "I don't want to talk, Taber," she says through tears she's trying to fight.

"It's Toby," I whisper, because anything louder seems invasive.

"I don't want to talk, Toby," she corrects.

That's fine, talking isn't my favorite thing. So, I walk with her.

For blocks and blocks, I walk with her.

I don't pick the route.

I don't try to guide.

When she turns right, I turn right.

When she speeds up, I speed up.

I walk beside her until she stops in the middle of the sidewalk and turns to face me. Tears are pooled, swelling along the ledge of her lower lids. Sad Alice is so wrong.

It's just become my mission to change that. "Will you go somewhere with me? I want to show you something."

Her affirmative and trusting answer is a hand held out between us for me to take.

I do.

My palm aligns with hers and my fingers and thumb secure her cold skin against mine.

We've been walking several blocks when she says, "That feels nice. Thank you."

It's the *thank you* that snaps me back to reality. Because apparently, holding Alice's hand makes me lose my mind. Without thinking, I'd wrapped my free hand around hers too and was rubbing the back of it to warm her up. The *thank you* makes me tense and stop immediately.

Ten or twelve steps down the sidewalk Alice counters by readjusting our grip. Her fingers urge the release before slipping between mine and capturing them. The move is confident and graceful. Her easy, gentle way with touch and words, all interaction really, is new to me and it's disconcerting, but I don't fight it. Because it also feels so damn good.

I glance down at our hands, fingers interlaced, and watch her thumb sweep across the back of my hand so softly that it feels imagined instead of real. The pattern varies from brushing back and forth, to tracing circles. Easing my constant worry, solidifying friendship by seeing me in ways others don't, and confirming that Alice makes me feel more than anyone I've ever met—all with the pad of her thumb. I know this is completely platonic on her part—it's just Alice being Alice—but for a loner like me, there's intimacy in weaving my fingers with someone else's. It's a union that feels naked and vulnerable, intrepidly sexy. Which is why I always choose the emotionally boundary based, I'm-not-letting-you-in palm to palm, non-finger-weaving grip.

I decide there are other ways to set boundaries with Alice, because her hand was only made to be held with the full commitment of my fingers between hers. Even if her heart belongs to someone else who deserves it more than I ever could.

She makes the rules.

She defines friendship.

I follow it to the letter.

When we get to our destination, I almost walk past it and add another trip around the block to spend five more minutes touching her, but I don't because Alice pays attention and will know I've done a loop. Opening the door, I guide her in behind me and say, "Welcome."

A smile blooms when Joy Division stuns her ears, and leading her down the first narrow aisle of vinyl, it only grows.

"Where are we?" she asks loudly to compete with the music pulsing through the overhead speakers.

Releasing her grip, I grasp her wrist and place her hand palm down on top of dozens of records. Once there I let go and watch her stroke her fingers across the top edge of the stack several times like she's petting a cat. The motion is inquisitive but also reverent like she knows how much this place means to me. She leans her white cane up against the display and picks up the album closest to her, holds it to her nose, and inhales deeply.

"You brought me to a record shop? You have no idea how much I love music."

"I do," I whisper too quietly for her to hear. I'm an expert when it comes to eavesdropping.

"Which album is this?" She's loud again, which normally would make me shy away because I don't like attention of any kind focused on me, but in this moment I don't care. She reacted exactly like I hoped she would. She's in her element and it's stunning to watch.

I lean in close to answer and her wavy hair tickles my nose and lips. "Iggy Pop's 'Lust for Life.'"

"Oh!" There's immediate recognition and it's cute. "My dad had this album. I love 'The Passenger.'"

She puts it back in place and does a one-eighty, reaching out for what she assumes will be more records behind her. There are. I watch her repeat the ritual, adoring strokes on the covers until she begins flipping through them, stops, and pulls one out.

"Which album is this?" Her excitement is like a can of RC Cola that's been shaken up and opened, fizzing out. I'm sticky in it and I don't want to wash it off.

"Duran Duran's 'Seven and the Ragged Tiger,'" I tell her.

She sighs and the sound scatters goose bumps up my arms and down my legs. "I had such a crush on Simon Le Bon in ninth grade. I used to run home after school every day to watch the Top Twenty Video Countdown on MTV so I didn't miss 'The Reflex.' God, I loved that song. And blonds. I definitely had a thing for blonds."

Even the grouchy looking goth dude dressed in head to toe black in the next row is smiling listening to her.

Caught up in her excitement, I ask without thinking, "And now?"

Unoffended, she answers, "Now I have a thing for deep voices that reverberate behind my ribs long after I've heard them; innate kindness; and people who see *me*, not the fact that I can't." She walks, dragging her fingers along the front of the display case. From what I can tell, she's just described Taber. When she reaches the end of the row, she asks, "What about you, Toby?"

I have a thing for you, Alice, is the first thought that comes to mind. The second thought is, *I bet she's as intentional, detailed, descriptive, and thorough with her kisses as she is with her words.* Followed quickly by the answer I give when I catch up to her: "I didn't have a crush on Simon Le Bon in ninth grade."

She laughs. "You aren't truly doing life justice if you haven't experienced a Simon Le Bon lusting phase." Entering the next aisle, I think she's going to let me off the hook, but she doesn't. "What makes your pulse race, Toby?"

Not, *What's attractive?* or, *What's your type?* but, *What makes your pulse race?*

She hasn't touched the albums, she's waiting. When she listens, she listens with her entire body.

"I don't know." It sounds lame when I say it, but it's true, I've never really thought about it.

"Nope. We're not moving on until you answer the question." She crosses her arms disapprovingly, but she's smirking. "Friends answer friend's questions. They have conversations. They get to know each other. Start talking."

"Give me a minute," I say to pause the moment. When I'm ready, I step to her, tuck my nose into her hair, and lower my voice so no one else can hear. "A genuine smile, especially if I know I put it there; someone who listens when I have nothing to say; sharing the same taste in music; and blondes. I have a thing for blondes." Nothing I said meant anything to me before I met Alice. It's a very short list of the things about *her* that make my pulse race. The rest I'll keep to myself because this could get incredibly inappropriate in no time and then Taber will use the steak knife on me instead of threatening me with it.

"The most important time to listen is when words are missing, that's when hearts cry out the loudest." She smiles softly and then changes the subject. "I want you to show me your favorite album in this store and tell me a story about it."

I hesitate, not because I don't know, but because I don't know if I want to share. I could easily make something up—there are plenty of bands I like—but I decide to go with the truth. "It's over here."

"I should go back for my cane before we move on. I got excited and left it on the last aisle," she says.

"I have it," I tell her, and when she reaches out, I place it in her grasp.

"Thanks," she says before she holds out her left hand. "Show me."

I slide my fingers between hers, moan internally, and walk us down the aisle, over two, and loop back to the spot where we began. Yes, we were, coincidentally, standing five feet from section L when she asked the question. But as soon as she offered me her hand, a longer route was necessary.

She smiles slyly when we come to a stop. "We just walked in a circle, Toby."

"I forgot where it was," I lie.

"Mmm-hmm," she hums, a smile still in place.

I'm only mildly embarrassed until I look up and goth guy is giving me a mocking thumbs-up while mouthing the word, *Smooth,* and then I'm mortified. Annoyed, I shake my head at the taunter in black because I can't tell him to shut up, and flick through the stack of vinyl until I find what I'm looking for.

"This is my favorite album, *Physical Graffiti*," I say, freeing it from the others. I haven't looked at this cover for years and my throat is suddenly closing off. Why did I do this?

"Can I hold it?" Alice asks. I see her lips move more than I hear her because she's speaking so quietly.

When she outstretches her hand, I place it within reach and she takes it. Leaning her cane against the display, she runs her fingertips reverently over the cover. "How old were you the first time you heard it?"

I cough to try to find my voice, but it cracks on the only syllable I can force out. "Nine." My sister, Nina, had just come to live with us again. She was in and out of our lives a lot. That time she'd overdosed and my mom insisted she come and live with us after she was released from the hospital. She said she was sick and it was an accident. I was too young to understand addiction and I believed her. I always believed her. I loved it when Nina was around, probably because it was an unexpected treat. She paid attention to me, made me laugh, taught me how to draw, watched cartoons with me on Saturday mornings, read me comics before I could read, and during that stay with us she played her Led Zeppelin album and unknowingly made me fall in love with music. All of this I don't tell Alice, of course. I don't talk about Nina with anyone. Ever.

She's nodding her head, giving me time to compose myself because the emotion erupting is hard to conceal. And then she does something unexpected. She sets the record down on top of the others and she turns slightly, finds the sleeve of my arms crossed over my chest with her hand and tugs it gently, her other arm extended out in invitation.

That I step into. When her arms slide around my waist and mine rest on her shoulders and gather her in around her neck, I press my face into her hair and the inhalation of air that's involuntarily dragged into my lungs is the precursor to a sob that I stifle with everything in me by clamping down my lips and biting down from the inside to keep it trapped.

I hold my breath.

The sob leaks from my eyes instead.

I do not cry in front of people. I save it for when I'm alone in my room, or in the shower, or in a bathroom stall at school if it's a particularly shitty day. I feel like such a goddamn failure right now. No one is supposed to see this. It's supposed to remain hidden. My sadness is mine and it shouldn't bleed all over anyone else.

Holding me to her with one arm while running the other hand up and down my back, she presses her lips to my ear and the whisper of a kiss touches it before the whisper of the words do. "Breathe, Toby. *Just breathe.*"

I can't.

Not yet.

Because it will be loud and tortured. It's clawing fiercely to be let out.

"Breathe," she repeats.

I bury my face in my elbow resting on her shoulder to muffle the embarrassing ugliness that escapes. I'm usually a silent crier—I can mute the sound and let the pain of encapsulating it burn me from the inside. Today is different, I guess. The ugly bursts out in the open before I'm able to sniff and clear my nose, and breathe deep as Alice coached. She's still rubbing my back when I finally swallow down the lump in my throat and apologize into my elbow. "I'm so sorry."

Her hand moves up to cradle the back of my head, holding it in place. It's a comforting gesture and I can honestly say that no one has ever held me, touched me, cared for me like this. I wasn't raised in a family that showed affection. We didn't touch. I hugged Nina twice. In this moment, I don't ever want Alice to let me go, because even though it still hurts like hell—it hurts a little less.

"Don't be," she whispers against my neck. "Just promise me that someday, when it doesn't hurt so much to talk about, you'll tell me the story. I want to hear it, Toby. I want to hear all of your stories."

I lift my head and press the side of my cheek to the side of hers so she can feel my answering nod.

Stroking the hair on the back of my head, she nods in agreement.

And then Alice starts to sway, and before I know it, we're slow dancing to U2 in the middle of Wax Trax on a Sunday afternoon. My eyes are still wet and hers are still red.

Despite everything, I don't care what anyone thinks because this is mine.

Until the song ends and I open my eyes to everyone staring at us or diligently trying hard not to. I can't decide which is worse.

As if Alice notices the tension swell in me, she whispers in my ear, "I should get home, Toby."

Grabbing her cane, I lead her out the door and give her directions so she can lead us back to the Victorian on Clarkson, that way she'll be able to come back here on her own anytime she wants. I also add that this isn't the safest neighborhood after dark and she should avoid going out alone then.

Taber is sitting on the front steps when we approach the house. His arms are folded, resting on his knees, and his forehead rests on his arms. He's a still frame of worry until he lifts his head, sees Alice, and every inch of him relaxes.

"Getting to know the neighborhood?" he asks. The casualness of the question is telling. It's trusting, knowing, supportive, and thoughtful.

"Yeah. Toby took me to a record store a few blocks away. It's called Wax Trax, you'll love it," Alice answers as Taber pulls her into a hug.

"A record store? Perfect," are the words Taber's mouth says. *Are you okay?* is the question his hug asks.

"Is she gone?" Alice asks in answer.

He releases her. "You know how much Rachel enjoys quality time alone with me." He tries to sound light when he says it, and then adds, "The conversation after you left was riveting, we chatted about cross-stitch and puppies over coffee for an enjoyable hour. I didn't want it to end, but sadly, she had to get to work."

A smile breaks out on Alice's face and it reminds me why Taber deserves her. He saves her from sadness. I am sadness. "She hates dogs. And coffee."

"Does she at least still have a deep and wholesome love affair with cross-stitch?" Taber asks to prolong Alice's smile.

She answers on an amused snort. "The deepest."

"Thank God or my lies would have no merit." That's where he leaves it and turns to face me mouthing the words, *Thank you,* before he asks, "You like music, Toby?"

I nod and add, "Yeah," to include Alice in the conversation.

"Our band plays Saturday night, you should come. Alice is amazing." He glances at Alice and smiles knowingly when her cheeks brighten and blush at the compliment.

"Yeah?" When I realize that sounded like I'm questioning her talent instead of the fact that he's inviting me to their show, I add a quick, "Okay."

Alice smiles but says nothing.

"Listen, I hate to bring this party to an end, but we really need to get to band practice," Taber says apologetically.

Alice nods and reaches out until her hand makes contact with my sleeve. Pulling me to her, she wraps me in a hug and whispers in my ear, "Thank you for Wax Trax...and the dance...and for not leaving me alone to get lost in my thoughts."

My grip on her is awkward given our audience; it feels forced and unnatural. The opposite of how this felt less than twenty minutes ago. I want to melt into her and bury my face in her hair. Instead, I'm rigid and distant. A boyfriend looking on will do that. I'm also starting to sweat. I can't ignore the *thank you* when she's hugging me though, so I repeat what she said about Simon Le Bon in the store.

"You aren't truly doing life justice if you haven't experienced Wax Trax."

She gets the reference and smiles when she releases me.

"Ready?" Taber asks Alice. "Our gear is already in the van."

"Yup," she answers, before she adds, "Bye, Toby."

"Bye." One word. It doesn't feel like enough after all she's given me today. I'm suddenly plunged back into reality when I hear Taber speak.

"Later, Toby."

When I pry my eyes from Alice and dart them to Taber, he mouths, *Thank you*, again while he pokes out an elbow and prods Alice gently with it. I think he's messing with her until she grips his bicep and he leads her down the sidewalk to an old panel van that's beat to hell. It's white and says *Bob's Appliance Repair* on the side in faded red, cursive letters.

As I walk back inside, I'm kicking myself for accepting the invitation for Saturday night. I don't have any spare money for a ticket. I don't have any spare courage to actually show up. And I don't have any spare hope that I can do friendship worthy of Alice.

Because I don't do friendship.

I'm counting out, that's a bad time to invite people in.

That thought opens the door to guilt and it stampedes me in a relentless barrage.

Guilt that I'll let her down.

Guilt that I'll hurt her.

Guilt that I like her as much as I do.

Guilt that she has a boyfriend who's perfect for her.

Guilt that I can't stop thinking about that Siouxsie and the Banshees T-shirt.

Guilt that I felt more today with her than all of my recent Friday nights rolled up into one.

Guilt that I'm even thinking about any of this because I'm a piece of shit who only has eighty-eight days left.

Guilt...

Guilt...

And more fucking...

Guilt.

JOHNNY COMES HOME AROUND MIDNIGHT STUMBLING drunk. So much for short-lived sobriety.

CHAPTER NINE

The cock clock reads five twenty, which means I have ten minutes to make a few sandwiches and eat them. There are three pieces of bread left, a half teaspoon of mayo, and three cheese slices. I stack and layer everything I have to work with and the result is a pathetic Big Mac. Minus the burgers. And lettuce. And pickles. And special sauce. I make a mental note to stop at the grocery store near school and pick up some food on my way home tomorrow afternoon.

Cliff wanders out of his room looking dazed. I assume he's stoned but don't ask.

"Babysitting tonight, Daddy?" he asks, though the normal sneering chuckle that usually accompanies this question is absent.

I take a few deep breaths before I answer simply, "It's Tuesday."

Every Monday and Thursday morning and Tuesday evening, Chantal waits tables at a diner a few blocks away. During her morning shifts her coworker comes over with her kids and takes care of Joey and Mrs. Bennett, and when she works, Chantal watches her three kids. The trading of care works out for both of them. The evening shift is mine. I'll never forget the look of humiliation on Chantal's face when she knocked on my door a little over a month ago and asked if I could help her out with Joey on Tuesday nights so she could pick up the extra shift. I've known Chantal for several years and though everything changed between us when she got pregnant, she's still one of the proudest people I know. She clings to it, it's her essence. Her defining trait. So, accepting help, let alone asking for it, makes her feel like a failure. I know what that's like and don't want her anywhere near failure because it's destructive and she has too much to live for. But as much as she doesn't want to admit it, she needs help. She needs a lot of help. You can't care for a baby and an ailing, elderly woman on your own full-time. Everything has to be on her terms though—when she gets to the breaking point and desperately needs help, she asks.

"Is it weird being a dad at seventeen?" Cliff asks as I'm chewing the last bite of my sandwich.

He almost sounds sincere, which immediately puts me on high alert. Why would he ask a question like that unless...I turn to face him and scrutinize his eyes to figure out how messed up he is. "Did you smoke after school?" I ask.

He shakes his head and I believe him. "Wish I had, but no. Nobody could score any weed today."

When I walk to my room to unlock it, he paces behind me and asks again, "Well, is it weird?"

I huff, because this is quickly turning into a Sex Ed talk that I would rather cut off my right nut than give. My back still to him while leaning in and grabbing my backpack and sketchpad, I ask, "Did you get someone pregnant, Cliff?"

His hesitation to answer churns the cheese sandwich in my stomach and I freeze mid-squat.

"No."

When he finally says it, the air rushes out of my lungs in a gust of relief. Johnny would murder him if, while under his lackluster guardianship, Cliff knocked someone up at fourteen fucking years old.

Slinging my backpack over my shoulder, I lock up. "Good, keep it that way."

"You didn't answer my question," he says, as I open the door to exit the apartment.

Normally I'd walk out the door without another word because that's how Cliff and I communicate—he talks and I don't—but for some reason, I give him the most honest answer I can. "You have no idea." And I close the door behind me.

Chantal is wearing her pink uniform dress and name tag that reads, *Trixie,* pinned to her chest. It's funny because Chantal could never be a Trixie. Trixie is a name people don't take seriously. This woman is the opposite. From the stories Mrs. Bennett has told me, Chantal's been through a lot. She's the child of a mixed-race marriage who's endured lifelong racism and prejudice but thrived in the face of it. She lost her parents at thirteen and Mrs. Bennett, her maternal grand-mother, took her in. She entered the University of Denver at eighteen, the first in her family to go to college, and on scholar-ship no less. Her junior year she got pregnant, her future forever altered by an asshole who had no right to touch a woman like her. Two semesters short of her degree, Joey was born.

And here we are...

"Hi, Toby." She sounds tired but determined as she slips on

her jacket. It's her demeanor ninety-nine percent of the time. When it's not, you know it's time to worry. "Joey just ate so he should be good until bedtime. Formula and bottle are on the kitchen counter. Make sure it's not too hot."

I nod. This is the standard drill every Tuesday night. "I know."

She smiles that smile that tells me she knows she's needlessly worrying. "I know you know. Sorry. See you at midnight." She raises her voice over the volume of the TV to Mrs. Bennett, who's sitting on the couch behind a TV tray with a half-empty plate of food and an almost empty glass of milk. "Bye, Grandma. Toby's going to stay here with you while I'm at work. You remember Toby, he lives upstairs?" It must be a bad day if an explanation is needed.

Mrs. Bennett turns her head toward Chantal's voice and I see the vacant look in her eyes and know recollection isn't likely, reminders or not. "Who?" She's studying me, but it's the assessing of a stranger.

I nod toward the door, subtly giving Chantal the permission I know she feels like she needs to leave. "She'll be fine," I whisper as I watch Mrs. Bennett's gaze snap back to the TV.

She always feels guilty leaving them both. Guilt is a burden we both carry, though she allows it to fuel her these days and I've always let it destroy me, but it's harder on the days that her grandmother's Alzheimer's is in control of Mrs. Bennett, instead of the other way around. "I know," she whispers before she slips out the door.

Walking to Joey on the floor, who's holding a brightly colored plastic block, I sit down beside him on the blanket and set my backpack and sketchpad on the floor out of the way. I'll do my homework after Joey goes to bed in two hours.

"That taste good?" I ask as he gnaws on the corner of the red block.

His hands and the block are covered in slobber. He stops momentarily and grins at me and the sound of my voice. He's never done this for me. Chantal can prompt smiles from him all the time because he's a momma's boy. But this is new and it makes me feel not quite so invisible. Picking him up and sitting him on my lap, a sudden swell of emotion creeps into my throat and before I know it tears are blotting my eyes. I'm glad I have my back to Mrs. Bennett, because even in her current state of bewilderment, I don't want her to see me like this. This is similar to the common surge of emotion that comes on several times every day, but especially at night. It's the overwhelming rush of disappointment in me, my actions, and my life. It's the constant reminder that I'm an asshole who deserves nothing and no one. It's the message that runs on a loop through my brain, reminding me that I'm hopeless and everyone would be better off if I wasn't around. Looking at this little boy, it's also the unjustness that someone so pure and sweet wasn't fathered by someone who should be the mentor and role model he'll need down the road.

I let the paralyzing helplessness flow until the taps are dry, while Joey chews on his fist and his tiny fingers on the other hand fiddle with the drawstring on my sweatshirt. When the tears stop and I feel like I can breathe without hiccupping in air, I run the sleeve of my sweatshirt across my eyes and cheeks to clear away the evidence of my failure. I stand holding Joey and walk to Mrs. Bennett. She's resting back against the couch cushions, settled in to watch the rest of a *Three's Company* rerun that's playing.

"Are you finished with your dinner?" I ask her.

There are a few bites of mashed potatoes and meatloaf left on the plate.

When she looks up at me and asks, "Where's Irvin? Is he

still at work?" I know I'm not going to get an answer out of her and that I should clear the dishes.

Irvin was her husband. He died in World War II, over forty-four years ago. When all else escapes her, the memory of Irvin always seems to swoop in. I like to think it's merciful comfort on her mind's part to reunite them.

"Yeah, he'll be home late."

Chantal says when this happens, I should remind her that Irvin's been gone for years to try to bring her back to the present, but I can't do it. So, I lie because it brings her fleeting happiness. It won't last; she may as well enjoy it while she can.

I cover Mrs. Bennett's leftovers in foil and put them in the refrigerator so she can eat them tomorrow and then I return to the living room. Figuring Joey will be ready to return to his blocks on the floor, I try to lay him down, but he clings to me and starts to whimper, the precursor to actual tears. Changing my mind, I sit on the other end of the couch and ask Mrs. Bennett if she needs anything.

She responds with, "No, thank you, Toby." Mrs. Bennett is back. "I'm tired, I'll probably turn in when this program is over."

"Okay," I respond as Joey snuggles into my chest, rests his head on my shoulder, and drools all over it while he tries to gum his fist off.

The room is quiet except for the TV for the next ten minutes. When the final scene plays and a commercial appears telling us how much Mikey likes Life cereal, Mrs. Bennett announces she's heading to bed.

It's only six thirty, but who am I to begrudge anyone getting some extra sleep if they can? I'd probably go to bed early every night if monsters didn't keep me awake.

She's standing in front of us, staring at us. She does this a lot, stares. It makes me unbelievably uncomfortable, but if I don't meet her deep brown eyes and engage her, it's easier.

"When you hold him it always reminds me of my husband holding Chantal's mom when she was that age. There is not much in this world that makes my heart sing like watching a child transform a man into a father. Good night, Toby. Good night, Joey."

That was a compliment. That I haven't earned. "Night, Mrs. Bennett."

She smiles sweetly, pats Joey's back gently, and disappears behind her closed bedroom door. Since the baby is content, I grab the paperback I'm reading for an English assignment from my backpack and lie on the couch with Joey stretched out on my belly, his head resting on my chest. And I read "Moby Dick" aloud to him for thirty minutes. My sweatshirt is soaked with drool by the time my voice grows hoarse from use, and I can tell Joey is fighting sleep when he starts rubbing his eyes.

Fresh diaper and onesie on for bed, I make his bottle. Usually I sit in the rocking chair in Chantal's room next to his crib to feed him, but I'm extra tired tonight and afraid that the chair will only make it worse, so I feed him standing instead. I walk the living room, Joey in my arms on his back looking up at me through half-lidded, milk-drunk eyes. Every minute the struggle to pry them open after they slip closed is harder and harder, until he gives up the effort and concentrates on drinking instead. His puckered, pink lips working in earnest. Bottle empty, lips still trying to coax more in their sleepy mission, I slowly slide the nipple from his mouth and begin swaying, rocking him the rest of the way into slumber. It's not long before his breathing slows and deepens into that space where only dreams can touch him. Placing him in his crib without waking him is getting more and more difficult every week. After four failed attempts, and an hour of trying, I give up and sit down on the rocking chair with him in the dark.

I sit there until I hear keys rattle in the front door, and Chantal walks in looking exhausted.

"He wouldn't go down in his crib?" she asks through a wide yawn.

I shake my head, a yawn copycatting its way out after hearing hers.

"Did you finish your homework?" She's worried, I can hear it in her voice.

"Yeah," I lie. I have about two hours' worth of work to do before I go to bed, but I would never tell her that.

She turns on the nightlight next to her twin bed and returns to scoop Joey from my arms. "Thank you," she whispers before she expertly transitions him to his crib without incident. She follows me out to the living room, where I gather up my book, backpack, and sketchpad from the floor. "Was Grandma okay? Any issues?"

"She went to bed a little early, but other than that she was fine. Nothing unusual." It escapes on another yawn.

She's standing at the door holding it open for me, and for some reason, it's always awkward when I leave like this. I don't know if it's the fact that I've just spent several hours with Joey, or if it's the fact that I've been inside this woman, or if it's the fact that our arrangement is murky, but leaving her apartment late into the night always doubles the guilt for me. And she always acts like she isn't quite sure what to say either.

So we've come to a mutual unspoken agreement that we won't say anything.

I leave in silence.

And she lets me.

CHAPTER TEN

Present, March 1987
Toby

The knocking is muffled but grows louder when the second round of it starts up. I set aside my sketchpad and rise to open my bedroom door. The kitchen is dark, but when I flick the light on, the cock clock reads three in the morning. I glance at Johnny's and Cliff's doors before answering the knock. Johnny's door is open and he isn't in it. And Cliff's is closed, which means he's snoring behind it.

Two more raps on the door register as I open it.

Taber is standing on the other side, looking as tired as I feel, but fully dressed and wearing his wool coat and contrasting snowflakes in his dark hair. "Sorry, man, but Johnny is passed out inside the front door at the foot of the stairs. You wanna give me a hand and we'll carry him up? I tried to wake him, but he wouldn't budge."

I think most residents who have been here for a while know

Johnny is a drunk based on his absence. It's never been on full display like this, at least not since I've lived here. He either stays somewhere else, or he manages to make it upstairs and into his bed before he passes out. Something about him outing himself with such a grand gesture makes me embarrassed for him.

"Yeah, let me grab my shoes."

Taber waits in the hall while I slip them on and when I return, he asks, "This happen often?"

"The drinking or the passing out?" I question, not wanting to answer.

"Both?" He shrugs and paired with softness in his voice it screams compassion.

Which prompts me to answer, "The drinking is daily. The passing out downstairs on the floor isn't."

He nods and licks his lips like he's thinking as we walk down the final flight of stairs.

"Jesus," I say under my breath. "He's lucky he wasn't on his back or he could've died." He's facedown. Vomit on the floorboards is pooled around, and under, his face.

Taber sighs sadly and agrees. "Yup."

"You take his feet, I'll take the top half," I say, cringing at the sight. And the smell.

"I appreciate that," Taber says with his trademark grin.

We hoist his deadweight and make it up the first flight before we have to stop and put him down to adjust our grip. We're both dragging in air loudly, exertion taking its toll.

"I should probably quit smoking. Moving a dead body is exhausting. I could never be a serial killer," Taber jokes quietly.

I laugh on the inside, but it doesn't make it out. I'm relieved he's joking instead of judging, it's making all of this easier to deal with. "Me too."

Final flight assailed, I lead us into his bedroom where we

put him on his bed, take off his coat, and roll him over on his belly in case he gets sick again. Taber stuffs his hands in his pockets and lingers for a few seconds like he's trying to decide what the next move should be.

"I'll take it from here." I'm not good at reassuring, but I'm trying my best.

"Sorry I had to wake you," he apologizes.

"You didn't. I don't sleep much. Insomnia," I explain.

He looks me over like he wants to say something, but he stops short and I'm left with a contemplative, "Good luck, Toby," instead. I don't know if he's talking about Johnny, my insomnia, or something else altogether.

I nod and he leaves.

Cleaning up Johnny, the puke downstairs, and myself takes another half hour.

I doze for two hours before my alarm goes off to wake me for school.

Johnny's still asleep when I leave and I'm grateful because I don't want to have to face him and tell him what happened if and when he asks.

He probably won't because avoidance is our game.

He's getting even better at avoiding life and everything in it than I am.

That's quite a feat.

CHAPTER ELEVEN

Different

PAST, January 1985
Nina's Protector

KEN *IS* DIFFERENT.

In turn, Nina is different. They've been dating for four weeks and the changes in her are miraculous. The forced smiles are gone, replaced with real ones. I've watched his attention and compliments—which I'm generally reluctantly cautious of —breathe life into her. Transform her. Nina has never been a confident person. I've known her forever and her life has been hard. Early on, difficulty and cruelty were thrust upon her, out of her control. She grew up used to expecting the worst out of life, and the worst continued to find her.

I oftentimes liken Nina to driving past a car accident—I know that sounds awful, but bear with me. No matter how badly I want to cover my face with my hands and avert my attention from the wreckage, I can't. I can't because I love her. So, instead, I grip the first thing within reach tightly with both hands and squeeze until I'm white-knuckled, focus unblinking on the disaster, and scream at her to stop. Or to make changes. Or to pay attention.

But like I said, Ken is different.

He relaxes her. Which relaxes me. There's no high alert *Danger! Danger!* status with him. Which in itself makes me a bit edgy because that's what I'm used to, but I roll with it. Because he takes her to dinner. He brings her flowers. He picks her up from work. He tells her she looks pretty. It's been sixteen years since anyone told her that other than Toby when he was five. Hearing it from your blood is different than hearing it from someone you're romantically linked to.

Tonight, when he picked her up from work, the first words he spoke to her when she got in the car were: "I want you to move in with me. What do you say?" His hand cupped her cheek lovingly.

Her trust transuded into the palm of his hand. And she agreed instantly. "Okay."

In that hasty agreement is the first niggling of *Danger! Danger!* I've felt in weeks. I know Nina is only looking for a way out of her mom's apartment. She's been living with her for months now and she yearns for independence. No thirty-one-year-old wants to live with their parent, but a series of poor choices, which I railed against loudly, put her there.

At her agreement a smile seeps into his cheeks; like a drop of ink dispersing through water it fans out gloriously until his face is animated and bright.

"Yeah?" he questions. There's no surprise in his tone, in his expression, only joy. And maybe a little satisfaction. "This weekend?"

"Yeah," she agrees with a smile that matches his.

Danger! Danger! is called off completely again. I think she should do it. I don't say so, but I think getting away from her mom would be good for her. Her mother has always been controlling, manipulative, and a bad influence. She should have been protective, watchful, and guiding like me. Yes, I'm judgmental and a bit egotistical, it's who I am. It's then that the idea hits me: Nina should take Ken home to meet Toby. Toby and I are allies, an army of two who want nothing more than what's best for Nina. I love that kid. And he's like one of those police dogs trained to sniff out drugs; he can smell shady ten miles away. If Ken passes the Toby test, he's golden.

Just like that Nina looks at Ken and says, "Can we go by my mom's so I can change clothes?" Then she adds, "And you can meet my brother," like she's a mouthpiece for my thoughts.

Yes! I cheer quietly to myself.

Though his cheeks are still tugged back in a smile, the brightness snuffs out. I chalk it up to nerves when he reaches across the seat and squeezes her knee lovingly. "Okay. Sure, let's go meet your brother."

I study Ken closely when they pull up and park down the street from the Victorian on Clarkson. There's a light sheen of sweat on his forehead and his expression is schooled and unreadable. My Sherlock Holmes hat is firmly in place and my eyes are narrowed as I try to figure him out.

Nina is fidgety, that's nothing new, but anxiety is pulsing through her as she reaches for the handle and hesitantly pushes the creaky door of his old Chevelle open. When they come together on the sidewalk and join hands, I forget that these are two grown adults about to walk into a house and engage a fifteen-year-old boy. I know the only thing going through Nina's mind as she shuffles along is how desperately she wants Toby to like Ken. It's like this every time she dates someone new. Toby never thinks they're good enough for her. He's been correct every time. And Ken? I have no idea what Ken is thinking, but there's no confidence in his gait. His usual swagger is gone, his steps aren't fluid. As if hesitation is tripping him up.

Led Zeppelin's "Kashmir" is pulsing loudly like a heartbeat from behind apartment 1A's door when they approach. Toby must be alone; he never turns the record player up this loud when their mom is home.

"Robert Plant is a pussy," Ken mutters as Nina unlocks the door.

Nina chuckles to herself before retorting, "We can't all be AC/DC fans, Ken," with a dash of sarcasm and a wink, despite Nina being Zeppelin's biggest, lifelong fan. This flirty side of Nina is a relic from the past. It hasn't seen the light of day in years. Most past boyfriends haven't appreciated her well-placed humor. I marvel at it; her sarcasm is fierce. I'm happy she's dusting it off and putting it to use again.

A relaxed smile graces him as he accepts her teasing and kisses her on the cheek. "But you should be," he whispers in a serious tone that betrays the smile, before the door opens and judgment day descends upon him.

In the pause between "Kashmir" ending and "In the Light" beginning, Nina yells, "Toby!"

"In here!" Toby yells from his bedroom.

I notice the stumble in her step as she moves toward his door, it's a giveaway. She's rethinking this plan. She's rethinking the second opinion or affirmation she's just realized she's after, because if Toby doesn't approve of Ken, she doesn't know what she'll do. Will she look at Ken, who she tells herself she's fallen in love with, differently? Will she suddenly see in him what Toby sees?

Toby meets her in the doorway of his room; he's on his way out to greet her. Toby's ghost smile is in place. I call it that because Toby never smiles outwardly, he never really has, but every once in a while, happiness burns bright in his pale green eyes and they light up, while his lips refuse to curve upward and join them. Even when he was little, he was serious. Inquisitive, quietly observing and sifting through people's actions and words to decide if what someone projected on the outside matched who they were on the inside. It's unnerving how perceptive he is.

"I thought you were going out tonight? Wanna eat—" he trails off when he notices Ken standing by the front door.

The atmosphere in the room shifts in an instant. It's bloated; there simply isn't enough space within the four walls of the living room to hold the judgment that's expanding within like a balloon. It's pushing in from opposite sides of the room, equal in weight and force, and Nina is stuck helplessly in the middle. The air being forced out of her lungs, Ken and Toby's stare down is constricting from the back and the front. I don't know if Ken's aware his posture has changed. He's standing up straighter. He's looking for respect from Toby even though he hasn't earned it; it's an age-based assumption it will be given.

If Ken is waiting for Toby to introduce himself first, he'll grow old where he stands. It won't happen.

Toby is blinking slowly. He's starting to sweat, but other than that, there's no tell that his nerves are blistering. He's doing his thing—assessing—with the music blaring all around them like a siren call.

Nina shifts from one foot to the other—words stuck in her throat, nerves tightening—as time slows to mimic the uneven rhythm of the room's tension. The music is suddenly too loud, her beloved Robert Plant's voice too eerie, and her only mission is to turn it off. When the music is muted surely the universe will right itself and Ken and Toby will stop the pretense and be civil. Nina is holding her breath, but I already know how this is going to end. There's no amount of righting itself the universe can do to make Toby change his mind. I can see the disapproval in his eyes and so can Nina.

The needle skitters across the vinyl as Nina lifts it with a shaky hand.

"Shit," she mutters, hoping she didn't scratch it. This album is hers. It's also her favorite.

When she turns to face the showdown, she decides the sudden shock of an audible void has done little to remedy the situation. If anything, it's amplified it and has demanded it be addressed.

Nina's eyes instinctively go to Toby first but bounce back to Ken instantly. Ken is standing closer to her and it seems proximity has chosen him for her. "Ken, this is my little brother, Toby."

Ken remains stoically still for an uneasy three or four seconds, before he takes a few steps forward into the living room where he stops halfway and raises his chin slightly in greeting. "Hey, man."

Toby blinks twice and takes one step forward into the living room, leaving several feet between them. This is it. I know it; Nina knows it. Toby is shorter than Ken, he hasn't hit a growth spurt yet, but he looks up at him and valiantly holds his gaze. In all the years I've known Toby, I've only known him to act bold on Nina's behalf. All he's ever wanted is to be her protector. "You're Nina's boyfriend."

It's not a question but the way he says it, an odd juxtaposition of doubt and certainty, prods Ken to answer anyway. "Yeah."

Toby's eyes drop to the floor and he licks his lips before his eyes bounce back up to Ken's. "What's your favorite thing about her?" he asks without further hesitation.

This approach is new. Nina doesn't like it, she's a rubber

band ready to snap. *Wait him out, see where this goes,* I coach silently.

Ken tilts his head and gives Toby a puzzled look. "What?"

Toby repeats slowly, emphasizing every word like their importance is paramount: "What's your favorite thing about her?" The pause that follows is short, like Toby's patience for Ken. Toby glances pointedly at Nina before turning and stepping back into his room. One hand on the door, he looks over his shoulder at Ken and says sadly, "It shouldn't take that long, Ken. That was an easy question." The door shuts before Ken or Nina can reply.

Nina's thoughts stall out.

It was an easy question! I echo loudly.

"What the hell was that about?" Ken asks angrily. "Is your brother always such a little prick?"

Nina is still in shock and coupled with letdown it feels oddly like betrayal. Nina's happy for the first time in forever. *Because of Ken.* When she finally looks at Ken, all she can do is shrug pitifully. "I'm sorry."

In those two hushed words, I'm brought back to all the times I've heard them uttered in that same tone. Sometimes it's warranted, most times it isn't. Nina has always been the type of person to apologize first and the vast majority of them are inserted needlessly into a situation to smooth things over. Saying, "I'm sorry," to someone, when they're the one who should be saying it to her instead, is a lifelong, chronic problem. Taking the blame for everything is a by-product of insecurity and a sense of worthlessness in Nina. Self-doubt has always been louder than her cheerleader...me. That's always pissed me off.

The current *I'm sorry* hanging in the room is pulsing and building steam. It's gingerly stroking Ken's ego like cautious fingertips trying to calm a riled cat. But it's working twofold on

Nina. Despite me backing up Toby and yelling again, *It was an easy question!* to prompt, if nothing else, a quick counterargument to the pedestal she's put Ken on, Nina takes the fork in the road she's never taken. Resentment toward Toby is rising. And second by second, she's embracing it. Dangerously welcoming it in. I know how dangerous this is, because Nina can hold a grudge like a champ. When resentment takes root, there's no chance of weeding it from the garden. It's there to stay.

Nina's glassy eyes blaze at Toby's door. "Help me pack. I'm moving in tonight."

I know, in the moment, that Nina is making a bad decision. I'm the queen of hunches. *Trust your gut* is my motto, my epithet.

Ken is different, I remind myself.

Only this time it feels ominous, instead of reassuring.

Ken is different, I repeat.

Trust me! my gut agrees.

Ken is different.

Different.

Different.

Danger!

Danger!

Ken is *different*.

CHAPTER TWELVE

Present, March 1987
Toby

Rap, rap...rap. The knocks are quiet like the person on the other side of the door is hesitant to initiate the contact. It's early on a Friday, they're being considerate. Considerate is alien in this building. In this part of town.

Which means it can only be one person.

Alice.

She's standing in the hall when I open the door.

"Hi," is the word I go with to let her know it's me greeting her. There are so many other things on the tip of my tongue, but they would all involve spilling thoughts about her that are better left locked inside where only I can ponder them to the point of torture.

"Morning, Toby. I was hoping you would answer. Sorry it's so early, but I'm headed to school and wanted to let you know that the toilet is acting up again. Taber says it's the flapper thingy. He tried to fix it, but he thinks it needs to be replaced because the toilet won't stop running. I would've called you this afternoon, but I have an appointment right after school." She's talking quickly and I want her to slow down so I have more time with her, but I realize Taber is probably waiting on her and I need to get going too.

"I'll take care of it."

"You're the best. Thanks." She's already turned and is walking down the hall. "Sorry to rush off, Taber's waiting in the van. Have a great day," she calls from the stairs.

For the first time ever I almost reply with, "You too," but my natural instinct to not respond to niceties wins out and I don't.

As soon as I get home from school, before I even listen to the answering machine, I hoist the toolbox down from the top of the fridge, grab the master keys, and head down to apartment 2A to look at Alice's toilet. Alice said she has an appointment, so I assume that means band practice. I'll have the place to myself and be in and out. Maybe I can even get it fixed before they get home so it's not a bother to them tonight.

Unlocking the door, I slip in and leave the door open. I head straight for the bathroom but stop mid-path through the living room when I hear noises coming from the bedroom on the left. Noises that shutter my eyelids and take a stab at my gut. The rhythmic squeak of bedsprings accompanied by ecstasy-induced moans and the deep rumble of unintelligible words—an in sync symphony of pleasure that fills me with boiling jealousy. For seconds I stand in shocked suspense, listening like a masochist...or a pacifist. I can't decide which because the jealousy is raging and blending with my self-loathing. *You could never have her. She's too good for you. They belong together. Your days are numbered anyway, let them be happy.* And then my inner monologue morphs into the familiar repetitive, all-consuming chant of my truth...

You're nothing.

You're nothing.

You're nothing.

As if on cue, everything climaxes behind the thin, pine bedroom door coated in layers of peeling paint in contrasting colors. Their bliss in perfect time with my hate. Hate directed solely at me. Their bliss directed solely at each other.

I need to leave.

By the time I reach the stairs, I only make it halfway up before I stop and sit down. I can't go back into the apartment because Cliff is home. I'm a disaster and I don't want him to see me like this. I don't want anyone to see me like this. I'm shaking, my heart is racing, and when I drop my face into my hands to hide my malfunction and inability to cope from the world, I realize my cheeks are wet. I'm crying and I didn't know it. That happens a lot. Sometimes the tears are there long before I'm aware of them. Pain has an inexplicable way of making that possible, a remarkable way of making sure you don't forget it and give it recognition even when you don't want to.

The sound of a door opening brings me out of my thoughts and forces me to surface and acknowledge the land of the living. The panic of being caught in the middle of a meltdown will do that. Wiping the tears away with a swipe of the collar of my T-shirt, I want to sniff and rein in the snot that's running free but that would make me known and I'm trying to hide. So I wipe my nose with my T-shirt too.

Voices drift down the hall and up the stairs to me, undisturbed and clear. "I'm sorry we couldn't spend more time together, but I have to pick up Alice from her appointment and then we need to get to band practice." It's Taber. The bastard doesn't even sound ashamed. His voice is soft and loving, what a fucking imposter. I was actually starting to like the guy.

"I'll take any spare minute I can get, you know that." She sounds so different than Alice. Her voice is higher and she has an obscure accent.

"God, I can't wait until you graduate and we can be together, Inga. Fort Collins is too far away, this whole distance thing is killing me." He sounds sincere and it makes me want to punch him in the goddamn face. This whole thing is killing *him*? What's it going to do to *Alice* when she finds out? It will kill her. *Bastard.*

A pause punctuated by the faint sound of three staccato kisses and finally a sigh. "I know. Me too. We knew when we started this it was going to be hard, but I promise it will all be worth it. I love you." *Bitch.*

They're a united front joined to destroy Alice's world.

"I love you, too. So much. Drive safe, I'll talk to you tomorrow." Declarations and promises that should belong to Alice.

Her footsteps gain volume before they ghost away down the stairs and out the front door.

I'm not a violent person, but I want to pummel Taber. I thought there was only enough room for two varieties of hate within me: the hate for my mom and the hate for myself. They fill me to capacity. It seems I was wrong. There's room for Taber too.

I listen to his door open and shut again, followed by hurried footsteps to pick up Alice.

Maybe hate isn't a strong enough word for what I'm feeling.

I need to get out of here. Thank God it's Friday. Dan's. Escape.

There's only one message on the answering machine when I return to apartment 3A. It's Mrs. Bennett. There was a raccoon in the dumpster outside when Chantal took the trash out today. I weigh the call for a second and decide to ignore it. It's likely untrue since raccoons are nocturnal. Even if it did happen, there's nothing I can do about it now.

I pull the T-shirt I wore yesterday out of my laundry bag and swap it out for the one I'm wearing now—a ketchup stain is better than snot—and zip up my sweatshirt over the top of it to hide the red splotch. The stain is over my heart, which seems appropriate since it feels like I've been stabbed there.

Locking up both doors behind me, I'm out of the house and on pace for a record arrival at Dan's, the adrenaline still coursing, driving me into a frenzy.

Johnny is sitting on his stool surrounded by cigarette smoke, a cranky Joe Cocker tune, and the touchstone degeneration that only Dan's Tavern can provide and somehow bask in. His eyes look haunted and hollow, dark and sunken, like rest has been evasive. His entire life.

Normally, I would ask for my money so I can sink into inebriation like the sea of lost and forgotten humanity around me, but I wait him out and we wallow in our shitty moods in unison.

Johnny slides the bills across the bar in front of me without prompting. "You should go home, Toby," accompanies it. When he calls me Toby instead of *Asshole*, I know he's serious.

Stunned, my reply is paused, but when I find my bearings, it's an inquiry more than a challenge. "Why?"

He shakes his head, his intense gaze drifting out across the bar but choosing not to zero in on anything in particular because the thoughts filling his mind won't allow it. "You shouldn't be here. I told Dan you're only seventeen and asked him not to serve you anymore." He doesn't sound happy to say it, but he does sound resolved. Like he's sad, sorry, and resolute all at once. He slides his pack of cigarettes and Zippo in my direction and adds, "You can have one. When it's done, you go home."

A cigarette between my lips, I ask, "Why would you do that?" while I bring the flame to life and inhale.

"You should go home, Toby," he repeats like it's the only explanation I need. Like he has the authority to make the command.

"*You* should go home," I volley back. That brings his eyes, underscored with weariness, to mine, and I lift my eyebrows in response and hold him in a stare. It's not something I usually do. Eye contact like this makes me squirm, but I'm pissed and if he's going to call me out then I'm going to call him out too. "You were blackout drunk; you could've died the other night."

When the dark truth hits, the connection severs and his eyes drop to his lap. I think it's because he's mad, but when he asks, "Did you get me into bed?" I know it's subdued humiliation.

I nod. "Taber came home late and found you downstairs by the front door. He knocked on our door and told me and we carried you up together."

His big, calloused hands scrub over his face like he's trying to erase the past...or maybe he's trying to erase the present. "Did Cliff see any of it?"

I flick ash into the ashtray in front of me and take another drag before I answer. "No. He was sleeping."

Running his hands through his hair, he rests his head against the wall behind him and shakes it in disgust. "I figured he didn't, he would've rubbed it in my face until the irony was tattooed. Hypocrites make horrible disciplinarians. I'm not cut out for this," he mutters, scolding himself.

I finish my cigarette and as soon as I snub it out, I want another one. I throw Dan a look to make sure Johnny wasn't bluffing about snitching on me, but when he gives his head a single, irrefutable, hard shake, I know he wasn't. I sigh, because tonight of all nights I need this. I need to dive headfirst into diversion. To feint reality. To *forget* reality.

Which Johnny brings front and center when he asks, "Any calls today?"

I huff, and it almost sounds like a humorless laugh. Except I don't laugh. "That son of a bitch Taber needs a new flapper for his toilet."

"Son of a bitch? Those are fighting words." Johnny sounds mildly intrigued.

I give him nothing but a shrug and swivel on my stool. Crossing my arms, I wait out tonight's redemption.

Ten minutes later, a group of three women walks in. When they immediately stop and a trio of discerning eyes travel a loop around the room, I know they've stumbled in here by mistake and they're two seconds away from deciding this was a bad idea. Or maybe not such a bad idea, when they take a seat at the nearest table and order a round of beers. They look out of place, like a full color rainbow in a sepia photo. They're dressed for a night out and it makes me wonder if they're tourists who ended up in the wrong part of town, or maybe they're waiting on the music venue a few blocks away to open and are having a drink or two beforehand.

I'm watching the two guys playing pool and replaying the sounds of Taber cheating on Alice in my mind, until it turns into an insane, tortuous soundtrack that's competing for my attention with The Rolling Stone's "You Can't Always Get What You Want" playing on the jukebox. The song wins because it's an accurate synopsis of the past, near and far, as well as prophetic of the future. That, and it's less depressing than Taber's betrayal.

I'm lost in thought, my anger, and the song, when Johnny's voice brings me back to the present. He's leaning forward on his stool and he's talking low. "Don't do it. You need to go home."

I turn my head, but not my body, to look at him. He's leaning back into the wall, and I'm about to ask him what that's supposed to mean when his eyes jump pointedly over my shoulder. When my head swivels back around, the blonde from the pack of three is standing in front of me. Her smile is a strip-tease. "We're getting out of here, do you wanna come party with us?"

The offer of escape.

It's like she's answered my prayers.

An uncharacteristic, *Yes*, is on the tip of my tongue.

Until the blonde morphs into another blonde.

The only blonde who matters.

I shake my head and mutter, "No," before I turn to face Johnny and mutter, "I need to go. There's something I need to do," while shaking two cigarettes from his pack. Stuffing one in my sweatshirt pocket and lighting the other. "These are illegal for minors too, you know?" I say, holding up the lit cigarette in my hand.

Johnny's eyes slide to the side to meet mine. "I'm choosing to ignore that one for now, don't make me change my mind."

When I hop off the stool, the girls are gone. Dan tips his chin to me on my way out. I do the same in return. I'll be back soon, you can drink in Colorado when you're eighteen and I have a birthday coming up.

When I walk outside, the sun is low in the sky, setting over the mountains in the distance. The Victorian on Clarkson is only down the street from Dan's so I haven't even finished the cigarette by the time I get there. Each stair passing underfoot amplifies my anxiety. She's going to be heartbroken. I don't want to deliver the news that breaks her heart.

And by the time I'm standing in front of 2A's door, hand

raised and poised to knock, my courage plummets and I can't do it.

I can't break Alice's heart. I can't watch the revelation dissolve her.

My Friday nights are spent dealing with the aftermath of situations like this. I don't think I can be the agent who provokes the disclosure of it.

Blissfully unaware is still blissful.

I know that's complete bullshit.

But, I'm a coward.

So, I walk up to 3A and finish the cigarette in my hand. Followed by the one in my pocket. And then I force myself into a sleep so unsettling and hostile that I'm brutalized when I wake from it.

CHAPTER THIRTEEN

PRESENT, March 1987
Toby

SATURDAY IS HELL.

The conscience is profound and unforgiving when self-preservation is lacking. It's unguarded, a bully that antagonizes toward action, even though I have a plan in place to end this in June. Sometimes I consider forgetting the plan and acting on the impulse to stop the pain now instead of later. Today is one of those days. Standing on our fire escape, I look at the ground three stories below and wonder if the hard landing would be enough to stop my body and release my soul.

I decide that it probably wouldn't and I'd only end up in the hospital with a plethora of broken bones instead. I can't finish school and graduate from a hospital room in a full body cast.

I've kept busy trying to ignore the guilt chant in my head and dodge the occupants of 2A. This morning I cleaned the leaves out of the gutters and fixed a fence post that's been loose for over a month. This afternoon I've been hiding out in the basement rearranging and sorting the spare parts and hardware on the shelves in the locked supply room where no one will find me. I told Cliff to come and get me only in case of an emergency. His idea of an emergency is dicey at best, so I'm surprised he's complied. There's a lot to do. Johnny keeps adding to the junk pile in the corner. If it has moving parts and is abandoned, he rescues it and dumps it here. I can't blame him; I fix a lot from this stash without spending a dime.

I brought my boom box and one of my cassettes down with me to keep me company. Occasionally, I hear someone on the other side of the door putting a load of laundry in the washer or dryer, but for the most part, it's solitary. When I'm done and the floor is clear, the shelves are orderly, and I'm covered in the filth of grimy old parts and avoidance, I sit on the floor with my back against the cool, stone-foundation wall and I hide.

I hide from the world.

I hide from the residents.

I hide from Alice.

I hide from Chantal and Joey.

I hide from Nina.

I hide.

That is until I hear a knock on the door. I pause, unmoving, and wait to see if they'll go away.

"Toby, I know you're in there! No one else in this house has the good taste to lock themselves away with The Smiths!" It's Alice yelling through a smile. Her voice is more playful when her grin is wide and toothy.

Opening the door, a greeting would be appropriate, but guilt makes me irritable and instead I ask, "How'd you know I was down here?"

"Cliff told me."

Of course he did. Guilt, the instigator with impeccable timing, drops the needle on the track of Taber and Inga in my mind and turns up the volume until it's deafening; I want to cover my ears even though I can't block it out because it's coming from the inside.

"What do you need?" I blurt. That sounded harsh and blunt and I regret it even before I see the subtle recoil of her reaction.

"Umm..." She fumbles as the smile tumbles from her lips. "I came to see if you wanted to ride with us to the gig, that way you can come in with us and won't need a ticket." She sounds hurt, like she already knows I'm going to bow out and flake on her.

Her words are kind.

Her tone is wounded.

I am an asshole.

I pinch the bridge of my nose because I can't punch myself in the face to exact some punishment and then I talk over my filter that's usually airtight. "I'm sorry." That was for being a dick. And holding back the truth. Sighing, because she's *so* fucking good and I'm *so* fucking not, I put the filter back in place, temper my voice, and I lie. "Something came up, Alice. Johnny's friend in Greeley is giving away a freezer and he needs me to ride with him and help him load it. If he doesn't pick it up tonight, she's giving it to someone else. So, I can't make it to your show." My God, that felt horrible.

Her lips rub together, an act of disappointment, as she nods slowly. "Yeah...no problem...I understand..." It's preoccupied contemplation masked by stunted phrases of misunderstanding.

Deciphered, it's *No. It is a problem. I don't understand*, in my ears, because she knows I'm lying. On the inside I'm down on my knees in front of her apologizing profusely, *I'm sorry. I'm sorry. I am so sorry,* but on the outside, which is the only place that matters, I'm silent. Delivering silence to Alice is cruel denial. She can't see the shame filling my eyes and threatening to spill out. She can't see the crease of self-hate in my forehead and between my eyes. She can't see the frustration of my lies balling up my fists. I manage to croak out, "Good luck." It sounds misplaced and questioning because I've messed everything up.

She makes me wait for her reply. Or maybe she's trying to decide if she's going to reply at all. "Thanks," she finally calls back from the foot of the stairs. It sounds misplaced and questioning because I've messed everything up.

CHAPTER FOURTEEN

PRESENT, March 1987
Toby

I DIDN'T SLEEP LAST NIGHT.

It's eating at me from the inside out.

Alice. Making things right.

Taber. Bringing things to light.

My omission is a lie; it's blatant elusion void of choice by the affected.

Protecting the innocent.

By protecting the guilty.

Blissfully unaware is a teetering breath away from being sucker punched with an alternate reality. I'd rather she hears it from me than hears it in motion like I did.

I'm sitting on my sleeping bag tying my shoes when Cliff stops in front of my open door, rubbing the sleep from his eyes in only a pair of sweatpants, his overweight physique pinched in the middle by tight elastic. His mohawk is flopped over from a night of sleep, rigid but spiritless. Like Cliff. "Where are you going so early?" he asks.

"It's noon. And none of your business," I snap. I can't blame my quick temper on my lack of sleep; a night of sleeplessness is a drop in the bucket for an insomniac. It's the heaviness of this secret I'm carrying. I'm full of secrets, I don't need another one.

"I just asked a question, you don't have to be an ass about it." There's a fine line between putting up with Cliff and lashing out at him. It's subtle for me, but he heard it loud and clear and shuffles on toward the bathroom.

I put on my sweatshirt and take it off twice before I decide wearing it is a good idea in case this goes badly and I end up taking a long walk alone afterward.

I'm sweating by the time I click the padlock on my door into place.

And I'm grumbling under my breath, "This is a horrible idea," as I descend the stairs.

But by the time I'm walking down the hall with the door of 2A in sight, a switch flips and the slow simmer of anger begins.

When I knock, louder than I intended, the anger is a steady, rolling boil.

Alice answers, draped in an oversized gray sweatshirt over the infamous blue and white striped boxers.

Before she can say anything, I barge in conversationally, "I lied, Alice." It's poorly executed and rushed, lacking in context and grace, because I'm seething as I watch Taber walk out of one of the bedrooms in his underwear with his sights set on the kitchen. He looks like he just woke up. So does Alice.

"Toby?" she asks sleepily.

"There was no freezer, I lied," I divulge, more softly than I thought my anger would allow. But as I watch Taber pour himself a glass of orange juice through the kitchen doorway, I can't contain the rage, and everything starts to blur and tilt on its axis. Etiquette, rules, right, wrong—it all flies out the goddamn window.

Alice asks, "Why?" She sounds hurt like she did last night.

I say, "Excuse me," and squeeze past her into the apartment; my body in control and my mind unable to stop it, I head for Taber.

Who, conveniently, is heading for me.

Three things happen at once to stir this shitstorm up into a monumental clusterfuck.

Taber says, "Hey, Toby. How's it going?" without a care in the world.

A surge of rage-fueled adrenaline drives my knuckles into his face.

And a white blonde head pokes out from Taber's bedroom and asks, "Where are your clean towels, babe?"

The trio of simultaneous events feels like a concussive joke. That I'm the butt of.

The pause to process what just happened should be longer, more dramatic, but it's not. There's an immediate rapid-fire succession of questions, one followed up by another so quickly that answers have to wait until they're all out in the open to sort through and prioritize.

Taber folds in half, holding his cheek in stunned surprise. "Son of a bitch. What the hell, man?" I'd expect to hear fury from him, but it sounds, oddly, like this has happened before.

"Are you okay?" The pale blonde runs to him, while tossing deadly daggers at me with her murderous eyes.

"Who are you?" I ask the blonde.

And somewhere behind us, in a voice that's controlled and practiced in chaos, Alice demands, "Somebody tell me what's going on." She needs a play-by-play to catch up.

The answers flood in out of order. Or maybe they only

sound out of order because I've lost my mind. I've never punched anyone in my life and my knuckles are throbbing.

"I punched Taber because he's cheating on you."

"I'm fine. Nothing's broken."

"I'm Taber's girlfriend."

Followed by a fresh speed round of questions:

"Cheating on *who*?"

"Your nose is *bleeding*, are you *sure*?"

"Taber's *girlfriend*?"

Alice is still quiet, I'm sure this is a lot to process when you can't see the debacle.

More tumbling answers to the previous questions:

"Alice."

"I'm sure. I'll probably have a black eye."

"Yeah, I'm Inga. Taber's *girlfriend*."

Finally, there's silence as we all look at each other, appraising, all of the puzzle pieces clicking into place.

I am an asshole.

And a fool.

Alice clears her throat. "Toby, Taber isn't my boyfriend. He's my brother."

I don't want to respond, I want to run out the door of this apartment and never come back. This is yet another stunning example of why I shouldn't get involved with people; I interfere in spectacularly shitty fashion. "Yeah, I just figured that out," I whisper, from behind my hands that are covering my face as I try to conjure some dignity out of thin air. "I'm such an idiot."

When I drop my hands, Alice is beaming and I can't tell if she's about to laugh at me and make this whole thing worse, as if that's possible. But then she says, "Come here, Toby," and motions with her hand for me to advance on her.

In a daze, I do.

When I reach her, she finds my face with a hand gripping

THE OTHER SIDE • 117

each cheek and pulls my ear down to her mouth. Into which she whispers, "Did you just defend my honor?"

I sigh and answer quietly, "No, I'm pretty sure I just gave your brother a shiner for no reason," before raising my voice, "Sorry, Taber." An apology is definitely in order.

He laughs good-naturedly because he's a maniac. "It's cool. Inga loves the whole bad boy thing. I'll probably get lucky before she leaves because she can't resist the black eye. I should thank you."

I hear Inga swat at him somewhere behind me and her giggling, "Shut up."

Challenged by his, "*Ouch*. What? It's true."

And her agreeing, "I know."

I hear feet shuffling toward the bedroom and just before the door clicks shut, Taber calls out, "Remember when you asked if I thought Toby was a good idea, Alice? Yes, I think Toby's a good idea."

I CONSIDER ONE LAST TRIP TO THE COMIC STORE BUT trade it for a trip to Wax Trax with Alice instead, while Taber and Inga christen the black eye. I hold her hand again, fingers interlaced. There's no rehashing of the recent fiasco, no questioning to re-clarify my misunderstanding. Most of the time when something like what happened today happens, people want to analyze it to death. They ask questions like, *Why would you think that? Or, Why would you do something like that?* When the only real, honest answer is, *I don't know. I just did.* It feels like Alice understands that sometimes people just *did*, and doesn't expect, or even need, explanation. She's curious by nature about getting to know people, but her curiosity doesn't come with a side dish of scrutiny. I get the idea that she respects people for who they are, and where they've been, and what they've been through. I've never met anyone in my life like that. Judgment is part of the game. It's *always* part of the game. Sometimes it *is* the game. The never-ending dodging and hiding to avoid it, which is tiring as hell when everyone is always watching and waiting for me to mess up. Again.

And again.

So trusting Alice is hard.

But goddamn, right this minute, do I ever want to.

We talk about their band, which is, ironically, called Wonderland. She downplays her talent and talks up her brother's. The same way I've overheard Taber talk about her. They're a well-paired team.

We talk about music in general.

But not once does she make me feel like my past is part of the present conversation. We live in the moment.

And living in the moment feels so odd, so selfish, but also so...*good*.

CHAPTER FIFTEEN

PRESENT, March 1987
Toby

ALICE STILL DOESN'T KNOW WE GO TO THE SAME SCHOOL. I haven't said anything for a few reasons. I want her to make friends and if she starts hanging around with me, that's unlikely to happen. I'm a loner. Two years ago I pushed the few friends I had away. Well, my anger, resentment, and the perpetual black cloud hanging over me did it for me, and I became known as the asshole. Depression plus introversion equals pariah. No one wants to hang out with the guy who's dead inside and I don't want to hang out with them either, so it works out fine.

Which brings me back to my current dilemma—to tell Alice or not to tell Alice.

I agonize over it through English.

While I stare at her.

And think about how much I want to walk over and sit in the chair next to her, rest my hand on her thigh under the table, and slip my fingers between hers like they were less than twenty-four hours ago.

Pros and cons are weighed. Two minutes before the bell rings, I decide on the way out of the room I'll stop and tell her.

When the time comes, I chicken out and walk past, sparing her a label she doesn't deserve and leaving her with the potential she does.

CHAPTER SIXTEEN

Present, March 1987
   Toby

Two days later, my willpower is fading. It takes everything in me not to follow Alice into the library during lunch.

CHAPTER SEVENTEEN

PRESENT, March 1987
Toby

BY THURSDAY IT'S UNBEARABLE BEING IN THE SAME ROOM
with Alice and not being able to talk to her. I miss her and she's
sitting two tables away.

I'M STILL THINKING ABOUT HER WHEN THE SUN GOES
down. Normally, I would go in my room and get started on my
homework and draw until sleep makes the fight impossible, but
I find myself on the fire escape instead, staring up at a starless,
cloudy sky punctuated with a swelling full moon. The air is
cold, I can see my breath and it makes me crave a cigarette. I
guess I've turned into one of those people who doesn't just
smoke when they drink. Pulling my sweatshirt hood up and my
sleeves down, I tuck my hands inside to keep them warm.

That's when I hear the door open and shut below me, footsteps, and singing. It's Alice, I can see her through the metal slats that make up the floor of the fire escape. She isn't singing every verse of the song, she's picking and choosing and humming the rest.

When the song I've never heard dies out, I make my way down the ladder and sit on the second rung from the bottom, my feet resting on the platform. Alice is standing at the railing not far from me, her Walkman in her hand and headphones tucked into her hair at her ears. "Hi, Toby," she says. A faint smile colors her lips and then it fades just as quickly as it arrived, and she takes the headphones off and sets them with the Walkman on a small table.

It startles me. "Hey. I didn't think you could hear me."

She turns toward the ladder. "I couldn't. My music was turned up. I could feel the fire escape shudder when you walked on it and climbed down the ladder."

"Oh, right." Of course she could, that was stupid of me. "Is your brother home?" I ask to draw the attention away from me and my insensitivity.

"No, he's begrudgingly having dinner with our mom. Trying to smooth things over for me, I think. Taber's always been the unlikely peacemaker in our family. The Eliot family Gandhi...if Gandhi wore leather and eyeliner." Even through the joke, she doesn't crack a smile. It seems Alice harbors all of her negativity and saves it up only for her mom. Not that I can blame her after the argument I overheard a few weeks ago. She shakes her head. "Sorry, sore subject. Let's talk about something else. Are the stars out tonight?" She's sad and deflated and I hate it.

I lie without hesitation because I will do anything to lighten her mood. "They are and the moon is full."

"I miss seeing the stars." When I don't answer because I

don't know what to say to make this better, she makes her way over to me. "What's your last name, Toby?"

"Page," I answer as her right knee bumps into my left.

"I thought so," she says as her head tilts back like she's looking at the sky.

I'm sitting too low to see her face, but there's sadness all around her. I can feel it and I need to make it go away, but I don't know how to do that. I can't manage my own emotions, let alone someone else's. "How did you know?"

Her head drops down to face mine and the corner of her mouth quirks up like something amuses her. "I heard some girls at school talking about you, the *infamous* Toby Page."

I don't even want to know what that means. "I should've told you we go to the same school," I whisper.

"They were talking about you in Contemporary Living class. They said you had a nice ass and pretty eyes and that it's a shame you're such a dick. Though I got the impression that they didn't really mind that part either. And yes, you should've told me we go to the same school. Why didn't you?"

"It's complicated, Alice."

Ignoring my self-assessment, Alice counters my cryptic answer with another question to see where she stands. "Are you embarrassed to be seen with me?" She's not the type of girl to put up with bullshit, if she sensed I was that type of person she wouldn't be standing here talking to me.

"Absolutely not." My hand is shaking when I reach around the back of her leg that's touching mine and run my hand up and down her calf to reassure her.

She holds up her palm facing me and I press mine to it, watching her fingers alternate between mine and dropping to secure them in place. "Then why?"

Everything about you makes my pulse race, I think as my heart starts beating double-time at her touch. "You don't know me, Alice. You hang around me and you'll never make any friends. I keep to myself and I'm kind of an asshole. Those girls were right about that part at least."

"Lucky for me, good guys disguised as assholes are my favorite," she says with a smirk as she rubs circles with her thumb over the back of my hand and I rub circles with mine over the back of her calf.

I know there's a hole in these tights about eight inches north and my fingers are begging to find it, so I hold my breath and let them travel in search of it. When I brush bare skin at the back of her thigh, it's pebbled with goose bumps from the cold but it's still so soft. I'm watching her chest and shoulders rise exaggeratedly through her puffy coat, like her only job is to get maximum amounts of air into her lungs. "I'm not a good guy," I warn as I widen my legs and guide her between them.

Her free hand finds my hood up and lowers it. "I don't believe you. What color is your hair, Toby?"

"Brown," I answer as my fingertips tuck inside the torn edge of her tights and my palm flattens against the skin exposed by the hole.

She runs her hand through my hair and it feels like she's reached inside me and her fingertips are skimming nerves and bringing them to life. "Be more specific. Is it light brown like an almond? Or is it dark brown like chocolate?"

I don't want to think about anything except what Alice's lips taste like, but I answer, "Dark chocolate," while I squeeze the back of her thigh.

Her breaths are coming quicker now, but she keeps up with the line of questioning. "What about your pretty eyes?"

I give her the most accurate description I can, "Seafoam green."

She smiles and traces my forehead lightly with her pointer

finger, followed by cheeks, chin, nose, and finally lips, where it lingers.

"Alice?" Her name tastes sacred and sounds divine. I'm breathless.

"Yeah." Her response should be questioning, it's not. It sounds like agreement. It also seems we're in competition to find out who can talk the quietest. "Kiss me." It isn't a question either.

The air fogs out of her mouth twice before I release her hand and leg and cup her cheeks instead, coaxing her forward. "We shouldn't," I warn.

She ignores my warning with a breathy repeat, "Kiss me," and follows my physical lead and leans in. One hand grips my thigh where it rests against the outside of hers, and the other finds the back of my head. Her touch is a gentle demand that makes me thrum with anticipation.

Tilting my head slightly, I don't close my eyes until we're close enough that our visible misty breaths tangle and I give her one final warning, "We can't be together."

I let my eyelids drop and touch my lips to hers as she repeats, "Kiss me," a third time.

Her lips are soft and there's no hesitation. She welcomes the connection like she knew it was always going to happen, like she's been waiting for it.

The first kiss is slow as we test this out, test each other out, but I can feel her seeping into me while I fall headlong into her. *Goddamn, I love kissing.*

Her face in my hands, I pull back ever so slightly and shift positions, my nose brushes hers as we trade sides. But our lips are eager to reconnect and when they do it's rushed. My tongue glides along the seam of her lips, and her hand at the nape of my neck squeezes and urges me forward even though I have nowhere to go. But then she parts her lips and I realize I do and the possibilities are endless. When our tongues touch, the gentlest hum of satisfaction radiates out of her, and I decide there is nothing I want more than to hear that sound again.

Our tongues flirt. They tease and retreat. The reunion intensifies with each tangle until it reaches a fever pitch. "Sit down," I whisper into her mouth because I'm not breaking this kiss for anything more. I pull my knees together, slowly forcing her out from between them and I expect her to sit across my lap. She doesn't. Still facing me, she lowers, straddling me.

And I mentally chuck the *What makes my pulse race* list and start a new one. It's called *How Alice ignites me*. The hum in her throat when our tongues touch and her thighs wrapped around the outside of mine top the list so far.

I want more of her.

I want to explore her.

I want to figure out what else makes her hum.

So my mouth makes the journey toward her neck. A kiss at the corner of her mouth, followed by another feathered across her jaw. I've always been reserved, but not when I kiss. When I kiss, I don't hold anything back. The tip of my tongue catches the skin just below her ear and that's when the hum begins. It amplifies when I ghost a path slowly down her neck. She blooms into the contact and tilts her head back and to the side, handing herself over to me. Alice is the type of person who should be worshipped and I can't believe that tonight, right now, that honor is all mine. The hollow indentation at the base of her throat invites me in and I kiss it before dipping my tongue in and tasting it. The hum turns into a moan when the taste ends in my lower lip dragging against her skin. Moving back to the side of her exposed neck I place an open mouth kiss, sucking gently and nipping with teeth, before soothing with my tongue.

Her hands have slipped underneath my sweatshirt and are

flush against my stomach. The air creeping in over my bare skin is cold, but I'm burning up.

When my lips find hers again, it's blistering. It seems Alice has a few tricks of her own and I let her take the lead. I was right about Alice's kisses: they are intentional, detailed, descriptive, and thorough. My mind is spinning, yet I've never been so singularly focused as I am on her and the things she's doing to me. Sucking my bottom lip in between hers, she captures it with her teeth and releases it slowly. The drag is delirium-inducing, and I'm pretty sure I just released a hum of my own. The impression of her smile when she kisses me confirms that I did.

"I like that," she whispers and continues her blissful siege across my cheek toward my ear. Her tongue traces a loop around the hard, outer edge, and wraps up with a nip of my lobe.

I can officially cross the kiss off my list. I feel this one all the way to my soul and back again. Jesus, I don't ever want it to end.

Until it does, when I hear the door open above and Cliff yells out, "Toby! Phone! It's Chantal!"

I sigh internally and then irrationally bargain with myself, wondering if I ignore everyone except Alice, they'll all go away.

I hear Cliff walk across the fire escape. I'm sure he's peering over the side at us. Alice's forehead is resting on my shoulder now. She's catching her breath and so am I when Cliff's chuckle rains down on us. "Oh shit. Sorry, Toby, but Chantal says the smoke alarm keeps beeping, and it's scaring Mrs. Bennett and making Joey cry."

I sigh again, outwardly this time, and my hands that have ended up on her hips squeeze an apology before I say, "I have to get that."

Her hands shift from my stomach and slide around to hug

me under my shirt. "Every kiss eventually ends. The memory of them doesn't. I'll still feel that one when I'm ninety," she whispers so Cliff can't hear, because the bastard is still watching us.

Hugging her back, I agree inwardly, *The memory of them doesn't,* and whisper outwardly, "I'll see you tomorrow at school, Alice. First hour."

When she stands, there's a small smile playing at her lips.

It matches mine. Yes, I'm smiling.

"Tomorrow," she echoes, followed by, "Good night, Toby." And then louder, "Good night, Cliff."

When I climb up the ladder, Cliff looks dumbfounded that a pretty girl is talking to him, so I say, "Don't be rude—say something." I'm never one to prompt manners, but I don't like Alice going unanswered anymore.

"Good night," he hurriedly fumbles.

Alice raises her hand to wave as she disappears into her apartment.

"She's hot," Cliff says as he opens the door into our kitchen.

I don't acknowledge the comment because I'm not discussing this with Cliff. But yes, she is. The fact that I have to adjust myself in my pants behind my sweatshirt when Cliff's back is to me as we walk into the apartment is glaring proof of that.

CHAPTER EIGHTEEN

PRESENT, March 1987
Toby

ALICE BEAT ME TO ENGLISH THIS MORNING. I STOP AT HER table and say hello—that's a first at school. I don't think I've ever uttered the word within this building.

She asks me to sit with her. When I hesitate, she knows I'm trying to shield her from my reputation, and insists, "I'm the blind girl they're all ignoring because they don't know what else to do with me. Nobody cares who I sit with...*asshole*." She says *asshole* in such a mocking way, throwing my own label back at me, that it almost makes me laugh and I can't resist taking a seat.

"You've just blacklisted yourself," I whisper.

A smile breaks out, broadcasting that she likes the idea. "I guess it's a good thing I don't care what they think then, huh?"

Alice is Alice—confident.

And I am still Toby—catastrophic.

How did it come to this?

I have a friend.

A friend.

And instead of making me happy, it makes me anxious.

I don't know how to do this.

I *shouldn't* do this.

You're nothing. You're nothing. You're nothing, the reminder demands to be felt.

Just let me have this, I beg.

No, it answers authoritatively.

I pretend to ignore the answer, my reality. We'll see how long this lasts until the guilt wins.

Because it always wins.

CHAPTER NINETEEN

PRESENT, April 1987
Toby

"I THINK BONNIE IS LYING." A THICK CURTAIN OF REM sleep separates me from the words drifting in from the periphery of wakefulness.

"That's nice," I mumble into my pillow, not wanting to give in to the pull.

The intruder repeats the message.

I don't want to engage. My subconscious attempts to appease with a mollifying, "Everyone lies." This voice needs to go away and leave me alone. I'm sleeping. And tonight it's not beating me up, it's cooperating, and the nightmares are unexpectedly being kept at bay.

Go away.

"Toby, are you awake?"

I am now. Thanks, Cliff. "Yeah," I answer.

When he repeats the message for a third time "Bonnie" turns into "Johnny" and "lying" turns into "dying."

My eyes open and fix on the red numbers glowing on my left and I squint to read them, ten minutes past four. "What?" I ask to confirm.

"I think Johnny is dying," he repeats.

Cliff is standing in my open doorway and points to the bathroom. "I couldn't sleep and needed to take a leak and found this." He tosses me an envelope, only instead of pitching it underhand, he holds it like a paper airplane and it nosedives into my lap. My name is written on it in all caps.

Rubbing my eyes, partially to rouse them and partially to shield them from the assaulting light of the kitchen outside my door, I pick up the envelope. That's already been opened. "Didn't realize T-O-B-Y spelled Cliff," I say under my breath as I rise to a sitting position.

Cliff shrugs to rebuff the invasion of privacy allusion while I unfold the letter and begin to read it. Cliff is usually sloth-like, but he's almost tap dancing in place and it's driving me nuts.

Toby,

I'll be gone for a few days, maybe a week. There's some shit that needs to be dealt with. Should've done it a long time ago.

Keep an eye on Cliff and make sure he doesn't get himself killed or thrown in juvie while I'm gone.

Johnny

I read it twice, because I don't trust my foggy brain with only one pass. I'm not sure what to make of the vague message other than to take it at its word. It's not my job to analyze Johnny, it's my job to make sure this building doesn't fall down around us.

Cliff is eyeing me when I refold the letter and stuff it back in the envelope. "What does it mean?"

"I think it means he's going to be gone for a few days," I say dryly. "And that you shouldn't do anything dumb or reckless while he's away," I add to paraphrase and remind.

Cliff sinks to his knees on my sleeping bag, narrowly misses crushing my feet in the process, and rolls his eyes with all the flair of someone truly scorned.

I shake my head because it's way too early to deal with a cross-examination, but then I zero in on his eyes now that they're this close to me. His pupils are blown wide-open. Rubbing my temples, I pinch my lids closed to block out the flagrant accumulation of bad late-night choices squatting in front of me.

"He's dying, isn't he? He's not coming back." He shakes his head furiously. "They can't make me go to foster care. I don't even like waffles. Why is it so hot in here? I need to get this shirt off." He's not wearing a shirt. The words tumbling out of his mouth are an incoherent stream of consciousness fueled by whatever chemicals are in charge. I knew Cliff smoked weed, but this is the first time I've ever seen him cranked up on something more.

"Jesus Christ," I mutter.

As if prompted by all things biblical, Cliff makes the sign of the cross over his chest and clutches the beads hanging there. I've never seen him pray but apparently blow, or speed, or acid, or whatever he's on, brings out the Holy Ghost.

I put the brakes on the rosary because I know it's a time-consuming process. "Cliff, why don't you go lie down and do that in your room? Maybe you could try to go to sleep?"

His hand slips from the tiny cross resting on his protruding belly to the floor beside him like it's useless to him. "I can't sleep," he confesses.

No shit. "Watch some TV," I suggest vocally. *Leave me alone*, I beg internally.

All at once he jumps to his feet with the enthusiasm, but not the grace, of a cheerleader. "Good idea, I'll bake a pizza and we can watch S*id and Nancy.*"

Watching him preheat the oven, I whisper just in case Cliff grabbed his attention and there is a God still listening, "Please don't let him set the house on fire. He's on your watch tonight, I'm going back to sleep."

I sleep in until eight after the early morning, manic, drug-induced wake-up call from Cliff and then make my Saturday rounds. Cliff is finally asleep, he crashed in spectacular fashion. He ate the pizza he baked and watched S*id and Nancy* alone, alternately reciting the lines of the movie along with the actors and crying while repeatedly declaring, "Legend," to the sad tale unfolding on the TV. When all went quiet, I knew he was finally out.

"Son of a bitch," I mutter to myself as I walk by the shed in the backyard on my way to the trash dumpster in the back alley. After I toss the garbage bag, I return to take a better look. Some douchebag tried to break in the shed last night. They didn't get in, but they busted up the wood on the bottom corner of the door trying to pry it open. My trip to take out the trash turns into a two-hour long repair to the shed. I take it off the hinges and do my best to patch it. It may not be pretty, but it's weathertight and solid with a backing plate of metal on the inside now.

On my way back inside, I gather the mail. There's a small box for me. It's finally here.

Back up in apartment 3A, I make sure Cliff is still among the living. He's made it easy for me, his bedroom door is wide open and he's lying on his back, stark naked. The girth of his pale torso, that looks like it's never seen the sun, inflating and deflating. Satisfied he's breathing, I shut the door quickly, wishing I could unsee what I've just seen.

Tearing into the box, I find ten bright white envelopes and ten bright white cards stacked atop each other and wrapped in a band of cellophane. My graduation announcements.

Slipping one card and one envelope out, I let the rest fall into the kitchen trash can. As I watch them settle into their demise between a frozen pizza box, an empty gallon of milk, and cigarette butts, it feels fitting. Some people are born to do great things, to leave a mark, to simply *be* great.

And some people, like me...aren't.

Have I left my mark? Yeah, I've left a few.

None I'm proud of.

So, it's fitting that the culmination of almost eighteen years, graduation, ends up in the bottom of a trash can.

I set the one remaining defiant invitation on a shelf in my room where it will have to wait until Johnny comes back.

CHAPTER TWENTY

Different unfolds, tragically

Past, February – May 1985
Nina's Protector

Ken is different.

If only I'd known what a prophetic proclamation that was from the very beginning.

Ken is different.

Ken *is* different.

Ken is *different*.

No matter how it's dissected, the outcome is the same.

Week one living with Ken:

"Babe, I want you to quit your job. I'll take care of you." Nina hates her job. She thinks Ken is the answer to her prayers.

You have your GED now, you can enroll in nursing school like you've always wanted, I urge.

Nina agrees with both of us, quits her job the next day, and while Ken is at work she calls and requests information from two local nursing programs.

———

WEEK THREE LIVING WITH KEN:

"How do I look?" Normally, Nina wouldn't ask this question. She wouldn't invite the potential for criticism. But it's Valentine's Day, she's wearing her favorite dress, and Ken's taking her out to dinner. She hasn't left the apartment since she quit her job. Ken says it's not safe for her to go out without him. She thinks it's chivalrous.

I bet you know me well enough by now to deduce how I feel about that. I feel itchy. Chivalry isn't supposed to feel like confinement.

"Dress looks a little tighter than it did last time you wore it," Ken answers offhandedly.

It is. Nina's gained a few pounds since she quit working. Her weight and appearance are an endless battle, more mental than physical. Nina has always looked in the mirror and seen legs that are too short, a butt that's too big, a chest that's a cup size too small, a nose that's too wide, a bottom row of crooked teeth, and hair that isn't straight enough. I've always looked at her in the mirror and seen a beautiful person—no flaws, just Nina being Nina the way no one else can. That's the reason Ken's comment raises my hackles. If he's been paying attention since the first day they met, he would know this is a hot button issue and something she needs to be built up, not torn down.

How dare he! I rage. She put herself out there asking that question. He should've told her she looks gorgeous...because she does. Instead, he planted the seed of doubt. Nina will dwell on this comment. For all the confidence she's gained the past two months, that one sentence was a devastating blow that will negate it all. A single negative can wipe out one hundred positives.

"It is," she agrees, and I watch pride drain out of her while shame pours in.

Week four living with Ken:

Ken shakes a large white envelope in Nina's face the minute he walks through the door. "What the hell is this?" His tone is accusatory, which makes her nervous because even though he's never talked to her like this, other men have.

Nina takes the envelope with a trembling hand. It's addressed to her from Denver College of Nursing and it's already been opened. "You opened my mail?" This is the first piece of mail Nina's received here at Ken's.

He ignores the question and raises his eyebrows waiting for her to answer his demand.

"I've always wanted to be a nurse. I thought this might be a good time to follow my dream. I qualify for tuition grants and—"

And then everything happens so fast it's a blur.

Hands grasp Nina's upper arms.

Those same hands squeeze down like a vise until the skin and tissue beneath throbs and capillaries rupture.

Her feet leave the ground, suspended and flailing.

What the flight lacks in distance, it makes up for in speed and ferocity.

Nina is on her back, pain radiating out in bursts from the back of her skull and so many other spots it's hard to pinpoint them all.

Before her vision comes back into focus, Ken is sitting on her stomach straddling her, his finger wagging aggressively an inch from her face. "I don't think you understand how this works, woman. You live here with me. I take care of you. I tell you what you can and cannot do because *I know best.* You're not going to nursing school." He stands up abruptly, done with his sermon. But as he walks into the kitchen, he adds, "You're not smart enough anyway."

I'm stunned. Unfortunately for Nina, this isn't the first horrific thing that's ever happened to her that's stunned me. She's been slapped, she's been shaken, but this is the first time someone has inflicted this particular brand of physical pain. Good thing I'm equipped for emergencies. The shock, panic, and embarrassment are hot in the tears streaming down Nina's cheeks, which is the reason I need to remain calm. *Leave, leave, leave, leave, leave, leave, leave, leave, leaveleaveleaveleaveleave...*I command it so many times that the words run together. I know I'm competing with his last comment that's looping itself through her brain. "You're not smart enough." She's heard it many times from her mother. There was a time she believed it. When confidence is as shaky as Nina's is, all it takes is the tap of the first domino and they all start falling down.

Ken returns to the room.

Helps her up off the floor.

Hugs her.

"Sorry, babe." The wild outrage that was in his eyes only minutes ago has died away, but I don't buy it and I hope Nina doesn't either. "I had a really shitty day at work. And then I come home to that." He gestures with a gentle tip of his chin to the papers strewn all over the floor as if they're offensive. "I promise it won't happen again. We just both need to do better, okay?"

We just both need to do better? What is that even supposed to mean? I shout at Nina.

She's stunned, but there's a vacant look about her that scares me to death. I've seen it before in her darkest days. When she lets depression take hold and take over, this is what it looks like. It's been visiting her more and more frequently lately, but it just buried its claws in and I know I'm in for a fight. I have a sinking feeling it's not going to let go this time.

———

WEEK SIX WITH KEN:
Ken is a liar.
He hit Nina again.
He apologized again.
She accepted again.
I'm furious.
Again.

———

WEEK SEVEN WITH KEN:
Nina didn't refill her prescription. She takes pills daily to balance her bipolar disorder. Yeah, did I mention that? She's bipolar. Diagnosed when she was a teenager. The medication works. I argued loudly for the refill. She ignored me. When she stops taking the meds she plummets. I think she does it to punish herself because she doesn't think she's worthy. This is a bad sign.

———

WEEK EIGHT WITH KEN:
Nina's depression is a dictator. It changes her, molds her into what it wants her to be.

It also allows Ken to mold her into what *he* wants her to be.

WEEK NINE WITH KEN:
Nina hasn't talked to her friends in weeks. She hasn't been out of the house for weeks.

WEEK TWELVE WITH KEN:
Nina has cried all day thinking about Toby. She hasn't seen or talked to him since that night she took Ken to meet him. The night that everything changed.

When Ken walks in the door at seven o'clock, she's still in bed in her pajamas. There will be hell to pay when dinner isn't on the table, but she's too tired of life to even care. I'm still chanting, *Leave, leave, leave, leave, leave,* but she tells me it doesn't matter because it's all going to end soon anyway.

By "it's all going to end," she means *she's* going to end. I get that. I've been in this spot with her before. She's not one to mess around with empty threats. The last time she filled her belly full of pain pills. The only reason she survived is because her mom found her and called 911. Stomach pumped inside out, she recovered under psychiatric evaluation and was released to her mother and Toby. She was seventeen. Toby was two. Her mother was a train wreck.

"Nina!" Ken yells from the living room. The sound deadens when his footfalls still on the hardwood inside their bedroom.

She looks at him through blurry eyes and before he can start in on her, we both notice how different his eyes look. They're glazed over. He's high, but he doesn't smell like pot.

She's always known about the pot. This is something different. For weeks she's chased away suspicions that he might be dealing drugs, but she didn't realize he dipped into his supply.

She's braced for the worst, the beatings are daily now. She's covered in bruises.

So when he climbs in bed and pulls her into his chest, she stills rigidly like a frightened animal being stalked like prey.

Stroking her hair gently, he says, "I love you, Nina. You know that, right?" When she doesn't answer, he doesn't notice and goes on with his petting. "You've been so good lately, Nina. *So good.*" The only thing scarier than the cruel Ken Nina has come to expect, is nice Ken.

Different gets scarier every day. Ken is different.

CHAPTER TWENTY-ONE

PRESENT, April 1987
Toby

JOHNNY'S BACK.

He's sitting on the wooden chair by the phone in the kitchen like a sentinel standing guard when I walk in the door from school. We exchange nods, and then I begin the covert assessment to try to determine where he's been all week.

He looks different.

His eyes are clear, the constant ruddy cheeks are gone, and his skin has color. And he's lost weight, or more than weight, he's lost bloat. That puffy layer is gone.

When he clears his throat, I drop my eyes and walk to unlock the padlock on my room. Throat clearing by Johnny is usually followed by something he'd rather not have to say out loud. "I quit drinking." I stop in my tracks. More throat clearing and I keep my eyes trained on the floor because I know Johnny well enough to know if he's being this frank, he doesn't want eye contact of any kind. "Thought I could do it cold turkey and ended up in the hospital sicker than a dog." More throat clearing. "Spent the last three days at my sponsor's house trying to get my head on straight before I came back here to you guys. I joined AA," he says as an add-on to explain the "sponsor" comment, I guess.

I chew at my thumbnail for a moment before I ask, "So this was the shit that needed to be dealt with, getting sober?" referencing the note he left for me.

"Yeah," he says grimly, his tone laced with shame. When I look up at him, there's remorse in his eyes. "I've been fucked up for so long that I don't know if I can do this or not." He shrugs like it's an apology for showing weakness. "But it's either try or eventually die. I'm trying."

I don't know what to say. I was prepared to come home, listen to the messages, and get to work. I wasn't prepared for soul-baring on Johnny's part. Communication isn't my strong suit, especially when feelings are involved. Johnny and I don't talk about personal stuff, the line was drawn the day I moved into his apartment and we've never crossed it since. I don't want to start now.

"That's good," I say because my silence is awkward. This whole situation is awkward. "Does Cliff know?"

"No, I wanted to talk to you first."

I nod but feel slotted in the middle of a strange family dynamic. Shouldn't he talk to his nephew before he spills his guts to his employee and tenant?

"He's still alive? And a free man?" he asks in only a half-joking tone.

I start to unlock the padlock, sensing this conversation is thankfully coming to an end. "As of this morning he was. Give Cliff a few hours and anything's possible, though."

Johnny's subdued sigh is audible. "You're right about that."

When I set down my backpack on my sleeping bag, my gaze falls on the graduation invitation on one of my shelves. "You wouldn't happen to know where Marilyn is these days, would you?"

His eyebrows pull together in confusion at my random change of topic. "Nope, haven't seen her in years. Why?"

I snag the envelope off the shelf and hold it up like it explains my madness. "I need to mail her this."

"What is it?" he asks curiously.

"My graduation announcement." I'm going for aloof, but the resentment in my voice wins out.

He nods solemnly. "Give it to me. I'll ask around."

I'm reluctant to surrender it to him, but at the same time it will be a relief to get it out of my hands, so I make the decision to hand it over. I almost say thanks, but I stop myself because Johnny likes being thanked for anything about as much as I do, so I skip it.

It's then that I notice the light isn't flashing on the answering machine. "No messages?" I ask.

"Nope, Curtis Street called earlier and I took care of it. And Mrs. Bennett called a little while ago and said her dog needed to be walked. I didn't remember them having a dog, but I went down to her apartment anyway." I can see in his eyes that the severity of her decline had escaped him these past few years and he feels bad about it. Life went on in this big, old house while he was somewhere else ignoring it. "They don't have a dog," he says somberly. "It's sad, isn't it, watching her memory fade away?"

I nod because it's beyond sad. "I'm going to start my home-work." I don't have any homework, but I need to get away.

"Okay," he agrees, and just like that, I have the night off.

I sit in my room all night and draw and listen to my New Order tape, only taking a break to make a couple of bologna sandwiches. And I think about Johnny and hope he doesn't fall off the wagon. But because my faith in everything is woefully lacking, I wonder how long it will take before he does. My pessimism honestly answers my own suspicions, *I give him two weeks, tops.* I can't help but agree.

CHAPTER TWENTY-TWO

PRESENT, April 1987
Toby

THERE'S A TEACHER WORKDAY TODAY, WHICH MEANS NO school for us. It's rare that I accept idle downtime. When I'm not busy my mind takes over and the depression always wins the mental wrestling match, and I submit, but my work is done, and Alice knocked on my door and invited me to come outside with her.

So I did.

Because I can't seem to say no to her.

We're lying side by side on our backs on the small patch of crabgrass in the backyard of the Victorian. It's warm today and the sun is directly overhead. The shocking rays force my eyelids closed and the backs of them look like molten lava, a fiery red.

"Why are you so sad all the time, Toby?" Alice asks out of the blue.

I wear my depression like a winter coat, zipped up tight to

my chin and bulky—a barrier that smothers out the rest of the world. No one has ever asked me about it because I hide it. I like to think that people are layered and if you don't care, if you don't get to know them, if you don't question, you can't peel back the layers and find out what's deeper. And when your outer layer is entirely made up of asshole, no one digs deeper to see the depression just underneath. The depression and the asshole are explicably linked—cause and effect. Effect and cause...and effect. Repeat, repeat, repeat. I don't know how to answer this question. I don't *want* to answer this question.

So, I lie. "I'm not sad." Or maybe it isn't a lie, depression is different than sadness. Sadness is melancholy. Depression is a black hole of despair. I always imagine it's like drowning. There are short bursts of fresh air, like Alice, but the past, the hopelessness, the guilt, and self-loathing is a pair of lead shoes that always pull me back under.

Finding my hand, she slips her fingers between mine and squeezes hard. So hard that her fingertips seat between my knuckles with purpose and the tendons on the back of her hand tauten under the tips of mine. I know she doesn't accept my answer. She lets her face drop to the side until her cheek is resting on the grass and she's facing me. She does this a lot when she says something important, even though she can't make eye contact, she attempts it. I wonder if the gesture is habit or voluntary.

And then she says something that raises goose bumps on my skin. "You know what I miss most about losing my eyesight?" I don't answer because I'm not supposed to. "Looking people in the eye when I talk to them. Because looking people in the eye achieves many things. I can gauge if what they're saying with their words aligns with how they really feel. Mouths can lie, but eyes can't. There's intimacy in eye contact. Not creepy level intimacy, but human level intimacy. You know what I like most about losing my eyesight?"

Again, no answer from me but mostly because I'm hanging on every word in stunned silence.

"Truly hearing what people say when I talk to them. Strike eye contact and sight from a face-to-face exchange and it forces me to listen to words, tone, and inflection. It's added dimension that I didn't pay much attention to when I had eye contact to lean on. Contradiction in words, tone, or inflection is telling. It's information-gathering. I like that. All that being said, Toby, you're a terrible liar. Your sadness is deep. It's old and aged and I can't begin to hear where it began. But it isn't permanent." She squeezes my hand tight again and whispers, "I'll help you slay it."

"I'm not sad," I repeat, but my voice betrays me. There's shock, hesitation, and agreement in it that makes it sound shaky and uneven.

She smiles, but it's the kind of smile that kindly accepts what she's being told, knowing it's complete bullshit. "Someday that will be true."

For a second, I believe her. I want it to be true.

But then I remember I'm Toby Page and that isn't possible.

CHAPTER TWENTY-THREE

Present, April 1987
Toby

The knock on apartment 3A's door rouses both Johnny and me out of our rooms and creates a near collision in the middle of the kitchen. I acquiesce right-of-way even though no one has come knocking on the door for him in two years. He opens the door, offers a quick, "Let me just grab my coat," to the person outside and returns to his bedroom.

Taber is standing in the hall, wool coat on, hands tucked deep in the pockets until he lifts one and raises it in my direction. "Hey, man."

"Hey," I say in return. We get along pretty well these days, all things considered. I'm trying to keep it that way.

His hand returns to the warmth of his pocket and he rocks up on his toes and back down again like he's trying to be patient but is running late. "We're late for our meeting with the friends of Bill W.," he says to me like that means something.

From behind me Johnny says, "I'll be back in an hour or so," as he slips on his coat and walks around me to the door. It sounds ridiculous, like he's a child and I'm the parent. Since when are we checking in with each other in this house?

I nod but give him a puzzled look. "Leave the door open, I'm right behind you," I add. It comes out all wrong because I'm confused.

Alice is ready when I knock on her door: jacket on and white cane in hand. "I'm so excited and I have no idea where we're going."

I warn her our walk will be long and she doesn't mind.

Conversation starts out surface level but digs deeper when I ask, "Do you know where Johnny and Taber were going?"

"AA meeting," she answers matter-of-factly.

"Taber is in AA?" I ask stupidly.

"Yeah." If she's shocked by my question, it doesn't show.

Which encourages me to continue, "I thought Taber was a bartender? How does he do that job if he's a recovering alcoholic?"

"'Keep your friends close and your enemies closer,' that's what he always says. I think he's trying to prove to himself that he's strong, mind over matter and all that."

"Do you worry about him? That he'll start drinking again?"

"Not at all." Faith is kind of refreshing when it's as sincere as hers is. "He made some mistakes when he was younger and he paid the price. When people learn from their mistakes it matures them; when they don't, they stagnate. Taber's probably the most mature twenty-two-year-old on the planet."

What kind of mistakes? I wonder, but I don't ask because it would be rude and I've already asked my fair share of private questions.

When we finally arrive at the Natural History Museum, I guide her in through the planetarium entrance. The lobby is packed and there's already a line forming to get in to the two o'clock showing. "Wait here, I'm going to grab our tickets," I tell her. I don't want her to come with me and hear me or it will ruin the surprise.

She smiles widely. "A movie, huh?"

I gasp, feigning offense. "Give me some credit, Alice. I'm not that cliché."

She laughs at my teasing as I walk away.

I purchase two tickets, and when I return to her, we get in line with the masses. I'm worried the entire time the flow weaves back and forth, as we're corralled between velvet ropes on either side, that she'll overhear someone around us talking and guess why we're here. And then I start worrying that maybe this was a horrible idea and she won't enjoy it. I've never been to one myself, but I've heard kids at school talk about it and hope I'm not overestimating the potential of the entire sensory experience for her.

The planetarium is dimly lit inside, and as we settle into our semi-reclined seats, the announcements begin, "Welcome to Laserium at Gates Planetarium."

Alice interrupts with a whisper, "I've never been to a planetarium, Toby."

She sounds excited and it's then that I remember how much she said she used to love looking at the stars. The thought makes me both happy and sad. If we were here to stargaze at constellations, she wouldn't be able to see them.

The announcer continues with warnings about light, sound, and motion sickness, and finishes up with, "If you need to exit during the show, readmission is prohibited. Now sit back and enjoy *The Led Zeppelin Experience*."

I wish I could see Alice's face, but the room is pitch black.

Until the synchronization of primary colored lights flashing across the ceiling and the first notes of "Whole Lotta Love" assault me. The combination is visceral. As laser lights dance above us, I pry my eyes away to look at Alice and I'm instantly in awe.

Her lips are parted. No hint of a smile, just the arch of an upper lip and the rounded out bow of a bottom lip forming the guileless, unmistakable expression of someone who has been thoroughly stunned. Eyes open and unblinking, she sits statue still. The room momentarily goes dark for a pause in light and sound and I lose her. But when the choreographed swirl of color and thump of bass simultaneously burst back to life, she gasps and reaches over the armrest searching for my hand, fingers curling between mine, securing us.

Song after song the lights flash above me and the music reverberates through me, but I can't take my eyes off of Alice. The shock receded and conceded to a smudge of a smile indicative of someone truly in the throes of wonder. And for the second time since I've known her, I'm struck breathless by her —her openness, her honesty, her beauty, and most of all, her unabashed willingness to feel intensely and not care if anyone's watching.

When the room falls quiet and the house lights illuminate and cast the room in a lusterless, almost foggy glow, Alice turns in my direction and for the first time I notice tears streaking her cheeks. "There was light, Toby." The wonder has slipped from her eyes into her voice.

"What could you see?" I ask hopefully.

She pauses like there's so much she wants to say and doesn't have the words. "There were faint flickers of light..." She pauses again and her eyes drift up like talking about the memory will recall it visually to life. "And they...they..." An errant tear escapes the corner of her eye and trails over her cheekbone to her earlobe where it pools before her chin drops and she finishes her thought. "They pulsed in time with the music. I felt like I was inside of the rib cage of the song, watching its heartbeat. It was—"

Her joy is interrupted by a timid employee adorned in all black, including the yeti-like bushy hair covering his face and scalp. "Hey, dude, sorry to interrupt, but I'm going to have to ask you guys to please—"

I side-eye him without moving my head and glare; it's an effective deterrent. He walks away and stands near the door like he's cowering. Gaze back on Alice, I prompt her to continue, "It was..."

"Incredible. I'll never forget this." She sighs and it's pure contentment. "Thank you." After a short pause, because she knows I won't acknowledge the thank you, she says, "Let's go back to my apartment, I'll make you dinner."

AFTER THE LONG WALK BACK TO THE VICTORIAN ON Clarkson, I'm starving. I haven't eaten all day. I was too nervous earlier. The apartment is empty and the solitude feels recklessly magnetic, like if I sit down and hand myself over to it, I won't want to leave. Solitude and Alice are a dangerous combination; they lull me into serenity and make me believe things might be possible that aren't.

Like happiness.

And girlfriends.

"Do you like turkey or ham?" Alice inquires as she opens the refrigerator door.

My mouth waters and I want to say, *Both*, but I go with, "Whatever you have the most of is fine," because when it comes to food, I've never been picky. I guess that's what happens growing up with a mom who forgot to buy food half the time because she was either drunk or gone.

She feels around inside the fridge and pulls out two plastic baggies, the kind you get from the deli counter at the grocery store. The kind that costs twice as much and tastes twice as good as the Oscar Mayer packages in the cold-cut section. After setting them on the counter, she goes back for the mayo jar in the door and a bottle of mustard.

"How do you know what's what?" I ask, because I can't fathom navigating the world in the dark.

"Taber buys condiments in different sizes and shapes so I know which is which without opening them. Mayo is the small jar, ketchup is the big bottle, mustard is the little bottle, and the salsa jar is shaped weird...if we have any. We usually run out though because Taber puts it on everything."

I like that. I like that Taber goes out of his way to make his sister's life accessible and as easy as possible, at least the little things like food.

The plates clank and rattle against each other when she takes two out of the cupboard. The noise is loud in the silence. As if everything she's doing is amplified because my senses are so intently focused on her.

"I'll grab the bread," I say because I need something to do. Something to take my mind off the fact that her independence, her confidence, her disposition—everything about her—is attractive. I've never been the type of guy who's attracted to women for typical reasons. It's rarely about looks with me. My first crush was on our neighbor. I was nine, and she was in her twenties. She had frizzy brown hair that she never combed, political bumper stickers all over the back of her Volkswagen Beetle, and a smile that made you feel like she put it on just for you. I was always outside because I didn't want to be inside with my mom, and when she came in or out of the apartment building she always said hi and asked how I was doing, or asked if I'd eaten anything lately, or asked to see my drawings and then told me how good they were. We only lived in that building for two months, and I don't know what happened to her, but I'll never forget her smile and how a few words could make me feel human.

I find myself taking my time making my sandwich. I can't remember the last time I had ham or turkey, let alone both. And lettuce. And tomato. I haven't eaten a vegetable in months. They're too expensive and the convenience store I usually shop at doesn't sell fresh produce unless you count brown bananas. This sandwich is a masterpiece.

"We can eat in my room," Alice says.

I follow her in and two things strike me instantaneously: how at home I feel and how much I want to leave. Immediately. Comfort and discomfort are clashing inside my mind and my chest. My knee-jerk reaction is to make up an excuse to leave, so that's what I do. "Hey, Alice, I need to check the answering machine. I've been gone for a few hours and Johnny's probably gone, so..." I trail off because I don't want to stretch this out into a full-on lie.

She's sitting on the end of the bed, her legs dangling over the edge of the footboard, and taking a bite of her sandwich. "Oh," she says with a full mouth. I know it's not ladylike, but it's just one more thing about her that's cute. It's cute until I hear the hurt in her voice.

"Will you be around later? When I'm done with my work?" I don't know if I'll have the courage to come back, but I'm uncharacteristically trying to give myself an in if I do.

The corner of her mouth curves up in hope before she says, "Sure, I'll be here."

I leave her eating the best sandwich that's ever ended up in my stomach.

THERE WERE NO MESSAGES ON THE ANSWERING MACHINE,

but it's three hours before I psych myself up enough to go back down and knock on her door. Waiting for her to answer, I repeat the reminder, *You're nothing. She deserves better. You can't be with her.*

When she opens the door, I know it's true, but I stay anyway.

Her room feels, once again, like home. It makes my heart beat erratically and my palms perspire. I can't acclimate to home or the idea of it, and my nerves spiral.

When she sits on her bed, I remain standing because there isn't a chair in the room.

"My brother won't be home tonight, he's staying at Inga's."

I immediately drop and sit on the floor because I'm not sure if that statement was purely informational or purely invitational. "Okay," I say, slipping out of my sweatshirt because now my pits are starting to sweat too.

"What do you want to do, Toby?"

Because I'm alone in an apartment with this beautiful, kind, fierce girl who sets me on fire, I want to say, *Kiss you. For hours.* But because I know I shouldn't, I say, "Listen to you play one of your songs." Because I really want that too.

That smile emerges, the one that's a little shy and a lot playful. "Really?"

I nod, still in the habit around her, and then answer, "Of course."

She brings her hand to her mouth and taps her bottom lip with her pointer finger before running the tip of it back and forth; she's thinking. "I've been working on something new, do you want to hear that?"

"I want to hear everything," I answer earnestly. I don't want to lie to her tonight. I don't want to hide from her tonight.

Her smile grows impossibly wide. "Good answer, Toby. Can you please hand me my keyboard? It's on my dresser."

I stand and retrieve a smallish keyboard that's already plugged in to an outlet and set it on the bed in front of her.

"Thanks," she says as she turns it on and presses a few buttons. Before I can sit back down on the floor, she pats the bed next to her. "Sit by me. If we're touching, I don't feel like I'm alone playing for myself." The pause is significant enough that she prompts a second time. "I won't bite." As my butt depresses into the mattress next to her and my shoulder grazes hers, she adds loud enough that I can hear her, "Unless you want me to."

God help me, she's flirting. The sound in my throat is almost a laugh.

That makes her laugh. "This one is still rough. I'm struggling with the intro, so I'll skip that part for now."

I don't think a response is necessary, but I say, "Okay," anyway because I always try harder with her than I do with anyone else in the communication department.

She plays it through and even though the volume is turned down, the hairs on my forearms stand on end. It's good. "Reminds me of The Cure," I tell her when she's done.

"Nobody sounds like The Cure. The universe would never allow it." It's joking and self-deprecating, but she also sounds like she really means it.

"I didn't say it sounds like The Cure, but that it reminds me of them. Their darker stuff."

She nods. "It's probably the darkest melody I've ever written. Taber loves it so far, the guitar is broody. He thinks he's a badass when he plays it, I can tell." A sheepish smile that's pride with a little humor mixed in appears on her lips, and I love more and more how layered she is. She never gives herself over to one emotion one hundred percent. She's a dichotomy, a division, a blend of contradicting (sometimes harmonious and sometimes not) emotions that are always a revelation of exactly who Alice is at any moment in time. I've never met anyone like her. She's not guarded, she's ardently forthcoming. Naked. Exposed. I always feel so flat. Her dimension is awe-inspiring. Tonight, I want to soak it up.

"I like it," and then because that isn't enough, I add, "I *really* like it. What about the lyrics?"

She sighs and the smile fades as she sets the keyboard back on her dresser and returns to the bed. "I'm struggling with those too. It's a dark song that needs depth, but everything I write just sounds like unrefined rage or cheesy angst. It sounds manufactured; I want something organic. I want delicate, raw despair because that's what I hear in the keys and guitar. I'm kind of in a good place for the first time in a long time, so those words are elusive right now."

It sounds like she's inside my head. It's not always delicate, but I live in raw despair. And then a thought occurs to me, and I know I shouldn't, but tonight I've let Alice crawl inside me and I want to give something back. "It probably won't help, but I wrote this poem for English last week..." I pause then because I shouldn't share this.

She shifts and all of her attention is on me. "I need to hear it. *Now.*"

I shake my head. "No, I shouldn't have brought it up. It's stupid. You write song lyrics, real poetry. This was just an assignment."

She makes a *Pfft* sound to dismiss my dismissal. "There is nothing amateur about the depths of your soul, Toby. Tell me." When I don't say anything, she adds, "Please," and searches for my hand with hers.

When her fingers slot with mine and her thumb doesn't wrap around the back of my hand but instead curls and slips between our palms, the knuckle and nail stroking my palm whisper soft, I ask, "You sure you want to hear it?"

She leans in until I can feel her lips touch my hair. "More than anything," she whispers.

The words, the feel and the sound of them, make me shiver. The kind of shiver that begins down deep in the pit of my being and spreads like adrenaline-based lust through my veins. This. Girl. I close my eyes, carve out my black heart, and bare it for her to see, feel, and hear. It's absolutely terrifying.

> *"Darkness is passive denial of light.*
> *And aggressive denial of self.*
> *Thoughts rearranged,*
> *Emotions relabeled,*
> *Personality retracted*
> *By a thief*
> *Until all that remains*
> *Is a delicate, reluctant cacophony of shame.*
> *Screaming,*
> *So much blame.*
> *So much blame.*
> *Conscience profound.*
> *Self-preservation drowned.*
> *So much blame.*
> *So much blame.*
>
> *It all fades into oblivion*
> *When everything goes black.*
> *My sacred companion, disregard,*
> *She soothes.*
> *Like the dull blade of contempt,*
> *She maims.*
> *Whispering,*
> *So much blame.*
> *So much blame.*

A mercenary with an end game.
A victim with my name.
So much blame.
So much blame."

She's unmoving except for her vigilante thumb still sweeping, determined to encourage me, comfort me, and arouse me—because it's doing all three. Which is at odds with the silence—it's crushing me, humiliating me, and filleting me.

Unable to bear my unease, paired with my boner, I make a move to get off the bed while hurriedly saying, "I should go—"

Her grip tightens on my hand and before I can rise, she's pushed me on my back and is hovering over the top of me, her long hair like curtains on either side of my face. "No, you most certainly should *not* go." She pauses and swallows. "I've never wished I could touch someone's voice before, but I want to touch yours so badly my fingers itch." Her statement has the reverse effect and I feel tactile-lessly touched by her words. Stroked. Tempted. Stimulated. "You wrote that?" she whispers like the moment won't allow for anything more.

"Yeah. It's stupid, I know."

She shakes her head and puts a hand over my mouth so I can't talk. "No, it's not stupid. It's gut-wrenching, and sad, and painful, and severely gorgeous. You have no idea what you reciting poetry does to me. That was *sexy*."

"Really?" I ask from behind her hand.

"Come on, Toby. You know you're sexy, poetry or not."

I shake my head, bewildered by her response. I've never been called sexy in my life.

She releases me and says, "To your core," while she climbs off the bed and walks out of the room only to return seconds later with a spiral notebook and a blue Bic pen with a gnarled cap that's been chewed unmercifully. "Please write that down.

And then read it to me again. And again. Poems flirt like hell with my mind." The flush in her cheeks tells me she means it.

I feel the same way about songs I love.

I write the poem down.

Then I read it.

Again.

And again.

And again.

At her request.

I'm sitting on the bed. She's standing. Pacing in the narrow space between the wall and the bed. And she's smiling—it's contemplative, and turned-on, and melancholy. After the fourth reading she asks, "Is that how you really feel? Deep down where you don't hide?"

Yes. "No," I lie before I can stop myself.

She nods but ignores my denial. "Is it ever too much? The guilt? The blame? The darkness?" There's genuine concern in her voice.

"No." So much for not lying to her tonight.

"Would you tell someone if it ever gets to that point?" She's always so bold.

I'm not. "Yes," I lie again. Effectively, apparently.

Finally satisfied with what she presumes is the truth, she sits down on the bed next to me and changes gears. "I have a bottle of vodka hidden in a shoebox in my closet. Well, half of a bottle of vodka. I took it from the open bar at my cousin's wedding last year. Do you want some?"

"No." It feels like a lie, but I immediately know that it isn't, because there's something I want even more.

"You don't drink?" she questions curiously.

I let the truth go. "I do. But I'd rather kiss you instead."

She licks her lips and her quick comeback stalls and turns into a slow, thought-out counter. "We can do both."

I take her hands and press her palms to my cheeks and shake my head slowly so she can feel it.

"Why not?" she says it on a deep inhalation of air meant to calm her.

I'm staring at her mouth, expectant like it's ready and willing to grant wishes and make dreams reality. I end the lies. "Because I don't want anything between my mind and your lips. I want to remember it all. Clearly." She rises up on her knees and with my cheeks still covered in her hands that are still covered in mine, leans in. A second before our lips touch, I answer the question she asked me weeks ago at Wax Trax. "*You* make my pulse race, Alice."

The first brush of lips isn't tentative; we jump right in where we left off the last time. This isn't a kiss that's going to smolder until it ignites. It's an inferno from the start. Intent established on both sides, her fingers free from my hold and slide to the nape of my neck, cradling my head to angle up toward her. Before I know it, I'm up on my knees too. My hands on her waist, our bodies pressed flush. The kiss is entirely visceral, all-consuming. Our breathing is accelerated and purposeful, chests expanding and retracting in an erratic rhythm. And when my lips touch her neck, the quiet sigh she releases incites a riot inside me. When her hands find their way under my shirt, I don't waste any time and pause the kiss to strip it over my head. The move is unconscious and instinct-driven and I immediately question myself. *Is this moving too fast?* I really like Alice and don't want to scare her.

"Is this okay?" I whisper.

She places her palms on my chest and slowly drags them reverently over bone and muscle. She's looking at me with her hands. If this wasn't so hot, I'd be self-conscious. But I'm not. Hormones must be my superpower because I've never felt embarrassed when I'm physically intimate with someone. It's like all the doubt temporarily suspends.

"It's more than okay, Toby. Does it make you uncomfortable when I touch you like this? I've wondered for a long time what you look like." Her eyes are focused on my chest like she can see what she's touching.

"No," is buried in a satisfied moan.

The kissing resumes, slower this time. It's exploratory, to match what our hands are doing.

Time ticks by slowly.

Her shirt is removed by me.

Her bra is removed by her.

At some point, we lie down.

On our sides facing each other.

Legs weave together.

And while our lips worship and hands inquire and please, hips begin to slowly engage.

Which leads to a shifting of bodies.

An alignment to address the throbbing need.

Me on my back.

Alice on top, her skirt pulled up to allow her legs to part.

Chests flesh-to-flesh.

My hands guiding her hips.

Her hips guiding my hands.

The grinding blissful.

Through my jeans and her panties.

The red ones.

Kissing alternates between languid and frenetic.

Touching alternates between adoring and fanatical.

I'm *so close.*

And I'm lost.

Lost in *her*.

Lost in *this*.

Lost in *us*.

And that's when the soundtrack starts up.

You're nothing.

She's everything.

You don't deserve this.

She deserves more.

Than you.

Than this.

Don't lead her on.

You're nothing.

You're nothing.

You're nothing.

Slowly, I still my hips.

And my hands.

And my lips.

And I drag in the deep breath my lungs desperately need.

Eyes still closed, I listen to Alice inhale and exhale like she's been underwater.

Once.

Twice.

Three times before I open my eyes.

I don't know what I expected, but she's smiling. It's hazily euphoric and fearlessly shy. She rolls off me and puts her shirt back on without a word, skipping the bra, but with the smile still in place. Then she walks to her closet and pulls out a shoebox from underneath a pile of notebooks and extracts the bottle of vodka. I search for my T-shirt on the floor and tug it on, watching her the entire time. She returns to the bed and sits next to me before she unscrews the lid and hands it to me. While I'm taking a swig, she says, "I'm not sure where you learned to kiss like that, but I'd like to offer her my sincere and undying appreciation."

I almost spit out the liquid in my mouth but manage to swallow it back.

She smiles when she hears me splutter and holds her hand out for the bottle.

"Ditto," I say when I hand her the bottle. I mean it, that kiss was everything a kiss should be. And more.

She tips it back, takes a sip, and cringes as she swallows. "He was a bastard. Kissing was his only saving grace."

"First boyfriend?" I ask.

"Yeah," she replies as she props up a pillow against the headboard and leans back into it. "Ninth grade. Ryan Lopez. We went out for three months."

"What happened?"

"I found out he'd been kissing Melinda Tompkins for three months too." Her tone is sour, the years' old malice fierce.

"I hope you broke up with him and not the other way around."

She nods proudly. "Killed him and buried him in the woods behind our house."

I snort; it's not a laugh but it's close.

Which makes her laugh and change her story. "Okay, I didn't kill him. But Melinda and I did publicly humiliate him when we both broke up with him at the same time during a pep assembly at school."

"Good. For not committing murder and the breakup public humiliation style," I encourage.

"What about you? Tell me about your first girlfriend."

She hands me the bottle and I take a big gulp. "I've never had a girlfriend," I answer truthfully.

Her head turns my way and the look on her face is incredulous. "*Really?*"

"Really," I confirm. It's true; I've never had a girlfriend. I've never been interested in having a girlfriend. And no one has ever been interested in having me fill that role. Fill other physical roles? Yes. But never the boyfriend role.

"But you've kissed girls, *obviously*." She wiggles her eyebrows in an adorable cartoony villain way. "And there's no way you're a virgin," she adds, shaking her head. "*No way*."

"A gentleman never tells." The tone of my voice was supposed to be serious, but it comes out teasing instead. I guess the vodka is starting to work its magic and loosen me up.

That makes one corner of her mouth lift in admiration. "Good answer, Toby." Then she motions with her hand for the bottle and after taking another sip, followed by the same cringe, she asks, "Who was your first kiss?"

"I'm a gentleman, remember?" I counter.

Her features are softer, slackened the tiniest bit. She looks more approachable than anyone I've ever known. Even Nina. Like I could tell her anything and she would never judge me for it. "You are." It's sincere affirmation.

"Her name was Isabelle. She lived in the apartment across the hall from us." My voice is quiet as I dust off the memories. I haven't thought about her in years.

"How old were you?" she asks as she hands me back the bottle.

I pause to throw back one last shot's worth and set the bottle on the nightstand because we've both had enough for now. "Fourteen, almost fifteen."

She shifts to face me, propping her head up on the pillow. "How old was she?"

Reaching behind her I take hold of the quilt draped over the side of the bed and pull it over the top of her. "Thanks," she whispers as she snuggles in.

"Older than me," I answer vaguely.

"Seventeen?" she guesses.

"Close enough," I answer. She was twenty.

She opens her mouth to say something but then stops.

I'm watching her closely because my thoughts and words are flowing freely thanks to the vodka and I'm worried this is where the judgment begins. "What?"

"Was it consensual?" she asks quietly like she fears my answer. Like she fears for me. For what I may have been through.

"Yes," I answer honestly. "The first time she asked me to help her move a big chair she'd bought at Goodwill into her apartment. I did and she kissed me."

"Was that the only time?" The concerned look is still on her face.

"No. It went on for a few weeks. And then one day she was gone. Evicted. I never saw her again."

The truth is we had sex the second time I went to her apartment. And many times thereafter. I knew it was wrong. I knew it was illegal on her part. But at the time, it didn't feel that way. It felt like an escape. It felt good to be needed. To be wanted. To make someone happy. I was always the invisible kid outside our apartment and the focus of my mom's rage inside it. In Isabelle's apartment, in her bed, I wasn't either of those. She saw me and there was no rage.

"Did you love her?" The concern is still there. Not jealousy, just concern.

"No," I answer without remorse because I didn't.

"Did she love you?" she asks.

I pause for a few seconds because I've never thought about it. "No. I think she was just lonely. Like me." It's an alcohol-laced, free-flowing add-on.

She nods in understanding. "Have you ever been in love, Toby?"

Sadly, I don't have to think the question over before answering. "No. Have you?"

"You mean other than Simon Le Bon?" she teases to lighten the somber mood I've draped over us.

I almost laugh. "Yeah, other than the Simon Le Bon lusting phase."

She shrugs the shoulder that's free and the quilt moves over it. "I've had three boyfriends and each time I thought I was in love. I thought they were *the one*," she sings the words to emphasize how silly the idea was, "and that we would be together forever."

"What do you think now?" I probe. My inhibitions have been freed; inebriation will do that.

"I think I lent my heart to boys who didn't know how to treat it or me." There's a touch of melancholy in her voice.

"And they returned it to you worse for wear?" I don't like the thought of Alice being mistreated.

She readjusts and tucks her hands under the pillow to get comfortable, and Alice's confident side shines bright in the smile that peeks out. "I like to think they returned it to me wiser. Because I know I won't settle in the future—that I deserve all of the effort, attention, and respect that I show them in return. It's a two-way street. Love isn't lopsided. Infatuation is."

"You deserve all of it," I tell her. She does.

She pulls a hand from its hiding place under the pillow and rubs my forearm that's resting on the bed next to her. "I know that now. So do you."

I change subjects because this one is at an end. "Why don't you live with your parents? I mean, I know you're eighteen, but you're still in school."

She sighs, but it isn't irritated, it's tired like the thought of them drains her. "Do you want the short version or the long version?"

THE OTHER SIDE • 171

"I've got all night," I tell her. I mean it. I would sit here all night and listen to her talk about anything.

"Where to begin?" she says, mostly to herself as she slips her hand down my forearm and slips her fingers between mine. The gesture isn't suggestive; it's friendly. "My parents are divorced. They never really got along. They argued a lot and I don't ever remember seeing them hug or kiss as a kid. When Taber was in high school, he was kind of a hellion. He partied a lot, and when my mom found weed and pills in his dresser his senior year, she kicked him out. My dad didn't agree with her parenting and that started World War III. Dad moved out and tried to get Taber into rehab. Taber refused because he wasn't ready, he hadn't hit rock bottom yet. Around the time the divorce was finalized I started having problems with my vision. You know how that part of the story goes.

"My dad got a promotion at work and was transferred to their Colorado Springs office where he met Suzanne and remarried. My mom lost her shit and became more tyrannical than before. She forbade Taber from her house and from seeing me, saying he was a bad influence. Of course that didn't work because we just met up at the mall, or for lunch, or after school. He always kept in touch with me, and even though his life was really messed up, he always looked out for me. I couldn't go live with my dad because I worried about Taber and didn't want to be two hours away from him. My mom started taking me to a series of doctors. They all gave the same diagnosis. The same prognosis. She wouldn't accept it. I saw twenty-four doctors the first year of my diagnosis. So not only was I struggling with losing my sight, I was struggling with my mom's inability to accept it. To accept me. She obsessed about finding a doctor who could fix me."

The conversation I overheard makes so much more sense now.

"Which made me feel like shit because adjusting to losing your sight is no picnic, but when your own parent doesn't accept you the way you are, it's crushing. I felt like a disappointment instead of a daughter. So, I started acting out: ditching school, drinking, smoking. Because if she didn't think I was the same old Alice anymore, I was determined to not be the same old Alice anymore and really show her. That was short-lived because I didn't like me like that either. So instead of acting out, I argued. A lot. I was bitter and jaded and started to hate myself. That was about a year ago. By that time, Taber met Inga and decided to go to AA. He got sober and secretly got me into a free counseling program offered through a church near my school. We aren't religious, but they welcomed me anyway. He took me once a week for almost a year. My mom didn't know."

"Did it help?" I ask, knowing the answer must be yes.

"So much. But my mom wouldn't give up on the new doctors, and I couldn't deal with what life had in store with my blindness and her constant need to fix me. To fix what can't be fixed. That's when fate and Taber intervened."

"What happened?"

"The band had been wanting to move to Denver and give the scene here a go, because we'd been getting a lot of gigs down here. Taber found this apartment and a job at the bar he works at all within a week. He called me and told me he wanted me to move in with him."

"Your knight in shining armor," I interject.

She smiles knowingly and corrects me. "My knight in leather and eyeliner."

"Right," I agree to accept the correction.

"Do you know why I wanted to drink tonight?" She sounds apologetic for bringing the conversation down.

"No, why?" I ask curiously. I know this isn't the acting out she mentioned earlier. She's way too even-keeled for that. Too responsible.

"I guess I just wanted to feel like a normal eighteen-year-old. The past two years have been a roller coaster. I feel like I'm finally in a good place. I like myself again." She tries to smile, but it looks sad. "Taber is doing really well, he's thriving in Denver. His girlfriend is great; I think they'll get married as soon as she finishes nursing school. Our band is kicking ass; we have gigs booked for the next three months. I'll be graduating soon and I'm so glad to get that behind me. But the one thing I've missed is having a friend who isn't my brother or a band-mate. The friends I had in Fort Collins, we drifted apart over the past two years. I changed, I know I did. I couldn't cope with me and they couldn't either. It's been months since I had a true friend. But with you, I feel like I've finally found one. You make me feel normal, Toby. I have fun with you because I can be myself."

"You can always be yourself with me. I wouldn't want you any other way," I whisper.

"Thanks," I can hear the smile in her voice. "What about your family? Why don't you live with them?" she asks.

I should've been expecting the question, but it catches me off guard. I slip my hand from hers and reach for the bottle on the nightstand and take in so much that it requires two swallows to get it all down.

"I could use some more of that. Pass it here, please," she says, motioning with her fingers.

I do and my eyes fall absently on the patchwork quilt underneath me and on top of Alice. "My mom is an alcoholic," I say with little emotion. I'm drunk and it's having a lovely numbing effect on just about every part of me. I don't know why I said it, but it seems the best place to start when it comes to my family.

Alice hands me the bottle, and I don't miss the irony of both of us getting sloppy drunk when alcoholism runs in our families. Like she can feel my instant guilt, she says, "Do you ever fear you could be someday, too? Because it runs in families?"

"No." I won't live long enough. "Do you?"

"No. At least, I hope not. I honestly don't like the taste of it. I don't think I ever will. And being around Taber I never drink, to be supportive of his choices and his health. That's why I've had this bottle hidden away for so long. I'll throw it in the dumpster outside before he gets home tomorrow so he'll never know." She pauses and circles back to the conversation I'd like to avoid even though my drunk mind won't let me. "Is that why you don't live with her, because she drinks?"

"I don't live with her because she left." I don't sound angry. I don't sound sad. I sound indifferent because right now, I am.

"She left?" Alice sounds confused and shifts on the bed until she's lying perpendicular to me and her head is in my lap. I love how comfortable she makes herself.

I brush the hair back from her forehead absentmindedly. "Yeah. Johnny evicted her. She left and I stayed."

"Wow." I see her lips move more than I hear it. "What about your dad? Couldn't you go live with him?"

"I don't know who he is. My mom always said he was a deadbeat and never told me his name. She just told me he didn't want anything to do with us."

"I'm sorry," she says sincerely. "He missed out on you. Maybe not on her, but definitely on you."

"That's debatable." I shouldn't have said that out loud.

She reaches up and presses her palm flush against my chest so I hear her words. "No, it's not. You're a good person, Toby." She then clasps both of her hands over her stomach. "Do you have any siblings?"

I clam up. Despite the alcohol, I clam up.

She must feel me tense. "Toby?"

"A sister," I force out.

"Older or younger?" Her voice is quieter, like she knows we're heading into uncharted territory.

"Fifteen years older. We didn't really grow up together because she wasn't around a lot, but she's the only person I've ever loved. She was great." Now that I'm talking, I can't seem to stop. "She had the best laugh. The kind of laugh that sounded like it bubbled up from somewhere deep inside, and once it started, she couldn't stop it. Hearing her laugh always made me laugh when I was little. And she was an incredible artist. She could draw anything I asked her to draw. She also loved music. When I was nine, she brought home an album and played it for me and it was like someone flipped a switch inside me. I didn't just hear the music, I felt it. It was like everything else in life blurred in comparison. Music was clear and precise and dauntless and honest, its message and soul intact despite everything else fading into oblivion. It made me feel connected to it. To her."

Alice hasn't missed the fact that I'm talking about Nina in the past tense, but her smile is warm. I think she likes that I've opened up and that I'm sharing myself with her. "*Physical Graffiti?*" she asks knowingly, remembering our first trip to Wax Trax.

"Yeah," I answer, lost in all the good that was Nina, and for a moment, blocking out the rest.

"It sounds like you had the best big sister in the world."

I nod. "I did." She wasn't perfect, nobody is. Her demons were many and she fought them daily: drug addiction and an abusive mother. On the good days, she won. And on the bad days, they won, but she tried to hide it. "Nina was one of those people who hid her hurt when you were around her and all you felt was the weight of her love instead. She put all of the attention on others, even if she never received it back in equal doses. She was great at asking questions and really listening to the answers. I loved that about her." It's one of my favorite things about Alice too.

"When did you lose her?" The words are support, pure and simple.

"Almost two years ago," I whisper. I'm suddenly tired. So damn tired, like the past two years have caught up with me. Again.

Alice looks tired too, her eyelids are droopy.

I maneuver around on the bed so that I'm lying on my side behind her, my front pressed against her back. She's wrapped up in my arms, and we're both wrapped up in the quilt. "Who made the quilt?" I ask. It looks old and handmade.

Covering my hands on her belly with hers, she answers, "My grandma. It was a wedding gift to my parents. My mom threw it away after the divorce and I pulled it out of the trash and kept it because I liked it. And my grandma. She's gone now."

"I like it." I do. It's sewn by hand and the seams are crooked. It's imperfect. Like everything in life. My eyes are getting heavy. I can't fall asleep with her. I have no idea if I lash out when my nightmares come to terrorize and I don't want her near them. "I should go, Alice." The words are muffled even to my own ears.

She tightens her grip on my arms and whispers, "Just five more minutes, Toby. I don't want you to leave yet."

"You need to sleep."

"I need a reason to *lose* sleep more," she counters and her voice trails off.

I smile at her admission and relax because this feels so good being here with her.

She relaxes too.

"What have you always wanted more than anything else, Toby?" It sounds dreamlike and far away.

The answer is easy, but the words are hard for my sleepy mouth to form. "To be someone's hero." I don't know if I only think the words or if they made it out in the open to her.

I WAKE SEVERAL HOURS LATER, GROGGY AND DISORIENTED, but calm. No nightmares. And then I feel Alice in my arms and realize I did exactly what I intended not to do and fell asleep in her bed. Disentangling myself from her, I ease off the mattress, trying not to wake her. A quick read of the alarm clock on the nightstand tells me it's 4:37 a.m. I grab the near-empty bottle of vodka and walk as quietly as I can to the front door and let myself out, making sure the door is locked behind me. I throw the bottle in the dumpster outside like she wanted and return to apartment 3A. It's dark and silent except for the symphony of lumbering snores coming from behind both closed bedroom doors. After using the bathroom, I unlock my door, undress, and slide into my sleeping bag, thoughts of Alice, and deep restful sleep. No nightmares. Only Alice-induced calm.

CHAPTER TWENTY-FOUR

Present, April 1987
Toby

"Cliff said you watch Joey on Tuesday nights while Chantal works," Johnny says, his back to me while he butters a piece of toast to go with the cereal he's eating for dinner.

"Yeah," I answer quietly.

I assess my food situation in the fridge before closing it and by default reach for the loaf of bread on the counter and my go-to jar of peanut butter in the cabinet above the sink. I can feel his eyes on me as he turns, bowl in hand, and rests his back against the counter to dig into his Raisin Bran. I prepare two sandwiches in record time because though this is casual, it feels...inquisitive. Sober Johnny is chatty. I don't think I like it. I stack the sandwiches, wrap them in a paper towel, and head for the door since my bedroom is already locked. My backpack is slung over my shoulder, prepared to sit in the corner of Mrs. Bennett's living room, the homework inside ignored and put off until Chantal gets home around midnight and I come back up here to do it. I don't know why I bring it with me anymore.

"How old is he now?" Johnny asks after crunching into his toast and talking through it, the crumbs dusting his beard and the front of his flannel shirt.

I'm distracted by how burned his toast is when I answer, "Seven months." It must taste like ash though he doesn't seem to notice.

He shakes his head like he can't believe it. I guess being nonstop drunk makes the passage of time unreliable and indefinite. "Wow," thankfully is all he says as my hand finds the doorknob on the door leading out to the hall.

Coincidentally, as I pull on it, someone else is pushing his way in. I hear Cliff before I see him.

"I'll see if he's home," Cliff calls.

Alice's voice drifts in from the hall. "Thanks."

When Cliff's eyes meet mine, he's smiling that smile that I know is going to end in trouble for me. I'm really beginning to resent Cliff. "The hot chick from downstairs is looking for—"

I cut him off because I have no patience for him anymore. "—Alice. She has a name, Cliff."

"Hey, Toby," Alice greets when she hears my voice.

I squeeze past Cliff into the hall but can't close the door because he's standing in the way. I don't want to initiate conversation with ears listening, but I don't have a choice. "Hey, Alice."

"We're heading to band practice and I wondered if maybe you wanted to come and watch. We're going to play that song I've been working on for the first time as a band, and I wanted you to be there since you helped with the lyrics." She looks nervous to ask.

"Don't you have to watch the kid tonight?" Cliff asks from over my shoulder as if he's part of this discussion. It's one of my biggest pet peeves about him—he sticks his nose in everyone's business.

I reach back to pull the door shut and he doesn't budge. The look on his face is innocent, I wonder if he knows he's being a douche. The look on my face is murderous. Johnny sees it and clears his throat before his voice rumbles low with authority. "Cliff, shut the damn door and go get started on your homework." He almost sounds like a parent—he's been working on it.

"Watch the kid?" Alice asks as the door finally closes with a benevolent click.

The boundary eases my anxiety slightly. Until I have to answer her question. I've avoided telling Alice about Joey. About Chantal. I never expected to be in this situation, to care about someone and what they thought about me. I don't want to be judged and I know that sounds shitty and makes me a hypocrite because I judge people all the time, but... "Joey," I answer because I have to say something.

"You babysit?" she asks skeptically.

As if on cue, I hear footsteps making their way up the stairs and I know who it is because I'm late. When Chantal crests the stairway and comes into sight, she's in her uniform and holding Joey in her arms. He's fidgeting. The stiff kicks of his legs tell me he's less than five seconds away from crying. When he's pissed about something, his arms and legs go rigid and he pumps them like he has to wind himself up to really put on a display. She walks directly to me, ignoring Alice, and the look on her face tells me it's been a long day and she just needs to get away for a few hours and decompress. Joey's cry erupts and she holds him at arm's length, facing me. He's an offering from a tired mom.

The moment I accept him into my arms and hold him

against my chest, I whisper, "Hey, it's okay. Don't cry, little man."

He quiets immediately at the sound of my voice.

Chantal shakes her head. "Of course he calms down for you," she mutters, but she sounds grateful. Then she looks me in the eye. "Grandma has been pretty good today and she finally finished dinner. Joey ate too, but he's been fussy all day. He isn't running a fever though." She's looking at him like she's not sure if she should leave him or not. The guilt is taking over.

"It's fine. Go," I urge.

She's staring at Joey wistfully when she nods. "I know. The diner phone number is on the fridge if you need to call me. If he gets worse or if a fever starts." The worrier in her is making her talk fast.

"I know," I echo.

Her eyes climb from Joey against my chest up to meet mine and they relax slightly. "I know you know." She says it all the time, but this time she adds, "You're the best, Toby," and kisses me on the cheek.

I stiffen when she does because this entire situation is already awkward, and this isn't us. It's not what we do.

I'm stunned when her gaze bounces immediately to Alice and she says, "We haven't been formally introduced, but I've seen you around. We both live on the second floor, we're neighbors. I'm Chantal."

Alice extends her hand in the direction of Chantal's voice and they shake. "I'm Alice. It's nice to meet you. How old is your son?"

"Our son is seven months." I didn't miss the *our* that began that sentence. Why is she doing this? She never acts like this.

Alice nods, but she looks stunned. She caught the *our* too.

Chantal smiles innocently and it looks all wrong on her.

"Well, I'd better get going or I'll be late. I'll be home around midnight, Toby."

I nod and the, "I know," that accompanies it sounds sour. Chantal heard it and I don't miss the darkening of her cheeks before she turns and walks away.

Alice waits until she hears Chantal descend every flight of stairs and walk out the front door before she whispers, "You have a baby, Toby?"

I nod, embarrassment flooding in. "Yeah," I whisper back. This is where I lose her. People, even nice people, are watching when we make what they perceive to be mistakes. They don't like mistakes.

"That's a pretty big deal. Were you ever going to tell me about him?" She sounds a little annoyed, shocked—hurt? I can't tell which. When I don't answer, she asks a follow-up, "Are you two together? You and Chantal?"

"No," I blurt out. Finally something I can be truthful about.

"How long were you together?" She's still whispering and it makes my stomach ball up.

"We never were." I sound ashamed and I'm not sure how she's going to take that.

She nods and a short, derisive bark of laughter that isn't laughter at all escapes. "Does she know that? Because it didn't sound that way to me."

I sigh because my life is a shit show. "Yes, she knows that. We had sex once—"

She cuts me off. "—You had sex *once* and she got pregnant?"

"Yeah. It *does* happen, you know? Sometimes what you think is a good choice in the moment turns into something you didn't ask for in the end." There's a clip in my voice, but truer words have never been spoken. My cheeks are burning. I don't want to talk about this anymore. "I need to get downstairs to their apartment; her grandma has Alzheimer's and can't be left alone."

She nods and it softens her, but I can tell the news is bothering her. I should explain more but I can't.

"I need to get to band practice," she says.

"Yeah," I agree because I'm tired, and Joey is starting to squirm in my arms.

"Yeah," she whispers in hesitant agreement, turns, and walks away.

I can feel the judgment and I want to scream, *Yes, I'm more fucked up than you could ever imagine! You should stay away from me!* But, I can't. Because I can't stay away from her.

MRS. BENNETT HAS BEEN ASLEEP IN HER BEDROOM FOR three hours and Joey has been asleep in my arms for two when I hear a timid knock on their door. When I open it, Alice is standing there and I can see the apology on her face before she opens her mouth.

"Alice," I say quietly. It's relief and gratitude and surprise.

"I'm sorry." I think she's going to say more, but she stops abruptly. "Are we alone?"

"Except the sleeping baby in my arms, yes," I answer. The irritation from earlier is gone, I'm just happy to see her.

"I'm sorry about earlier. I was jealous and I shouldn't have been, but I was. I was a little surprised too, but mostly just jealous," she rambles.

I shift Joey in the crook of my arm so I can free up one hand and touch her cheek because it's been days since I touched her and I need that right now. Touching her skin makes me feel like I'm not alone. Her head tilts and she leans slightly into my hand like she's missed it too.

"You don't need to be jealous. Surprised, yes. Jealous, no. I should've told you. I should've told you a long time ago." My fingers have threaded into her hair above her ear, and I'm stroking my thumb softly across her cheek. Her eyes are closed. And my God, she looks so pretty it hurts.

"You should've told me, but I should've behaved differently—"

"Chantal should've behaved differently. She's never like that," I interject.

She shrugs. "She just has this deep voice and she sounds older. She sounds mature and confident and..." she trails off then lets out a sigh. "I'm sorry, my self-conscious side is rearing its ugly head and I know how unattractive that is. I tend to compare myself to people, women especially, and I always come up short in the comparison. I'm working on it with my therapist, but I failed tonight. I'm sorry."

"It's okay. I'm sorry too."

"Listen, Toby, I don't know what we are to each other and I honestly don't want to put a label on it because then I overthink everything and I know I'll mess it up, but I do know that you're my friend. My only friend and the best friend I've probably ever had and I don't want that to change. Are we good?"

I'm not used to honesty like this. I'm not used to people caring.

My thumb brushes her cheek one more time before I release her and return to a two-armed hold on Joey before leaning forward and whispering, "We're good," against her temple before I kiss it. "This whole friendship thing is new to me too and I suck at it."

Her smile transforms into something dreamier. "Night, Toby and Joey."

I smile too. "Night, Alice."

. . .

When Chantal arrives home around midnight, I'm so tired I can hardly see straight. She looks sheepish. She never looks sheepish. I know she feels bad about what happened earlier with Alice, but she's not one to come out and apologize either. We are so similar. Usually, I avoid confrontation, and for the most part I plan on doing it tonight, but I can't leave without saying something. We do the ritual handoff, and I watch her effortlessly lie him down in his crib without waking him—I still think there's some sort of motherly witchcraft involved in the process because he wakes up every time I even look at the crib with intention, let alone try.

When she turns and walks back out to the living room, she asks, "Did he cry a lot?"

I shake my head. "Not at all."

She nods slowly like she's thinking a lot harder about that than she should, her eyes downcast. "You always seem to calm him," she says, lifting them to meet mine.

I raise my eyebrows and shrug because this is getting uncomfortable.

And then she changes the subject. "She seems nice." Her eyes have dropped back to the floor.

"She is," I answer, solemnly, knowing this conversation has shifted to Alice.

"I don't know why I acted the way I did. I shouldn't have."

Like I said, apologies aren't our thing. I know this is hard for her.

"You shouldn't have," I agree.

Her eyes dart up to meet mine before they drift off over my shoulder, and she huffs like she doesn't know how to say what she wants to say.

"You don't have to—" I start to let her off the hook, but she proceeds right over the top of me.

"I do. I've never seen you with anyone, but the way you

were looking at her, I knew that you've kissed her. And that you want to again. And again. Not many people are as guarded as you..."

I nod in agreement.

She continues quickly, "I saw you let your walls down tonight and instead of being happy for you, I got territorial and protective." She shakes her head, admonishing herself. "I had no right."

Normally, I would keep my mouth shut but not tonight. "You had no right."

She sighs like she's even more disappointed in herself. "I didn't. I'm seeing someone too, you know?"

This is news to me. "I didn't know that."

She shrugs. We both shrug a lot. "He's come into the diner as long as I've been working there and always asks to be seated in my section. A few weeks ago he asked me out. Every Monday he comes in at the end of my shift and we have coffee for thirty minutes."

"Is he a good man?" That's all I want for her. It would help put my mind at ease.

She nods and smiles. "He is. He's a widow, lost his wife to cancer at twenty-four. That was three years ago. He has a seven-year-old daughter, and works as an X-ray tech in the ER at Denver General Hospital."

This is what she needs. Someone who's stable, responsible, and has a future. Someone who's a complement to all of her strengths. "He sounds great."

She can't help the smile that creeps into her normally guarded expression. "He really is."

Lifting my backpack from the floor by the door, I heft the strap over my shoulder and tell her, "I'm happy for you. And Joey."

Her eyes finally lift from the floor to meet mine. Her hand

reaches out toward me but then retracts just as quickly. "Thanks, Toby." I think she's going to say more, but we just end up looking at each other awkwardly for a few seconds. Everything is back to normal it seems.

I turn and exit, leaving behind our oversharing exchange, but I can't help feeling like a shift is happening, and in the end, I'll be forced out when I'm no longer needed.

CHAPTER TWENTY-FIVE

Present, April 1987
Toby

It's Saturday. I've already done my rounds of the house and helped Mrs. Bennett chase away the imaginary bear she was convinced was trying to climb in her bedroom window. It's cold outside, so I'm drawing in my room until Alice gets home later. They're playing at the Mammoth Events Center tonight and I'm going along so I can finally see her perform. It's been a long time since I've looked forward to something like I'm looking forward to this. To seeing Alice in her element.

I'm an hour into a pencil drawing of Spider-Man suspended mid-air between two skyscrapers, when there's a knock on my bedroom door.

Cliff doesn't wait for me to answer. I think he knocks with one hand while the other is already turning the knob for entry. I'm desensitized to it now.

"What?" I ask without looking up, pencil shading a web.

THE OTHER SIDE • 189

"I'm bored," he announces like it's my job to rectify his predicament.

"So do something," I offer.

"I'm hungry. Let's go to QuikMart and get some pizzas."

I never go anywhere with Cliff, but he sounds down. I found out from Johnny a few days ago that Cliff's dad got into a fight in prison and there was a weapon involved. Which means his dad has new charges brought against him and an additional sentence. He won't be a free man until Cliff is well into his thirties. Cliff didn't take the news well and spiraled and has been a bigger jackass than normal. Ditching school, vandalism, drugs, shoplifting—he's teetering about a hair's breadth above rock bottom.

I'm sitting on my sleeping bag with my back resting against my propped-up pillow, legs outstretched.

He steps in and kicks my socked foot with his boot. Not hard enough to hurt, just hard enough to get my attention. "C'mon, Toby."

My eyes move to his dirty boots on my sleeping bag. "Boots off my bed," I command and he steps back onto the linoleum. "I don't have extra money this week." I don't. Joey needed diapers yesterday.

"I do." I know he's lying because his lips are moving.

I keep drawing and he takes my silence as disbelief.

"I do. My grandma sent me some this week for my birthday." He's really selling it.

I set my pencil down and look up at him, tilting my head so he knows I'm not buying it. "Your birthday is months away," I challenge.

"She's old, she forgets." He pulls a wad of bills out of his pocket as proof.

I sigh and rub my eyes because they're sore; dim lighting and deep concentration are a bad combination. Against my better judgment, I set my pad of paper and pencil on the shelf next to me and grab my shoes. "Wait for me downstairs. I need to use the bathroom before we go."

Obeying the request by heading directly to the front door tells me he's desperate to get out of the house. I pull a thermal on over my T-shirt and grab my sweatshirt off the hook on the wall before I step out and padlock the door behind me. I try to talk myself out of this field trip while I pee. It doesn't work, and minutes later we're stepping through the door of QuikMart. Cliff walks to the refrigerated section with the soda and grabs a root beer, while I walk to the frozen section and pull out a Canadian bacon Party Pizza. It's the cheapest pizza they have and it's on sale again. Bonus. Cliff walks up next to me and I hold the door open while he decides. After an agonizingly long internal debate between cheese and sausage—I know it's happening because he touches each of them at least six times— his hand finally commits to the sausage. When we turn to walk toward the counter, I notice my least favorite QuikMart employee is working. The guy always gives me a hard time and I'd rather not have to deal with him today, so I tell Cliff, "I'll wait for you outside, this guy's a dick."

Cliff takes my pizza and says, "Okay, I'll be out in a minute. I'm gonna grab a candy bar too."

The second Cliff meets me on the sidewalk, chaos erupts, and it becomes glaringly clear why I should always say no to Cliff.

"Stop!" QuikMart Dick yells.

At the same time, Cliff yells, "Run!"

I hesitate, but only for a split second before I find myself running next to him like an idiot. "What did you do?" I ask as adrenaline courses through my veins.

"Stole a pack of cigarettes," he says, his short, thick legs struggling, and failing, to keep up with me.

QuikMart Dick is gaining on us and when he shouts, "Stop or I'll shoot," I look over my shoulder.

"He has a gun, Cliff. What the hell?" I'm panicked now. QuikMart Dick is sketchy at best, and seeing him wielding a gun brings me no comfort. "Give me the cigarettes," I command.

"What?" Cliff puffs out. He's fading, the kid isn't built for physical activity.

"Give me the damn cigarettes," I grit out. *"Now,"* I add because we don't have much time.

I'm ahead of him, but he slips the pack out of his coat pocket and into my sweatshirt pocket with the precision of a seasoned pickpocket, and when it's secure, I stop in my tracks and put my hands up over my head.

"What are you doing?" Cliff pants and stops a few strides past me, doubling over with his hands on his knees.

"Shut up, Cliff. For once in your life, *just shut the fuck up.*" I'm whispering, but he knows I'm seething and he's never seen me like this, so he does.

QuikMart Dick is on us in no time. "I finally caught you, you little punk," he says to Cliff. He's waving the gun around like he's qualified to do so. I know the QuikMart has been robbed several times and that's why they have a gun, but that doesn't mean that Dick knows how to handle it safely.

"Hey, Dirty Harry, you caught us. Now put the gun down." I hate guns and the sight of it is making me nauseous.

He waves it around in my face and I have to close my eyes because my vision is starting to go black at the edges. "You steal from my store and you think you get to tell me what to do? *You don't.* What you get to do is come with me back to the store while I call the police. And then you get a trip to the station."

"Fine, let's go. But put the gun down and let him go. He didn't take anything, it was me," I plead. My body is shaking, not from the fear of being caught with stolen goods, but from the horrific memories playing out on the back of my eyelids. It's the nightmare that haunts me every night. I stick my hand in my pocket and pull out a pack of menthols. "See? Here. Let him go, he paid for all of his stuff."

They're ripped violently from my hand and my upper arm is locked down by his other hand, which tells me he's stashed the gun, so I open my eyes. "I know it was your friend. You sure you want to take the rap for him? I don't care which one of you I take with me."

"It was me," I repeat and my depression eggs me on. *You're nothing, Toby. No one will even miss you. Cliff has family. He's young, he still has a chance.*

"Toby—" Cliff starts, but I cut him off with a sharp, definitive, "*Cliff. Go. Home.*"

He drops his head and shakes it but turns and walks away slowly with his plastic bag of pizzas dangling from his hand.

Dick yells, "Don't you ever think about stepping foot in the store again! You're banned, you hear me?" after Cliff, and then happily strong-arms me back to the QuikMart. He seats me in a chair in the back office and hovers over me like I'm going to make a break for it while he calls the cops. He's getting off on this little taste of authority, and it makes me wonder if he was the bully or the bullied before he dropped out of school. I'm guessing the bullied.

When the officer arrives, I know him. His name is Jefferies. Johnny knows him from way back; they went to high school together or something. Cliff's taken several rides in his cruiser over the past year he's lived with us. He asks for my ID and I give it to him. As he's writing down my information and filling out the form, recognition dawns when he writes the address. "You're Johnny Stockton's kid, right?"

"He's my guardian," I answer. We don't have that in writing; it's not legally true, but we've resorted to using the title when I'm unable to forge my mom's name on documents and a living, breathing person is required to make an appearance.

He nods. It's not a disinterested gesture, but I can tell that QuikMart Dick isn't impressed that Officer Jefferies' level of enthusiasm doesn't match his own.

The way Dick describes the theft you would think it was armed robbery. It's very dramatic.

When Officer Jefferies asks me to describe the events, I simply say, "I pocketed a pack on the way out the door."

He nods his unbiased nod again.

Which makes Dick fume. "He's going to jail, right?"

Jefferies answers, "He's a minor. I'm guessing this is his first offense. So, no. It will go on his record." Jefferies calls the station and they run my name to see if I have any priors. I don't. Then he asks me for my home phone number and calls Johnny while Dick goes out front to help a customer. I tune out their conversation, but it's brief. When he hangs up, he asks me to stand and he cuffs me. They're loose on my wrists. Gripping my upper arm for Dick's benefit, he guides me out of the office and through the store. "I'm taking him down to the station to finish the paperwork and file charges. You can never come in this store again." He looks at me and raises his eyebrows to make sure I understand I'm not welcome here anymore.

I nod. I understand, which sucks because it's the only store like this for blocks.

Dick points his finger at me from behind the counter and parrots Jefferies' words, but his version is much angrier. "You can never come in this store again!"

I nod again.

Jefferies walks me outside and puts me in the back seat of his cruiser, and as soon as the door shuts, I think, *I am such a loser.* Before, nothing mattered except making it to the fifth of

June and graduating. My life had an expiration date, nothing beyond that mattered. But now Alice matters and she deserves better than hanging out with guys who end up in the back of police cars.

Instead of driving to the station, Jefferies pulls up to the Victorian on Clarkson and double parks in front, next to Mr. Street's cab. Once freed from the back seat, he walks me, hand on my upper arm, up the front walk to the porch. At the porch, I put my head down and pray I don't run into anyone on the way up. It's not that I need a lesson in shame. I've lived with shame every day for two years, but this is a fresh round of it and it hurts.

We make it past Mr. Street's door unseen and I close my eyes as we walk up the first flight of stairs. Rounding the turn to take the second flight I let out the breath I was holding as we leave Mrs. Bennett and Alice's apartments behind us.

But when I hear a knock on the door from above my stomach clenches. The door creaks open before we crest the stairs and Taber's voice pinches my eyelids closed again, as if I can block him out while my heart plummets. "Can you tell Toby we're leaving in two minutes for the venue? We'll be out in the van waiting for him. Also, the lock is jammed on the door out to the fire escape and I was wondering if you could come look at it tonight while we're out? I tried to fix it, but my tool selection is pretty bleak. As are my handyman skills."

Johnny sees us out of the corner of his eye coming into view when he says, "I'll be down in a bit to look at the lock."

"Okay. Thanks, man," Taber answers.

When we reach the landing, I meet Johnny's eyes—I don't want to, but I do—and he sighs. The sigh kills me. I don't know why but the idea that I've disappointed him in such a cliché Cliff way is killing me.

"No problem," he replies distractedly to Taber.

Before I can drop my eyes and avert a second round of judgment, I catch Taber's gaze when he turns for the stairs to exit. After he takes in the humiliation on my face, his eyes dart to Officer Jefferies and the handcuffs, both a neon sign advertising I've fucked up. That I *am* a fuck up. The shock on his face is evident, and though there's something else in his eyes, I don't hold the connection long enough to puzzle it out. I look the other way when he approaches.

"What's going on?" Taber asks, the shock still winning out. I'm not sure which one of us he's asking.

When Officer Jefferies and Johnny both remain quiet, I man up. "Shoplifting." I look him in the eyes when I say it.

Looking from me to Officer Jefferies to Johnny he seems at a loss. He settles on, "I'm guessing this means you won't make the gig tonight?"

I shake my head. Letting Alice down kills me more than Johnny's sigh just did.

He rubs his lips together; he's thinking, but I have no idea what those thoughts are. I can take a pretty good guess though, and in the pit of my stomach, I know my friendship with his sister is over. He's protective. As he should be. Finally he nods. It's a solemn gesture, disappointment or pity, I can't tell. Either suck. And then he says to Johnny, "The door can wait. Take your time," and disappears behind me down the hall toward the stairs.

I want to argue my story. I want to tell him what really happened, but nothing I say is going to erase the image of me in handcuffs from his mind. Alice deserves better than me. She always has. I've been living in a fantasy the past few weeks. Guys like me don't belong in fantasies. I suddenly feel like I've lost everything. Again. I'm too sad to sweat, even though I'm as nervous as I've ever been.

"The door will be fixed before you get home tonight!" Johnny yells after Taber.

We all stand silent until Taber reaches the second floor and returns to his apartment. When privacy is achieved, Officer Jefferies says, "Johnny, I just need you to sign this paperwork so I can release him to you."

Johnny backs away from the doorway, and we follow him into the kitchen where he signs the form in triplicate on the counter, and Jefferies uncuffs me. Paperwork and handshakes are traded between Jefferies and Johnny. "Thanks for bringing him home instead of down to the station, I appreciate it."

Jefferies nods and then turns to head out, but before he leaves, he says, "I don't ever want to see you in the back seat of my cruiser again, Toby."

"Understood," I say and I mean it.

When the door shuts behind him, I hear Johnny mumble, "Jesus Christ, I need a drink," and notice Cliff's bedroom door is shut. I can hear his TV playing. Johnny scrubs his hands up and down his face and runs them back through his hair. It's an act of frustration, and his face looks ancient, like he's lived a thousand lives consecutively and they've all been miserable. "What were you thinking, Toby?"

I shrug.

"Why would you steal?" he asks. Before I can answer, he adds, "As if dealing with this one wasn't enough?" while gesturing to Cliff's door. "Did he put you up to this?"

I shake my head. He didn't. He's a moron who makes horrendous choices, but this choice was entirely mine.

He crosses his arms and leans back against the counter, and even though he looks dead tired and monumentally disappointed, he also looks intimidating. I don't often notice his size, but right now I feel two feet tall. "Shit." He heaves in a breath and a rattling cough forces him to release it. "What am I supposed to do?" He's talking to himself, not me.

"Am I fired? Do you want me to move out? I can move out if you want me to." I mean it. If I have to live my final month on the street, so be it. I don't want to, but I'll make it work.

He rubs the thick, dark scruff on his chin. "No. That's not what I meant, Toby. You're just better than this. You don't steal. You don't break the law."

"I broke the law every Friday night when I drank at Dan's," I correct him.

He shakes his head. "That was my fault. I should've told Dan sooner. He just assumed you were older because you looked it. And you were with me." Picking up his pack of cigarettes off the counter, he shakes one out and lights it. After an agonizingly long first drag, he clutches it between his knuckles and points it at me. "Promise me this is the last time, Toby." He pauses when I don't answer him. "Look me in the eye and promise me I don't have to worry about you ending up in jail."

Guilt. So much guilt, but at least I don't have to lie because I don't have much time left. "I promise. But why do you care? This isn't what we do, Johnny. We coexist—you're my landlord, my employer."

He walks toward the fridge, grabs the toolbox from on top of it, and heads for the door, probably because I've just made him uncomfortable, but he stops before he shuts the door and ends this. "Everyone cares about someone, some of us are just shit at showing it."

That's where it ends when the door closes behind him.

He's right though, some of us are just shit.

CHAPTER TWENTY-SIX

The road to Hell is paved with good intentions

Past, June 1985
Nina's Protector

Ken is different.

But so is Toby.

Toby has always been a clever kid. Crafty. I would say sneaky, but to be sneaky there has to be motive and devious intent. And Toby isn't devious, he's straightforward and to the point. He doesn't have any cards up his sleeve; they're always out on the table. Even I think he would benefit from holding some of them a little closer to the chest, but I also admire him for putting it all out there. What you see is what you get.

Speaking of clever and crafty, it's brought him to Nina's front door. He's found her. I'm not religious, but I may have just shouted, *Thank God!* like I was literally giving thanks to a sentient being for the intervention. He's knocking on the front door, while Nina's watching him with her hand frozen on the living room curtain she's pulled aside to peek out.

Her heart is racing out of excitement, something her depression hasn't allowed in a while. But it's also racing out of fear. Fear that someone will see Toby here and tell Ken. Fear about what Ken would do to Toby.

The second set of rapid knocks sets her heart racing into overdrive and even I'm holding back on input at the minute, waiting for more information before I weigh in. Nina's safety and self-preservation make me want to command, *Open the door! Run away with Toby!* but Nina's concern for Toby is what holds me back.

In the end, self-preservation wins. It always does, it's something I can't ignore. I settle for, *Open the door!* and let her figure it out from there.

Though panic is rising, she listens and opens the door with a shaky hand after his third round of knocking. The scene that immediately follows would be almost comical if it wasn't for the backdrop of heartbreakingly real emotion on both ends.

Nina reaches for Toby's hand and yanks on it before words are exchanged. Her strength in this moment is spurred on by adrenaline and surges, sending him tumbling over the threshold and landing on his side at her feet. Forcing the door closed with an obstacle on the floor in front of it is difficult but not impossible.

"Jesus, Nina. Calm down—" Toby's plea dies on his lips when he looks up at her face: tearstained cheeks; bloodshot, lifeless eyes; lips turned down into a hopeless frown, the depths of which he's never seen. More than anything, that's what scares him. He's seen her sad before. She's always been a melancholy individual, but the set of her mouth looks incurable, like hope has been traded in for an eternity of damnation and despair. I've been watching it progressively get worse for the past few weeks—Toby seeing the rare, happy Nina a few months ago and transitioning to this must be gut-wrenching.

Toby, in a single motion, jumps to his feet and reaches for her, but when she involuntarily flinches at the near contact, he freezes. "What's going on?"

I can tell by the look of shock and horror in his stunned expression that this is not what he expected to find. He probably came by to check on her and find out why she left without saying goodbye, find out if she's mad at him—which would kill Toby, by the way. Nina's always been his constant supporter. Petty arguments and disagreements between the two of them never lasted more than a day or two before one of them called a truce. She's never truly been angry with him.

She shushes him, "Shh," like there are ears listening. She's paranoid now. Being punished for anything and everything for weeks on end, when you already have a history of punishing yourself, will do that.

"What's going on?" Toby repeats. His voice remains desperate, though his saucer-wide eyes have softened with compassion.

Second-guessing her need to see him, she swipes at her eyes with her sweater sleeves pulled down over her palms, and evades his question with a question. "How did you find me?"

Which he answers with another question, this one tilted toward a plea. "Why are you hiding?"

"Why are you looking for me?"

"Why shouldn't I?"

The ping-pong inquiry provides telling information, which is strange given the complete disregard for actual direct answers on both sides.

When Nina revisits, "How did you find me?"

Toby finally loses it and shouts a demand. "Tell me what the hell is going on, Nina!"

She flinches again and it's not lost on him. Toby's always been gentle with Nina. Because their mother has never been.

Mothers should safeguard their children's fragile vulnerability; instead, theirs wields shame and guilt like a machete. Slicing through them with words meant to wound when she feels the need to reinstate her sense of absolute authority. Or when she's jealous of something they've accomplished that she never could, she cuts them off at the knees in an attempt to make herself feel better. Toby has always been honest with Nina, but he's never been cruel. Her flinching from him is like a physical slap to the face.

The tears are still trickling down her cheeks, leaking out of lifeless eyes. The incongruous combination all the more haunting when she pairs it with the words, "I'm waiting." She holds back from tacking on more to spare Toby's feelings.

I'm surprised by her filter because she's started using again this week. Whatever Ken gives her. Falling out of sobriety was easy when depression felt like two giant hands pushing her face-first off the side of a cliff. I think Ken's trying to numb her, placate her, keep her placid for the next part of his plan, whatever that is. He's an idiot, but he's smart enough to scheme and manipulate. And Nina is too tired and beat down to care.

While Toby's deciphering that answer, he notices for the first time the bruises on Nina's legs. He skips questions and goes with a declaration instead. "He's hitting you."

Nina shakes her head adamantly, as fear fights its way in again. "No. No, he's not. I fell taking the trash out a few days ago."

Toby calls her bluff. "I saw you at 7-Eleven yesterday and you didn't have those bruises."

The lightbulb goes off, though the heroin in her system has dulled it to a dim flicker, and she narrows her eyes. "You followed me." It's not accusatory; she says it like she's just nimbly solved a riddle.

Toby narrows his eyes quizzically in return. "Are you high?"

"No," she immediately, and ineffectively, denies.

He sighs in frustration. He's seen her like this before. "Nina, you need to come home with me. I got a job washing dishes at The White Spot, and we can find an apartment. I'll help with rent. We don't have to live with Mom."

Do it! I scream. But when I hear the words, "I belong here," robotically spoken, like they've been rehearsed, I realize that Ken's won. He made threats, not against her, but against Toby. One night two weeks ago, during a fight, she threatened to leave Ken in a fit of rage and rare courage. He threatened to kill Toby if that ever happened, because he knows Toby is the only chink in her armor. And then he proceeded to choke her until she passed out.

She's trying to save Toby. I get it and I commend her because Ken is volatile enough to do it. Couple that with the fact that she's already checked out—in her mind she's living on borrowed time—and it's a recipe for disaster.

Leave, leave, leave, leave, leaveleaveleaveleaveleave, is my incessant war cry again. Do I care about Toby? Of course I do. But I have to think about Nina first, she's my priority. Not that I would offer Toby up like a sacrificial lamb, but there has to be a way to save them both.

"You don't," Toby responds with watery eyes as he wraps his arms around her motionless, slight body. "I'll be back tomorrow," he adds and then turns and walks out the door without closing it behind him.

Relief floods Nina as she watches him step onto his skateboard and disappear down the street.

Fear floods me as I watch the same scene. *Ken is different!* I scream at Toby's dissipating figure. It's bloodcurdling. *Ken is different!*

. . .

Toby returns the following afternoon as promised.

He pleads with her to leave with him. He's openly crying. "*Please*," he repeats over and over. I've never seen him like this.

"I can't," she refuses over and over.

When he acquiesces and moves on, exhausted, to plan B, he unzips his backpack, pulls out a revolver, and hands it to her.

She shakes her head defiantly, just like she did yesterday, and refuses it. "No. Put it away." It's the knee-jerk reaction to danger.

"You need to protect yourself. Either you leave with me or you take this." His eyes are a mixture of sadness, determination, and remorse. He doesn't want to do this. He doesn't like guns, he never has. There isn't a violent bone in his body; he's an artist and was born to wield a drawing pencil not a weapon. But he's squashed every impulse of right and wrong for Nina, to be her protector because she's failing to do it herself. Sweat is trickling down his temples; this whole situation from start to finish is torturing him. Desperation has driven him to do something he would never do, to be recklessly reactionary, and it's hard for me to watch. It's also comforting from my perspective because I know she's not alone, even if this is an extreme measure.

On the other hand, it *is* an extreme measure. And knowing Nina as well as I do, I offer a hushed caution, *Don't take it.*

As the fear begins to morph and twist her thoughts, I can already see that my caution is warranted. *Don't take it, Nina!* I yell. *Please, don't take it!*

I'm still begging when she extends her hand and he shakily hands it off. *Don't do this, Nina!*

And then I turn my attention to Toby. *Don't do this, Toby! Take it back! Take it back! Take it back!*

Stuffing his hand back into the backpack, he pulls out a clear plastic baggie with six bullets inside and hands it over without a word.

She takes the bullets with her other hand. "Thanks." She means it.

Shit, I think while I take a momentary pause in my rant. And I dive back in, *Nina, you can't do this! You have your entire life ahead of you!*

Toby hugs her like he did yesterday, but then he whispers something he's never said out loud before, "I love you."

The tears are streaming silently when she hugs him back, but she says nothing. Instead, Nina holds on tight and tries to return the sentiment with the pressure of her hold. She's never said it out loud either. They've never been the sort of family who says stuff like that.

When he releases her, he looks her dead in the eye for ten seconds like he wants to say more. Or like he wants to pick her up and throw her over his shoulder and carry her out of here kicking and screaming.

In the end, he decides to say nothing and walks out the door.

While I'm screaming until I'm blue in the face, *Don't go, Toby! Don't do this! Nina is different! This is different! Nina is different!*

CHAPTER TWENTY-SEVEN

PRESENT, May 1987
Toby

ALICE IS SITTING NEXT TO ME IN ENGLISH. I DIDN'T HAVE the heart to say anything when she sat down. Neither did she apparently, she just looks sad. Not like she's disappointed in me, just sad. I haven't heard from her since I missed her show Saturday night and Taber saw my disaster firsthand. I'm assuming she's pissed and agrees that I'm a bad idea.

The silence stretches on.

And the connection between us snaps.

I clipped it.

Mentally I clipped it.

With shaky hands.

And an aching heart.

Because confident and catastrophic can't coexist.

One will destroy the other.

I am the destroyer.

I am catastrophic.

And I don't have many days left.

We're quiet the rest of class while I dwell on it.

I clear my throat when the bell rings.

I can't do this.

Her nearness, her scent, her Alice-ness is agonizing.

What was I thinking?

Gathering my books from the table, I hastily stuff them in my backpack. I'm sweating like a fiend. Mentally, I'm already out the door and down the hall running away from her as I stand from my chair, but I can't walk away without saying something. Even though the heaviness of misery and self-loathing feels like it's crawling up my throat and I'm about to be sick.

"I'll see you around, Alice." It sounds like goodbye and not the kind of goodbye that means you'll see the other person in a few hours. Or even in a few days. It sounds like the kind of goodbye that's indelible.

Standing, she slings her backpack over her shoulder and grabs her cane from where it's propped up against the desk. "You okay, Toby?" she whispers. She's concerned. About me. She knows I'm off. More than normal.

Clearing my throat again, trying to keep the bile at bay, I answer as steadily as I can, "Yeah. Fine."

"Well, I'm not. And I know you're lying. We should talk." She sounds and looks on the verge of tears.

I can't handle sad Alice and knowing that I'm the reason for it. So I walk away.

By the time I make it to the hallway the masses are a blur of color and motion through the helplessness filling my eyes and perching on my bottom lashes ready to tumble free. Head down, I swipe at them with the cuff of my sweatshirt. *Get your shit together!* is a blaring command from within, but it's muffled by the quieter, but intimately bossier, *You're nothing. You're nothing. You're nothing*, on repeat.

"I know," I whisper in response to both. I'm standing in the last toilet stall now, behind the barrier of metal that I often use to divide my tears and breakdowns from their eyes. I can usually purge it quickly, the stone in my throat that comes with the wet cheeks and runny nose loosens and settles in my stomach where I carry it around unnoticed. But not this morning. The bombardment grows until my self-hate takes over every thought. Nina drifts in, the most angelic image of torture imaginable, her smiling face from my memories distorted by a coat of blood red. The color of death. And then the images that haunt my nightmares begin an unbidden slideshow to torment.

Nina.

My hands compress her rib cage begging for a miracle.

Nina.

My breath forced from my mouth to hers failing to inflate her lungs.

Nina.

Her frail body lying atop a pool of blood.

Nina.

Nina.

Nina.

I CAN'T DO THIS.

I can't do life.

Without her.

Like my mom said...

It should've been you.

YES. IT SHOULD'VE BEEN ME.

CHAPTER TWENTY-EIGHT

PRESENT, May 1987
Toby

"TOBY'S HERE IF YOU NEED ANYTHING, GRANDMA. I'M going to work, but you get some sleep and I'll see you in the morning. I love you." The words are hushed. Chantal's talking in the soothing voice she usually only uses on Joey. That means Mrs. Bennett's having a really bad day.

When Chantal walks out of the bedroom the sadness in her expression hardens to the stoic mask she puts on for the rest of the world. She's wearing her uniform and I can't help but notice that her name tag is upside down. Much like her life. Gathering her coat and purse, she doesn't meet my eyes but talks quietly to give me the babysitting rundown. "Grandma's having a bad day. She should be asleep any minute."

"Has she eaten dinner?" I ask because she's always finishing up when I get here. Mrs. Bennett is a creature of habit and follows a routine down to the minute.

Slipping into her coat and throwing the strap of her purse haphazardly on her shoulder, she answers distractedly, "Yeah, an hour ago." She looks like she has a million different things on her mind.

Walking to the playpen in the corner next to the TV, she bends over and kisses Joey on the top of his curly head. He's sitting up by himself, that's new and I can't help commenting on it. "He's sitting."

She straightens and repositions the purse strap that's slipped down to the crook of her elbow back up to her shoulder. "Yesterday." A wistful smile bullies its way through every other emotion and comes out on top. The oversaturation of warring emotions tamps it down, but it's there.

I nod.

"I'd better get going. I'll see you around eleven. I'll be home a little early, I need to talk to you."

I nod again and when she's in the hall and the door's almost shut behind her, I call out, "Name tag," loud enough that she'll hear me. Because everyone at work doesn't need to know where her head's at. Hopefully escaping this apartment for a few hours will allow her to clear it a little.

Dropping my backpack next to the couch, I walk over to Joey in the playpen. I know it's a necessity to safely contain him when Chantal needs a few minutes to take care of her grandma, but I hate seeing him in it even when he looks content like he does now chewing on the slobbery trunk of a stuffed elephant. He looks up at me expectantly with his big eyes that darken by the week. Before I can lean over to pick him up, he does something he's never done before. He reaches for me, arms extended and little chubby fingers flexing in anticipation. He only does this to Chantal. The gesture makes me freeze bent at the waist and I can't help but smile.

Yes, smile.

And then I pick him up and hold him high above my head. He squeals in delight like he does every time I do this, but this time it's followed by a giggle. That's new too. I've never heard him giggle like this and it's the type of sound that demands voluntary, even enthused, reciprocation. Before I know it, I'm laughing with him.

Yes, laughing.

It's not until I lower him against my chest that it hits me how natural the laughter felt at the onset but how it felt equally as foreign. Almost like we're both laughing for the first time in our lives. And as it fades, I just feel hollow again.

Before I sit down with him, I walk to Mrs. Bennett's bedroom door and peek in to make sure she's fallen asleep. She hasn't. Her twin bed is parallel to the door, and she's lying on her side looking at me like she's heard us laughing and it made her happy.

"Come in," she says, sweetly.

I take a few steps inside the doorway and squat down so I'm eye level with her.

She reaches out and strokes Joey's cheek with a shaky hand. "I love the way you've always been able to make her laugh, Irvin." Her milky eyes shift to mine, and even in the darkness of the room, I can see the innocent distance in her stare. She's not living in the here and now, she's lost in her mind, in a distant past that she retreats to more and more.

I can hear Chantal's instructions in my head telling me to correct her and try to bring her back to the present, but like every other time, I can't bring myself to do it.

"Do you remember when I was pregnant? I was so sure she was going to be a boy and you were so sure she was going to be a girl."

When her faraway eyes flick to mine, I do the only thing I can do—nod.

The gesture makes her smile. "You were right. You were always right about everything, my love." She pauses and I try to think of something to say, but she beats me to it. "I should get up and make you some breakfast so you can get to work."

It's my turn to pause because no matter how much I want her to have this necessary, self-created comfort, I don't know if I can talk through the lump in my throat. She looks so frail today. Not only is the light draining out of her eyes, it's draining out of the rest of her too. I know she won't be around much longer. I clear my throat and adjust Joey to the opposite hip to stall.

When I finally speak, my voice cracks, "I already...ate." The muscles in my jaw are tense, working stiffly against the tears sitting in the back of my throat.

"Okay. You look so tired. Are you having trouble sleeping again?" The concern in her voice is so real. I know she thinks she's talking to Irvin, but it feels like she's talking to me.

I shake my head and avoid using words that I know will fail me.

"It's not your fault, Irvin," she whispers.

I don't know what she's referring to in their past, but her consolation is so heartbreakingly comforting that I want to believe it for myself. But I can't.

There's a heaviness in her eyelids and I wonder if it's natural tiredness or a side effect of the extra medication bottles I noticed alongside the regular ones on the coffee table.

"Maybe I'll just go back to sleep for a little bit?"

It's a question, not a statement. She's waiting for permission from her husband who's been dead for decades.

Afraid I won't be able to speak, I lean forward and kiss her on the forehead gently. Her skin is cool to the touch and has an almost waxy quality to it, like the fake fruit on display in the wooden bowl on her kitchen table.

When I pull back, her eyes slide closed and she murmurs, "Thanks, Irvin."

"Sleep well," I manage to whisper.

Joey is uncharacteristically clingy after that, and I wonder if he can feel her slipping away like I can. Every time I try to set him down so we can play with his blocks, he cries. So I sit on the couch and I hold him like I'm trying to shield him from it all. He rests his head on my shoulder like he does when he's tired, but instead of sucking his thumb or rubbing his eyes, he starts jabbering. It's welcome in the silence of the sad apartment, so I join the conversation to try to keep him going.

"Oh yeah? Tell me more, little man."

He does. The sounds are more guttural this time and gurgle their way out like there's conviction behind whatever it is he's trying to tell me.

"Wow, that sounds serious," I say, hoping he hears how much I want him to continue.

He lifts his head from my shoulder and I adjust him to sit on my lap so we can look at each other. When his eyes meet mine they crinkle in the corners and his gummy smile appears, excitement in his high-pitched, almost-sounds-like-real-words words.

I can't help but think that apart from Alice, this is the best conversation I've had in the past few years.

Twice he giggles.

And twice I laugh, unable to resist. Because every once in a while, life gives you a sliver of happiness...however brief.

Far too soon he's rubbing his eyes that are beginning to droop like sleep has already come for them.

After changing him and feeding him his bottle, I sit in the rocking chair in Chantal's room and hold him while he sleeps. I can't help but think about how much I'm going to miss him when I go. I won't see him grow up.

. . .

As promised, Chantal is home early from her shift. And as promised, she wants to talk. Her tone, her posture, put me on edge. When she reaches for Joey like she always does to put him down in his crib, I reflexively ask, "Can I hold him while we talk?" like I need to feel his warmth and smell the purity of him to get through this.

She nods. "I took Grandma to the hospital today. She's been bad all week. Really bad. I thought I was going to lose her last night. I met with her doctor and a counselor before we left. They're encouraging me to put her in a facility..." Her eyes glaze over at the thought.

I didn't know sadness could induce goose bumps, but it can. My arms are covered with them. "What kind of facility?" I whisper.

"A nursing home." Her voice breaks and it breaks me because I know that would be her last stop. When she enters, she won't leave.

This woman isn't my family, but it's still hard. People age, I get that. She isn't just aging, she's decaying like a bouquet of flowers whose vibrancy has run its course and is wilting away to dust. I nod, waiting for her to say more.

She covers her face with her hands to hide the tears and the shame. "Am I a horrible person for agreeing with them?"

"Do you feel like you can provide the medical attention and care she needs?" I ask.

Face still hidden behind her hands, she sniffs and I watch her entire body heave upward with the effort to clear her nose and calm her down. "I used to be able to, Toby, but I can't keep up anymore. She's worse every day. She has trouble eating, she can't bathe herself anymore, she's wearing adult diapers now— it's not fair that someone so strong and smart and fun can have their life stripped away from the inside out. I feel like my grandma is gone. She forgets who I am far more than she remembers and I know that shouldn't upset me, but it does. It does. I want my grandma back." She shakes her head and purses her lips to hold back a sob. "I miss her, Toby. I'm in this apartment with her all day, but I miss her so damn much..." she trails off because when you're this worked up, there isn't room in your throat for words and shame and sadness. Only one of them wins that battle and it's never words because shame and sadness steal your breath.

"Sometimes in life, you do everything you can and it still isn't enough. And that sucks," I whisper. It's true. It's so true.

She nods and drops her hands to reveal wet cheeks and watery eyes. "Yeah, it does."

I nod. I've never been the type of person who gives or receives pep talks, and I don't think Chantal is either. I'm the last person who should give advice, so I always stick to straight talk instead. And with Chantal at least, it works.

CHAPTER TWENTY-NINE

PRESENT, May 1987
Toby

TWO DAYS LATER CHANTAL KNOCKS ON APARTMENT 3A's door and tells Johnny and me that Mrs. Bennett is moving into a nursing home in Lakewood that specializes in Alzheimer's patients.

That same afternoon she's gone. To the nursing home, not from existence. I didn't get to say goodbye; that was intentional. I've never said goodbye to anyone that I knew I would never see again. I don't want to start now. And yes, I know how shitty that sounds.

CHAPTER THIRTY

PRESENT, May 1987
Toby

CHANTAL'S COWORKER AT THE DINER WHO TRADES babysitting with her, and her kids, are moving into Mrs. Bennett's old bedroom today. She's only been gone two days, and though I know Chantal needs the roommate, it feels like Mrs. Bennett is being replaced and I don't like it. I know that's illogical, but it's how I feel.

I'm walking down the stairs to Chantal's apartment because she called thirty minutes ago and asked if I could help put her roommate's kids' bunk bed together.

The walk there is numb.

The introduction to them is numb.

Putting the bunk bed together is numb.

I'm just going through the motions, counting down the days that are so few they could technically be measured in hours. And I'm missing Alice. So much it hurts. She left a message on

THE OTHER SIDE • 217

the answering machine this morning to tell me she got The Cure's new cassette and to ask if I wanted to come down and listen to it.

I wanted to so badly.

But I didn't.

I couldn't.

And now I'm just missing her instead.

Gathering up my tools, I ignore the roommate's thanks. I can't even remember her name and she told it to me ten minutes ago.

Chantal catches me at the door. She looks rested for the first time in months. "Toby, I changed my schedule at work because I'm going to take some classes this summer. So, I won't need you to watch Joey on Tuesday nights anymore." The words that I would've taken at face value before, plunge in and twist the knife today. I have been dismissed.

No more Joey.

No more Mrs. Bennett.

There's absolutely no point in Tuesdays anymore.

CHAPTER THIRTY-ONE

PRESENT, May 1987
Toby

I KNOCK ON CHANTAL'S DOOR TUESDAY NIGHT, NOT because I'm on autopilot and forgot that our arrangements have changed, but because I just want to see Joey one last time.

They aren't home.

So, I hang the plastic bag with the diapers and a bib I bought on the way home from school on the doorknob. He'll be eating real food soon and he'll need it.

When I walk away, I know I won't have the strength to knock again.

Because like I said before, I've never said goodbye to anyone that I knew I would never see again.

And I will never see them again.

I only have a little over a week left.

CHAPTER THIRTY-TWO

The following week is dark.

Darker than normal.

When I'm not at school, I'm in my room.

Alone.

Light off.

No drawing.

No comics.

And when I am at school, I watch Alice.

From afar.

I ache to be near her.

But I avoid her.

Even when she comes to apartment 3A and knocks on the door, I don't answer.

Which is hard.

So hard.

Because I'm the moth.
And she's the flame.
Everything about her is ethereal.
She is light.
And hope.
And beauty.
Fearlessness embodied.
I am none of those.
I am her corruptive antidote.
I am light-less.
And hope-less.
And beauty-less.
Fear embodied.
I am the moth the flame should burn.
Out of existence.
Because confident and catastrophic,
the living and the dead,
don't,
shouldn't,
coexist.

I TAINT.

I AM NOTHING.
I am nothing.
I.
Am.
Nothing.

CHAPTER THIRTY-THREE

The final siege

Past, June 1985
Nina's Protector

Nina is different.

Today is different.

She told Ken she would have a surprise waiting for him tonight when he left this morning. The way she said it, he thinks it will be something good.

I know it won't.

Which is the reason my pleas have reached a fevered pitch and have been relentless all day. I'm used to living in stress management mode—I'm Nina's subconscious, it's what I do. But this is different. She isn't listening, she's tuning me out. I know she's been planning this since long before Toby gave her the gun yesterday, but I thought I could talk her out of it.

It's obvious now that I can't.

Subconsciouses don't like to be silenced.

We fight.

Until the end.

Nina, think about what you're doing. Please, think about what you're doing. I know you think there's no other way, but there is. There's always another way. Please. I've never wanted to cry before, but I do right now.

Instead, she's crying for both of us.

While she's loading the gun.

With all six bullets.

For the most part her tears are silent, but every so often there's an inhalation of air so deep it's soul-splintering.

When the cylinders are loaded and it's clicked back into place, I prompt her to check the time on the clock on the kitchen wall. It's 4:15.

Call Toby. He'll be home from school now. Please just do this one last thing for me before you change our life forever. You need to hear his voice. I need to hear his voice.

Surprisingly, she walks to the phone and picks up the receiver from the wall mount and dials her mom's phone number with the hand that's still holding the gun. Her breath is shallow and recedes to nothing while she holds it, waiting for him to answer. He doesn't. After the fifth ring, the answering machine greeting of her mom comes on the line instead and fills her ear with the tinny voice of the woman who not only terrorized her but who kept her biggest secret. Holding the phone away from her until she hears the beep to prompt her to talk, she almost hangs up.

Say something. Say something to Toby.

"Goodbye, Toby." And then she adds something that breaks me, because I know it's all over. "I love you, too."

Rather than return the receiver to its cradle on the wall, she drops it and watches it crash against the wall before it yo-yos up and down on its coiled cord. She watches it, completely engrossed and unblinking. The tears have dried up and the room is eerily quiet until the phone starts the modulated beep that indicates the answering machine stopped recording and the call's been disconnected. And as if that was the signal she was waiting for, she raises the gun.

Rests the barrel against her right temple.

Don't do it, Ni—

And pulls the trigger.

Toby

I CAUGHT THE RTD BUS FROM SCHOOL AND AM HEADED TO Nina's. I sat in school all day worrying and can't help but regret giving Nina that gun. She needs to protect herself against that asshole; I thought it was my only option since she refuses to leave. But *I* should be the one protecting her. I'm going to sit on her front step until Ken comes home and confront him myself, even if he beats the shit out of me. It's what I should've done before.

My skateboard ride to her house is short from the bus stop.

My heart is pounding like I'm going into cardiac arrest when I walk up the front steps. Something doesn't feel right.

The knock on the door goes unanswered, so I peek in the front window through the slit in the drawn curtains.

My heart drops into my shoes.

It stops beating.

And I know I will never be the same again...

CHAPTER THIRTY-FOUR

PRESENT, May 1987
Toby

"TOBY, WAKE UP!" THE COMMAND IS FAR AWAY, MUFFLED. A split second later, it's not. It's loud and in my face. "Toby, wake up!"

It's accompanied by shaking, hands rattling my shoulders, another pair jostling my feet.

My final breath of sleep merges violently into my first breath of wakefulness on an exhale—a seamless scream that begins unconscious and finishes, embarrassingly, conscious.

Johnny is in my room leaning over me, hands braced against my shoulders, eyes wide. Cliff is squatting in my bedroom doorway, hands gripping my feet through my sleeping bag, eyes wider.

My throat is hoarse, my cheeks are wet, my heart is galloping, my muscles are tight, and I can't catch my breath. The nightmare is dissipating like smoke, fragmenting until all that's left is my guilt, Nina's pain, my failure, and Nina's fulfillment. And the horrible realization that my nightmares now have the power to gain volume, purpose, *and* an audience.

Suffering should be a secret.

Shame should be a secret.

Guilt should be a secret.

I should be a secret.

NO. YOU SHOULDN'T EXIST AT ALL.

CHAPTER THIRTY-FIVE

The fallout

Past, June 1985
Johnny

I SPEND MY LIFE HIDING. IT'S THE REASON I SPEND AS much of my day as possible tucked away inside Dan's Tavern. The windowless interior and dim lighting cocoon me from the outside world, and the steady flow of alcohol divides me from my thoughts—it's how I cope. And yes, cope is a generous description. Hiding someplace even *I* can't find me is my approach. Am I embarrassed I can't function in society? Yes. Am I embarrassed I can't get over what happened? No. I did unforgivable things in the name of war. Three tours of endless survival-induced adrenaline supplemented with drugs led to paranoia and fear. Tour one, I was a soldier. Tour two, I was a machine. Tour three, I was a monster. Over a decade later, when I close my eyes every night to sleep, I'm haunted by faces. Some I fought beside, some I fought against—but the thing all the faces have in common is death. A hellish death, the result of bullet, knife, explosive, or fire. Their screams all blend harmoniously, because if there's one thing that's universally human no matter your nationality, it's pain and agony. Those screams all sound the same. The unyielding reminder of all I've done that's wrong.

I stay at Dan's until last call most evenings, because at that time my walk home is quiet and I can pretend I'm alone in the world while most of the city sleeps. It's after midnight when I step in the front door of the Victorian, the chill in the air flirting with inebriation and urging it toward sobriety. The decibel level of sound coming from inside 1A is enough to urge it a few more degrees, and I'm not happy about that. Raising my fist to pound on the door and tell them to quiet down, I'm stopped short by someone standing on the stairs to the right of me. It's Chantal from 2B, her arms are crossed over her chest. She's worrying at a hole in the sleeve of her sweater with her fingertips, and at the corner of her bottom lip with her teeth.

"She's been yelling like a banshee at him for a while now. I knocked an hour ago and asked her to please quiet down so my grandma can sleep, but she slammed the door in my face. She's saying awful things to him, Johnny. Just awful."

My unfocused eyes aren't my greatest ally when it comes to discernment, but even they can't deny the fear in her eyes.

I press my ear to the door first—unnecessary given that Marilyn is yelling again. Her voice unhinged and tremoring through sobs. *"You stupid, useless piece of shit, you're dead to me! Do you hear me? You're dead!"*

Silence. Which is helpful because I need a moment to dissect what she's said. This is the point at which I know I should knock, but my mind isn't firing on all cylinders and begs me to wait another minute to hear what she says next.

"It should've been you, Toby! If you thought a gun was

such a goddamn good idea, you should've just used it on yourself!"

That's it, I've heard enough. I pound on the door at the same time I look at Chantal and tell her to go back upstairs to her grandma's apartment. I pound until the soft flesh on the side of my palm begins to radiate bruising pain. When she doesn't answer, I yell, "Open the door, Marilyn!" while I continue the assault on the hardwood.

When the door finally creaks open, there's a two-inch slot held from further advancement by a short string of brass chain, and her bloodshot eye rimmed by blotchy, shock-red skin is fixed on me. "This ain't your concern, Johnny. Leave me be."

I take a deep breath, because it's either that or kick the door in, and then I say calmly, "It is my concern." That's a truer statement than I would like to acknowledge. "When you're keeping the whole building awake, it's my concern. You need to quiet down, Marilyn, or I'll call the cops."

She barks out a bitter laugh. "You'll call the cops? You know they won't do shit."

She's right, they won't. They'll come, tell her to quiet down, and leave. And then she'll start up again before they make it to the curb to get in their car. While I'm thinking through the next step in this mess, I break eye contact with her and look over her head into the apartment. She's a little over five feet tall and I'm a little over six; I have an unobstructed view. Toby is sitting on the couch, curled up into a ball, his face buried in his arms. His shoulders rising and falling as sobs violently shudder through him.

My eyes still on him, I ask, "What's going on?" Marilyn has never been the poster child for motherhood, far from it, but I've never seen her like this.

I can't see everything she's doing due to the limited view the two-inch peek into the room provides, but from what I can make out she's thrusting a finger accusatorially at the destroyed boy on the couch as she declares, "That little shit killed my daughter!"

The words punch me in the face. "Killed your daughter?" I repeat, in my head or aloud, I'm not sure.

She presses her face tight against the opening, the door and doorjamb pressing deep creases down her cheeks on either side of her mouth, and she screeches in my face, "He fucking killed my Nina!" The tirade is accompanied by spittle that her drunken state and anger can't contain, pelting the front of my T-shirt.

"Shh," I reflexively answer, because she's going to wake up the entire block if she keeps this up. "Open the door and talk to me." My voice is masking the anger that's boiling inside me.

Her mouth disappears and she takes a long pull from a bottle of clear liquid, gin judging by her breath. It won't take much more of that before she's passed out cold, so I let her take two more swigs before I try again. "Open the door, Marilyn."

"No," she whisper-shouts defiantly, like a mouthy child, her lips pressed against the opening again. At least she toned down the volume this time.

I wait. I'm an impatient man, so the wait is tortuous, but I do it. I have to take a leak and my lower back is starting to ache, but I remain with my feet planted in place. When her body finally slumps against the wall and slides down into an unflattering heap of unconsciousness on the floor, I whisper, "Finally. Jesus Christ," before I call out, "Toby, open the door." When he doesn't look up, I call out louder, my nerves urging me not to yell and make this all worse for him, "Come open the door, Toby. Let me in."

He looks up, and I'm not prepared for the eyes that meet me. The swollen eyelids of someone on the losing end of a brawl, circling the dying eyes I see in my nightmares. Eyes filled with horror, despair, self-loathing, and agony so deep it looks like something that can't be survived. He just turned sixteen; no one this young should ever wear those eyes. Slowly, he unfolds his limbs that he's been using as a shield and makes his way cautiously to the door. He closes it and I hear the chain slip off its track and rattle against wood before the door opens again. I don't say anything as I bend over and pick up Marilyn. When I deposit her on her bed, I whisper, "You will never talk to him like that again, you bitch." I know she can't hear me; the words are more for me. This is the night it stops and I do what I should've done a long time ago.

Returning to Toby is heartbreaking. He's a flesh and bone shell filled with so much raw emotion it's leeching out of every pore. "What happened, Toby?"

He fixes me with blurry, familiar green eyes and echoes Marilyn's words. "She's right, I killed her. I killed my sister." His words are soft, but there's conviction in them. He's staring at me, but he's looking through me like his eyes are fixed on a horrific memory only he can see. "Ken was a monster. He was beating her, keeping her away from us...she was using again..." He pauses and I wait. And when he finally blinks it's as if I come into focus for the first time and his features twist, anguish wringing them out while a guttural cry claws up his throat. "I gave her a gun. But instead of using it to protect herself and leave him—"

I finish the sentence to spare him having to say it. "She used it on herself."

He nods as the tears stream steadily down his cheeks. I've never seen someone cry this hard in all my life, and I've seen some messed up stuff. His soul is bleeding out. I want to wrap my arm around him. I want to offer comfort. But I can't, so I don't. Broken people like me just can't, we aren't capable of it.

Instead, I clear my throat and say, "Do you have a backpack or a bag you take to school?"

A puzzled look drifts across his features and then he nods once.

"Go get it. And grab a change of clothes, too."

With little hesitation, he walks to his bedroom to follow my instruction. While he's gone my mind goes to his sister, Nina. In the years I'd known her, her demons were plenty and unrelenting —drugs and depression—a pairing that waxed and waned, one spurring on the other. I give myself a moment to grieve and say a silent prayer. *Please welcome her to heaven and relieve her of her suffering.* I'm not a religious man (Seeing Hell on Earth has all but stripped away any faith I was raised with, because what kind of God would allow that kind of suffering to exist?), but it's something I unconsciously thought the first time I watched a young man die in a village in Vietnam in 1970. He was fighting for the other side, and my buddy shot him a second before he shot us. For some reason, the prayer entered my head then, and I've said it every time someone has died since, whether it was during the war or afterward, because suffering is an unspoken, unfortunate truth of life. I'm not sure why I do it—it doesn't help anyone or anything—but I do it anyway.

Toby returns with his backpack slung over his shoulder and hopelessness corrupting every fiber of his being.

I open the door and he follows me up two flights of stairs and into my apartment on the third floor. His steps are eerily quiet behind me, he's like a ghost. My apartment is small: a kitchen, bathroom, and two bedrooms. I point at the empty bedroom on the left. "You can sleep in there tonight. There's no bed, but—" I stall the thought while I walk to the pantry closet and pull out my old sleeping bag, "you can use this."

He nods as he takes it from me, his gaze glued to the floor. I can see his mind racing, the worst day of his life is refusing to give him up, as he shuffles into the room and closes the door behind him.

"Bathroom is yours if you need it," I offer to the peeling yellow paint on the door.

He doesn't answer. I didn't expect him to.

I'm beat and need to sleep, but I need some fresh air and a cigarette more, so I walk to the door next to the refrigerator that leads to the fire escape, step out on it, and light up. The cool air chills my skin, but I take my time, willing some peace out of the unfiltered Pall Mall slotted between my fingers.

It doesn't come.

It never does.

So I snub it out and go to bed.

And for the next six hours, I listen to the boy on the other side of the wall cry out with night terrors as his sleeping mind torments him after it traitorously allowed him to cry himself into oblivion.

WHEN THE SUN BEGINS TO LIGHT UP THE ROOM LIKE A flame flickering to life outside, I grab the pad of paper and pen on the nightstand next to my bed, and write the following:

Notice of Eviction

I, Johnny Stockton, hereby declare tenant, Marilyn Page, has until noon, June 6, 1985, to vacate the premises of 1261 N. Clarkson, Apt. 1A, Denver, Colorado, or the authorities will be called and legal action will be pursued to collect six months of unpaid rent.

Signature of landlord: Johnny Stockton

Date: June 6, 1985

Is this legal? No, definitely not. There are steps that must be followed in the process of eviction, and it takes months to jump through the hoops. You can't just tell someone they have a few hours to leave. Does she know that? Probably. Can I find it in me to be persuasive when I want to be? Yes, I sure as hell can. And she owes way more than six months' rent.

I hope this works.

I peek in on Toby. His entire body is inside the sleeping bag and it's pulled up over his head so he's hidden away. The steady motion of the quilted fabric's rise and fall tells me he's finally settled into a restful sleep. Good.

I leave the apartment quietly and walk down to face Marilyn and her wrath. Three rounds of knocking forces her to the door. Her squinting lids tell me her hangover doesn't agree with wakefulness. "What do ya want?" she snaps.

I hand her my handwritten ultimatum and wait for her to digest it and regurgitate fury.

The wait is unexpectedly short and she's blazing as she shakes it in my face. "What the hell is this? You really gonna put a grieving woman and a teenage boy out on the street, Johnny?" She's playing the sympathy card, quite confidently at that.

I shake my head and it almost makes her smile. She thinks she's won. "You're the only one leaving. Toby's staying here. He'll live with me."

The smile fades and all the things that a mother should say when faced with someone threatening to split her from her child, the kicking and screaming fight that should ensue, never materialize. This is the true test. She fails miserably when she says, "The little bastard is cursed. Good luck with that."

Inwardly, I cringe at her label for Toby, but outwardly, I stand my ground. "Marilyn, I'm only going to say this once, so listen closely." My voice is so menacing I almost don't recognize it. I'm never particularly friendly, but I'm rarely outright threatening. "Leave and never come back. Now that Nina's gone, I will not allow you to poison him any longer. I know she was Toby's mother—"

Her eyes widen in disbelief as their secret is outed and she cuts me off, "How do you know?"

I bend over, hands on knees, until I'm eye to eye with her and I grit out, "*She. Told. Me.*"

She shakes her head and denial floods her. "Impossible." More head shaking. "That's impossible. Why would she tell you?"

I don't answer her question, the indignant stare I pierce her with does though.

"Oh," she whispers. "Oh," she repeats as the realization sinks in.

She's been defeated and she knows it.

"You have an hour to pack your shit and get out of my sight."

THIRTY MINUTES LATER, I WATCH MARILYN PAGE PLACE A cardboard box and a duffel bag in the back seat of a cab, climb in beside it, and disappear from Toby's life for-what-I-hope-is-ever.

She took a knife to her mattress and destroyed it, as well as breaking every last glass and plate from the cupboards on the floor. The place is a disaster, but I don't care. I gather everything from Toby's room, which is depressingly very little, in one trip and take it back up to apartment 3A. And I hope to God with each step that I don't ruin him further.

CHAPTER THIRTY-SIX

Present, June 1987
Toby

It's your last Friday, asshole.

"I know," I answer aloud to show it I'm not scared of it anymore and am resigned to my fate. I've accepted and welcomed it.

I'm out the door, sweatshirt in hand, my pocket stuffed with the two dollars I have left. I haven't seen Johnny this afternoon, so I haven't been paid yet, but I'll make do without digging into my savings. It's not like I need much with less than twenty-four hours of existence remaining to endure.

Dan's Tavern is as dark, dreary, and dismal as I remember it. It's also unusually busy for six o'clock. Head down, I skirt the outer perimeter of the room and land on a stool at the far end of the bar. Johnny's old stool—I guess it's habit to gravitate to it. When I'm situated, I lift my eyes to find Dan in front of me. He doesn't look mad that I'm here; he looks almost nostalgic, like he's missed me or something. People don't look at me like that. I'm not a person who's missed, so I immediately drop my eyes back to the bar top and slide my state-issued ID across the counter toward him. "I'm legal now," I add. My birthday was a little over a week ago. I ignored it. Until now. In my periphery I see his big, gnarled hand pick it up for inspection.

"Happy birthday, but the law changed to twenty-one this year. Your eighteenth birthday had to be before January first to be grandfathered in."

I drop my forehead to the bar top and mutter, "You've got to be kidding me."

I see my ID out of the corner of my eye when he sets it down.

"Nope. You want a Coke? It's on me for your birthday."

I nod slightly, my skin sticking to the tacky spillage of those who sat in this seat before me.

The familiar semi-clean pint glass filled with dark carbonation is offered up a minute later. "How's Johnny doing?" he asks.

I lift my eyes to answer him because Dan has always been nice to me and he doesn't deserve my attitude or silence. "He's still sober."

Dan nods in understanding. "Glad to hear it," he says like he means it. Then he turns to tend to his congregation, the other patrons awaiting a refill of libation and hope that will never come.

Glancing in the mirror behind the bar takes more effort than it should. Everything takes more effort than it should. I just want to sleep. Forever.

But the night carries on as I seek out my target and do what I came here to do, despite the lack of beer.

She arrives an hour later.

Her name is Bethany.

She has secrets like all the rest.

And like every other woman, she shares them with me after she drinks a few beers.

Dan calls a cab for us two hours after that.

Mission complete.

ALICE IS SITTING ON THE SECOND FLIGHT OF STAIRS INSIDE the Victorian on Clarkson when I arrive. It's after one in the morning, she should be asleep. So should I. We graduate later today.

Her boots are crossed at the ankle and her arms are wrapped loosely around her knees. She looks casual, relaxed. Until I see her face. It's a portrait in tears, layers of fresh streaks over those hours' old. Each layer a record of swells—anger, sadness, disappointment—that have muddled together to create a watercolor of emotional catastrophe painted by the haphazard hand of fate.

I stop on the landing and consider turning around and leaving, but I know she's already heard me, so what's the point.

"What are you doing, Toby?" she whispers.

Repentance, I answer in my head, but the honesty doesn't find its way out. I say nothing.

"Listen, I know you warned me that you're no good at friendship. I know you got caught shoplifting and that's why you missed our show. And I know you well enough to know that you're punishing yourself for that because you haven't talked to me since. I know you're pushing me away because you think I deserve a better friend than you. But guess what? I'm stubborn, and you don't get to call our friendship off. You're still my best friend and I care about you."

Everything inside me has tightened up; muscles, tendons, and bundles of nerves are all retracting and balling up and settling inside my chest, squeezing until pain radiates and pricks tears in my eyes.

Her voice grows. "I knocked on your door earlier but you weren't home, so I've been sitting here waiting for hours. Taber came home a while ago and said he saw you leaving a bar with a woman when he was walking home from the QuikMart. I know you're not mine, Toby. I know that." She sniffs. "But does the thought of you with someone else still break my heart? Yes, because selfishly, I wish it would've been me whose hand you were holding instead. There are a few things I've experienced in my life that make my heart soar: music, laughter, and being near you. Talking, listening, kissing—no one kisses like you do, Toby. I can still feel each and every one like your lips are still on mine. And to know that someone else got them tonight hurts. Because, like I said, I'm selfish. I want your lips all to myself. But more than that," she pauses and wipes the tears from her cheeks, "I want more for *you*. Even if that doesn't include me. You graduate today. *You graduate.* I want you to have a life that's filled with pursuing dreams that are so mind-numbingly radiant you don't even know they're possible yet."

You *are the mind-numbingly radiant dream that isn't possible!* I want to cry out but I can't.

"I want you to not only watch your son grow up but to be the role model I know you can be," she pleads.

My stomach knots at the mention of Joey, and guilt takes another stab at me and leaves the knife buried to the hilt in my side. Where it will remain for the hours I have left. The tears are running down my face now, eyes pinched closed because I can't look at her while she spills her truth.

"Johnny, Cliff, Chantal, Joey, me—we need you." She sighs and it's exasperation and defiance. "Will you please say something so I don't feel like I'm just talking to myself?"

I wipe my running nose with the sleeve of my sweatshirt. I

don't want to sniff back the snot or she'll know I'm crying. I'm holding my breath. I can't say anything, or I know a sob will escape.

"Are you drunk?" she whispers.

No, I answer in my head, but my vocal cords don't cooperate.

She rises to her feet. She towers three steps above me, wild blonde hair glowing under the single exposed light bulb in the ceiling directly above her and unseeing eyes vaguely focus on nothing and everything all at once. I'm not a religious person, but the sight is tragically angelic and eerily prophetic, like she's peering into my soul looking for a flicker of light amongst all the dark and decay.

"Some people aren't worth fighting for, Toby. You're not one of them. There are people we meet in this life who anchor us. They reassure us with their presence. They bring us comfort *simply by being*. They love by osmosis, radiating it out and diffusing it in effortlessly. Quietly, they walk among us, treading lightly but providing stability and influence because it's second nature. The thing that's so special about these people is that they don't even know they're doing it."

Tears are streaming again as I involuntarily gasp for the air my body is demanding to feed the torrent. I immediately bury my face in the forearms of my sweatshirt to muffle my breakdown.

"That's you, Toby. *That's you.* You're worth fighting for." Her voice cracks before she adds, "You have *no fucking idea* how much I wish you realized it and started fighting for yourself."

With that, I hear her turn and ascend the stairs and walk down the hall to her apartment.

I don't know how long I stand on the stairs soaking my sleeves with her hope and my hopelessness, trying like hell to hold on to her words. *You're worth fighting for,* repeats in my head over and over in Alice's tearstained, warbly voice. Deep down there's a part of me that desperately wants to entertain that fighting is even a possibility.

Until it goes to war with the darkness.

You're worth fighting for.

No, you're not worth fighting for.

You're worth fighting for.

You were never worth fighting for.

You're worth fighting for.

Alice doesn't really care about you.

You're worth fighting for.

She doesn't even know you.

You're worth fighting for.

You're incapable of being loved.

You're worth fighting for.

You're incapable of love.

You're worth fight—

The world will be a better place when you're not in it.

You're wor—

You should kill yourself now and get it over with. You know your mom won't show tomorrow. Stop lying to yourself.

You—

I knew you'd see things my way.

CHAPTER THIRTY-SEVEN

Present, June 1987
Toby

I've been awake for twenty-five hours. I couldn't sleep. It seems when you know that years have turned into months, then days, and finally hours, your body refuses to shut down and forces you to face mortality head on. To dwell on it at length in the darkness, hyperawareness dawning that my life is now a series of final moments and events. I am a dead man walking. At six o'clock, I decide to get up and let the finality commence.

I thought there would be relief in knowing it's almost over and that all I need to do is survive a few more hours, but the hopelessness and helplessness I've felt for two years has transformed. It's gone from crushing to an entirely new level of pain.

I shower for the last time.

I shave for the last time.

I dress for the last time.

I brush my teeth for the last time.

Each task is done with a perpetual knot in my throat and tears streaming unchecked like the bullies they are. My traitorous face displays the telltale signs of sleeplessness, hours of unhinged crying. All-time high self-loathing reflects in my pathetic swollen, red eyes and blotchy cheeks like a pitiful billboard for all to see.

Slipping on my shoes, I grab the plastic bag with my cap and gown off the hook on the back of my bedroom door, toss a Sharpie in with them, and exit, unnecessarily padlocking my door. Thankful Johnny and Cliff are still sleeping. I cross the small space of the kitchen to the front door before backtracking three steps to snatch Johnny's sunglasses off the counter. They don't cover up the tears intermittently trailing down my cheeks, but they do conceal the train wreck in my eyes.

When I exit the Victorian on Clarkson, it's only six thirty. Graduation doesn't begin until noon. So, in a fog, I start walking. My feet are heavy, exhaustion adding what feels like fifty pounds to my frame. Progression of everything is slow: thoughts, movement, hindsight, foresight. I'm not sure where I'm going until my feet slow to a stop an hour later, and I'm standing outside the tiny house of horrors that takes a starring role in my nightmares. It looks different, like an old leather shoe that's worn and cracked, but that someone's taken a liking to and tried to polish with the hope of resurrection without actual repair. There's a fresh coat of pale yellow paint glossed over the battered siding hiding the decades-old dirty, white paint that lives underneath. The eaves, shutters, and downspouts, though functionally and aesthetically worse for wear, are cloaked in bright white. The house looks optimistic, like the guise of a cheery façade negates its history of sadness.

The longer I stare, the more the glamour of the makeover wilts. My vision blurs and memories emerge, drifting out from beneath the front door and drafty windows. They surround me —specters with swelling mass, hardened weight, and blame so sharp I would swear it's piercing my skin. They're crowding me, smothering. The sensation of claustrophobia peaking. My lungs constrict. It's hard to breathe.

"I'm so sorry, Nina. I'm so sorry," I whisper.

When the voices inside my head respond with a barrage of monstrous memories and truths, I drop to my knees and cover my ears to ward off the invasion. It doesn't work. Each voice is distinct and loud, so very loud, one competing to be heard over the other. They're the soundtrack to a macabre slideshow of Nina's life leaking out in a river of red from the hole in her head.

Either you leave with me or you take this.

It's all your fault, Toby!

My mom's blame: *He fucking killed my Nina!*

If you weren't such an asshole, maybe your mom could've loved you.

He's hitting you.

Ken hit her. He. Hit. Her. And you let him, you little pussy. You're worse than him.

Nina's pleas: *No, he's not. I fell taking the trash out a few days ago.*

You should've fought for her, not armed her.

My mom's declaration: *If you thought a gun was such a goddamn good idea, you should've just used it on yourself!*

You should've never been born. Think of all the devastation that could've been avoided if you'd never been born.

My mom's wish: *It should've been you, Toby!*

It should've been you, Toby!

It should've been me. It should've been me. It should've

been me. *It should've been me. It should've been me*, until every-thing else is a cacophony of blended angry white noise beneath the incessant bloodcurdling scream of my own persecution. With each iteration, something I already believed to be true morphs into a desperate need to make it reality immediately. Solutions to end this flash interlaced between the nonstop visions of Nina lying on the floor bleeding out: stepping out in front of a bus, jumping off an overpass into highway traffic, hanging myself in the basement of the Victorian on Clarkson.

Rising to my feet requires a feat of strength and I have none left. I'm completely and utterly drained. The required gradua-tion attire of black dress pants and white button-down shirt are no longer pristine. The hole in the knee of my pants feels symbolic. I've never been a clean slate, why should I go out looking like one? It's fitting. I lift the sunglasses and wipe my eyes and nose with the back of my shirtsleeve, because fuck it, it doesn't matter anymore if this shirt gets filthy.

The sun seems brighter and my eyeballs burn as I squint down the sidewalk and try to decide which way I need to go to finish this.

"Excuse me?"

I hear the voice, but I don't think for one second that the question is directed at me.

"Excuse me, young man? Are you okay?" The voice is closer and louder this time.

No, I'm not okay, a part of me wants to answer, but I keep my mouth shut and my head down, lowering the sunglasses back into place.

A quick side-glance tells me there's an elderly woman standing on the porch of the sunshine yellow house and somehow it looks cheery again through blurred eyes. She's waving at me like she's trying to get my attention, gentle and friendly like Mrs. Bennett. "Do you need help?" she calls out.

"There's no helping me," I mutter too quietly for her to hear and shake my head in answer before I walk away.

"Young man, you forgot your bag," she calls after me.

I return for the bag with my irrelevant cap and gown and pick it up off the ground. Two blocks down the street, I take a right because I know it's a major thoroughfare on the bus route. When I hear the first bus approaching from behind, my heart rate increases to what feels like unsustainable levels before it will burst. The fact that my body and mind are beyond exhaustion only amplifies the sensation of life beating through my body at breakneck speed. Stepping down into the gutter ratchets everything up: the need to end this, the fear because I've never been brave, the hopelessness that never relents. The bus is so close now, I can hear it roaring as I glance back over my shoulder and take two shaky steps toward the lane of traffic. Closing my eyes tight, my stomach wrings itself in two and the sensation forces fear to leak from my pinched lids.

I pull in a quick intake of breath.

Hold it.

And take the final step preparing for impact.

This isn't the plan! I shout at myself.

Instead of moving forward, I move back toward the curb and a powerful gust of air connects abrasively with my flesh like a rasp.

You could've ruined that bus driver's life! I shout.

Shaken, I walk to the curb and sit.

I promised myself from the beginning that my end wouldn't be a mess for someone else to witness and/or clean up. I want to disappear from existence and never be found because no one deserves the visual memory of suicide and death haunting their future. I don't want to hurt anyone, even if I don't know them, because you can never unsee death. I know.

I almost brought that bus driver, who probably has a wife

and kids at home, into my shitshow. I almost forced him to make *my* problems *his* trauma.

Before long, I'm looking at the bag in my hand and bargaining with myself. *You've made it over two years; you can do a few more hours. This isn't the time to go off script. Go to graduation. Give the middle finger to Mom if she shows. And then stick to the plan. No bringing others in, this is yours to finish.*

An hour later, I'm lying on the wide concrete rim circling a big fountain in City Park. The park is deserted except for the random dog walker or jogger. My body wants terribly to sleep, but I won't allow it, because lately when I sleep, I wake up screaming and thrashing in the grip of night terrors. I'm not putting on that display outdoors in the middle of a park.

My mind is preoccupied with Nina. What she would be doing now if she was still alive. I picture her married to a nice guy with a decent job. A little baby with dark hair and hazel eyes like hers in her arms and a smile free of worry, doubt, or sadness touching her lips. I don't know if she ever wanted kids, but I like to think she did, which is torture because it's yet another possibility I took from her when I handed her that gun.

Brevity is always the companion of good thoughts. They're cut short and I'm reminded that I'm not worthy of them. While my thoughts turn dark and the internal monologue begins to play, I roll over on my stomach and take the hat and marker out of my bag and try to lose myself in something for my final hours. On the top of my hat I draw Batman in profile. I prefer drawing with pencils, but I can make do. The voices are still berating me, but when I'm drawing, I don't have to give them my full attention. It's an escape. Escape that I don't deserve, but I take it anyway.

When I'm done, the surface of the mortarboard is covered in art except for a strip along the top edge that I intentionally left blank so I could fill it in with a message for my mom. I was going to write, *Fuck you, Marilyn*, but now that the time has come, I can't.

I write *I'm sorry*, instead.

And then I put it on along with the white gown. The red sash with Honors embroidered on it in white letters that came with my gown remains in the bag; I drop it in a trash can. I exit the park and walk two blocks west toward the school and the stadium behind it, where the ceremony will take place. I tell myself that I'm walking intentionally slow, but I don't think I could move any faster if I tried.

I take my place in line behind a girl who was in my PE class junior year. She's buzzing with excitement and her hair is so big in the front that her hat is pinned to the back of her head, instead of resting on top. It's defying gravity, clinging to her ratted hair with strategically placed hairpins. I distract myself by counting them, twenty-seven bobby pins that I can see by the time I take my seat amongst a sea of red robes. There are nineteen other white robes like mine, the top twenty GPAs in our graduating class are required to wear them. Along with the ostentatious sash I threw in the trash. I worked hard for this robe. It's amazing what you can do when you have a point to prove and a grudge to hold. My mom always said I was stupid and would amount to nothing. She was right about a lot of things, but I'm not stupid.

Our principal steps up to the podium on the stage and I try to listen, but after the first cursory line in a speech that feels like he wrote it ten years ago and has delivered every year since, I tune out. I think about scanning the crowd for my mom's face, but who am I kidding? Anything ten feet from me is distorted, and the further my field of vision extends from there, the more it blurs. The people in the stands are a kaleidoscope of muted color, a combination of other people's families cheering them on. Not mine. The isolation of the thought makes me close my eyes and tune them out. There is no one here for me. I'm going out alone. I know Alice is somewhere in the rows ahead of me. We're seated in alphabetical order, but there are over four hundred in our graduating class, the gap between Es and Ps is immense. I can't see her. And I can't feel her either.

In the darkness behind my closed lids, the voices coming through the loudspeaker vary in pitch, but they're all monotonous droning. The valedictorian's speech is the high-light. I don't hear words, but I think it's valiant that the pride and excitement almost mask the fear in her voice. People like her don't bask in accomplishment, they beat themselves up over tackling the next hallmark before it even comes into view. Stress is a way of life. The future is a way of life; the constant carrot dangling within view but just out of reach, is a way of life. There is no present. Only future.

What feels like hours pass before the presentation of indi-vidual diplomas begins. I still haven't opened my eyes hidden behind Johnny's sunglasses. Unbidden, the knot in my throat tightens and thoughts bombard me consecutively and uncen-sored: Nina coming to visit when I was five, acting strange, and leaving soon after a fight ensued with Mom. I hated that our mom fought loud, her anger amplified her voice to unbearable decimals. And I hated even more that Nina fought quiet, her anger muffled her voice to unbearable decimals. Nina's eyes looked vacant, a look I would see many times in the years to come, but the first time left a scary impression. It was like her body was there, but *she* wasn't. The moment the door clicked shut and Nina left, my mom looked at me and roared, "It's all your fault she's like this!" I loved my sister and the words crushed me, because even though I didn't understand them, I felt the weight of them in my soul. My mother parented with tone. Hearing something enough, I believed it—and have turned into it. Reflecting back, I feel the guilt of my five-year-old self compound and blend with the guilt of my eighteen-year-old self. And then I see Nina's body lying in a pool of blood. My mother's screeching continues, "It's all your fault she's like this!"

"I know," I say the words out loud. They blend in with the cheers and clapping that surrounds me and no one notices. Me in the midst of a singular meltdown, the rest of the world in the midst of a mass reverie. The juxtaposition sums up my life: there's everyone...and then there's me. Knowing from a young age that I didn't fit in.

Just then the loudspeaker cuts my thoughts like scissors snipping a string. "Alice Eliot," it booms.

The same obligatory, polite, congratulatory clapping continues, but I hear a loud whistle and a faint, but mighty yell from somewhere in the stands. "Way to go, Alice!" Taber. And it makes me do something I haven't done in a while. I smile. I smile with cheeks still streaked in fresh tears. I smile despite myself, because Alice has her entire life ahead of her. And I know it's going to be beautiful. The smile gives way to a few chuckles that feel foreign. My mind and body don't know what to do with them and quickly they morph into what still sounds like laughter but is fueled by despair and accompanied by tears. I'm so tired it's making me delirious. That's my only explanation.

It's a long time before the alphabet and ceremony proceed to my row. Lost in my thoughts, I take my cue when the girls sitting on either side of me rise, and I stand, mimicking them. I'm sweating like mad. I mop my face with the flared cuff of my robe sleeve to clear away the evidence of my crying, though the mania driving it remains etched in my features, I'm sure.

I wait: outwardly calm, inwardly growing more impatient by the minute. When I ascend the three stairs of the stage, I'm acutely aware of three things: how much I dislike the sound of my own name amplified and drawing attention to me; how clammy my hand is when it accepts Principal Scott's proffered, robotic shake; and how I know, without a doubt in my mind, that Marilyn Page is not here.

My mom didn't come.

Of course she didn't, I think sarcastically.

Of course she didn't, I think accusatorially.

Of course she didn't, I think hopelessly.

And it's at this exact moment that I realize maybe I didn't have something to prove to her.

But that I just wanted her to be proud of me.

Proud.

Of.

Me.

With that final revelation, I descend the three stairs on the other side of the stage, and instead of turning left and remaining in line to return to my seat for the remainder of the ceremony, I walk straight ahead, set on a path toward a gate— any gate—that will get me out of here.

"Young man, you need to sit down. You can't leave until it's over." The woman walking next to me is intermittently walking and jogging because her short legs are no match for the pace I'm suddenly keeping.

I don't even look at her when I answer so many things at once: "It's over." And then I run. My cap falls off before I make it to the gate and I leave it behind. At some point, I unzip my gown and shrug it off, leaving it behind too. There's a desperation like I've never felt thrumming through my veins. It's terrifyingly persistent, high alert, need to take action. I don't stop running until I'm standing on the front porch of the Victorian on Clarkson.

My legs are shaky when I walk up the stairs to the third floor. Unlocking the door, I'm grateful Johnny and Cliff are both gone. I don't have it in me to interact, even minimally. When I remove the padlock on my bedroom door, I toss it, with the key still inserted, on a shelf next to my cassettes. My backpack is empty on my sleeping bag where I left it this morning. Unzipping it, I throw in only essentials: the money I've been saving for two years, and the sleeping pills I took from the medicine cabinet in 2A after the tenants were evicted last year. One will buy me a bus and cab ride to the mountains, and the other will buy me oblivion. Next I throw in a few things that I'd like with me when I go out because they remind me that sometimes the universe creates remarkable beauty: Nina's *Physical Graffiti* album because it will forever remind me of her; my first edition *Dark Knight Returns* comic book because getting lost in someone else's imagination and art provided a necessary coping mechanism for years; and a pencil drawing of Alice standing on the fire escape staring unseeing, but all-knowing, at a sky filled with stars only she can behold.

Zipping up the backpack, I leave it on the floor and quickly change out of my dress clothes and into jeans and a long-sleeved T-shirt. Everything is moving in slow motion now, maybe because the adrenaline has worn off and I can't keep up with reality. Each movement is exaggerated, my senses dull and gauzy. Physical sensation feels sedate, like I'm so tired that my extremities are numb. I'm always tired, but this is a new level.

Before I leave, there's one more thing I need to do. I need to leave the letter I wrote to Johnny last night in his room. It's not a goodbye, it's an *I'm leaving to start over somewhere new, thanks for everything* letter. Short enough that he'll think I've moved on now that I'm done with school, but long enough that my heart won't have to take on an extra dose of guilt because I know he won't suspect anything and look for me.

I'll disappear and never be heard from again.

And everyone will assume I ended up as far as a bus ticket would take me and made a new life.

That's all I want.

I don't want people to worry.

I don't want people to question.

I just want people to forget and keep living their lives. I'll slip out of the daily flow the same way I lived in it...unseen.

Leaving the letter and the sunglasses I've been wearing all morning, but apparently don't have the constitution to steal, on Johnny's dresser, I walk back for my backpack in my room. I consider putting the padlock back in place on my door but then leave it where it is on the shelf because it doesn't matter. Shifting my eyes from the padlock to the box of Nina's stuff on the bottom shelf, for a moment I consider opening it one last time and looking at her things. But then I realize I'm stalling.

Delaying the inevitable.

You're nothing, is the rallying cry from within that pulls me out of the past and into the moment. That and the phone on the kitchen wall is ringing shrilly. It's instinct to answer it, to do my job, but then I remind myself that I'm on a mission. And that broken appliances aren't my concern anymore.

By the time I reach the front door, the answering machine has answered the call. And by the time I open the door Johnny's greeting that isn't much of a greeting has ended and the caller is speaking, "Johnny..."

I'm pulling the door shut on what is no longer my problem when I stop. An internal war is being waged. *Shut the fucking door and leave!* is screaming over the top of, *Something is really wrong!*

I'm shaking my head because this cannot be happening. I

have plans. This is it. I'm so close. And I'm so fucking tired. The tears have come again. They're warm but the flesh they're trailing over is beginning to feel raw and chapped. It's burning.

I'm listening to the message through what is now only a crack in the door. I know the voice. I don't understand the words. But I can hear the pleading and desperation and it cuts to the bone. It's the kind of pain that's almost impossible to talk through, but worst of all, it's blinding fear. He's terrified. He wants Johnny, but Johnny isn't here. Clicking the door shut, I walk toward the stairs.

The first flight I descend, I tell myself, *Johnny will probably be back soon.*

The second flight I descend, I tell myself, *You are such an asshole.*

And then I'm knocking on his door and yelling his name, "Mr. Street, are you okay?"

No answer.

Thinking back, I haven't seen him in over two months. He hasn't called with any issues. His cab parked out front hasn't moved.

I try the doorknob, but it's locked.

I knock again. "Mr. Street?"

Nothing.

Anxiety has flooded me. I can hear his voice from minutes ago in my head. *Do something!* my brain screams.

My run back up the stairs is an out-of-body experience. I don't know how my legs are moving but they are, and by the time I walk back into apartment 3A my lungs are protesting vehemently. I retrieve my keys, padlock and all, and run back down. My legs, lungs, and hands are shaking when I fit my master key into the lock on Mr. Street's door and push it open.

"Mr. Street?" I yell again.

He's not in the living room or kitchen, and the bathroom

door is open and the small room is empty. Which only leaves the bedroom. When I open the door, I am not prepared for what I'm about to see. There's a man in the bed who bears only a slight resemblance to the man I last saw months ago. Thin has transformed into gaunt. His eyes are ringed in shadows and sweat sheens his brow. Painful looking sores adorn his face and arms.

"Toby, thank God," he whispers in a southern drawl I've never heard. Looking at him, not only can I hear the desperation, pain, and fear...I can *see* it. The pairing is shocking.

I find that I'm nodding without making a conscious decision to do so. Frozen where I stand, I ask, "Should I call an ambulance?"

He wheezes and covers his mouth with the sheet to cough. "No, don't call. Just drive me to Denver General, please."

"I don't have a car," I tell him.

"You can drive my cab; it's parked right out front," he says weakly.

"I don't have a license," I counter and for the first time in my life, I regret not having one.

He slowly strips back the sheet covering him. Movement is a struggle. "Beggars can't be choosers." If he didn't look so sick, I would swear he's trying to make a joke.

"I don't—" I begin, but swallow *know how to drive* and walk to him with my hands extended so I can help him stand.

Looking at my hands, he pauses and speaks to them like he can't look me in the eye. "You should know that I have AIDS, Toby. Most people don't want to touch—"

Without hesitation, I cut him off with a whisper, "I'm not most people," as I grasp his hands with mine and hoist him to his feet. I don't think he's ever liked me, so I assume he agrees with what he interpreted as a sardonic reply. But when he's upright and his eyes are almost even with mine, they're shining with unshed tears.

I can't take seeing the tears, so I shift to his side and wrap my arm around his waist to keep him upright. He's weak, so weak. He lifts his arm behind me and cups my shoulder with his hand, but the pressure is slight, his strength is gone.

"Where are your keys and wallet?" I ask. And then I add, "Do you need anything else?" because I can't think straight immersed in this crisis. Adrenaline is making motion possible, but my mind is static.

"My keys and wallet are on the table by the front door." A raspy, damp cough is expelled into his free hand before he can continue. "I don't need anything else."

I nod because all I'm focused on now is getting him out to his car and to the hospital as soon as possible. His cough sounds awful and his skin, now that I'm looking at it up close, has a grayish cast to it.

Bearing his weight as we walk down the porch steps to the car isn't a burden at all. He weighs nothing. He's a framework of bones his clothes hang from. In the car safely, I run around and unlock the driver's door and jump in. I've ridden in cars on occasion, I understand the mechanics of driving even though I've never been behind the wheel. And it looks like literally having someone's life in my hands puts doubt on the back-burner for the moment. Pulling out into the northbound lane of Clarkson, I ease the gas pedal down gently at first to gauge its touchiness. From there, the short drive to Denver General Hospital is a blur of intense concentration on the road and the acute emergency in the seat next to me. His breathing is shallower now than it was inside his apartment and I wonder if it's from the exertion of the walk to the car or if whatever is wrong is accelerating.

Pulling up under the ER portico in front of two sliding

double doors, I throw the car into park and run inside. When the doors slide closed behind me, my eyes dart from one side of the lobby to the other, frantically searching for someone who looks like they can help. There's a check-in desk twenty feet from me and I bolt toward it. "I have someone in the car who needs to be seen right away. Do you have a wheelchair? He shouldn't be walking."

She's efficient and flags down a man in scrubs who follows me outside with a wheelchair. As we're helping him out, Mr. Street grips my arm and the desperation, fear, and pain have crept back into his eyes and voice. "Will you stay with me, *please*? I'm afraid this is it and I don't want to die alone." His bottom lip is trembling and he's trying not to cry.

Naked vulnerability is all I see and I can't say no, so I nod and try not to cry myself. "I'll go park your car and I'll be right back."

He nods once and pulls his lips in, biting down with his teeth in an attempt to trap the emotion inside. Traitorously, it seeps from the corners of his eyes.

By the time I walk in through the ER double doors again, I don't remember parking the car seconds ago, but I'm here. My life is now a dazed succession of moments in real time, one second leading to the next.

Mr. Street isn't in the waiting room, but the man in scrubs who helped us is walking toward me. He's talking, but I only hear the last bit. "...examined. Someone will be out to speak with you as soon as we have an update on his condition. Would you mind filling out these forms while you wait?"

I want to say, *I don't even really know the guy other than fixing his fridge; I can't fill them out*, but I take them and say, "Sure." Sitting down on one of the uncomfortable plastic chairs, I feel like a thief flipping open his tri-fold wallet and rifling through the contents: a two-dollar bill, a Colorado driver's license, a health insurance card, a MasterCard, a well-worn piece of paper that looks to be a library card from Huntsville, Alabama, and a photo folded in half with writing on the back, *I love you. Now, always, and forever.* I don't open it because it feels too private and slip it back into the wallet.

Filling out everything I can on the forms doesn't take long because I don't know much. When I hand it to the women at the check-in counter, I shrug. She nods when she sees most of the questions on the form are blank and smiles. "It's okay, thanks for getting us started. I'll take it from here."

I nod and I don't know if it's gratitude or shame or an apology. Maybe it's all three. And then I sit back in the same plastic chair to wait. I don't know why I sat back down in this one when there are several empty, especially since it has a crack down the middle that flexes open and bites at my jeans and the flesh underneath. It's pain that gives me something to focus on, maybe that's why.

Minutes, a few or dozens I don't know, pass before there's someone standing in front of me. They're saying, "Sir? *Sir?*" like they've said it several times with no response. When I finally look up, the irritation in her voice doesn't lighten. "Can you follow me? I'll escort you to Curtis Street's room."

I rise and follow her obediently even though I don't like the tone she's using. It sounds demeaning and critical. I shouldn't be here. Family should be here. Friends should be here. I'm neither. We walk in silence. We ride the elevator in silence. We walk some more in silence. When she stops in front of a door, I assume it's his room and walk in without a word, happy to be away from her.

He still looks ashen. A cannula is delivering oxygen in through his nostrils, and an IV is delivering meds and/or fluids in through his arm. "Do you need anything?" I ask, because I'm at a loss.

"My wallet," he says and tries to smile, but when the corners of his mouth turn up it's the melancholiest expression I've ever seen.

Pulling it from my back pocket, I hand it over belatedly. "I had to open it. To fill out the forms. Sorry," I explain lamely.

He takes it weakly and rests it on his chest while he opens it like he doesn't have the strength to hold it. Taking out the photo, he lets the wallet fall away next to him on the narrow bed. Unfolding it, he looks at the image inside and the defeated smile turns wistful as he lovingly strokes the paper once and then presses it face down against his chest. One palm resting atop the other over his heart. "Don't be sorry, Toby. I'm the one who's sorry. Thank you for staying." He coughs and this time instead of being raspy, it's watery and doesn't relent for almost a minute. He's doubled in half when the coughing fit ceases, the photo still clasped to his chest. It's disturbing to watch.

I pick up his wallet that's fallen to the floor and place it on the bedside table, and when he regains his faculties, I ask, "Should I get someone?" It's painful to watch him struggle. I don't know if I can handle this.

"No. They think it's pneumonia," he says like that explains everything. When I don't comment, he continues, "AIDS isn't what kills you, you know? It's something else that your immune system can no longer fight that finishes you..." he trails off.

Which is cruel, isn't it? It's like a muscle-bound bully who beats the shit out of you until you can barely move and then lets a child step in and deliver the final blow to knock you out.

He flips the photo over again and stares at it and the loving smile returns.

I can see the photo now. It's a younger version of Mr. Street with his arms around a man a few inches shorter than him and a few years older. They're both laughing. Their eyes are closed and their mouths are open. Sometimes a photo captures emotion so palpable that it can still be felt every time you look at it. That's this photo; it's pure joy.

Mr. Street catches me looking and turns it toward me. "This is my Henry."

The way he says it and the way he's looking at the photo with such love and pain in his eyes, I know Henry isn't with us anymore. "How long were you together?" I ask because he needs to talk. And I need to sit down.

"Total, almost eight years. We met in Huntsville, Alabama in 1978 at a mutual friend's Fourth of July party. Henry was charismatic, handsome, and had the politest Southern drawl I'd ever heard, and manners to match. I was smitten immediately. We lived together until he took a job in Miami in '83. I made the choice not to go with him and we broke up. I was crushed and knew the moment he walked out the door that I'd made the biggest mistake of my life. We reconciled a year later because we were miserable without each other and decided to start fresh in Denver. I lost him nine months ago. Not long before I moved into my current apartment."

I know it's probably impolite to ask, but he's sharing and it feels rude not to participate in his story. "AIDS?"

He nods and a tear slips from the corner of his eye. Wrinkles form across his chin as sadness crumples it. "Henry got sick first. Watching someone you love suffer is the wickedest form of torture there is. It was horrible watching him wither away." When he looks at me, his eyes are brimming with unshed tears and the pain in them is unbearable. His heartbreak is killing him far more than his body is.

I don't know how to comfort when I can think clearly, and I most definitely cannot think clearly right now, but I do feel sad for him. I can't imagine what he's been through, what he's going through. So I give him the truth. My truth. "He died knowing he was loved completely, and that was a gift. A gift that most people won't get." I won't.

"Enough about me, Toby." His breathing is shallow, even with the oxygen, and I want him to stop talking and not strain himself. "You look like I feel. What's going on?"

For a second, I contemplate spilling it all, but I end up saying, "I've had a really shitty..." I pause when I almost say, *life*, but go with, "week," instead because I don't need to unload my dirty laundry on anyone, especially him.

His eyes are on me. Assessing me. I have to look away. "Yeah, me too," he whispers.

I nod. His words hit me like a punch to the gut. Not that he meant them that way. He said it like he was commiserating. There was empathy in his voice, like what we're going through is similar. Every minute this goes on drains me. The adrenaline spike that got me through the past hour or so has faded and I'm standing at the precipice of complete delirium.

"When did you last sleep?" he asks.

Without thinking, I answer honestly, "Two nights ago."

"Why didn't you sleep last night?" he probes.

"I had a lot on my mind." When I say it my voice cracks. When I look him in the eye, I know that he heard it. I look away, ashamed. I want to leave; I'm going to lose it and I don't want to cry in front of him.

"Like what?" he asks it gently like he already knows the answer.

I shake my head and I can't stop. I keep shaking it while my lips pinch together and my face contorts in an effort to hold back the sobs.

"Holding it in gives it power, Toby. Talking about it takes that power away."

The sob I let loose physically hurts. The single sob is followed by crying that has no sound. It's crying so deep it's bone-jarring, but by the time it reaches the surface, it's mute. This emotion is immense, it's an eruption deep inside me that can't be fully expelled out into the light of day. I can't focus. My eyes are blurry. My mind is blurry. My existence is blurry.

The hand on my shoulder is not.

It's firm and grounding.

I didn't hear the person behind me approach, but when they guide me to stand, I do.

And when they guide me to step into their arms, I do.

The hug feels unconditional.

And for a moment I let myself believe it's my mom.

And that she's proud of me.

And I cry some more.

The harder I cry, the harder I'm hugged.

"She didn't show up," I gasp on an intake of air.

"I know," is his apologetic reply.

"How do you know?" I ask as I try to stifle another sob.

He pulls back just far enough that he can look me in the eye. "I never mailed the invitation, Toby."

"You couldn't find her?" I ask, suddenly afraid to hear the answer.

"No. I found her," he says as he pushes the hair back from my eyes. "I didn't give it to her because I was selfish. I wanted to be there instead."

"What?" I ask because this doesn't make any sense. And then anger starts to boil in the pit of my stomach. "That wasn't your choice to make, Johnny."

His eyes drop to the floor.

Mine follow his there.

We can't look at each other.

When I try to pull away, he won't let me. "Let me go," I insist quietly.

His eyes are still on the floor, but he shakes his head. "I can't do that."

"Let me go," I repeat. The anger swelling. The exhaustion unendurable.

He's still shaking his head, but now it's accompanied by tears sliding down his cheeks. "No," he says softly.

"*She* was supposed to be there! *Not you!*" I shout.

Which brings in my favorite nurse. "Sir, I'm going to have to ask you to keep your voice down or leave," she snaps.

Mr. Street's quiet voice drifts in behind hers. It sounds distant. My body wants so badly to sleep. "Take him home, Johnny. He needs to sleep. Badly."

Johnny is still holding my arm when he answers him. "I heard your message when Cliff and I got home from graduation, but your apartment was empty, so I figured you drove yourself to the hospital. How are you?"

"Pneumonia," Mr. Street answers on a cough. "And Toby drove me."

Johnny's attention shifts back to me. "You don't have a license."

The effort it takes to shrug is too much and my eyes drift closed despite the anger still pulsing through me. "I don't know how to drive either, but we made it."

Johnny looks back to Mr. Street. "How's your blood count? Have they talked to your doctor?"

I'm beginning to think I'm in an alternate universe. How does he know all of this?

"They've drawn blood, I'll know more soon. They've put a call into Dr. Thomas. Take Toby home. He needs you right now." He's putting my needs ahead of his fear.

Johnny nods. "Do you need anything before we go?"

Mr. Street's brave smile emerges, and he holds up the photo in his hand. "I have everything I need."

Johnny puts his arm around me and guides me toward the door. I want to fight, but I can't. So I go with him.

At the door Mr. Street says, "Thank you, Toby. You saved my life today. Go get some sleep. And when you wake up, talk to Johnny. He's a good listener."

I nod, or at least I think I do.

"Johnny?"

Johnny looks his way. "When Toby wakes up, talk to him. He's a good listener."

Johnny nods.

We walk out of the hospital side by side. When we hit the fresh air outside, I consider making a run for it, but the pull is short-lived because I don't have the energy. I promise myself that when we get home, I'll get my second wind and leave from there.

In Johnny's truck, I close my eyes.

Just for a minute...

When I open them, we're parked in front of the Victorian on Clarkson.

I wasn't supposed to come back here.

Ever.

But I'm so tired that I can't stick to the plan.

I shuffle inside ahead of Johnny because he walks behind, probably in case I fall. Two flights of stairs feel like twenty-two when you're navigating them half asleep. When we reach the apartment door, I stand to the side of it and let Johnny unlock it because I don't have keys to this place anymore. I left them behind earlier knowing I'd never need them again. Unlocked, I drag myself through the open door of my bedroom.

I hear Johnny say, "You need to eat something before you go to sleep, Toby," but I ignore him and shut the door behind me.

I contemplate kicking off my shoes and getting comfortable,

but then decide I don't need to be comfortable for this and sling my backpack to the ground. Lying down on the sleeping bag, I unzip my backpack and with trembling hands pull out the pill bottle.

Open it.

Shake out a handful.

Put all thirty-one pills in my mouth.

And close my eyes.

Alice flashes across the back of my eyelids.

Her words ring in my ears.

Tears spill out.

This wasn't the plan.

I'm supposed to be alone.

Not in this house.

I didn't want it to end like this with Johnny just outside the door.

But I know better than anyone that sometimes you don't get what you want...

PART TWO

There are two sides to every story.
This is The Other Side of Toby's.
The side that lends perspective.
And changes everything.

CHAPTER THIRTY-EIGHT

Past, 1985
Tiffany

I know I should be on my way home.

I know I'll pay for this.

And that it will hurt when I do.

Because when he's not happy with me, it always does.

When I showed up at work tonight, my boss, Roger, told me there was an error and that Shannon and I were both on the schedule for the eight to four shift. He only needs one of us. I work the front desk at a motel in Capitol Hill, and it's not a two-person job. Shannon beat me here by five minutes. I understand, but I'm still a little sad. This motel isn't paradise, but it's my escape. That's just been taken away for tonight.

So, I'm going to find another escape. I walk several blocks before the soft glow of kitschy script in ancient neon, *Dan's Tavern*, beckons me.

The internal battle within begins when I grab the long

brass pull on the heavy wooden door and heave it open: *You shouldn't be here. He'll know you've been drinking. This is a bad idea. Go home!*

I ignore the warnings, and as a direct result self-preservation, and walk inside. Even though I'm knee-deep in a terrible decision, I can't seem to stop. Two steps in, my hands are shaking so bad that I have to cross my arms over my chest to hide my nerves.

Eyes are roving, I can feel them assessing me. I'm an outsider and they all know it.

I sit down at the free table in the corner. The table is a barrel with a glass top and the two chairs are horseshoe shaped and covered in fake maroon leather. They're both sporting duct tape repairs to what I'm guessing are cracks underneath. Once seated, I quickly realize that this isn't the type of establishment with a waitstaff and that I should've ordered something at the bar before I sat down. Head bent down, I know their stares are still on me. I'm getting hot. I don't like scrutiny. I don't like attention. Good or bad. I should leave, this was a bad idea.

But before I can stand up.

He sits down.

He's younger than me but not by much.

"Do you mind if I sit with you for a while?" He's not smiling, but he's not leering either.

Yes? No? I don't know. "I don't mind." I'm not smiling either, I'm too nervous.

"What's your name?" His voice is raspy and low, his frame is tall but not imposing, and his eyes are harmlessly intense but filmed over with the hint of inebriation.

Without thinking, I give him my real name. "Tiffany." Stupid, stupid, stupid.

"I'm Toby," he says and I believe him.

I like his voice and his face way too much. "I need to get a beer," I blurt.

He nods. It's not the permissive nod I'm used to from men I've been with, it's simple agreement.

When I return, his glass is empty.

I empty mine.

Then I empty another.

And another.

I'm drunk, but not so drunk that I don't know what I'm saying.

And I'm saying a lot.

Toby's easy to talk to.

Surprisingly easy to talk to.

Dangerously easy to talk to.

He's a good listener.

So good that I tell him things I've never told anyone.

Like how my boyfriend, Steve, slapped me last week because I burned his Hot Pocket. And last month because I didn't have money to pay the electric bill and it got cut off.

He doesn't look at me like I'm pathetic.

He doesn't look at me like I'm a target.

He looks at me like I'm a human being worth more than I give myself credit for.

And he tells me so too.

For the first time in a long time, I feel like I might be.

I think it's the beer. But what if it's me?

When the bartender announces *last call* it's almost midnight. I need to go.

"Where to, Tiffany?" he asks, and it sounds like the most important question anyone has ever asked me. "Do you need a cab?"

Looking down at the tabletop, I think for a minute.

He doesn't rush me.

"I need a cab."

Without a word, Toby stands and walks to the bar. When he returns, he holds out his hand. "Dan's calling for one. I'd like to ride with you only to make sure you get home safe, if that's okay? I promise I don't have any ulterior motives."

I take his hand and I do something I haven't done since I was young, I put my trust in someone else. My blind, but wholehearted, trust. "Okay."

We don't talk while we're waiting out front on the sidewalk, but he never lets go of my hand. His fingers clasp firmly in the space between my forefinger and thumb. It's a protective gesture that makes me feel brave.

By the time we slide into the back seat of the cab, I'm ready for change. I'm ready for more.

I give the cabbie the address and we ride in silence, still hand in hand.

He pays the cabbie a few minutes later when we pull up in front of a brick apartment building.

I hug Toby tight, knowing that I will never forget him. "Take care," I whisper as I release him.

Stuffing his cold hands deep in the pockets of his sweatshirt, he nods. "You too. Go be you...*for you.*"

I smile but it's distorted, because I'm on the verge of tears. Confusing tears that are happy and sad, and optimistic and terrified. "I don't know how to do that."

He tilts his head and his eyes go soft like he doesn't know how to either. "Just because you haven't done it, doesn't mean it can't be done. Good luck."

And then he turns and walks away.

While I wonder if it was all a dream.

I walk up the stairs to my aunt's apartment, knock on her door for the first time in over a year, and ask if I can stay with her for the night.

ONE NIGHT TURNS INTO TWO.

THE THIRD NIGHT I SLEEP IN MY CHILDHOOD BED AT MY parents' house in Rapid City, South Dakota. They drove down and picked me up after I called and asked them for help. We hadn't talked in years.

All of this thanks to the stranger who asked the right questions and listened when I most needed to be heard.

He'll never know he changed my life.

But he did.

CHAPTER THIRTY-NINE

Past, 1986
Chantal

I can't deny it anymore. I thought I could.

But I can't.

The first month I missed my period I knew it was due to stress.

The second month I missed my period I hoped it was due to stress.

The third month I missed my period I *prayed* it was due to stress.

There are so many things I blame on the stress: my lack of patience, my short attention span, my inability to tolerate bullshit even in the smallest doses. I can no longer blame my missing periods on it too.

I'm pregnant.

I haven't gone to a doctor.

I haven't taken a test.

But I know.

I know.

I opened the door and let the revelation in this afternoon because I can't ignore its incessant knocking anymore. I've been crying ever since. I told my grandma I needed to do our laundry and came down to the basement where I can be alone. No one in the building does laundry on Tuesday nights. During the past two hours, the roller coaster has taken me through a range of emotions, none of them helpful. All of them antagonistic and vengeful.

When I was twelve, my mom sat me down to have the dreaded birds and bees discussion. She made me promise that I would get my college degree, get married, and get pregnant in that order. She had dreams for me. *I* had dreams for me. I promised.

Now here I am feeling guilty on top of everything else.

And scared because not only am I letting my mom down, but I'm letting my grandma down too. In her eyes, I'm perfect. Always have been. If she finds out what really happened, she'll never look at me the same way again. That would destroy me.

The washer is in the middle of its noisy spin cycle, so it's not until he's at the foot of the stairs that I see him, and it's too late to wipe my eyes and try to compose myself. So much for hiding, I can't even do that tonight.

Toby doesn't talk much. I've always liked that about him. He pays attention and he listens. He figures people out. People who don't know him think he's detached and unfriendly, but if there's ever an apocalypse, Toby is the first person I would pick to be on my team. Because he always has your back.

His hands are tucked deep in the pockets of his jeans and his eyes are tucked deep into the disheartenment permeating my being. He's trying to school his features, but when his head tilts a few degrees to the right, concern siphons in. I don't know how to explain it, but when Toby looks at you like this, you feel seen to the marrow of your bones.

I'm just realizing how much I need that right now.

He raises his eyebrows, and paired with the worry in his bright green eyes, he asks, *Are you okay?* without saying a word.

I can't look at him when I answer, "I'm pregnant."

He lowers himself to sit on the stairs and drops his face into his hands, scrubs it twice, and then raises it to catch me looking at him expectantly. I don't know what I need him to say because there's nothing that will make this better.

"Have you been to a doctor?" he asks quietly. Toby's always been soft-spoken. You'd think that would contradict his tall physical stature, but his gentle nature complements it.

I shake my head.

Elbows resting on his knees and hands clasped loosely in front of him, he drops his eyes to the floor and nods slowly. After an extended pause he asks, "Does your grandma know?"

Knowing I won't answer him verbally, he glances up in my direction and I shake my head again. But then I add, "She'll kick me out when she finds out who the father is." Trying to blink back tears doesn't keep them at bay.

His eyes begin to aimlessly roam the room, he's thinking.

I let him.

"You can still go to the police," he whispers. He doesn't want to bring it up because it will upset me, but that doesn't stop the burn of embarrassment from creeping up my neck and the bile to rise in my throat.

I shake my head fiercely and my tone gets defensive. "No, that's not an option."

"Why not? He's a professor and he took advantage of you," he pleads.

"Exactly," I say exasperatedly. "He's my professor and no one would believe me." My words have dissolved into a torrent of tears. "*I went out to dinner with him when he asked me to. I let him kiss me in his office at school knowing he was married—*"

"You also said *no* when it mattered most," he cuts me off to gently remind me.

I'm shaking my head again. I don't know if it's to ward off the awful memory of what happened or to get him to stop talking. "I shouldn't have been there to begin with."

He stands and walks toward me slowly. When he's directly in front of me, he stops and says, "He *raped* you. That *will never* be your fault."

I remember that day like it was yesterday. I was in shock, numb, when I came home and I couldn't go to our apartment because I couldn't bear the thought of facing my grandma. Going through something like that changes a person: physically, emotionally, psychologically. I felt like she would be able to tell what happened with one look at me, and things between us would never be the same again. My shame drove me downstairs to the basement of the house instead of upstairs to our apartment. That's where Toby found me crying, shattered. He's probably the only person in the world who could've gotten me to tell the truth that night about what happened, because for some reason, I knew he wouldn't judge me. Toby might be a loner and have no one, but I think he's also one of the most compassionate people I've ever known. He's perpetually melancholy and that somehow translates into being perpetually in need of taking sadness from others, like he's willing to harbor sadness for the world so others have a chance at happiness because he thinks he doesn't.

Covering my face with my hands because I've always believed I was strong and I hate feeling weak, I say, "I could lose my scholarship if I reported him, Toby. You don't understand. My parents had nothing. My grandma has nothing. *I* have nothing. This degree is my only hope to change that. It was my mom's dream for me to go to college. I want to make a difference someday. That's not going to happen if I tell the world my English professor raped me and I'm having his baby." This feels like a nightmare that I can't wake up from.

"Are you keeping the baby?" Toby asks.

The thought never crossed my mind that I wouldn't. Abortion isn't something I can do and adoption isn't either. Half of this baby is mine, no matter how it was conceived.

"*It's mine*," I plead soberly, like that should explain everything.

He nods thoughtfully. "Do you really think your grandma would kick you out if she found out?"

"I can't tell her I was raped. I can't." The tears have stopped, and I look up at him so he knows how serious I am. "*I just can't.* You're the only one who knows my secret and it's going to stay that way."

He nods again, but he doesn't agree with my logic. "She needs you, she can't kick you out. She wouldn't do it."

"My grandma is the sweetest person I know, but if she found out the baby's father is a married man, she would never forgive me. Marriage is sacred." The final words stick in my throat. I always thought it was sacred to me too. I watched my parents, a white man and a black woman, endure prejudice and racist remarks in the name of love and the sanctity of marriage. Their relationship in the late sixties and seventies in this country was marginalized, rare, and inexplicably misunderstood by the majority. Which is bullshit, love is love, but that's how it was. I feel like I've betrayed them and the love they were forced to fight for. Guilt, I have so much guilt.

I'm looking at Toby's hands hanging at his sides. There's pencil lead smudged on his fingertips; he was drawing before he came down here. That small thought is a distraction that I grasp onto because I've seen his drawings and they're unbeliev-ably good.

His voice pulls me out of my thoughts like a swimmer trying, but failing, to tread water. "Hear me out before you say anything."

It wasn't a question, but I nod anyway.

"What if your grandma thought the baby was mine?"

I'm stunned, but I find the words to cut him off. "No. Abso-lutely not. I can't let you do that for me."

He tilts his head and licks his lips. "Hear me out," he repeats patiently. "She caught us kissing on the couch the day we...you know..." he trails off and shrugs and lets *slept together* go unsaid. "She already assumes we were dating. Maybe she still thinks we are."

She does. Neither Toby nor I have ever talked about what happened that day. It was two months before the incident with my professor. Toby came to our apartment to fix the stove. Grandma was taking a nap. We commiserated in our unspoken loneliness. It was profound that day, a driving force. We went from staring at each other, understanding and empathizing completely without words, to kissing with the same conviction within moments. One thing led to another; it was like we both turned our brains off and let emotion guide us into the blissful whirl of connection we both so desperately needed. Neither of us intended for it to go that far, but it was a combined force that neither of us wanted to stop. I will never forget the look on his face when he was inside me; it was devastatingly beautiful and tragic at the same time. He looked like someone who was suspended in the imagination of another person's vivid dream, taking in every detail because it didn't belong to him. He was curious but also knew it was impossible and wouldn't last. I felt the same way. So like a soap bubble, we both floated on it, inside it, until it burst and disappeared. Afterward, we dressed and kissed on the couch, trying to regain the magic. The magic didn't return because it wasn't supposed to. Grandma caught us, and we ended up standing in the hallway wholeheartedly thanking and apologizing to each other with our eyes, while awkwardly saying nothing with our mouths because that's how we both are. He may be quiet and I may be outspoken, but neither of us talk about feelings. We keep that shit bottled up tight. His eyes are soulful and honest. I'm looking at them now.

"I can't do that to you. *You* can't do that to you."

"Why not? Are you embarrassed of me?" He doesn't really ask the question as much as he determines it to be a universal truth. "I understand," he whispers, and all I hear is the lonely heart that's lived inside this broken boy as long as I've known him. It breaks my heart.

I should elaborate. I should tell him all the good I see in him that I'm sure he's never heard from anyone else. Because he doesn't *have* anyone else. And when he did have his mom, she was a bitch, especially to him. Instead, I go the logical route because, like I said, I don't do feelings. "If we said you were the dad, that's a lifelong job. Not that you would have to be responsible for the baby in a parental way at all, but you would be judged for not marrying me. You would be judged for us having different skin colors. You would be judged for not being an active father. There would be a stigma." I don't know what else to say, so I stop. *You're too good for that,* I should add, but I don't.

He looks like he wants to say something but then shakes his head to rearrange his thoughts, choosing his words meticulously. "What if...I wasn't around in a few years? I mean...what if after graduation I left...moved away...and you never saw me again? If we told your grandma now that I'm the father to get you through this and to get you through school, wouldn't that be worth it? I can just disappear in a few years...be the asshole...

unfortunately, that happens all the time, dads walking out on their kids. Especially young dads." He shrugs and it looks guilty because I know in my heart that if the baby were his, he would never walk out on them. "You can move on before then. I mean, you can date, obviously. We were never together, I wouldn't expect us to be now."

I smile sadly because I'm not sure where this guy came from, but I've never known anyone so selfless. I tease him because I can't do anything else, "No one is going to date a pregnant girl or a single mom with a newborn; I'm not worried about dating."

He almost rolls his eyes but stops short. "You know what I mean. I'm not trying to..." he searches for the right word, "...insinuate myself into your life. I'm just trying to...help."

I know, and my God, do I ever need help. My cheeks are mostly dry, but I mop my face off with my sleeve and sniff back my stuffy nose. "Can I think about it?" I ask him.

He nods, back to quiet Toby.

I wait until he goes to the locked storage room in the corner to grab a part and is walking back up the stairs before I say, "Thanks," because I know it makes him uncomfortable. He doesn't respond, I don't expect him to.

———————

TWO DAYS LATER, I KNOCKED ON HIS DOOR AND ACCEPTED his offer to step in and keep my secret. I was raised with religion, though most days I don't give it any thought. But today is the first day in my life that I've felt like guardian angels are real. And how lucky I am to have him as mine.

CHAPTER FORTY

Past, 1986
Stephanie

It's hard to focus when I'm flying like this.
I promised the last time that I was done.
That I was going to get clean.
Because I used to have dreams.
I still have dreams.
But then today happened.
And now I'm making the promise again.
Like I've done so many times before.
But still...
Still the promise, the dream, is gaining momentum and sometimes it feels like its pull is almost as powerful as the need to get high.
I want things to be different.
I want to change.
It's just so hard.

When I look into his eyes, the realization dawns that I'm not just thinking the words, I'm saying them out loud. I knew leaving the house in this state was a mistake, but I needed to.

"I just had to leave, I couldn't be there another minute," I say as I stand, the skin on the back of my bare thighs slick with sweat from sitting on the vinyl chair for too long.

Straightening my shorts that are too short to be straightened, I look him in the eye again nervously, and though he looks like he's trying to follow my free-flowing, disconnected discourse, I still feel like I need to escape.

"I should go," I blurt.

His voice is calm like it's been since he sat down. "Are you sure?" It's the calm, not the words, that lures me back into the seat without giving it further thought. I like listening to him.

Once seated, I stare at the scratches in the wooden tabletop under the glass covering it. I fixate on the ones that read *Frank was here* while he asks, "When's the last time you ate anything, Stephanie?"

I shrug. "This morning, I think." I can't say with one-hundred-percent certainty that's true, but I think it is.

"I'll be right back." I don't know how long he's gone because time races and creeps at the same time and my perception of it is unreliable. "Here, eat these." He slides a bowl of peanuts in front of me, and even though they aren't my favorite I dig in, because bar peanuts always taste better than regular peanuts.

"What's your dream?" he asks.

For a minute I think he's psychic because I've been thinking about it nonstop all day, but then I remember that I basically shared every secret thought with him not so long ago.

"I want to work with animals. Like at a vet's office. Or an animal shelter. I've always loved dogs." My stare pries from the tabletop to him. "They're easier than people," I admit. People cause pain. It feels weird to tell him all of this because I've never told anyone.

He nods. "I've never had a dog, but I can relate to people being difficult. I'm not so great with people either."

But you are, I want to say, but for some reason this is the one thought I don't let escape. He's listening. To me. People don't do that. They usually ignore me, especially my family. They used to listen. But then I started using and for a while all they wanted to do was talk at me. Not to me, *at me*. They told me all the things I already knew. All the things I was doing wrong. And when I didn't change—I didn't do the things they wanted me to do—they gave up, discouraged and angry. It took a surprisingly short amount of time for that to happen. You think your family is there no matter what. But *no matter what* is conditional and it has a time limit. It's like a messed up version of *cry wolf*—now that I want the help, their exhausted compassion won't let them hear it. So I don't bother.

"Have you applied for jobs at vet offices or animal shelters? You could even volunteer to get your foot in the door."

I shake my head. "I know they'll take one look at me and turn me away. That's what most people do." I didn't mean to say that out loud either, but I can't hold back.

"Don't give up on yourself."

People have said a variation on this sentiment many times before, but it's always been more about them than me. *Do you know what you giving up on yourself is doing to your father and me?* Or *It's killing me watching you give up on yourself.* That always made me feel worse, not better, because then it was crystal clear that I was hurting them more than I was hurting me. Which, by the way, is arguable because I feel like shit all the time.

My eyes are pulled back to him again, I think just to see if the look on his face matches the sincerity in his voice. It does. "I need to get clean."

He nods. It's merciful agreement that lacks pity. I like that. I like him. He's quiet and compassionate. Not at all what I came in here looking for tonight. I came into Dan's Tavern looking for a diversion, looking for someone who could help me forget who I am for a few hours. Instead, he found me and made me face who I am for a few hours.

"There are a few free programs in the city, or you can always go to Denver General Hospital—they can't turn anyone away."

I huff. It's not unkind; it's reflexive, ingrained doubt.

He tilts his head like he's trying to figure me out. "What? You don't think you can do it?"

I start to shake my head, but my dream screams at me from within to remind me it's still there and wants to be in charge. I shrug instead. "I don't know. I've been like this for so long it's hard to remember what I was like when I didn't need it."

He nods. "I understand." And it looks like he does. "But the thing is, you don't have to go back to who you were before. Time passes. People change. You just have to decide who you want to be today, and if you're not sure who that is, time and sobriety will help you decide."

It makes sense. This guy makes sense. "That kind of takes the pressure off," I say more to myself than to him.

He doesn't react, he understands.

From somewhere in the distance I hear, "Last call!"

"I should go," I say again, but it sounds different than it did before.

"Cab?" he asks.

I stall on the thought because my mind is still looping his words, *People change*, over and over in my mind. Distractedly, I answer, "No, I don't live far. I can walk from here."

"I'll walk with you. You shouldn't be walking around after dark by yourself in this neighborhood."

Normally I would be skeptical, guys only want to go home with girls for one reason. In fact, that's what I thought I was looking for tonight, so it's ironic that this is playing out the way it is.

He stands and offers his hand for me to take. I hesitate, not because I don't want to take it, but because no one's ever done this for me. Guys like him don't acknowledge girls like me. And they sure as hell don't walk down the street holding my hand.

When I take his hand, he must be able to tell I'm freaked out because he squeezes it once gently.

We walk a few blocks in silence and when I get my bearings, I stop in front of an apartment building and point with my thumb over my shoulder. "This is me."

He nods. "Good luck, Stephanie."

"Thank you." I don't even remember his name. But guarantee I will never forget him.

I walk toward the front door and he continues on in the opposite direction.

When he turns the corner, I backtrack down the sidewalk and don't stop walking until I step through the ER doors of Denver General Hospital.

And I tell them I need help.

THIRTY DAYS LATER, I WALK OUT OF A REHAB FACILITY. Clean. Program complete.

Six months later, I start a veterinarian technician program.

Forever thankful that I walked into Dan's Tavern that night looking for an escape.

Because I finally did.

Escape.

All thanks to a stranger who will never know what his words helped me find.

CHAPTER FORTY-ONE

Past, 1987
Cliff

There are things in life that have changed me.
Things I don't talk to anybody about.
Because I can't.
"Toughen up, boy," my pops would tell me.
My friends would laugh. And call me a pussy. Or a loser.
Or both.
When I was ten, my mom died. She'd been sick for a while and didn't go to the doctor because she thought she would get better. She didn't. Cancer doesn't get better on its own. She was the nicest person I've ever known. I wish I would've told her that when she was alive. I wish I would've thanked her for making me grilled cheese every Friday night because it was my favorite; and holding me when I was little and scared but trying to pretend like I wasn't; and asking how my day was when she got home from her job at the dry cleaners every night, even

though I only ever told her, "It was fine." She knew that was usually a lie. My mom always knew.

Losing her changed me. I was always kind of a brat when I was a kid, but losing her turned me into a dickhead. It's not her fault. She was the best part of our family. It's like taking the referee off the football field—the game turns into a free-for-all. My pops and I never got along, deep down I was a momma's boy, but I looked up to him. Because that's what you're supposed to do and I thought I had to. I didn't know I had a choice. He was the flashy one, the smooth talker, the tough guy. He hustled—begged, borrowed, and stole—while she prayed for him to change. Literally prayed on her knees every Wednesday night and Sunday morning at Cathedral Basilica of the Immaculate Conception near our apartment. I know because I went with her sometimes. Not because I thought he could be saved, or I could be saved, or even to confess my sins, I went because being close to her and her faith made me feel like maybe her good would rub off on me a little.

All the praying didn't help. She died and my pops didn't change. He stole a car at gunpoint, got caught, and went to jail instead. And I never stepped inside a church again. What's the point? There's no way her good can rub off now. It's gone.

Losing my pops changed me too. It's not like he died, but sometimes I think he may as well have. He doesn't want me to visit him. The first few months I wrote him letters. Dozens of letters. He didn't write back. I went from being a dick to being a reckless dick. My pops made me live with my mom's drunk brother because there was nowhere else for me to go. I drank. I did drugs. I picked the worst kids at my new school to hang out with. I shoplifted. I vandalized. Basically, I did everything I could to try to forget how alone I was.

Here's something I'll never admit out loud—I'm scared. Of a lot of stuff. I'm scared that I'll always be alone. I'm scared that this is as good as it gets. Hanging around with friends who aren't really friends and make fun of me behind my back. And sometimes to my face. I pretend not to let it bother me when they make cracks about my weight, but the fat jokes get old. I've heard them all because kids started telling them in kindergarten. That was a *long* time ago. It feels even longer when you're the butt of the joke. *Every joke.* I've never had a girlfriend, never kissed a girl, never even had a girl look at me and smile the way they do when they have a crush.

On someone.

Who will never be me.

Being alone sucks.

But today something changed.

Changed me.

Toby stood up for me.

He took the fall when I stole those cigarettes.

Because *he* didn't want *me* to get in trouble.

For someone with family and friends, it may seem small, but when you don't have either it changes you. For a minute, it felt like my mom was back. Like someone had *my* back.

I don't know why I steal. I guess because I figure *why not?* It's not like I'm going to graduate, or find a decent job, or find a good girl, get married, and buy into the house and white picket fence dream. That shit only happens in movies. In real life, in my neighborhood, people scrape by with crappy, minimum wage jobs if they're honest, and crappy, maximum risks "jobs" if they aren't. They hook-up because they're horny and desperate, and then fight, lie, and pray on their knees if they're Catholic, until one of them leaves, or dies, or goes to jail.

Then the cycle repeats.

But then Toby goes and saves me from myself and I'm sitting here in my room at twenty past two in the morning rethinking some things.

Here's another thing I would never admit out loud—I want to be like Toby. The first week I lived with Johnny, Toby annoyed the hell out of me; I think, because we're so different from each other. But the longer I shared an apartment with him and watched him, I slowly started to respect him. I didn't want to at first because that word is hard for me—*respect*. It gets stuck in my throat like it doesn't belong, maybe because my pops always said, "You *will* respect me," in our house. The more he said it, the less my mom and I did. If we ever even did to begin with.

But Toby is different. He doesn't demand it. He moves through this house, he moves through the neighborhood, *quietly*, but he's watching. He's always watching. For someone he can help. I've seen it. Because I watch him when he thinks I'm not. He helps, sometimes it's something small and sometimes it's something big that will change someone's life.

Not his own, someone else's.

He's smart. He always knows the right words to use that make him sound older and like maybe we didn't grow up in the same neighborhood, even though I know we did. He can draw, and I mean *draw*. Draw like people who have so much bottled up inside them that they have to let it out onto paper or it will start a fire inside and burn them alive. Then when it's on paper, people looking at it can feel all the feelings that created it and pay big money for it so they can get that high any time they want because it's theirs now. A little piece of him is theirs. To feed off of when they need a fix. He could be *that guy* someday.

I get it. I get wanting to feel what he feels. Because it's intense. Intense like I've never known intense. I see the way he looks at people, at things, at situations—like his life depends on it—and the fact that it's all done in silence most of the time only amps it up. Most people don't notice because they think he's kind of an asshole. It takes a dick to know a dick—*he's not a dick.* He just wants people to think he is.

I see him.

So I'm lying in bed, staring out of the dirty window at the roof of the house next door, thinking about how much I owe Toby for this afternoon. I would've gotten caught. I would've gone to juvie. I would've stayed there until I'm eighteen. That's a long time. I like to think I'd be tough and handle it okay, but deep down I know I wouldn't. I can't even watch *Sid and Nancy* without crying. I'm soft, that's what my pops always said and he sounded really, *really* disappointed when he did. I guess he's right. And soft wouldn't do well locked up with kids who aren't.

I'm also thinking about the fact that not only did Toby take the fall for what I did, but he didn't tell Johnny the truth. He could've ratted me out when the cop brought him home.

But he didn't.

I think that blew my mind more than anything. More than taking the cigarettes from me, more than telling me to shut up and go home, more than seeing him in handcuffs—*he didn't tell Johnny.* And now Johnny's pissed and disappointed in him. He could fire him. He could throw him out. He could ruin his life.

But Toby took that risk.

For me.

I owe him.

Someday I'll repay the favor.

Until then, I'm going to try to do better.

I'm going to try not being a dick for a while.

Fingers crossed, because I have no idea how to be anything else.

NOTE FROM THE AUTHOR:

I'm talking to you.

The one whose pain is unbearable.

The one drowning in hopelessness.

The one feeling completely unworthy of being loved.

The one who's lonely, even in a crowded room surrounded by friends.

The one thinking that the world would be better if you didn't exist.

I see you.

I've been you.

You are so loved.

You matter.

You make a difference in others' lives in ways you'll never know.

Just like Toby.

You fill a place in space and time that is yours and yours alone.

Because no other human being—past, present, or future—can be you.

You'll get through this.
I promise.

Talk to someone.
Right now.
Please.

You can call the National Suicide Prevention Lifeline 24/7 (1-800-273-8255).

Or log-on to www.suicidepreventionlifeline.org to chat anytime.

Or send a text to 741-741.

PART THREE

When The Other Side is introduced to reality, lives change.

CHAPTER FORTY-TWO

PRESENT, June 1987
Toby

WHEN I OPEN MY EYES, IT'S DARK.
My clock reads 12:12 a.m.
It takes several seconds for me to adjust to wakefulness.
And to being alive.
I'm lying, fully clothed, on top of my sleeping bag.
My head is thumping like a bass drum and I'm still tired.
So damn tired.
I don't know if it's fatigue.
Or the desolation that fills me.
Eight hours ago, I literally held my own death in my hand.
Thirty-one sleeping pills. I put them in my mouth.
Started crying.
And spit them out.
I couldn't do it.
After all this time, I couldn't do it.

All I could hear were Alice's last words to me: *You're worth fighting for. You have* no fucking idea *how much I wish you realized it and started fighting for yourself.* Suddenly, I wanted so badly to believe her. And to start fighting. For myself.

Feeling around for my lamp in the dark, I click it on. The pills and the pill bottle are gone. My backpack is gone. In its place is a paper plate with a ham and cheese sandwich, potato chips, and a glass of water. I drink the water first and then eat the food that I'm guessing Johnny left. When I'm done, my bladder is screaming. I don't want to face anyone, but the apartment is so quiet I figure Johnny and Cliff are asleep and the coast is clear.

When I push open my door that wasn't fully closed, I discover I'm wrong. The light spills out to find Johnny facing me. He's sitting in the dark in the middle of the kitchen about four feet from my bedroom door on the uncomfortable, rickety chair that the answering machine is usually perched on. Stepping out, the first thing I see is the pill bottle in one hand, and the letter I left him in the other. My eyes climb slowly to meet his: they're swollen, rimmed in red, and bloodshot like he's been punishing them for days. Neither of us say anything when I move quickly into the bathroom. After I pee and wash my hands, I put the stopper in the sink and fill it with cold water, plunging my face under. Scrubbing at it underwater in the hopes that it will bring alertness or some semblance of clarity for the conversation that I know is about to unfold. The world's two worst communicators are about to go head-to-head and I'm not looking forward to it. While I'm preparing myself, I hear Johnny ask Cliff to go wait out in the hall and give us some privacy. Which is considerate, but ineffective because the walls are thin. He'll probably be able to hear just as much from the hallway as he would from his room. But whatever.

When I hear the door to the apartment open and shut, I

walk out, pass Johnny, and go back into my room and shut the door.

"Please come out, Toby. I need to talk to you." His voice is hoarser than normal.

Leaning my back against my side of the door, I slide down and pull my knees to my chest. "I can't come out. Let's talk like this," I counter. I don't sound defiant, I sound defeated.

"Why?" He sounds defeated too.

"Because I can't take the disappointment in your eyes right now," I tell him. I guess I'm going for all-out honesty tonight. No more hiding.

"Toby, I'm not disappointed in *you*. I'm disappointed in *me*." It's the same brutal, aching pain I saw in his eyes searing through his vocal cords. "I'd like to talk to you face-to-face, but if this makes it easier for you, that's fine."

He pauses, I guess for me to answer, but I don't. I'm not trying to be an asshole, I'm trying to choose my words wisely and be selective. Because I know they matter.

"I've seen some horrific stuff in my life. I did three tours in Vietnam during the war, but nothing compares to seeing you lying on the floor in your room with this bottle in your hand and pills scattered everywhere. I've never been so scared in my life, Toby. I thought I lost you."

The unmistakable pain in his words forces me to say, "I couldn't go through with it."

A muffled sob tears through him, reverberating through the door and me. I've never heard a grown man cry like this. Well, except for me, I suppose. "Thank God," he says quietly.

We can come back to this, but I need to talk about something else before I start crying too. "Why didn't you mail my mom the graduation invitation?"

He sniffs. "Like I said earlier, I was selfish."

I lower my chin to my chest then gently rock back against

the door out of frustration and immediately regret it when the thumping starts up in my temples again. "That tells me nothing, Johnny."

"She didn't deserve to be there—"

I cut him off because I'm starting to get pissed all over again, "*Not your call to make*. I worked *my ass off* in school to prove a point to Marilyn Page. I wanted her there to see her *stupid* son graduate with honors." My blood pressure is rising, so is my volume. "*She should've been there!*"

The chair creaks and a few seconds later it creaks again and I hear him blow his nose. "You're the reason I quit drinking." Not what I expected him to say. He continues, like now that he's started he can't stop. "You're the reason I go to my AA meetings every week, even though I'd rather go to Dan's instead. You're the reason when I stuck a gun in my mouth six years ago, I didn't pull the trigger. You're the reason I try to redeem myself in some small way every day. I usually fail, but I try. You're the reason I want to get better. To *be* better."

I'm shaking my head and I'm crying. I don't know if it's because of the things he's saying or because of the way he's saying them. He genuinely means it, but it makes no sense.

When he begins to repeat, "I didn't mail Marilyn the invitation because I was selfish—" I cut him off impatiently.

Inside my head, I'm screaming to get his attention. Apparently, I don't have the discretion to filter myself and the screaming isn't confined to my mind. "Tell me what the hell is going on!"

He roars back in anguish, "*I wanted to watch my son graduate!*"

Silence ripples through the air between us like a shockwave.

That I absorb over and over...and over again. I want to reject the news, but I can't because deep down I know he's telling the truth. We're too much alike for this to be a lie. Same eyes, same shitty demeanor, same inability to show or share feelings, same avoidance issues—*we are the same asshole.*

It's been quiet for minutes before Johnny prompts, "Toby, please say something, even if it's to tell me to go to hell."

I'm still in shock. *"You and Marilyn?"* I can't picture him with my mom. I don't know how old Johnny is, but he's nowhere near my mom's age.

"No," he whispers regretfully.

The silence ripples again, but this time it only leaves me confused. "What do you mean, *no?*"

"Marilyn raised you, but she wasn't your mom."

I know he finished his thought, but it dangles just out of my reach because I refuse to process it. I'm hugging my knees to my chest so tight it's painful to breathe. My head starts shaking back and forth and I can't stop the compulsive denial. The tears have come for me and I close my eyes to blot out the blur. The pain of this new reality.

Johnny's voice is just on the other side of the door when he speaks again and it's brokenhearted. "I'm so sorry, Toby."

The image of her bleeding out is all I can see, my nightmares rushing in relentlessly, and I can't catch my breath. I croak out her name. "Nina?"

"Nina," he confirms. It sounds like two decades of regret. "She didn't want you to know."

I'm still shaking my head, but it's not relieving any of the torment, so I ball my fist and punch the wall with everything in me. The pain radiates out from my knuckles and pulsates up my arm when the drywall gives way. *"Fuck!"* It's filled with frustration, pain, confusion, grief, regret, guilt, and shame.

"You okay?" The question comes immediately.

Far from it. I know that question wasn't related to my

mental instability but was focused on the destruction he just heard. "No. Neither is your wall."

"I'm not worried about the wall, Toby. Do you need ice?"

He sounds worried, like he wants to open the door to check on me, so I shake my hand out and grit my teeth through the pain. "No," and then I ask bewilderedly, "How?"

He knows we're back to Nina. For the first time I hear the click of his Zippo light a cigarette, he usually doesn't go this long without one. "Do you want one?"

Before I answer, a cigarette and the lighter slide under the door. The floor is filthy, but I pick the cigarette up and place it between my lips without hesitation and light up. Closing my eyes, I breathe in the calm and blow it out several times before the tears subside. Wiping my nose on my sleeve, I slide the lighter back out to signal my shit is in check for the moment and we can proceed.

"I enlisted in the Marines the summer after I graduated from high school. Two nights before I shipped out to basic training, my buddy threw me a going-away party at his cousin's house not far from here. The place filled up fast with high school and college kids, a lot of them I didn't recognize. It didn't take long before I was wasted. I ran into Nina standing in line at the keg. I thought she was pretty and told her so. We started talking and even though she was a little shy, she was really funny and just...nice. Before long, we were making out and one thing led to another."

Flicking the ash onto the paper plate that my sandwich was on earlier, I stop him because I'm doing the math in my head. "She was only fourteen."

His inhale and exhale are long and loud repentance. "She told me she was eighteen and I believed her. She looked older. She acted older."

I believe him, but it's then that I hear Alice's voice in my head when I told her about my first kiss with my neighbor. I understand why she asked the question because rage is swelling. "Was it consensual?"

His answer is immediate. "*Of course*, I would never force myself on anyone. I can be an asshole, but I'm not a rapist, Toby."

I can't picture a fourteen-year-old Nina, but I believe him. "Then what happened?"

"I told her before we did anything that I was leaving town and wouldn't be back. We both knew it was a one-night thing. I left for basic training and then shipped out to Vietnam. I didn't come back to Denver for four years, and when I did, I was a disaster. The war changed me: I couldn't hold down a job, I couldn't go more than a day without a drink, I moved around a lot and slept on friends' couches or sometimes on the street. Then my parents died. We were estranged at that point, I hadn't talked to them in years, but their will was outdated and made while I was still in high school. They left me this house that was a rental property. Cliff's mom, my younger sister, got the house we grew up in. Their minimal savings was split between the two of us. I moved in and took over as landlord here. As you well know, I'm shit at the job.

"One day eight years ago, someone knocked on my door asking about the apartment for rent ad in the newspaper, her mom and brother were looking for a place. It was Nina. I recognized her immediately and she recognized me too. I showed her the apartment. You and Marilyn moved in the next day. As soon as I saw you, I knew you were mine. I confronted her and she told me the whole story. When she got pregnant, she told her mom she didn't know who the father was, only that he was a soldier headed to Vietnam, which was true. A month before she delivered you, she was diagnosed with bipolar disorder. She threatened suicide the day after you were born and was held under psychiatric observation until you were ready to be released from the hospital. Rather than putting you up for adoption, her mom took you, fearing that Nina would try to kill herself if you were taken away. Nina knew she was too young and too unstable to raise you and agreed to it.

"Marilyn always blamed Nina's mental health issues on her pregnancy with you, which is a crock of shit. That's why she always held a grudge against you. Marilyn was delusional. It got worse with time. When Nina found me, she wanted me to take you, but you were ten, and I was an alcoholic with night terrors who couldn't function in the real world. The thought of fucking up your life with my influence and instability was unconscionable. Instead, I insisted that Nina make sure that Marilyn stayed with you in this house until you graduated, and I promised to keep an eye on you. I only charged Marilyn for utilities and she never questioned why the rent was so cheap. From one alcoholic to another, I understood her detachment from reality."

My mind is reeling, but when he pauses to light another cigarette, I ask, "Nina was bipolar? Why didn't I ever know that?"

"They hid a lot from you. Obviously. But I'm not one to talk in that department. I'm sorry," he says solemnly. "When Nina was medicated, she handled it valiantly. She was just a nice, caring girl with a great sense of humor. But when she wasn't medicated, it's because she decided to medicate with something else, usually heroin, and that's when she went off the rails. Addiction consumed her. Toby, I really didn't know Nina that well. She lived like a gypsy, coming and going all the time. We talked occasionally, mostly about you. But through our interactions, I did see both sides of Nina and the difference was startling, like two different people. She struggled. She was in and out of rehab several times and OD'd twice that I know of."

"Three times," I correct him. "I knew about the drug use. She couldn't walk away from it for long before it lured her back in. That's when she'd disappear and we didn't see her for months on end. I didn't know that's what was going on until I was thirteen. My mom...Marilyn hid that too."

"Yeah. Two addicts covering for each other is a volatile pairing."

"I guess I never saw it that way. They were always at odds. Always fighting."

"I'm not going to pretend I know anything about their relationship, only what I witnessed firsthand. It wasn't healthy. The fighting or the covering for each other."

I feel like I'm in the *Twilight Zone*. I know I lived in chaos, but I didn't realize I lived in the middle of such a big lie. "Everything was a lie."

"The adults in your life tried to do their best, but their best was shit because they were a mess. That's not your fault, Toby. That's *our* fault. I'm sorry you suffered for it. I know the saying, 'Too little, too late,' is ironic and cliché in this situation, and you'd probably punch me in the face if you could right now, and I wouldn't blame you. But I want to make it up to you. I'm finally sober. I'm finally in therapy dealing with stuff I should've dealt with fifteen years ago when I was discharged. I want to be a dad to you. I want to be in your life. I want to be *involved* in your life. I want a chance to really get to know you because you're one of the toughest people I've ever met."

I huff out what sounds like a laugh but is anything but. "I was going to kill myself. I'm not tough."

"But you didn't," he reminds me. "And depression isn't about weakness, it's about battling and wanting to deaden the pain, not the person."

Which reminds me. "How did you know when you came in

my room and found me asleep with the pills that I hadn't taken any?"

Before Johnny can answer, Cliff yells from the hall, "Because I knew you had the pills and I knew how many you had. I found them months ago. I go through your room when you're not here, remember?"

I close my eyes and shake my head, but I'm kind of proud of him for admitting it out loud in front of Johnny and manning up. "I know. That needs to stop," I yell back.

"It will," Johnny answers with an authoritative edge to his voice. "Cliff and I had a long talk while you were sleeping."

The front door opens and closes and I hear Cliff's shuffling footsteps on the linoleum. "I also swapped out the sleeping pills for...what do you call it?" He snaps his fingers a few times to try to resurrect the word that's evading him.

"Placebos?" Johnny and I say in unison—Johnny's is said knowingly, and mine is suggested incomprehensibly.

He snaps one more time. "Yeah, I swapped them for placebos. Same number and color so you wouldn't notice." He sounds proud of himself. That's new for Cliff because it's not the jackass boasting he usually does.

"How did you get placebos?" I ask bewildered.

I hear Johnny clear his throat in fatherly disappointment, apparently this must've been part of this afternoon's come-to-Jesus talk.

There's hesitation before Cliff admits, "The dude who used to sell us weed sells other stuff too, mostly pills and acid. He mixes in placebos to stretch his inventory."

"Industrious," I deadpan.

"Right?" Cliff exclaims, as if he agrees with the compliment he thinks I just gave.

Johnny sighs in exasperation and I know he's scrubbing his

hands up and down his face like he does when he's frustrated. "That was sarcasm, Cliff."

"Oh," Cliff says.

Johnny brings us back to the story and my question. "When we found you, Cliff told me about the pills and going through your room. He counted the pills and made sure they were all the same ones he'd swapped out. Pills and amount matched, so we knew you hadn't taken anything. That you'd just fallen asleep."

I'm nodding my head absently. Thoroughly stunned by his thoughtfulness. "You could've saved my life if I'd gone through with swallowing them, Cliff."

His reply is delayed and quieter than usual. "Yeah, well you kind of saved mine too...so we're even."

I'm confused. "No, I didn't."

"The day you took the rap for me at the QuikMart. I would've gone to juvie and you knew that and you stepped in for me. I'm too pretty for juvie, Toby. It would've been ugly."

I can't help it and a chuckle silently vibrates in my chest. He's trying to joke because this conversation is too serious for him to deal with, hell, it's too serious for all of us to deal with, but we need this. We needed this a long time ago.

"Anyway, things changed that day. I realized some stuff. I don't want to be a fuck-up. I don't want to be like my pops. I don't want to be in and out of jail my whole life. I'm not the smartest guy, I know that, but I want to graduate and get a job afterward. I want to make something of myself."

This doesn't sound like the Cliff I've known for the past year, but I say the only thing I can say because I mean it. "Good for you, Cliff. That's all you."

"When you're used to being kicked down, I guess all it takes is that one person who comes along and stands up for you instead. That can change everything. Besides, now we're cousins, which means we have to be bros, right?"

"I'm still not watching *Sid and Nancy* with you." I sound serious, but he knows I'm just giving him a hard time. "I'll try not to act like an asshole since you're trying not to act like a dick."

He laughs, but it sounds watery like he might be crying. "Deal."

It's quiet for a minute before Cliff says, "Johnny, we should go out in the hall, there are a few more people who want to talk to Toby."

"What?" Johnny sounds weary but surprised.

Cliff pleads his case. "Yeah. I went and talked to a few people in the house earlier while you guys were discussing family stuff. People who I know care about Toby. I think he needs to hear them out."

The chair Johnny is sitting on creaks under his weight and screeches on the linoleum when he stands. Then I hear the door open.

"Hi, Chantal," Johnny's greeting is friendly even though it's after one o'clock in the morning now and I know he's exhausted.

"Hey, Johnny. I want you guys to stay, you should hear this too. And Alice, you should come in here." The nerves are evident, maybe not to people who don't know Chantal well, but I can hear them.

More footsteps enter the room. "Hi, everyone. Hi, Toby." I've thought it before, but sadness is all wrong in Alice.

I want to open the door and hug her. But I don't because even after everything that's happened the past hour, I can't face them. "Hi, Alice."

"Toby isn't ready to come out of his room yet and face this

full-on, but he's listening. I promise you, he's listening," Johnny explains.

Chantal half coughs, half clears her throat, she does this when she's ramping up to say something she doesn't really want to say. "I'm not quite sure where to start. Other than my grandma, Toby, you're the one person in my life that I always know I can count on. You've helped me more times than I can count and you've never asked for anything in return. Joey," her voice cracks on his name and then her voice breaks down, "is so lucky to have you in his life."

That's all it takes for the lump to return to my throat.

"That little boy loves you. You spend time with him. You play with him. You read to him. You feed him. You hold him for hours when he sleeps because you know you'll wake him if you try to put him in his crib. You buy diapers when I'm running low. And formula. I know whenever I find a plastic shopping bag hanging on the outside of our door that you put it there and it always seems to come just when he needs it most. I know when you do that, you go without so that he doesn't." Tears have distorted the words. She sniffles and then I hear her blow her nose.

"He's a good dad," Johnny says quietly. I picture him trying to awkwardly comfort her. They both aren't touchy-feely people, so I bet it's not going well.

She sniffles again. "He's the best person I know. Toby, I know that I get stressed and I get busy and that I worry about me and Joey and my grandma. Sometimes I forget that other people have problems too because our problems seem so big that I can't see past them. I let you down. I always knew you carried around this sadness, but I never realized how profoundly heavy it was. I never saw that it was smothering you. I guess I figured that because you always found it in you to be there for us that it wasn't that bad." She sniffles again and the next words are quiet. "But I never asked. *I never asked*," she repeats. "I should've checked in with you like you've checked in with me."

I interrupt her because she's being too hard on herself. "You have plenty on your plate. It wasn't your job to take care of me too."

"But I should've asked you if you were doing okay." It sounds like an agonizing apology. "Just once, I should've been there for you. I wasn't. And I'm so sorry for that." We're all quiet for several seconds before she starts in again. "Toby, tonight when Cliff came and knocked on our door and told us what happened, I felt like I'd been punched in the gut. The pain of what could've been was quickly followed up by the relief that it didn't. Don't you *ever* scare us like that again. I know I'm horrible at telling people how I feel, but I care about you, Toby. I care about your happiness and your future. I've been doing a lot of soul-searching the past hour and I've decided it's time everyone knows the truth, including my grandma. You've sacrificed yourself way too long to protect me."

I hear the chair creak again. I don't know if Johnny decided he needed to take a seat to hear the news or if Chantal sat down because she can't get through this standing.

"A little over a year ago..." She stops to quell the emotion that's rising.

"Chantal, you don't have to tell them. It's okay. Don't do this for me," I beg.

"I was raped," she continues as if I didn't speak, "by my English professor. I got pregnant. With Joey." I hear pacing, it's Johnny. He does this when he's trying to solve a problem. I hear the click of his lighter, followed quickly by another cigarette and the Zippo sliding under the door for me.

I gladly accept the calm, light up, and slide the lighter back out when I've taken a few drags.

Silence stretches on. Everyone is processing. I close my eyes and focus on breathing in the nicotine.

"Joey isn't Toby's?" Johnny finally asks.

"No." Chantal's guilt is a burden she carries with her every day. I know that. But I don't think I've ever truly felt the gravity of it until now.

"Chantal, you don't have to talk about this. It was my idea, Johnny. Chantal didn't want anyone to know what happened, so I offered to help. You know...so nobody had to know who his real dad was."

"Shit," Johnny says, and in that one word, I hear his shock at the situation and his alarm on Chantal's behalf.

"Yeah," Chantal seconds. "Shit."

More silence.

"Did you go to the police?" Alice finally asks.

"No," Chantal whispers. "You have no idea how ashamed I am to say that in front of all of you, but I couldn't do it. I knew no one would believe me." Her voice is thick again.

Johnny's voice is soft when he says, "I have a friend who's a cop. I've known him since we were kids, he's a good guy. If you ever change your mind and want to talk to someone, to report it..." he trails off like he doesn't know what else to say.

"I don't think I'm quite there yet, but thanks, Johnny." She's not, but I hope she gets there someday. "Everyone knows, so you're off the hook, Toby. You don't have to pretend any longer."

"I don't regret anything I did for Joey, I hope you know that."

She huffs out an almost laugh and it's admiration. "Of course you don't, because you're selfless. And good. You know, there are

310 · KIM HOLDEN

so many times I've wished that Joey *was* yours. So many times I've prayed that he grows up knowing you. That you never move on and out of his life. I don't know what your future holds or where it will take you, but I hope you'll only be a phone call away for him."

"Uncle Toby?" I suggest.

"Uncle Toby sounds perfect." She's smiling, I can hear it.

"Okay," I agree.

"I'm going to go now; I need to get to bed. Thank you for not leaving us tonight. We need you in the world because you make it a better place."

I don't say anything. I know she doesn't expect me to.

The front door opens and shuts amid shuffling and a myriad of goodbyes.

"Good night, Alice. We're going to leave you two alone and get to bed," Johnny says and then he adds, "Thanks for coming. You're the best thing that's ever happened to Toby."

"Good night," she says softly.

"Night, Alice," Cliff says, and I notice that he called her by her name instead of calling her *the hot girl from downstairs.* And then Cliff's voice is closer, like his lips are pressed against the crack in my door. "You know I always thought Joey wasn't yours, but I couldn't figure out why you'd lie for her."

"I just tried to make things easier," I answer.

"Yeah," he says in understanding. "I also know about all those girls you left Dan's with every Friday night, that you just took them home. That nothing ever happened." I would expect taunting from him, but it's not.

"Yeah, well, we can't all be a ladies' man like you, Cliff. How'd you know?"

"Johnny paid me a few times to follow you." He's laughing, the bastard.

"What?" I say incredulously.

"I couldn't do it myself," Johnny explains. "I was too drunk, but I wanted to make sure you were being safe. Turns out you were just making sure *they* were safe."

"Nina was abused. By several men. I saw her in all of those women. I just wanted to make sure that, at least for one night, someone was looking out for them." I've never talked about my Friday nights before.

"I know, and I've never questioned your integrity or character since. You're a good kid. A good man," says Johnny solemnly.

I want to open the door and hug Johnny, but my mind is still reeling and trying to process everything. I can't do the father-son thing yet; there's time for that later today.

I wait until I hear both of their bedroom doors shut and Cliff's TV turn on before I rise and open my door.

Alice is standing next to the refrigerator, her hands clasped in front of her. She looks a little unsure and I realize how weird this all must've been for her, with me in my room and everyone else crammed in the kitchen. I wonder if she even knew who was in the room with her. Let alone the conversations she overheard. My mind is racing and I blurt out, "I'm sorry, Alice."

Her face crumples and tears form in her eyes. "Toby." Her outstretched arms are an invitation that I gladly walk into.

I hug her.

The hug lasts minutes.

It's more than an embrace—it's apologies for the past and promises for the future. It's solace, and safety, and reassurance, and friendship, and want, and need, and acceptance, and forgiveness. It's contentment. It's love.

I've only ever felt like this with Alice. I never really knew what it was other than foreign. And disconcertingly lovely. I didn't know what to do with it.

Her arms are wrapped around my back and the material of my sweatshirt is balled up in both of her fists like she never wants to let go. I don't either. I kiss the side of her head and whisper, "I'm so sorry." The hitch in her breath is the first signal she's crying. I pull back and cradle her face in my hands, wiping away her tears.

Her bottom lip quivers. "Did you really want to kill yourself, Toby?"

I kiss her forehead before I whisper, "I had the pills in my mouth and you know what made me spit them out?"

A hiccupping intake of air precedes a fresh wave of tears. "What?"

"*You*. I heard your voice telling me, 'You're worth fighting for,' and I guess I believed it might be true and wanted to wake up another day to find out. I wanted to fight."

"You are worth fighting for," she whispers.

"And I wanted to see you again. To talk to you. I don't even know who your favorite band is. Or if you sleep with your socks on. Or if you've ever traveled outside of Colorado. I don't know where you want to be in two years. Or if you like pancakes. I have so many questions. You're the first person I've ever wanted to know everything about...I need more time with you."

"Depeche Mode. Yes. Not yet. In a studio recording a Wonderland album. And I love pancakes but only if they're unmercifully drenched in blueberry syrup." Her small smile is lopsided because the sadness is still clinging to her. "You need to talk to someone, Toby."

"I know. And I will." I will. After tonight's unearthing of secrets I know I'm not alone and that kind of changes everything.

She rests her head on my shoulder again. She's tired.

"How was your show tonight?" I ask.

She shrugs. "We didn't play."

I stiffen reflexively because I suspect it's my fault.

She must feel it because she rubs my back. "I came to see if

I could persuade you to come with us around four o'clock and Johnny told us what happened." Her chest rises and falls exaggeratedly with the pause. "I was a mess. So was Taber. We canceled."

"I'm sorry," I whisper again.

"Don't be. People we love are more important than a gig. There will be other gigs. There will never be another Toby Page."

I don't know what to say, but I don't let that stop me. "I know I'm a mess, Alice. And that I don't deserve someone like you, but after I deal with all the shit that's going on inside my head and get some help, can we start over?"

"You're not a mess, Toby, you're human. One of my favorite things about you is that you feel completely and you care endlessly. You just need to start talking. If you need me to wait and give you some space while you figure this out, I'll do it. But I'm not the type of person who abandons people while they're going through tough stuff. You don't scare me, Toby Page. People aren't perfect. It's not about loving them when it's easy and convenient; it's about loving them even more when it's hard."

"I'm so tired, Alice." Mind, body, memory, nerves, reasoning, will—it's all tired.

She presses her lips to the underside of my jaw and whispers, "I know. Someday soon you won't be though, I promise."

I know I shouldn't ask but... "I don't want you to leave."

"I can stay."

"I can stay," I repeat it quietly. Three words that mean something completely different than they did yesterday. I've given myself permission to stay. I don't have to leave. "Should we sleep out on the fire escape? We can share my sleeping bag."

"Absolutely." Her eyelids are drooping, but her agreement is ardent.

Releasing her, I kiss her lips softly. A quick peck. "I'll grab the sleeping bag and my pillow."

"I'm going to run down to my apartment. I need to grab something and let Taber know I'm staying with you tonight. I'll meet you outside in a minute." She's at the door before I can say anything.

While I'm waiting outside for Alice, I pull my wallet out of my pocket and take the familiar slip of worn paper from it. *The Count-Out*. Negative one day. I made it to the other side. The paper is soft and rubbed through in spots from being folded and unfolded so many times and slid in and out of my wallet for two years. When I tear it in half, it surrenders without resistance. I tear it again and again until it's nothing but confetti, and then I let it fall to the ground three stories below.

When Alice climbs the ladder, I'm teetering on the edge of sleep. "I'm right here," I whisper while reaching out to gently touch her calf.

She responds by reaching down for my hand and letting me guide her into the sleeping bag next to me. It's warm out tonight, so I have it unzipped. There's plenty of room because I'm hanging halfway out of it so she'll be comfortable. Lying on her side, she faces me and I do the same until our noses are touching. And then she pushes play on her Walkman and holds one headphone near her ear and I hold the other half near mine.

As the first notes of what I know is going to be The Cure's new album come to life in my ear, Alice whispers sleepily, "Are the stars out, Toby?"

My eyes are closed, but I know the answer because I looked at the sky the moment I stepped outside. It's the first thing I do every time I walk outside when it's dark now. "They're all out and they're breathtaking. Like you."

Her response is a kiss. It's slow and sleepy, but even

minutes before her body is sure to surrender to rest, she's intrepid and deliberate and loving.

As Robert Smith sings about *touching the sky*, I breathe the words I've felt, feared, and ignored for weeks, "I love you."

Alice's lips twist into a slight, knowing smile against my mouth. "Remember the first time you took me to Wax Trax and I asked you what made your pulse race, Toby?"

"Yes," I whisper against her lips.

"Were you describing me, the same way I was describing you?"

"Yes," I repeat.

Her smile grows. "That's the day I fell in love with you." I kiss her as she says, *you*.

The tug of sleep is relentless and before I give in to it, I murmur, "Most nights I have nightmares. Sometimes I cry out in my sleep. If that freaks you out, you don't have to stay."

"Sometimes I wet the bed." She's trying to lighten the mood and make me laugh.

"No, you don't," I counter.

"You don't scare me, Toby." Her reassurance, once again, is so unbelievably welcome.

And that's where we leave it.

Her warm breath feathers across my face for a count of nineteen before I lose track and drift off.

CHAPTER FORTY-THREE

Present, June 1987
Toby

When I wake, the sun is high overhead and I'm sweating from the heat in the air, the sleeping bag, and the body pressed against me. Alice is still facing me on her side, eyes closed, jaw slack, drooling. It's adorable.

"Feed the zucchini to the armadillos."

Shocked by the clarity of her voice, I shift back a few inches.

"She talks in her sleep when she's exhausted. She always has."

Shocked by the voice behind me, I shift forward to my original position. When I roll over, Taber is standing on the ladder leading up from their fire escape to ours and he's only visible from the shoulders up.

He laughs. "And she always says the funniest shit. I've

asked her about it when she wakes up, but she never remembers her dreams."

I blink a few times before he comes into focus. "Sorry about last night. That I messed up your gig."

"Nothing to be sorry about. We're the ones who are sorry we didn't see the severity of what you're going through." And then he shrugs and I know he's about to relieve the heaviness a bit. "Besides, the band we were opening for are a bunch of douches anyway. Don't sweat it. Sorry I assumed you were picking up women at the bar Friday night. Alice told me what you were really doing. You know I was only looking out for her by telling her about it."

I return his acceptance of the apology. "Don't sweat it. You couldn't have known. And thanks for not returning the favor and punching me in the face for the assumed betrayal."

He huffs out an unexpected laugh remembering the black eye I gave him, and then looks down for a few seconds before his eyes meet mine again. "Listen, I know we don't know each other very well, but sometimes those are the best people to talk to. I've done a lot of shit I regret, and I have no room to judge anyone's struggles. I'm here if you need an ear."

"He's a really good listener," Alice says to the back of my head before kissing it.

I nod at Taber to acknowledge the offer and reach back to find Alice's hand to acknowledge her concern.

"Come by anytime," Taber says and that's where it ends. I like that about Taber, he knows when to change the subject. "Rise and shine, Alice. Dad's heading out to drive home in a few minutes and wants to say goodbye."

Alice stretches like a cat behind me, limbs extended to maximum length, holding onto my hand the whole time. When she sits up, I stand and pull her up with me. Her eyes are still closed, but she's smiling a sleepy smile that looks sated. "Want to come meet my dad?"

There are few more intimidating questions than that. "Umm..."

Her smile grows at my stalling tactics. "Another time?" she asks, letting me off the hook.

"Next time?"

"Okay," she agrees. And then she leans forward slightly and says, "Kiss me."

I do. It's closed mouth but lingers just long enough to stir things inside me. When she backs away, I ask, "Did your mom go to graduation?"

A half smile emerges, but it isn't sad like it usually is when she talks about her mom. "Nope, and that's okay. I think it would've stressed me out if she did come so this was better. She's still upset I'm not living her version of my life." She kisses me one more time and then says, "I'll come by later," as I guide her to the ladder and Taber helps her climb onto it.

"Okay," I say as I watch her descend.

Gathering up my sleeping bag and pillow, I walk inside. It smells like frosting. Like when I was in elementary school and Doug Strickland's mom would bring cupcakes from Albertson's bakery in for everyone on his birthday. I loved it, because they were the kind of cupcakes that were more frosting than cake. There's a rectangular box on the counter next to my dirty graduation cap that Johnny must've picked up from where it fell off at graduation. When I peek inside, there's a small sheet cake with the same overabundance of white frosting and blue writing that reads, *Happy Graduation, Toby!* Dropping the lid closed I press my face into the sleeping bag and pillow in my hands and I try not to cry. But I fail. I'm eighteen years old and this is the first cake I've ever had that was mine, name written on it or not. We never had birthday cakes growing up. We never celebrated milestones. We never did a lot of things and it was okay because that's just how it was.

But this cake is *mine*.

When I wipe my eyes and turn around, Cliff is standing in the kitchen behind me, a bowl of mac and cheese in one hand and a big, wooden spoon in the other. I guess he couldn't find any other clean utensils. He doesn't wait to swallow the mouthful of noodles before he starts talking. "Johnny's in the basement fixing the washing machine. He said to come get him when you woke up and we'd eat it."

I nod. "I need to shower first." I also make a note to wash my sleeping bag because it's dirty from the fire escape.

"Okay," he says, his back already to me. When he gets to his bedroom door and I get to mine, he stops and turns around. "I'm glad you didn't do it, Toby. I lost my mom, and then my pops," his voice cracks, "I don't want to lose anyone else." He shuts his door but not before I see the first tear fall.

The shower is, as always, my sanctuary. My hand is throbbing from punching the wall last night and all of my muscles are stiff from holding the same position while I slept with Alice. But I'd wake every morning sore if it meant being near her. As I wash and soak up the heat, I think about the cake that Johnny obviously bought.

And then I think about the skateboard that he brought home five years ago and told me his friend threw it in when he bought a bunch of stuff off him at a garage sale. Or the time he said there was a pair of brand new, high-top Chucks in the bedroom closet of 2A after they left in the middle of the night. Or the clothes he's left in the kitchen for me that he claimed were abandoned by tenants who moved out or were evicted. It's always been stuff I needed. And it fit. I'm beginning to think it wasn't coincidental at all. He was always looking out for me, always trying in his own way to take care of me.

After I shave and dress, Johnny's back in the apartment. He's cutting the cake when I walk into the kitchen.

He tips his chin at me. His eyes roam over me like he's taking inventory to make sure everything is still intact.

I tip my chin in return and put my dirty clothes and towel back in my room before joining him again.

He's finished cutting and his hands are stuffed in his pockets.

So are mine.

We're so alike, it's not even funny.

He clears his throat. "I'm proud of you, Toby. I don't know if I made that clear last night, but I am."

I glance down at the floor. I don't do well with compliments.

"Do you like chocolate cake?" It sounds tentative, like he's embarrassed that he doesn't know and has to ask.

"Yeah." I pause before I ask, "You bought that skateboard when I was thirteen, and those Chuck Taylors, and all those clothes for me over the years, didn't you?"

He scratches at the stubble on his chin and shrugs. "They were from the Goodwill, but it's all I could afford. I'm sorry I couldn't do more."

We both pause, eyes averted from each other, thinking.

Until I break the silence. "Thank you. It mattered. And it was enough, I didn't need new."

His chin rises and I can feel his eyes on me. "I've been fixing up 1A. Painting it, cleaning it. I got a new mattress for the bed in the master bedroom. It's your graduation present..." He pauses like he's not sure how I'll react. "If you want it," he adds, like he's afraid I'll turn it down.

I meet his eyes, not sure what to say. It's the apartment I lived in with Marilyn for years. It's been closed up since she left and I moved up here.

"If you don't want it...if there are too many bad memories, I understand."

I shake my head, not because I want to refuse him, but because I can't accept it. "You should take it. There's more space for you and Cliff."

He looks contemplative. "I don't need more space. Cliff doesn't need more space."

"Speak for yourself!" Cliff yells from behind his closed bedroom door.

Johnny closes his eyes and inhales deeply like Cliff is testing his patience. Before he opens them he laughs and whispers so softly that Cliff can't hear him. "That kid is going to be the death of me."

I raise my eyebrows to agree. "You should take it," I repeat. "Or rent it out. Now that it's fixed up, you could probably get decent rent for it."

He shakes his head and pulls the pack of cigarettes from the chest pocket of his flannel shirt, shakes one out and lights it. "It's yours. You deserve a real bed, Toby. And some privacy—you've done without for so long. It's time."

"I didn't plan beyond graduation...for obvious reasons. I don't know what I'm going to do. But I'll need to get a second job. I'll pay rent, if I take it," I add.

Johnny inhales and I watch the smoke drift out in curls toward the ceiling. "No rent. You're my son, this is your house too. And you don't have to work for me anymore if you don't want to. When you find something better, something full-time, I expect you to quit working for me. What about college?"

I shrug. "I don't think I'm cut out for college."

"Why not? You're a smart kid; you can do anything you want. You could go to that art school on Ninth Avenue," he suggests.

I bite at the inside of my cheek because this conversation is too much. "I don't know what I want. My life was supposed to end yesterday. For two years, I just worked toward that..." I trail off and leave it at that.

He takes a long drag and then flicks the ash into the ashtray on the counter. "Well, think about it. Start making new plans. I'll help with tuition. I start a new job next week working for the city maintenance department."

"You'll need help with the house then, if you're getting another job—"

"I can manage, Toby," he cuts me off gently. "Don't worry about me."

Sometimes I forget he's a functioning, responsible adult now. I nod.

"Let's eat," he says.

The words aren't even out of Johnny's mouth before Cliff's door opens. "Finally," he says exasperatedly and marches into the kitchen.

The three of us eat two big pieces each. My teeth hurt when I'm done because it was so sweet, but I regret nothing. My first cake was the best cake I've ever eaten.

When we're done, Johnny hands me a key. "Go take a look. See how you feel. No pressure."

I hesitate like he's handing off a live grenade, but then I take it.

I walk down two flights of stairs.

When I slide the key into the lock with a shaky hand, I can hear Marilyn's voice screeching, *He fucking killed my Nina!*

Turning the key I don't tune it out, I let her in. *That little shit killed my daughter!*

And the familiar self-talk begins. *You're nothing. You're nothing. You're nothing.*

It's interrupted by Alice's voice, *You don't scare me, Toby Page.*

When I step inside, the voices quiet.

It smells like fresh paint.

And warmed-over, botched childhood.

All of the furniture is the same. Even the record player is still sitting on the metal TV tray in the corner with a milk crate of old albums beneath it. They're Marilyn's because Nina took hers when she moved out with Ken. Unless Johnny rearranged them, I can tell you what order they're in because I looked through them so often: Three Dog Night, Fleetwood Mac, The Carpenters, and Jim Croce. There is a new-to-me, ancient console TV sitting directly across from the couch though. The rabbit ears sitting on top of it are wrapped in duct tape to keep them extended fully, and the tips are covered in aluminum foil to help with reception. I've never had a TV and it's Sunday; *Teletunes* is on tonight.

My old room is empty except for the pine dresser against the wall by the window. The middle drawer hangs at an angle. It broke years ago.

The master bedroom is painted pale blue now. And the furniture is different, not just the mattress. The sheets and pillowcases and bedspread all match. They're all blue like the walls. I know it's no big deal, but I've never had sheets and pillowcases that match. Hell, I've never had sheets, I've always just used blankets or the sleeping bag I've had for the past two years. I touch the bedspread because I can't resist. There are creases in it like it's been recently unfolded. It's new. I've never had new either.

Then the dresser catches my eye. There are a few small cans of paint, some paintbrushes, and a piece of paper. When I get closer, I find that the paper is folded in half and my name is on it. Johnny's chicken scratch is inside.

Toby,

I hope you like blue. I don't know your favorite color, so I took a guess and went with mine.

This place is yours. Give it life. Paint a mural on the wall. Get a roommate if you want one. Or a dog. But not a cat, I hate cats.

Happy graduation.

Johnny

It's mine.

This bed.

These sheets.

This paint.

This life.

It's mine.

If I want it.

Without hesitation, I open the cans of paint—black, white, red, and blue.

Replacing the lids on the red and blue, I work with white and black only.

Normally I draw comics, but I want something on my wall that I can look at every morning when I wake up and every night before I fall asleep that is...I don't know...me.

You're nothing. You're nothing. You're nothing, the faint chant begins to remind me who's in charge.

Without thinking, I dip the three-inch brush in the white paint and slash the letter *I* three feet tall and almost as wide. I return to the can, dip the brush again to load it with more white, and add a refined *am* underneath it. I take my time with the letters: flowing cursive, smooth edges. The words are equal in size and weight and presence, but vary in aggression. I look at the space beneath *I am* and switch out brushes. This one is wider by a half inch or so. When I dip it deep into the black paint, the voice chides, *You're nothing. You're nothing. You're nothing.* I squat down and raise my hand, on autopilot ready to draw the *n* with the brush, but then I think about the people in my life who care about me. Really care about me. And I fight for myself.

I stand and paint a period behind *am* instead.

And I leave it at that. Because maybe I don't need a declaration. Maybe just existing today is enough. I'm here.

I am.

I wash the brushes out in the kitchen sink. In *my* kitchen sink. After I take the paint and paintbrushes to the supply room in the basement, I go back up to apartment 3A and make three trips to move my stuff to my new apartment. Each time I walk through the door I hear Marilyn's voice initially, but it gets a little quieter every time, and when I put Nina's *Physical Graffiti* album on the turntable and touch the needle to vinyl, all I hear is her:

Laughing boisterously. It bounced around inside her rib cage before it expelled and always made me think that she felt it intensely because it had to be allowed to build before she could release it.

Teaching me how to draw. "Don't strangle your pencil, Toby. Be gentle if you want it to cooperate with you." "Always shade, it adds depth." "There are no mistakes in art." "Don't be afraid to mess up, it's the only way you learn and get better."

Singing along to "Houses of the Holy." Her voice wasn't great, but she sang with conviction and that counts far more than perfection.

Reading aloud to herself in a whisper because she always said she understood the words better that way.

Offering to share with me. "Do you want half of this peanut butter sandwich, Toby?" "Do you want to split this cookie with me, Toby?" Whatever she was eating, she always shared.

Wishing me a happy birthday, even if it was late, because she's the only one who ever said it.

Commenting on *The Road Runner* cartoons when we watched them together on Saturday mornings. "Why can't the coyote win? Just once, I'd like to see him win."

"I'M SO SORRY, NINA," I WHISPER TO THE AIR. "I'M SORRY there was so much I didn't know. I'm sorry I couldn't help. I'm sorry that life was *so hard for you*." Pinching my lips together, I take in a deep, shaky breath through my nose. "I miss you. Every day I miss you. I've blamed myself for two years for your death. But I think I finally realize you lived with depression, the same way I live with depression. It's hard. It's *so hard* when you don't believe you're good enough. Or smart enough. Or just...*enough*. I should've told you that you were. *You were enough.* I should've told you that I loved you more than just once. I should've told you how funny you were. And how much I looked up to you. And that I love music because *you* loved music. I should've told you a lot of things. I think sometimes we take people for granted...or we just assume that they know how we feel about them because if it's so obvious to us, shouldn't it be obvious to them too? I know now that people don't know...*they can't know*... unless we tell them. Because saying it, or hearing it, can literally be the difference between life and death. I'll never go another day without letting people know how I feel, even though it's hard. I'm starting with Alice. I know I won't have the right words, or I'll be embarrassed, but I won't let that stop me. Because it matters. People need to hear it. Thank you for teaching me so many things. You were enough, even if you didn't believe it."

Pulling the collar of my T-shirt up, I wipe away the tears from my eyes, cheeks, and chin.

I turn off the record player and put the album back in its sleeve.

I walk to the answering machine that's still sitting next to the phone on the table. The phone is dead because the number's been disconnected for years, but the answering machine's light is still on and it's flashing like there's a new message. I hit play and I'm not prepared for what I'm about to hear.

"Goodbye, Toby. I love you, too."

I let the message play out in static for a minute before it cuts off. She must've not hung up the phone after she left the message. I hit rewind and listen to it again. And again. Her voice sounds weary and deconstructed, like she'd succumbed. I know she recorded this moments before she pulled the trigger, but it also sounds like she means it. Like she really did love me. She never said it before, but I know now that it's probably the last thing she said.

"I love you, too, Mom," I say to the silence as I push the off button on the answering machine.

I sit for a few seconds, but I can't sit here any longer. I need to do something.

I walk across the foyer and knock on my neighbor's door.

"Come in!" he yells from inside.

Turning the doorknob, I urge the door forward slowly. I don't know what state he'll be in, but he's home, so I'm guessing that's a good sign.

He waves from the couch. He's cloaked, as always, in the brown terry cloth robe. The pallor of his skin reminds me of skim milk, a hint of blue amongst stark white. The coffee table is covered with neatly lined up pill bottles, a glass and a pitcher of water, and two novels. *One Flew Over the Cuckoo's Nest* is playing on the TV. He mutes it.

"They let you come home?" I ask. And then I repeat what I thought a few seconds ago. "That's a good sign."

He smiles weakly, not because he's faking it but because he's too drained to generate the genuine article. "Indeed. They downgraded the pneumonia diagnosis after more tests. It appears I'm not going anywhere yet." I expect Jack Nicholson's voice, but it's Mr. Street's instead.

I take a few tentative steps in. I don't want to sit on the couch and disturb him, but there isn't anywhere else to sit. I'm so bad at this, so I stand in place. "We're neighbors now." I point with my thumb over my shoulder. "I mean, I moved in across the hall. So, if you need anything, just knock. I don't have a phone yet. I probably won't for a while, but..." I trail off because I'm rambling...and I don't ramble.

The smile remains. "Glad to hear it. It's been a bit lonely down here on the first floor. I'll take the company."

I stuff my hands in my pockets because I don't know what to do with them. I wish I could put my mouth in my pocket too because I don't know what to do with it either. "Do you need anything? Are you okay?" I add, dumbly. He's dying, of course he's not okay.

"I'm fine, thank you. Johnny's been down to check on me twice today." The news is delivered like it's unremarkable, like Johnny does this often.

Normally I wouldn't voice my curiosity, but I've vowed to make some changes, so I don't hold back. "Does he do that often, check on you? He obviously knew that you're sick since he came to the hospital to find you when you weren't home."

Mr. Street nods. "Johnny's known I have AIDS since I moved in. I find it's better to be upfront with people. It helps me sort out the hateful assholes from the start."

I've never heard Mr. Street cuss in his own polished voice. His bold directness makes me smile.

His smile broadens slightly when he sees mine. It's the equivalent of a high five. "Johnny has been taking me to my doctor's appointments the past several weeks. I told him I could drive myself, but he insisted. He's a bit surly, if you haven't noticed. I didn't have the heart to argue when he was trying to make a kind gesture."

"I'm familiar with his brand of surly. The apple doesn't fall far from the tree, apparently."

He laughs, which leads to coughing. I move forward and offer him the glass of water. After drinking half of it down, he sets it back on the coaster. "You're certainly a lot alike. The persona you present to the world is not who you truly are. Though I do admit that when we're out and someone directs a slur at us assuming Johnny and I are a couple, it is quite gratifying when his grouchy side rears its head and he tells them to, 'Fuck off and mind your own damn business.'" He chuckles to himself at the memory. "I think being sober has been difficult for him and keeping busy has been key. Checking in on me and Mrs. Bennett before she moved out, helped keep him occupied. And worrying about you and Cliff, of course."

"You knew he was my dad when you told him to talk to me yesterday at the hospital, didn't you?"

He nods. "Yes. We've shared a lot these past weeks during our car rides and long stretches spent in waiting rooms. He told me the whole story. He carries around a lot of shame about so much in his life. I think that's why he fills this house with people who need help. It's like he's trying to redeem himself."

I think about that. As long as I've lived in this house, Johnny's tenants have always been misfits, or sick, or down on their luck. They've always been people who struggle in one way or another. Maybe that's why he charges so little for rent too. He's just trying to help and I never saw it.

Mr. Street continues, separating me from my thoughts. "He

was afraid to tell you for fear it would make your life harder, or that you would reject him completely."

I shrug. "I wish he would've told me years ago, but I guess I understand why he didn't. Inviting people in when you're at your lowest isn't ideal because you don't want to bring them down too. My mom—well, my grandma, I guess—she always told me that I taint people. I believed her, especially after Nina died. I'm sure Johnny told you the story."

He nods contemplatively. "He did. It wasn't your fault that she took her life, Toby. We are all responsible for our choices."

I look down at my feet when I ask my next question because I know I'm out of line, but I need to know. "Do you blame Henry?" I leave the, *for infecting you with the HIV virus,* unsaid.

"We are all responsible for our choices," he repeats. "No. When we got back together, I never asked him if he'd been with anyone else while we were apart. I guess I assumed he hadn't because I hadn't. I should've asked. It was years later when he got sick and was diagnosed. We both knew I had it too. How could I not? We'd been together for years at that point. I was angry. Angry at him. Angry at me. Angry at the man who infected him. Angry that gay men dying wasn't a priority for government-funded medical research. But then I realized that my anger wasn't doing me or Henry any good and that if our time together was limited, I didn't want to waste it. So I focused on him, making sure he was comfortable, taking his meds, eating good food, getting rest, and making sure he knew he was loved, and forgiven. Because Henry never got angry—it wasn't in his nature—but he felt guilt intensely. He hated what he'd done to me. It broke his heart and his spirit. No one should be allowed to die with the burden of guilt like that."

I finally look up and his eyes are on me. "Did your forgiveness help ease it?" I know guilt, it's a fickle bastard.

"One can never truly know what goes on inside another's head, but I like to think it did. We had the best talks of our lives in his final weeks." He nods as if to reassure himself and the look on his face grows wistful. "I like to think it did," he repeats quietly to himself. He looks tired all of a sudden, but it's the content kind of exhaustion, not the ragged kind that's borne from stress or illness.

"You should get some sleep," I urge. "I just wanted to let you know that I'm across the hall now if you need anything."

"Thank you. And likewise, I'm here if you ever need to talk," he offers in return. "And Toby?"

I look back over my shoulder on my way to the door. "Yeah?"

"Release the guilt. Forgive yourself. Nina would want that."

I don't nod. I don't say anything. But eye contact tells him I heard him. When I'm out the door, I have to sit down on the stairs and think.

Sometimes in life, there are moments of clarity so blinding in their revelation that they change everything. It's usually something small, something obvious, that we wonder how we missed it before. If I put myself in Nina's shoes, would I blame me? Or what if Nina had given me my bottle of sleeping pills because she was worried I wasn't sleeping enough and was trying to help? Would I blame her if I decided to use them later to end my life instead? No, I wouldn't. Nina only ever had the best intentions for others. She was human, she made mistakes, but she never wanted those mistakes to affect anyone else. It's the reason she disappeared from our lives when she was using. She didn't want her demons to become ours. She saw distance as a shield, for us, not her. She tried to protect me my entire life from what she believed to be her flaws. I've done the same thing. I've hidden. For two years, I've hidden from everything and everyone. I thought if I didn't let people in, I was protecting them...from me. Alice was the exception. I couldn't stay away. I *can't* stay away.

With that, I rise and take the stairs two at a time to Alice's door. And when she opens it, I say, "Hi," to get the formality out of the way.

Her smile grows impossibly wide. "Hi, Toby."

"Are you busy? Can I steal you for a little while?" I ask.

"You can steal me for a long while."

I don't know how suggestive she intended that to sound, but it throws me for a second, and I temporarily forget about what I had in mind and can only think about kissing her instead. Before I stammer something that will only embarrass me, I reach for her hand.

"I'll be back later, Taber! I'm going with Toby!" Alice yells over her shoulder.

Little does she know that Taber is standing in the same room with her and that he overheard our entire conversation. "Use protection!" he yells back, smirking. I guess he heard the suggestive tone too.

I know my face is red, an inferno has suddenly ignited behind my cheeks. It's at odds with what's going on inside my jeans.

Alice laughs at his teasing and it eases my anxiety.

I take her to my apartment.

And tell her what I painted on my bedroom wall.

"I am," she whispers with a knowing smile. "You are so many things, Toby, an amalgamation that makes you, *you*. That's why I love this so much. It's owning it all, the triumphs and the struggles, the things you like and the things you want to change, because they all make you who you are. We're all a work in progress—hell, no one knows that better than me. Every day is new. Every day delivers a new challenge. But saying, 'Fuck it, *I am*,' feels good. I'm going to steal this. I might have you paint it on my bedroom wall too. Even though I can't see it, I'll know it's there."

Pulling her to me, I kiss her forehead. "Or you could just sleep here," I whisper.

When her chin tips up, her entire face is smiling. "I talk in my sleep," she warns.

"You don't scare me, Alice Eliot."

A laugh escapes her. "Touché."

And then I kiss her.

And she kisses me.

And it lasts for hours.

Until *Teletunes* comes on and we watch and listen and sing along. I describe the videos to Alice so she can get a visual, and she fills me in on random facts about the bands or songs when she knows something I don't. She knows a lot that I don't.

When the last song ends at ten thirty, I tell her she should go change into her pajamas and come back down to sleep.

She does.

It's the first of many nights that I share my new bed with Alice, Siouxsie and the Banshees, and a nearly nightmare-free sleep.

CHAPTER FORTY-FOUR

PRESENT, August 1987
Toby

"Do they have coffee, Toby?" Alice whispers, trying
to be considerate of others who might be in the waiting room
with us.

"There's no one else in the room, so you don't have to
whisper if you don't want to," I tell her.

She smiles wide, and it's the self-assured smile that makes
my crush on her swell, even though we've been dating and
inseparable for months now. "Do they have coffee, Toby?" she
repeats in a normal volume.

"They do. Do you want a cup?"

She was up late last night; she's tired. Wonderland played
an acoustic set at the Mercury Café. It was stripped down—just
her, Taber, and his acoustic guitar—and it was my favorite
performance yet. I haven't missed a show since mid-June, and
even though they're great, they get better each time. Alice

always tells me she won't accept a future that's nothing short of "fiercely passionate and wildly beautiful." I knew she was determined, but being with her nonstop for months has shown me she's pretty much Joan Jett-"Bad Reputation"-badass level determined about everything in life. Including me. It's humbling, inspiring, and, well...hot.

"Or in an IV, if it's available, that would be great." She laughs through a yawn, her hand covering her mouth.

I stand and walk toward the table in the corner where the coffeemaker sits. "Looks like you're going to have to settle on a Styrofoam cup. Unless you want to come over here and lie on the table and I'll just pour it directly into your mouth."

It looks like she's contemplating my idea. "That's tempting, don't tease me. And this skirt is probably too short to climb up on a table and still keep it halfway ladylike. A cup will do."

I pour two cups and tear open two packets of sugar and stir them into Alice's coffee, smiling the whole time because I can't believe she's mine.

She thanks me when I hand it to her and immediately takes a sip, humming in appreciation.

"Toby?" A voice calls from the opposite side of the room and my heart rate increases twofold.

Alice stands before I do and holds out her free hand.

I take it and when I do, she squeezes tightly to reassure me that I'm not alone.

When we're close enough to the balding man that an introduction is possible without raising my voice, I say, "Hi, Dr. Goldin. This is my girlfriend, Alice Eliot."

His eyes crinkle in the corners when he says, "It's nice to meet you, Alice," and his lips rise in the friendly smile that I'm beginning to think is a permanent fixture on his face.

I release Alice's hand and she offers it to shake his. "Likewise. It's nice to meet you, too, Dr. Goldin." Her confidence and ease with people, especially strangers, feels like a lesson when I'm with her. Like if I pay attention, I'll learn how to do it myself. I'm trying, *I'm really trying.*

When we're seated on a couch in Dr. Goldin's office, he starts in, "Alice, thank you very much for coming. As you know, Toby has been my patient for almost six weeks and I feel like we're making real progress." His eyes dart to mine. "You would agree with that assessment, wouldn't you, Toby?"

I clear my throat and tell the truth because I've promised myself to do that in here...and everywhere. "I feel like I've done so many things the past few weeks that are so uncomfortable they bring comfort." I pause and shake my head because I tend to give my thoughts a rushed, unrestrained voice in here and sometimes that means they come out wrong. "That probably doesn't make any sense..." I pause again and they both wait patiently and I'm so grateful for it. "What I mean is that I've tried new things, or opened myself up, or let people in, or just considered ideas that I didn't think were possible for someone like me. They were all things that scared me, things I wouldn't normally do, but when the nauseous feeling passed, it was replaced by a sense of...I don't know how else to explain it... except comfort. Maybe peace is the right word?" I shrug. "It's hard to put a label on it because it's new...and I've never felt it before...but I feel it. Intensely."

Dr. Goldin nods encouragingly. "That's definitely progress from your first appointment."

This leads to a succession of questions for Alice. They're all about me, what our daily life is like, and changes she's noticed. He said he doesn't always do this with patients, but for those willing, it gives him a different perspective into my life and offers insight into progress and future treatment. While they talk, I listen and remain quiet. It's strange being discussed while sitting in the room, but at the same time, it's the uncomfortable comfort I talked about a minute ago because I know they both want what's best for me.

When he's done, his focus returns to me. "How are you feeling, Toby? This is week five on the anti-depressants. Last week you said you were beginning to feel significant relief. Does that still hold true? Any further changes?"

I stop myself before I speak and arrange my thoughts. Alice squeezes my hand again. "The voice is gone, those perpetual thoughts of hopelessness. It was normal, like I've told you before, to tell myself that I was nothing, that the world would be a better place if I was gone, that I didn't matter. I haven't had those thoughts this week and I honestly didn't think about the fact that they're gone until this morning. You'd think that living with them for so long, that their absence would be more noticeable, wouldn't you? It's kind of like when you have a horrible headache and it starts to fade and when it disappears eventually, you're so thankful it's gone that you focus on what feels good and forget to miss the pain. Does that make sense?" I ask this question a lot with Dr. Goldin because I want to make sure I'm explaining myself well.

He nods.

"It's not that I've forgotten what the pain of hopelessness feels like. It's frighteningly vivid and it scares me that I'll wake up tomorrow and it will return. Because now that I know what it's like to live without it for a few consecutive days, I don't ever want to go back there." My eyes have dropped to my hand in Alice's, but when I lift them to Dr. Goldin, his are there waiting for me. "What if it comes back?" The fear in my voice is evident.

His eyes soften at my question, at my worry. "As we've discussed, depression is often something that returns over the course of one's life. Not always, but it happens. What we're doing now is filling your toolbox with the tools to manage it, instead of it managing you instead. You're doing so well, Toby, in regards to therapy and medication. But the other thing that's making a big difference is your support system and your willingness to open up to them. Communication is key. Strong, trusting, healthy relationships are key. There's unfortunately a misconception attached to depression and mental illness in general. People don't talk about it. They hide it. They're ashamed of it. But why? Imagine if we didn't talk about cancer, or heart disease, or diabetes, or any number of other ailments that affect the body? Thousands of people would suffer and die unnecessarily without treatment. The same should hold true for ailments of the mind. Societal compassion and understanding would go a long way in saving people's lives. Don't ever be ashamed to ask for help when you need it. And if you don't get it, ask someone else until you do. Your mental state is important, it drives your quality of life. Fight for it."

I nod. I understand all of this now. My support system is critical, just knowing that Alice, Johnny, Cliff, Taber, Chantal, and even Mr. Street, are there when I need to talk about important stuff, or nothing important at all, makes all the difference. I've never had friends and family like this. I never thought I could. "Will the meds be forever?"

He shakes his head. "We will reevaluate when I feel like you've stabilized in all areas, most likely around the six-month mark, judging by your progress so far. My approach is cautious but focused on healing through therapy rather than relying on medication. Every person is different, of course, but I anticipate removing the anti-depressants in six months."

I nod again. I don't like medication either, but I have to admit that whether it's solely the medication or a combination of everything I'm doing, it's working. "Okay."

"How are all of the jobs going? Are you still helping Johnny out now that you started at the museum?" he asks the question like we're friends and we're catching up, not like he's assessing my mental stability. I like that.

"All is well. I help out Johnny occasionally. And I really like being at the museum. It feels...I don't know...it feels empowering." I still help Johnny out with maintenance work when he needs it and I got a part-time job at Wax Trax because employee discounts are awesome. And I also got a part-time job at the Denver Art Museum because art is awesome, but it's also the persuasion of the soul to seek out self and I need that right now. Desperately. "I only sell tickets for exhibit admission, but there's something about being in that building three days a week that ignites a desire in me that I've never felt before. It makes me want to put myself out there the way every artist in the building has. Their fearlessness to share themselves is bold and terrifying and humble and implicit and galvanizing. *I want that.*"

"Good. Did you apply to The Art Institute of Denver?"

I nod and watch him smile encouragingly as he jots a note on his notepad.

"Yeah, I turned in my application Monday afternoon. The woman in admissions said I should hear something in four to six weeks. I'll start in January if I'm accepted."

"Good luck," he says. "I think you need that creative outlet. Art is inherently therapeutic. Our time is almost up, any questions for me, Toby?"

"No, not that I can think of," I answer, and I notice how clammy my hands are. I'm sweating. Being here always makes me feel equal parts nervous and better at the same time.

"Very good." His eyes shift to Alice. "Thank you so much for coming today, Alice, and for being so open and willing to be a supportive part of Toby's treatment. As I said before, Toby is doing the hard work, but a reliable support system is critical."

Alice politely extends her hand and he shakes it. "I'm not

going anywhere. And as much as I may be Toby's support system, he's also mine—we'd need another hour to discuss all the ways." She smiles. "He's a good person and so easy to love. I'm proud of him. He's my hero."

The right words, spoken at just the right time, make all the difference.

Alice always has the right words.

EPILOGUE OF HEALING AND HAPPINESS

Three years later...

PRESENT, July 1990
Toby

"I MISS YOU." ALICE'S VOICE IS SOFT IN THE DARK.

"You haven't left yet." My hands are wrapped around her hips, thumbs brushing back and forth over the soft skin under her Siouxsie and the Banshees T-shirt I love so much. I'm on my back, propped up on both bed pillows, and she's lying on me, her forearms resting on my bare chest, legs draped on either side of mine, socked feet curled back across my shins, and her long hair tickling every inch of exposed skin that isn't under the sheets.

Lowering her head, she kisses me, it's featherlight, a dusting of lust we both feel but won't give in to until we've finished talking. We've gotten really good at communication, with words and without. Because a conversation between two bodies is telling too.

"I know, but it's two weeks without you."

My hand curves around to her lower back and my fingertips trace the line of her spine. She shivers. I feel it even though I can't see it, and it makes me smile.

"We'll talk every day. Twice. When you wake up and before you go to sleep. And you'll tell me everything, so it's like I'm there with you. This is the coolest thing that's ever happened, Alice. You're going on tour. You get to see the West Coast. I'm so proud of you. Are you nervous?"

Their band has always been successful locally, but last year Wonderland recorded their first album. A few months ago, radio stations nationwide started playing their first single. They're getting noticed and it led to this tour—handpicked by the headliner to open for them. Small venues, sold out shows— it's the exposure they need. I may be biased, but Alice is a goddess onstage. And off.

She huffs like she's both amused and, well...nervous. "Of course, I'm nervous."

"Good, the nerves are there to remind you that you're doing something that matters." I'm only reciting her words back to her; she says this to me at least once a week. And it always helps.

"You do listen." I can hear the smile in her words and the subsiding of nerves. "Were you nervous tonight?" Her voice has dropped to a whisper. It's the tone she takes when she's serious. And turned-on.

"Yeah, could you tell?" I had my first exhibit at an up-and-coming art gallery in Boulder tonight.

"Only because you held my hand so tight and never let go." She sounds lighthearted and is teasing me, but there's truth. I held onto her hand all night like she was my life preserver and I'd drown without her.

"Sorry," I whisper.

She laughs once, throaty and unrestrained. "Don't apologize, I'm sure no one else noticed you were nervous." And then she switches back to serious, adoring Alice. "You were gracious and humble when people engaged you. I was proud. In awe. Toby Page in his element is unbelievably sexy."

I'm still not good at receiving compliments, so I change the subject. "Is there anything you need me to do for the wedding while you're gone?"

We're getting married next month. It will be a casual ceremony here at the house with family and a few friends. Johnny built a gazebo in the backyard, and it turns out Dan from Dan's Tavern is an ordained minister, so he's going to do the honors.

She's drawing lazy circles on my chest. Pushing her T-shirt up, I do the same on her upper back. "You can take Johnny to get fitted for his tux." He's my best man. "Taber went last week, so he's all set." He's her maid of honor. "And we should probably find something for Joey sooner than later." He's the ring bearer.

"I can do that." The lull in the conversation tells me it's about at its end.

"Oh, and Cliff too." He's the usher. We only sent out thirty invitations, so it's more formality than necessity, but I think it made him feel good when I asked him. The kid has done a one-eighty from where he was a few years ago. Except his obsession with the Sex Pistols, that remains fanatical. Yes, I finally watched *Sid and Nancy* with him. And yes, Sid Vicious is not a legend but Gary Oldman playing Sid Vicious is. He was fantastic.

"He'll probably cut the sleeves off the suit jacket because it's not punk rock enough for him and they'll end up keeping our deposit."

Her body rumbles against mine as she laughs soundlessly. "You're probably right. Maybe we should let him wear whatever he wants."

It's quiet now. The darkness feels safe like it always does when I'm with Alice. She is sanctuary.

Her lips press against my chest, the pressure behind them telling. It's intent. And loving.

There will be one more question because she asks it every night. It finds its way to me when her kisses climb up my neck to my ear. "What makes you happy, Toby?"

I give her a different answer every night.

And I mean them all.

"The girl who sees the stars despite the clouds taught me to do the same. And it changed everything."

LETTER FROM THE AUTHOR:

We never truly know what's going on in other people's minds. In their lives. Even those closest to us. Be gentle with each other. Talk to each other. Listen to each other. Tell your friends and family you love them every chance you get. Compliment a stranger. Initiate a conversation with someone you don't know. People need to be seen, heard, and loved—it's part of what makes the human experience so...human.

I'm a firm believer that we all affect people's lives for the better in ways we will never know. Think about it for a moment: how many times in your life have you been the recipient of kindness from a stranger that occurred when you were having a really shitty day and needed it most, or someone said something that resonated with you so deeply that years later you remember it word for word, or a conversation changed your point of view or educated you, or words read sparked a change in your perspective about life? It happens all the time. But do we ever tell the person how much we appreciated their kindness, wisdom, or love? Most of the time, we don't. And in some situations, we can't. The person who affected us will likely never know.

But they should.

Don't be afraid to share your gratitude, or feelings, or love, because the person on the receiving end may need to hear it more than you will ever know. Because like I said, we never truly know what's going on in other people's minds. In their lives. Kindness matters.

This book touched on many issues that are often hard to talk about. Times are changing, misconceptions are being clarified, the collective consciousness is more compassionate than ever before—my hope is that one day soon, the judgment disappears entirely. If you're carrying around something heavy, I encourage you with everything in me to talk to someone about it. You don't have to deal with it alone. Ask for help.

In 1995, I was twenty-two years old. I was also suicidal. I didn't tell anyone. I functioned, but I tried to hide—my depression and myself. For over a year, I carried the unbearable hopelessness around and listened to the constant inner dialogue of *You're nothing, you're nothing, you're nothing. The world would be a better place if you weren't in it*, just like Toby. I made a plan. I knew how, when, and where I was going to end my life. Days prior to my end date, a longtime friend of mine completed suicide. Sitting amongst his grieving family and friends at the funeral forced me to face my own pain and my own plans with a different perspective. Instead of going through with it, I talked to my fiancé (now husband) instead and asked for help. That changed everything. Knowing I wasn't alone to fight it was a game changer for me. And it still is to this day. Off and on throughout my adult life, depression revisits. Is it fun? Nope, it sure isn't. But those are the months I ask for help and I fight like hell to get back to happiness. I talk to the people I trust, the people I know won't judge me. And eventually the darkness lifts and the light on the other side returns and it feels like a gift. I no longer take happiness for granted. I no longer take life for granted. I look for the bright side in every situation. And I fight when I need to. I fight even when it feels impossible to do so.

If I can do it, you can do it. Fight. Fight. FIGHT. For yourself. For happiness. For life. You deserve it all, my friend. You are a precious resource that cannot be replaced.

Help isn't a four-letter word (technically it is, but you know what I mean), ask for it when you need it. Following is a list of amazing, selfless people who get up every day to be there for others in crisis, contact them if you need help or need to talk:

National Suicide Prevention Lifeline
https://suicidepreventionlifeline.org
Call 1-800-273-TALK (8255)

The American Foundation for Suicide Prevention
www.afsp.org

Crisis Text Line
Text 741741

More Than Sad Program (a resource for parents and educators)
http://morethansad.org

Seize the Awkward (a resource offering tips to start conversations with friends or family related to mental health)
https://seizetheawkward.org

The Trevor Project (a resource for LGBTQ youth)
https://www.thetrevorproject.org
Call 1-866-488-7386

Veterans Crisis Line (a resource for veterans)
  https://www.veteranscrisisline.net/
  Call 1-800-273-8255 press 1
  Text 838255

The National Domestic Violence Hotline
  https://www.thehotline.org
  Call 1-800-799-7233
  You can also contact a local safe house in your community.

RAINN (Rape, Abuse & Incest National Network)
  https://www.rainn.org
  National Sexual Assault Hotline
  Call 1-800-656-HOPE (4673)

SAMHSA (Substance Abuse & Mental Health Services Administration)
  https://www.samhsa.gov/
  Call 1-800-662-HELP (4357)

Or in the event of an emergency call 911.

A portion of the proceeds for every copy of this book sold will be donated monthly to a charitable foundation doing outstanding work to raise awareness and assist those in need.

ACKNOWLEDGMENTS

Otherwise known as a million heartfelt thank yous from a beyond grateful girl.

I'll start with you. *Yes, you.* There are so many books out there to choose—thank you for choosing this one. I appreciate you so very much. I'm hugging you tight.

Thank you to the following women, who I not only look up to, respect, and admire, but who spent hours reading this book in its rough draft form and offered thoughtful feedback and suggestions to help me write the best book I could: Beth Flynn, Brandy Toler, Diane Hambric, Gemma Hitchen, Lindsey Burdick, Peggy Tran, Rebecca Donovan, Shannon O'Neill, and Susan Rossman. This book is very personal and terrifying to put out into the world. You were my backbone when I needed it. Thank you for your support in all ways. Love you like crazy!

Thank you to Gemma Hitchen for being a legend in the friendship department. I probably wouldn't have started this book if you hadn't sent me that link to "Something Just Like This" by The Chainsmokers & Coldplay a few years ago and said, "I know you don't really like Coldplay, but you have to listen to this." That song turned into me thinking about Toby as a character and everything snowballed from there. Your friendship means everything to me. You are the Jama to my Tiaco. Love you, bestie!

Thank you to Beth Flynn, my soul sister, for always (and I mean *ALWAYS*) being there to listen and hold my hand when I need it most. I don't know what I would do without you. Love you, sis!

Thank you to Anne Eliot for coffee dates/writing time/Laini Taylor fangirl sessions/plotting wisdom/listening, listening, listening/teaching me all the technical things/cheerleading like a mofo. I wouldn't have finished this book without you. Love you!

Thank you to Peggy Tran for being my #soulduster and partner in crime when it comes to tacos, margaritas, and stalking authors locally. Your pure soul is such a gift and I feel incredibly lucky to call you my friend. I couldn't have finished this book without your kind offer to step in and talk it through with me when I needed it most. Love you!

Thank you to Rebecca Donovan for making my life brighter from the moment you walked into it. We share the same brain when it comes to health and wellness, and most importantly music. I'm thankful the book world brought us together, even if it's just a small part of the things that bond us. Love you!

Thank you to Susan Rossman for being the epitome of class, intelligence, bravery, and kindness. I know I've told you this before, but I have ALL the respect for you. The way you tackle the world is inspiring. Love you!

Thank you to Diane Hambric for having one of the most generous hearts I've ever known. And fantastic taste in music, thank you for that too. Love you!

Thank you to Lindsey Burdick for being the most honest person I've ever met. You wear your heart on your sleeve and would do anything for anyone. You continually teach me what it means to be a good person. Thank you for setting the example for the rest of us to follow. Love you!

Thank you to Shannon O'Neill for being nice personified. You welcome everyone into your life with kindness and without judgment. It's a beautiful thing. You are a reminder of everything that's good in the world. Love you!

Thank you to Brandy Toler for being my Love Mama. We get far too little time together, but every time we do, your gift for storytelling (because outrageous situations are the moth, and you are their irresistible flame) always astounds me. You never fail to make me laugh. Your friendship fills me to bursting. Love you, Mama!

Thank you to Robin Stonehocker for 30+ years of friendship. I've grown up with you and continue to grow with you. Your laughter is contagious, and your positive attitude always reminds me that we are surrounded by so much that is good in this world. Here's to another thirty years of friendship. Love you!

Thank you to Colleen Hoover for always being a stellar human being. The way you see the world and the people in it, from every perspective, is a rare and beautiful thing. Thank you for your friendship, you inspire me. Love you!

Thank you to Lin Reynolds for always making me smile. And laugh. You're one of those people who truly makes me feel better/happier/bolder when I spend five minutes with you. You are a precious human being and I'm so lucky to call you my friend. Love you!

Thank you to Ginger Scott for your sage-like wisdom in helping me navigate this release. And for just being awesome, thank you for that too. Love you!

Thank you to Bob Ault for gifting me the love of music. When we were in eighth grade, we were listening to music in your room and you played "Close to Me" by The Cure. I remember it vividly because I'd never heard anything like it. That was the exact moment that I fell in love with music. I haven't seen you in almost thirty years, but I want you to know that you are one of the best friends I've ever had. I wish you happiness, health, and peace wherever you are, my friend.

Thank you to Sara Moncada and her 2016-2017 eighth grade English students at Silver Hills Middle School. The honesty you shared with me when I visited your class, and the bravery and vulnerability it took to do so, helped inspire this book and solidify my determination to write about depression and suicide. I'm hugging each and every one of you!

Thank you to Andy Hull for writing the most thought-provoking, gorgeous lyrics and songs I've ever heard. Your words inspire emotion. And emotion inspires art, change, ideas, love, and life. The ripple effect is massive. Keep doing what you're doing. Please. All the gratitude to you!

Thank you to Denise Milano Sprung, who works closely with The American Foundation for Suicide Prevention and The Keith Milano Memorial Fund, for taking the time to educate me about the resources available for suicide prevention and for sharing your personal story with me. Thank you for making a difference in this world!

Thank you to Lori "Goddess of Editing" Sabin for your time, care, smarts, talent, and heart. I adore so many things about you, but I've added editing to the list. You took on this story as your own and put so much love and careful thought into your feedback. Toby, Alice, and I thank you for making us all better. Love you, superstar!

Thank you to Christine Estevez and Monique Tarver for putting your keen eyes on this manuscript and being the last line of defense in the proofreading department. I am eternally grateful because I could read this thing 5,000 times (it feels like I have) and miss the obvious. Love you both!

Thank you to Autumn Gantz at WordSmith Publicity for lending your expertise and making this release less scary. Many, many thanks!

Thank you to my agents Jane Dystel and Lauren Abramo at Dystel, Goderich & Bourret LLC. You make this girl's dreams come true. Your support and belief in my little stories mean the world to me. Love to you both!

Thank you to Mom and Dad for being the best parents/mentors/friends/cheerleaders a girl could ask for. Love you both to the moon and back!

Thank you to my husband, B. I, literally, wouldn't be here without you. Thank you for twenty-nine years of endless patience, friendship, humor, support, loyalty, love, caring, and kindness. And for making me pretty book covers, thank you for that too. I love you more than you could ever imagine!

Thank you to my son, Phoenix, for inspiring me in all ways. I have a million favorite things about you, but your heart is my *favorite* favorite. Your compassionate, gentle, kind approach to life is stunning. I'm so proud to know you, let alone to be the one you call Mama. I love, love, love, love you!

Thank you to readers, bloggers, bookstagrammers, and foreign publishers for spreading the love about my books. Word of mouth is the most genuine, authentic form of promotion— you've mastered it. Authenticity is my jam, so your kindness makes my heart smile on a daily basis. Love you all!

And last but not least, thank you to my closed group on Facebook, *Bright Siders*, for being the most awesome friends on the planet. We are truly a family in every sense of the word. You show me on a daily basis what kindness in action is and provide a safe environment where everyone feels accepted and valued for who they are. I feel incredibly lucky that you let me hang out with cool kids like you. Love you all so much!

PLAYLIST

Music inspires. Absolutely and endlessly. These are the songs
that brought Toby and his story to life.

"Sleeper 1972" by Manchester Orchestra
"Oats In the Water" by Ben Howard
"Sit Next to Me" by Foster the People
"Us Vs Them" by Spring King
"Overlap" by Catfish and the Bottlemen
"Kamikaze" by Walk the Moon
"Something Just Like This" by The Chainsmokers & Coldplay
"Someone to You" by Banners
"Particles" by Nothing But Thieves
"My Backwards Walk" by Frightened Rabbit
"Mother" by The Hunna
"The Maze" by Manchester Orchestra
"Next To Me" by Imagine Dragons
"Sorry" by Nothing But Thieves
"11 Minutes" (feat. Travis Barker) by YUNGBLUD & Halsey
"I See You" by Missio
"My Blood" by Twenty One Pilots
"Take on the World" by You Me At Six
"Two High" by Moon Taxi

"How Soon Is Now?" by The Smiths
"Problems" by Sex Pistols
"In My Room" by Yaz
"Lips Like Sugar" by Echo and the Bunnymen
"Close to Me" by The Cure
"Under the Milky Way" by The Church
"Kashmir" by Led Zeppelin
"With or Without You" by U2
"Strangelove" by Depeche Mode
"She Sells Sanctuary" by The Cult
"So Alive" by Love and Rockets
"Only You" by Yaz
"One More Time" by The Cure

ABOUT THE AUTHOR

I love reading, writing, traveling, music, tea, tacos, nice people,
my big dude (husband), and my not-so-little dude (son).
And lots of other stuff too.

I also love making new friends.
Please come and find me in one of these spots.

https://www.facebook.com/kimholdenauthor
(While you're on Facebook look for our closed group, Bright
Siders, that's where I love to hang out because it's jam-packed
with the nicest people on the planet.)

https://www.instagram.com/kimholdenauthor

https://www.kimholdenbooks.com

Email: kim@kimholdenbooks.com

Made in the USA
Lexington, KY
09 June 2019